THE BOMBSHELL 'DEVIL'S' ADVOCATE

A HELLION HARLOT NOVEL

WRITTEN & ILLUSTRATED BY

NIKKITA BELL

The Bombshell Devil's Advocate was developed from Nikkita Bell's *Bound in Pincers*. *Bound in Pincers* was originally printed and included in *Out of the Cauldron, a Fall Fantasy Collection* by Azala Press in 2023, and independently published in 2024.

Cover, interior artwork, and graphic illustrations by Nikkita Bell.

Nightwish – Disco Script Retro Font by Fortune Co, commercial license.

Developmental Editing by Stephanie Storm.

Line Editing by Lexi Smith McNicholas.

Editing and proofreading by Alexa at The Fiction Fix.

Proofreading by The Cauldron Author Services.

ISBN: 9798304114462 (paperback), 9798991924412 (hardcover)

First Edition, February 2025.

Published by Nikkita Bell and Scorpion Script Press.

www.nikkitabell.com

For those who've dimmed their flames to fit the mold—may this book remind you to burn brightly once more.

And to me, the little girl who always wanted to live forever and fought like hell to stay alive.

Greetings from
Hollywood
Califonia
circa 2003
YAMASHIRO HOLLYWOOD
THE HOLLYWOOD ROOSEVELT HOTEL
THE ROXY THEATER
ROXY
BAD DECIS
THE STARL
SANTA MONICA BLVD
West Hollywood

HOLLYWOOD
HOLLYWOOD SIGN
Hollywood Hills
GRIFFITH OBSERVATORY
HOLLYWOOD BLVD
OF FAME
SUNSET BLVD
THE VISTA THEATER
HOLLYWOOD FOREVER CEMETERY
101 FWY

THE BOMBSHELL "DEVIL'S" ADVOCATE

TRACK LIST

SCAN TO LISTEN TO THE PLAYLIST HERE!

Please be advised that this is a dark adult novel and may include themes that are disturbing to some readers.

I created this series to provide a fresh perspective on villainy, featuring bad gals you can't help but root for. It is important to remember that **this book is told from the perspective of a morally black witch**, a creature who should not be held accountable to the same moral standards as a human. While I invite you to explore their darker sides, the health, safety, and mental and emotional well-being of my readers is of utmost importance to me. Please make sure to read through this list of trigger warnings to help you make an informed decision before delving into this universe.

WARNINGS: Adult language, sexual content (18+ only), dubious consent, depictions and references of death/murder, religious/Satanic references, blood, gore & violence, fire/burn trauma, choking/drowning, PTSD, tobacco usage, alcohol consumption.

DEMONIC HIERARCHY

OF THE HELLION HARLOT SERIES

THE KING OF DEMONS

LUCIFER MORNINGSTAR / SATAN / THE DEVIL

THE THIRTEEN PRIME EVILS

HEAD DEMONS CREATED BY THE DEVIL WHO HAVE DOMINION OVER HUMANS AND SUPERNATURALS CREATURES.

DEMON OF CHAOS

DEMON OF DEBAUCHERY (CURRENTLY INHABITING LOS ANGELES, CA)

DEMON OF DECEPTION (CURRENTLY INHABITING LAS VEGAS, NV)

DEMON OF DESTRUCTION

DEMON OF DOMINATION

DEMON OF DOUBT

DEMON OF ENVY

DEMON OF GREED (CURRENTLY INHABITING MANHATTAN, NY)

DEMON OF MISFORTUNE

DEMONS OF NIGHTMARES AND FEAR (TWO-HEADED TWINS)

DEMON OF PESTILENCE (LOCATION UNKNOWN)

DEMON OF VENGEANCE

DEMON OF VIOLENCE

UNDERLINGS

HIGH-LEVEL DEMONS

MID-LEVEL DEMONS

LOWER-LEVEL DEMONS

HELLSPAWN

TRACK ONE
LIVING DEAD GIRL

TRACK ONE

LIVING DEAD GIRL

I KNOW WHAT HAPPENS WHEN PEOPLE LIKE ME DIE. There are no guiding lights, no pearly gates, and certainly no rosy-cheeked cherubs with outstretched arms. There is only darkness. Fire. Brimstone—whatever *that* is. Maybe I'll ask the Devil when we cross paths again.

Assuming he doesn't kill me first.

Déjà vu greets me like an old friend when I step out of my car, a candy-red '70 Camaro with an engine powered by dark magic. Thick boots hit hallowed ground as I slip on my trusty leather jacket, the perfect staple in my gothic wardrobe. The door slams shut behind me as I pull out a rickety shovel from the trunk and rest it on my shoulder. I remove my sunglasses, light the cigarette hanging from my lips, and gaze upon one of my favorite Tinsel Town watering holes—Hollywood Forever Cemetery.

The 90s weren't kind to the City of Angels, and its charm has long since faded, now marred by grime and decay. The streets, dimly lit and filled with shadowy corners, still offer refuge for the damned and deranged, where the good, the bad, and the ugly teeter on a knife's edge.

It has been a solid decade since I last set foot in the streets of Los Angeles, and I'm glad to see it hasn't changed.

It feels like home, and I'm glad to be back.

My welcoming committee—if you can call it that—isn't as glamorous as I would like. I'd imagined a warm welcome from a crowd of adoring fans, maybe a few brown-nosing witches and warlocks, even some love-sick vampires. Instead, I'm met with the incessant moaning and groaning of the dead. Their woes hit me like a sledgehammer as I creep my way through the graveyard, gripping the splintered shovel tightly.

Restless spirits watch me like I'm some sort of pariah, their translucent, human-shaped forms darkening and flashing red in my presence, while the palm trees seem to shudder as I pass. My heels sink into the damp grass, and my already-muddied soles slog through a sea of tombstones. The sooner I get this over with, the better. After all, I just need one: one wealthy dead person whose grave goods could make me rich, or at least afford me a place to lay low in this God-forsaken city.

Despite the restless deceased, the graveyard appears

desolate of any mortals. The setting sun casts a Hellish glow over Mount Hollywood, the tiny white letters barely discernible against the smog-choked horizon. The cemetery is overflowing with the dead, a final resting place for decades of Hollywood elite—actors, directors, producers, and the like. Their gravesites are unmistakably opulent and elaborate, glittering with freshly-polished marble and perfectly manicured landscaping. A decorative sculpture draws my attention as I trudge by— a lavish likeness of an actress adorned in expensive jewels from head to toe. Her husband's grave sits nearby, marked by a statue of him standing tall with a stiff upper lip, as if a foot is permanently lodged up his ass. Their spirits linger near their above-ground tomb, cowering as I approach, shovel in hand. The woman wails, her ethereal screech nearly deafening me as she begs for help.

"Your acting days are long behind you, lady." I smirk through my cigarette, glancing at her death date of 1973. Good year for me, bad year for the stock market. I eye her attire—a flawless fur draped over her ghostly form— and take one final drag before snuffing out my light. My grimy sole meets the rusted shovel as I start to dig up her grave.

The temperature around me plummets suddenly as a cold breeze cuts through my clothes, sending a chill across my skin. My hand clutches the shaft as I shake the wretched feeling. An army of spirits closes in as I sweat, my muscles aching from the unusual exertion. If this had been a year ago, I'd have simply wiggled my fingers, murmured a spell, and conjured a mound of dirt next to a magically dug six-foot ditch. But this isn't 2002, and my magic is a luxury I can't afford.

My skin tickles with the awareness of my audience, the grim apparitions who hurl insults and threats my way.

'Devil-loving whore.'

'Go back to the depths of hell you crawled out of.'

Funny—I've never been to Hell, and I have no intention of ever going there.

I groan as I reach the halfway point, dirt finally reaching up to my knees. I rest my arm against the end of the shovel, letting out a huff of frustration as I turn to face the dead.

"You're lucky I don't harvest you cretins right here and now," I mutter, disdain dripping like poison from my lips. "And believe me, there's no coming back from where I'll be sending you."

The spirits burn red with unrelenting fury, their voices muddled as their shadows swirl around me. I swing my shovel with reckless abandon, grunting and growling like a child thrashing at a piñata, daring them to challenge me. My muscles are out of practice, aching and screaming as I swing.

Fuck, this was *so* much easier when I had magic.

Spectral howls resonate across the twilight sky with decades of unrest. They're eager to bring this wicked witch to her knees. Try as they might, though, their efforts prove useless; magic or no magic, they should know better than to test me.

But it isn't my nefarious reputation thwarting their assault—it's that cold gust of wind, the same one that hit me the moment I set foot on this damned grave. It's not the usual chill that follows the dead—no, it's something far more sinister. Something familiar. Something *powerful*.

A voice rings in my ears, much clearer than those of the pathetic wraiths. It's a voice that grips my heart with thick, sharp claws, threatening to pull it out of my chest through my throat. A voice that has haunted me for nine centuries. A voice I've desperately been running from for over a year.

"October Winters," it calls to me, and a snake-like dread slithers up my spine. I swallow the knot in my throat and fight the building panic. While every fiber of my being tells me to run, to get the hell out of this cemetery and put the pedal to the metal, I simply shrug.

"I'm busy," I grit through my teeth as I continue digging the grave.

The spirits dissipate as the air weighs heavy with a disturbing presence and lingering dread—the kind that hits you seconds before plunging down a rollercoaster drop. *He knows better,* I remind myself. He could never set foot on hallowed ground, not without human sacrifice and archaic rituals. Not without *my* help.

My shovel finally bangs against a hardened surface,

and I realize my efforts have paid off. I descend into the poorly dug grave, boots colliding with the rotted wood of the actress' coffin.

If I could just whisper a spell to open the damn thing…

No. **No magic.** Especially not now.

The casket is malleable beneath me, a gust of dirt lifting as I bounce my foot over the festering timber. A brilliant idea strikes me; I rise to my feet and repeatedly crash my sole into the box. The chilling sensation returns then—that cold wind seems to wrap around me, as if threatening to choke me where I stand.

"October Winters."

"I heard you the first time," I growl. "Buzz off."

One final blow to the casket yields my victory. I peel away at the rotting wood, nearly gagging as I'm met with a heady stench. To say the scent is grueling would be a massive understatement; a whiff of death and decay assaults my nostrils, forcing a cough through my lungs. I hold my breath and reveal a moldy, satin-lined coffin. The remains of the dead are long gone, leaving behind an unrecognizable lump of dust and rags. What *does* remain, however, is a seemingly well-preserved fox fur coat and a pile of discarded jewelry. "Bingo."

I use the shovel to pick through the decay, sorting through the diamond, emerald, ruby, and sapphire accessories scattered throughout the case. A massive engagement ring catches my eye, and I grab it. A sneer curls my lips as disgust rises in my gut. This thing's weight feels like a shackle, as binding as any marriage vow. I pocket the jewelry and reach for the fur coat, only to find a clumsily stitched knockoff label inside.

The damn thing's fake. Figures.

I look up from the casket, my eyes meeting the spirit of the grave I've just robbed. She stares down at me in contempt, a small, prideful smile playing upon her features.

"Here lies a fake-ass bitch," I practically spit at her.

She hisses at me, spitting out a jumble of words I don't care to listen to. I fold the coat over my arm, patting the dust off. "Don't worry, it's pretty convincing. Some poor idiot will easily fall for my sales pitch. 'One priceless, vintage fox fur, previously worn by a silver-screen coke-head.'" The spirit hisses again, and I hurl my shovel in her direction, nearly toppling over my own feet in the process.

I throw the coat out of the ditch and climb out slowly after it. The army of spirits circles the tomb again, still trembling and cowering before a great evil. I'd like to think they're afraid of me, but their eyes are fixed on a blinding, burning glow.

The actress' tombstone erupts in flames, but this fire is different—nothing like the magic I wield or the fading ember of my cigarette. It rages with a Hellish intensity, reeking of sulfur, or whatever I imagine brimstone is supposed to smell like.

It isn't until a message magically carves into the epitaph that I feel my heart wrench in my chest. The words taunt me, serving as a deadly reminder of my fated demise. They burn into the headstone, cinders flaring as each letter curves in a haunting script.

Time is running out.

Darkness looms heavy with an unseen presence that clings to my skin. I shrug my new stolen coat over my shoulders, fighting the bitter cold and dread that threaten to suffocate me. A second tombstone—her husband's—burns before my eyes, yet another warning etched onto the granite.

You can't run forever.

Oh, really? Watch me.

Gravel crunches under my feet as I walk down the winding cemetery path. The Camaro finally comes into view as I fumble for the keys in my pocket, hands trembling when I finally slip into the driver's seat. My fingers struggle to guide the metal into the ignition, and I curse under my breath. It seems that even the easiest task proves too difficult under the shadow of impending doom. *C'mon, bitch, get the damn thing in.*

A final blast of fire sears the windshield, white-hot and threatening to melt the red paint off my enchanted car. The engine roars to life on its own—thanks to a lingering spell I cast on this hunk of metal before I went off the magical grid last year. I slam the accelerator to the floor, tires screeching against the asphalt as I try to make my escape. But the car stays rooted, the wheels melting into the ground with a puff of smoke.

I'm trapped.

I'm trapped like a fucking rat.

The fire blazes on, engulfing a new cluster of tombstones and bathing them in a scorching glow. This time, a third inscription materializes on white marble, but the letters form in crimson, bleeding into the stone.

I'm coming for you, October Winters.

The words hang over me, an eternal reminder. There's an itch in my fingertips no ointment can ease, an incessant prickling that spreads through every nerve, limb by limb, until it consumes my mind. Like a recovering alcoholic, I cling to my earring—a scorpion-shaped ear cuff—as if it's my sobriety token, a reminder I've been walking a mile in a human's shoes for far too long and my feet are failing.

I light another cigarette to calm my rising panic and take a long drag, awaiting the euphoria that comes with the pull. Instead, my throat closes in on me. I curse my lungs, easing the discomfort with a cough—seems like the terms and conditions of my employment are catching up to me. The realization hits me with a jolt when I catch a glimpse of my hand on the steering wheel: once flawless, smooth skin turns frail, littered with light spots and blue-green veins that trail from my wrist like the branches of a barren tree.

Fuck. I'm starting to age. Yet another price for my hubris—He's trying to teach me a fucking lesson.

I could make this all go away. I could use my magic, regain my youth, and continue as I have for nearly a thousand years—beautiful, powerful, deadly. The idea tempts me, tugging at my deepest, darkest desires as I yearn to reclaim the formidable witch the Underworld remembers me to be.

*No. Do **not** use your magic.*

The moment I do, He will find me—*truly* find me—and then, there will be no escaping Him. I close my eyes, trying to silence the endless voices of the dead and the relentless reminders of my poor choices. Out of sight, out of mind. It's easier to ignore your problems when you've been given eternal life, but immortality comes with a price, and the Devil has come to collect.

BAD DECISIONS
C'MON, BABE, WHO'S A GIRL GOTTA FUCK TO GET A ROOM AROUND HERE?
YOU'RE REALLY NOT IN THE POSITION TO BE MAKING DEMANDS, DOLL FACE.
TRACK TWO
DOIN' TIME

TRACK TWO

DOIN' TIME

My heart pounds in sync with the drums blaring through fading speakers, the radio static mimicking the raspy sound of my labored breaths. I slam the pedal to the floor, the roar of my Camaro echoing through the night. With the windows down, I leave a trail of burning rubber and desperation behind me, pushing sixty in a twenty-five. The wind whips through my choppy, freshly bleached hair as I glance in the rearview mirror, half-expecting to see the Devil hot on my trail.

But there's nothing behind me. No fire. No ghosts. Certainly no King of Demons. There's only darkness—the kind that threatens to swallow you whole if you're not fast enough. Relief washes over me, if only for a moment, and I pull over to catch my breath.

One year. One exhausting, relentless year.

That's how long I've been running. That's how long

He's been hunting me. No matter how hard I've tried to stay hidden from the Underworld, His wretched Underlings have always tracked me down, chasing me from state to state until I ended up back here—just another big city where I can disappear in plain sight. My fingers brush against my earring once more, eyes closing as centuries of dark deeds flash through my mind like a reel of old film. "Not much longer now, buddy," I sigh, speaking to the scorpion curled around my cartilage as if he can hear me—as if he needs reassurance more than I do.

I continue my drive down the famed streets of Hollywood, cruising the boulevard for a place to crash. Amid the gloom of shadowed alleys, I spot the usual nocturnal crowd; stilettos click on corners while hushed deals go down under buzzing streetlights. The roads are lined with lodgings of every flavor. Take your pick— seedy motel? Check. Overpriced Hellhole? You bet. Can't forget the old-school-landmarks-turned-tourist-traps.

The flickering of a bright neon light captures my attention—a tall motel sign that has seen better days. I was there the day this motel opened. I remember passing by as it was being built, watching it flourish from the ground up. I remember absolutely loathing the color scheme, the ungodly kaleidoscope of mismatched colors meant to draw people in. The 60s were a hot mess; don't let anyone tell you otherwise. Flower power and free love might've been groovy, but it sure as hell didn't do any favors for interior design.

The sun hasn't been kind to The Starlight over the years; its ghastly paint appears faded and chipped—thank Hell—giving off a haunting charm of sorts. My kind of look.

The words 'Bad Decisions' reflect in a freshly formed puddle of rainwater by the curb, and I can't help but snort at the pun. Attached to the motel stands a squalid, rundown establishment that feels like a relic lost to time. The exterior appears mediocre at best, with various posters of scantily clad women plastered over barred windows, lewd graffiti sprayed onto the façade, and a faded neon sign that flickers dimly under a single streetlight. It made perfect sense for a strip joint to be connected to a seedy motel—a forgotten corner of Hollywood where the glitz and glam are robbed of their pretenses and reveal their true nature: damned, demented, and deranged.

My possessed car parks perfectly into the first spot it finds. These streets, once familiar, now feel hostile—filled with dangers both mundane and supernatural. Demons lurk around every corner, and if memory serves me right, one of the Devil's sons has a firm grip on the entertainment industry. I need to tread carefully.

As soon as I step out of the car, I'm hit with a sordid racket: classic rock blares from the motel rooms, a heavy thump pulsing through the ground beneath me. Locals and visitors clash in a screaming match over the music, some threatening to fight while others catcall the barely-dressed women who blow kisses from the second-floor railing. Guests of The Starlight have a delicious flavor of their own, it seems. I know these walls have seen decades of lies and scandals and have provided refuge for lost souls, if only for a night. What was once a sanctuary veiled in secrecy now stands as a seedy halfway house for cheaters, drug dealers, and broken hearts—the perfect place for me to lay low.

With a deep breath, I enter the motel lobby, only to be met with a heady whiff of cigarette smoke, cheap liquor, and stale cologne. I smirk at management's feeble attempt to decorate the place for Halloween, the reception desk covered with rotting pumpkins, fake cobwebs, and plastic spiders.

I stop dead in my tracks as I come face to face with a striking but deadly creature, one whose aura pulses before me like a warning sign. She stands behind the front desk, expression grim as she flips through her books, scribbling notes on faded pages. I should have known a place like this would be filled to the brim with demons, specifically the staff. Hesitation builds within me as I weigh my options; I *cannot* be seen by a demon—not while the Devil's network is hot on my heels.

I look down at my hands as I turn to make a beeline for the exit. My other hand now looks wrinkled, fingers curling as centuries of dodged arthritis flare up in my joints. The pain radiates to my elbows and irritates my shoulders, soon followed by micro tremors and a persistent tingling that spreads across my skin. The Devil was right: my time is running out, and there's no turning back. This is the best option I've got.

I clear my throat and lean over the counter. "I need a room."

The woman—no, demon—regards me with a look of indifference. If she recognizes me, she doesn't let it show. "Did you miss the 'no vacancy' sign out front? We're full."

The she-demon is exactly what you'd expect—an intoxicating blend of beauty and danger, balanced on a razor's edge. Tip it one way, and you just might find yourself with a cut. Her presence demands respect; fiery amber eyes blaze like an inferno, daring to scorch anyone who steps out of line. The elegant curves of her ebony horns twist with an unnatural grace, a clear testament to her demonic lineage. She reeks of seduction and mystery, a prized sensation in the tawdry clutches of this unforgiving city.

The demoness retreats from the front desk, sauntering with a melodic sway of her hips. I instinctively follow her, unconvinced by her dismissal. "Well, did you check in the back?" My thorny humor goes unappreciated, naturally, judging by the roll of her eyes.

"This is a motel, not a Toys R' Us."

With an exasperated sigh, I add, "C'mon, babe. Who's a girl gotta fuck to get a room around here?"

The she-demon spins around to face me, hand on her hip and expression straight-laced. "Reagan, not 'babe.' I'm too high up the food chain for cheesy nicknames, and you're *way* above fucking someone for a room."

Ah, so she *does* recognize me. Fabulous—I hope. "Reagan." Her name rolls off my tongue. "Any relation?"

"Hell no. That would have made things *painfully* awkward." She winks, throwing her mess of crimson hair over her dark shoulder. Her skin glows faintly in this light as twisted, red-hot tendrils adorn her skin like a river of molten lava. It's no surprise she doesn't conceal her monstrous features, what with Halloween right around the corner. Plus, a strip joint is the perfect place to blend in while standing out. I bet there's some sick fuck out there with a demon fetish. In fact, I'm certain of it.

A screeching wail interrupts our exchange. "Not again," she groans, running her claws through her thick, red curls. "Fucking Violence."

Her statement sends a jolt of panic through me, and my breath catches in my throat. "Demon of Violence?" I ask, desperate to remain aloof.

Her fiery gaze burns as I follow her through the door connecting the motel to the strip club. "Fucker keeps sending his gangsters in here, and they keep getting a little too fresh with my girls, sometimes even end up killing the human ones."

Ah, how I've missed demonic turf wars. "How's your boss handling that?"

"He isn't," she practically growls. "*I'm* the one who ends up having to clean up their messes and replace my girls. I can't do both *and* run two businesses."

"Looks like you need to show them who's boss."

She barks out a laugh. "I'm a high-tier Debauchery demon. How exactly am I supposed to do that? Edge them to death?"

"It'll keep them from coming again, no pun intended."

"Aren't you funny?" Her voice drips with petulance as we walk through a dark, seemingly empty dance club with a handful of patrons. She pushes through a heavy black door, revealing a private room covered in blood… and the lifeless bodies of two dancers still clad in glittery thongs.

Reagan's exasperated groan echoes in the small space as she rolls up her fishnet sleeves and digs through a supply closet filled with cleaning supplies and black tarp. "You just gonna stand there, or are you going to help me get rid of these?"

I glance over the corpses. My fists ball at my sides, fingers itching to siphon the souls out of the freshly dead before they ascend to the *other* place. "Dead bodies aren't my style."

"Bullshit," she scoffs. "Can you at least use your magic to help me lift them?"

Do not use your magic. The reminder plays on a loop in

my head. With a heavy sigh, I remove my jacket, tie it around my waist, and help Reagan lay the tarp out on the dirty concrete floor.

"Look, I won't beat around the bush," I start as I roll the bodies over. "I need a place to stay, somewhere I can lay low and make a little cash to get around without getting into any trouble. Tryin' to fly under the radar."

"You? Under the radar?" She grunts as she wraps the tarp around body number one. "That's not your style."

"No, it's not. So, I'll make you a deal: you give me a place to hang low, and I'll take care of your gangster problem. Gives you time to recruit more girls and keeps the rabble away."

She ponders on my offer but doesn't seem convinced. "Tempting."

"But you're not sold," I grimace.

She glances at me, those fiery amber eyes sizing me up and practically burning a hole through my skin. "I know all about you, October Winters. I know that trouble follows you wherever you go, and if it doesn't, you always find a way to make it. A witch of your standing doesn't just show up in a city like this without a mile-long honey-do list."

"Under normal circumstances, you'd be right—" the last words sting as I admit them "—but in this case, it's exactly as I said. I need to lay low."

Her posture straightens for a moment, and she shoots

me an incredulous glance. "I know better than to make a deal with someone like you."

"And *I* know better than to make a deal with a demon, especially a Debauchery demon. But like it or not, my methods are effective and you know it."

We carry the tarp-wrapped corpses out the back door into a dark alley that reeks of trash and broken dreams. My muscles continue to ache as the tarp grows too heavy for my dismal strength, and in a span of five minutes, I feel my body age decades. Fuck, what I'd give to just cast a little spell right now…

Reagan and I hoist the bodies into an oversized garbage bin, groaning as the scent of decay mixes with the stale stench of week-old trash. The she-demon claps her hands to dust them off and turns to face me once more. "Motels are a dime a dozen in this town. Why don't you fuck off to The Valley and shack up there?"

"Valley's crawling with Hellspawn and Hollywood's more my scene. C'mon, Reagan. I'll throw in a vintage '73 fox fur, fresh from the grave. It'll really bring out your eyes."

Her gaze narrows. "And you said dead bodies aren't your style."

I flash her a coy smirk, shrugging a shoulder with the arch of my brow.

She shoots me yet another scrutinizing glance and finally sighs. "Take care of the thugs, hand over the coat, and I'll give you a place to stay. But until I can procure more girls, I need you to dance."

I could smack a bitch. "What part of 'lay low' didn't sink into that horny red head of yours?"

Reagan's chuckle echoes throughout the grimy alley. "You're *really* not in the position to be making demands, doll face. Doors open at eight. Grab yourself a pair of heels. Nothing too grippy; you want to be able to slip."

A shadow falls across the dim, flickering yellow lights in the alley. Two figures emerge, tall and brutish, as Reagan's stance stiffens. Goosebumps prickle over my arms as the air suddenly thickens with menace…and a sickening scent of sulfur.

"Pretty things like you shouldn't be out here alone," one of the demons says as he looms closer, all bulk and swagger through his human glamor. I fight to keep my breathing steady as my power instinctually tingles beneath my skin. Reagan steps out of the shadows, her amber markings glowing with a pulsing, ominous warning. The figures hiss, twin grins dripping with malice.

"Lookie-here, Jones. We've got ourselves a demon whore and her useless trash."

"You know the rules, boys," Reagan's voice rasps, low and guttural like a growling tigress. "I'm off-limits."

"Sure." The second one steps forward, his demented eyes raking over my body. "But your friend isn't."

"I wouldn't if I were you." Reagan steps in front of me. "Not unless you've got a death wish."

The demonic thugs continue to stare at me as they saunter closer. One's gaze falls to my ear, no doubt noticing the scorpion cuff clinging to me. His eyes widen then, and a triumphant grin spreads over his ghastly features.

"I know you," he mutters. "You're the —"

"—one the Devil's been after," his smug friend cuts him off. "There's a pretty price on that pretty head of yours, witch." They're just feet away now, and I can see the hunger in their eyes—the thirst for violence that drives their fury. My knees tremble at the sight, though I can't tell if it's another arthritic flare-up or pure fear coursing through me. The truth gnaws at my resolve like a flesh-eating parasite. Without my magic, I'm helpless, useless —*especially* against two Violence demons. It's either do or die, and I'm running out of time.

Well, Winters, I guess this is it; it was fun while it lasted. At the end of the day, my survival is paramount, to Hell with the consequences.

Literally.

I smile at the thugs. "And it's a pretty price you can't afford."

My magic flows through me, bursting through a dam, flooding with a surge of power I'd almost forgotten. The world around me sharpens; the lights are brighter, my vision is clearer, and my aches and pains fade as vitality returns. Tears well in the corner of my eyes as I relish in the heat that builds through my body, and the flames cast out from my hand. Hell, how I've *missed* my fire.

It's intoxicating, this rush of power. It's like a drug, one that pulls at my veins and fills me with euphoria that thrums through my core. The scent of burning, melting demonic flesh fills my lungs with a satisfaction I've yearned for for over a year.

The demonic thugs' mouths gape, revealing rows of serrated teeth as they scream their torment. I propel my flames at them, hurl after hurl, one after the other as they fall to their knees. I long for their ashes, to see their fiendish corpses disintegrate into the hazy, smog-ridden sky, but it's Reagan's voice that pulls me from my frenzy.

"That's enough, doll. They can't get any deader."

My fire extinguishes then, leaving us with a pile of burning flesh at our feet. I look at my hands, rubbing my fingers together as the magic still lingers. A small smile plays on my lips. While I know my demise is imminent, I savor the moment. I relish in the power I so deeply missed.

Reagan and I return to the club in a hurried silence, checking over our shoulders for prying eyes. Demonic turf wars are never simple, and I see the concern that builds in her gaze as she leads me into her office. Her skin wrinkles as worry lines form on her forehead and her brows furrow. She collapses into her large, red leather chair, letting out a sigh of relief as she runs her claws over her face.

"Thanks for that," she says, words muffled behind her hands. "Debauchery demons aren't exactly well-equipped with offensive powers. It's not easy to defend myself or my girls in this place."

I shrug, unwrapping my jacket from my waist and pulling it over my shoulders. I snag a cigarette from my pocket, and for the first time in a year, I use my magic to light the flame. Reagan yanks open a desk drawer and rifles through a jumble of clinking metal and crumpled receipts. She retrieves a key from the clutter—a rusty, ancient piece that looks like it hasn't been used in years.

"Remember our deal." She wags the rickety key in front of my face, dangling it like a cookie in front of a starving child. "You still need to take care of those gangsters."

"What do you think I just did back there?" I groan, shoulders slumping.

"That was just two of them. There are more—lots more." I reach for the key, but she pulls her hand back. "A deal's a deal, Winters."

"A deal's a deal," I repeat. My grouchiness knows no bounds.

Reagan drops the key into my hand, its faded tag marked with the number '666.' Of course. Of fucking course.

There it is again—a cold gust of wind, followed by the

unsettling feeling that every move I make is being closely watched. A dark figure shifts in my peripheral, one that wasn't there just moments ago. It's as if He's right here, scrutinizing me with those void-like eyes, patronizing me with that deep, menacing growl and husky voice, reminding me of our thousand-year exchange and my eternal promise. It's only a matter of time now…

"Hey, Your Excellence," Reagan calls as I head toward the exit. Her choice of words stings—just a little. "Who are you running from anyway?"

I flash her a demure smile before I run out of Bad Decisions. "That's my business."

TRACK THREE
SHOUT AT THE DEVIL
WHAT DO YOU HAVE TO SAY FOR YOURSELF, MY CHILD?
SORRY DADDY, I'VE BEEN A BAD GIRL?

TRACK THREE

SHOUT AT THE DEVIL

IRKSOME WORRY CLOUDS MY VISION WHEN I EXIT THE club and make way across the street toward a shopping center. There's also a hint of thrill, an excitement that builds as I feel my magic born anew. And damn, does it feel good—almost like the first time.

Fine, I'll admit it; I've missed the power. I've craved that release more than anything, even the air in my lungs. But despite the relief, despite the warm fuzzies urging me to light my fire and raise the dead, all I can hope is that my little inferno won't land me in a fuck-ton of trouble.

I push through the glass doors of a seemingly empty Blockbuster. The store is lined with aisles and aisles of boxed movies, everything from cult classics to new releases. I smirk to myself as I remember the evolution of entertainment when giant screens slowly replaced the elegance of outdoor plays and sold-out operas. I've had the privilege of witnessing the rise and fall of empires, the discovery of new worlds, and the genius invention of the pet rock. I've seen the unsinkable succumb to icy depths and held my breath as man took their first steps upon the moon. You can only imagine my elation when I discovered I could relive it all again through clunky cassette tapes, thick television sets, and a Blockbuster card. Hollywood sure loves to monetize on the trials and tribulations of mankind, and here I am, arms full of the latest and greatest, feeding the beast I so boldly criticize.

I slam a stack of VHS tapes on the check-out stand, idly grabbing one too many sweets and savories to go with my festive night in. The fluorescent lights flicker as the thin walls hum and shake around me. I look around, heart rate increasing as I realize I'm the only person inside this establishment, save the teenage cashier behind the desk.

"Hello, Toby."

My skin prickles at the mention of that stupid nickname. There's only one creature in the entire universe who could ever dare to call me that. My body grows numb as that familiar gust of cold air flurries past. A darkness fills the room, one that's unmistakably sinister, the same one I felt at the cemetery.

Fuck. He found me. I *need* to get out of here.

I glance over at the cashier. He's a young thing covered in acne and braces, with eyes so sickeningly black that I forget how to breathe. He smiles at me, a devious, demented smile that almost seems ill-fitted for his features. Thick black veins appear on his quickly-paling skin, creeping up his neck and cheeks as the Devil possesses him.

Candies and tapes crash onto the ground as I make my escape. My hands press against the icy glass doors, and I instinctively reach for my earring. The cool metal hits my fingers, and relief washes over me, grounding me, if only for a moment.

I pull my hood over my head to shield my messy, easily-distinguishable hair, shove my hands into my pockets, and make my way up Gower. The streets are packed tonight, car horns blaring while engines roar and speed up the streets of Hollywood. I reach a freeway overpass, keeping to the shadows as the uncharacteristically crisp fall night threatens to freeze me over. Last I checked, this was LA—the city of endless summer, where rain and snow are practically myths. But this chill? It wasn't just any cold front. I knew better.

Tent City looms ahead, a sprawling homeless encampment cobbled together from tarps and plastic sheets. I do my best to ignore the handful of figures huddled around a garbage bin fire, but one of them catches my attention with a gravelly voice.

"Got a cigarette, Toby?"

I can't help but stare at the woman. Her eyes and smile are like the Blockbuster cashier from earlier, with those eerie black veins covering her hollow cheeks. The way she shuffles toward me makes me quicken my pace and duck around the nearest corner.

No. No way. He is *not* fucking *body hopping*.

I'm desperate to find a hiding place, preferably somewhere crowded, where someone possessed by the Devil wouldn't stand out. Low and behold, a dive bar sign blinds me like a literal and figurative slap in the face. I sprint toward the bar with the possessed woman far from reach and slip inside. Bathed in a crimson light from lackluster neon signs, the place is full of people. I scan the room and take a quick headcount, pinning at least sixty patrons within the spot. The joint isn't much, but what it lacks in glitz and glam, it makes up with cheap booze and a hefty chunk of pitiful humans to disappear amongst. Plus, this witch could use a drink.

The bar is littered with desperate souls—touch-starved sports fanatics and tough women who think they can best said men in pool or darts. I take a seat at a barstool, quickly removing my earring and gripping it like my life depends on it. Hell, it practically does. I run my knuckles over the little thing, tempted to cast my spell, to bring my little scorpion to life, to finally have my best friend within reach again. The magic sparks at my fingertips, and I'm close—*so close* to whispering the words…

"Devil's Martini?" The bartender jolts me from my stupor, setting down a crimson cocktail that assaults my senses with spices and strong liquor. His reflection is clear through the liquid in front of me: a handsome man with graying skin, dark veins, and black eyes.

Fucker can't take a hint, can he?

I clutch my earring to my chest, swirling off the barstool and pushing past the sea of drunken nimrods. With fumbling fingers, I reattach it to my cartilage, eyes already scanning for my next refuge. I bolt out of the dive bar, the howling wind matching my pace as it whips through my hair.

My options are limited, as the world—or at least Hollywood—feels like the Devil's playground. I press my back against the cool concrete of a back alley, weighing my choices. The motel is a wash, especially with its demon management; he'd be welcomed there with open arms and bootlickers. Places like the Walk of Fame and the nightlife are out of the question, and the cemetery is too far to reach on foot.

I'm left with only one option: a house of God.

The nearest church in Hollywood is just a few blocks away, up Gower, if I remember correctly. It's just another useless factoid swimming in the cesspool of a 999-year-old brain, drowning in centuries of memories.

I move cautiously, my feet growing weary and my calves aching under the weight of my heavy shoes. While my magic gives me a burst of energy, it can't reverse the effects of aging—only the Devil can do that. But I'm not ready to face him, not yet—despite how tonight's events seem to push me toward that inevitability. I need one last chance to catch my breath and come up with a convenient excuse for avoiding him for over a year. The church will have to suffice.

I haven't set foot in one of these bad boys in—Hell, has it really been sixty-three years? Not since that mishap at Notre Dame. This cathedral is one of the oldest buildings in the city, all brick exteriors and stained-glass windows, with the world-famous Hollywood Sign just visible above the overpass of the 101 Freeway. As I push the heavy wooden doors open, an invisible force pushes back, trying to keep me out. I press forward, using my magic to shatter the holy enchantments meant to repel evil. I smirk, knowing I've got centuries of power on this building—and my magic wins.

An unsettling breeze whistles through the walls as ambient city lights pierce the stained glass. They cast a kaleidoscope of red and blue that covers the altar in a twisted glow—something far from pure and holy. Candlelight flickers, and the silence and emptiness soothes my frigid nerves. There's something unnaturally striking about it all, something impressive, even to a wretch like me. It's no secret that I was never destined to be a woman of God, not with so many wicked, dirty games to play in life. But this current game of hide and seek is definitely testing my limits.

My shoes echo with heavy thumps as I search for a hiding spot, hoping my boss will eventually give up his merciless chase. A confessional booth catches my eye, and

I dart inside, locking the door behind me. Breathless and weary, I lift my hood and rake my fingers through my hair, trying to calm myself, but a quiet throat clearing shatters my moment of peace. I'm not alone—a priest sits just beyond the intricate divider, separated by only a thin screen.

"What do you have to say for yourself, my child?" the priest's voice speaks calmly behind the latticed screen. The words come in an unnatural echo, as if teetering between the world of the living and the dead. And then, there's the cold again. Mother*fucker*.

I wince, my shoulders inching toward my ears, and I flash him a weary smile through the divider. "Sorry, Daddy. I've been a bad girl?"

"Close enough," he sighs.

My eyes dart to the door latch, ready to lunge for another escape, but the guttural timbre of his assertive voice has me in a chokehold. "Don't."

My body slumps against the booth, and I slap my hands against my knees in sheer and utter astonishment. "How the fuck did you manage to possess a priest?"

I can almost hear the smile in His voice as He huffs. "He's not really a priest. Maybe in name but not in practice. Let's just say his tastes make him better suited for Hell."

"Gross," I mutter under my breath as I grip my jacket tighter to fight the incessant chill that follows Him. "So, Luci, you're a long way from home. To what do I owe the pleasure, your Unholiness?" I know why He's here, but you can't blame a girl's thirst for banter, not when she's been on the run for over a year.

The possessed priest crosses His arms over His chest. "Now isn't the time to play coy with me, my little firestarter. This meeting is long overdue, and you knew it was inevitable."

"I couldn't tell, what with all the burning signs and body hopping."

The Devil sneers through shadows of the screen. "You've been avoiding me."

"Who, me? I would never."

"And yet, you have. For over a year. Did you really think our bond would weaken just because you stopped using your magic?"

It made sense to me—if I didn't use His gifts, maybe His hold on me would loosen...but I guess even the Devil knows how to find loopholes. Clearly.

He sighs when I remain silent, His breath coming out in a hollow resonance. "Remember about nine centuries ago, when you came into my service?"

I choke out a nervous laugh. "Cutting right to the chase, aren't we?"

"I granted you everything you could have dreamed of: beauty, invulnerability, power beyond imagination. I only asked for one thing in return."

Fuck me, it's like I'm a petulant child being scolded by her elder. "Souls. Lots of souls."

"That's right. And when I come to you with a very specific, very *delicate* job, I expect you to handle it. No questions asked, no procrastination, and certainly no betrayals." Guilt weighs heavily on my chest, unshakable, squeezing the air out of my lungs as I recall the past year. The deal I never made good on. The soul I failed to deliver.

"Look, I've been at this a long time, boss. Can't a girl muck it up every now and then?"

His voice deepens, rumbling like distant thunder. "Not when said girl is meant to be my right hand and most trusted acolyte. Your mistakes make me look weak. You can't possibly imagine the rumors I've had to silence, the backlash from my sons—"

"Your sons are idiots," I cut Him off.

He hums at my choice of words. "Not idiots, just in need of a little direction. And I must say, your absence in the past year made them all rather…*lazy.* I much prefer it when they're competing with you for my favor."

"What can I say? I have an unfair advantage; fathers *always* favor their daughters."

A deep, melodious chuckle resonates through the confessional, sending a delicious shiver up my spine. We sit in a comfortable, familiar silence for a moment, as we have for centuries, but I know it won't last long. There is still an elephant in this rather small booth.

"We have a deal in place, Toby—an *eternal* deal. My gifts are not for free, you know that."

And *there* it is. "Yeah, well, one year out of nine hundred shouldn't cost you much. Besides, you can't blame me for needing a break. That last job wasn't easy, y'know."

"You make it sound like I twisted your hand in all of this. If I remember correctly, you *begged* me for this life."

I squint. "I was a child. You manipulated me."

"Might need to revisit that memory." He moves closer to the divider, and I can almost make out the shape of His husk's form. "You need to make up for lost time, Toby. You know the repercussions."

I sure do. Deliver souls and live forever. Fail to do so, and it's bye-bye immortality. My aching muscles and wrinkling skin are proof of that.

"I'm giving you six sunrises and six sunsets to deliver a thousand souls to me."

I nearly choke on my own spit, rising to my feet in the cramped booth. "A thousand!?"

"One for every year you've walked this earth."

I push the doors open, barging out of the confessional and pacing the marble floors. Panic rises within me, and I can't subdue my high-pitched tone. "In six days? On Halloween — my birthday? How the Hell am I supposed to —"

"What better way to celebrate than knowing you've still got another thousand years ahead of you?" The Devil exits the booth, and I am met with the void-like eyes of a possessed priest. "You're my best employee and too smart for your own good. Running away from your responsibilities never did you any favors. Los Angeles is a big city. Figure it out."

Oh. He *really* wasn't kidding. I open my mouth to continue my protest, but He cuts me off. "And no cheating. I won't accept spirits or lost souls lingering near graves. That's lazy and you're better than that. Souls of the living *only*."

This just keeps getting better and better. I nod with an embarrassingly obvious gulp, accepting His terms while trying my best to keep calm. He extends His hand to me, just as He did nine hundred-some years ago when we made our very first deal. "Six sunrises and six sunsets, Toby. And if you fail, you can kiss your immortality goodbye." It's a fine line to tread, an impossible task under impossible circumstances. Six sunrises, six sunsets —six days. The numbers seem to follow me wherever I go.

The Devil regards me with one more look, raising a finger to trail along my jaw. "Don't disappoint me—I'd hate to see that beautiful face wither away as your years catch up to you."

The mere thought makes the bile rise in my throat. I've worked too hard to solidify my power and immortality. There's no way I can fail Him—or fail myself —now.

And so, I take His hand.

And the ground quakes beneath me.

Every candle flickers as a cold gust blows by, snuffing out the only light in the church. Darkness consumes us as we seal the deal with a shake. The cold wind twists and writhes around me like a snake, and my gaze falls to our hands. My lips twitch upward at the sight of my skin. Spotless. Flawless. Youthful. As it was always meant to be. I look up at my boss, whose darker than dark eyes peer down at me with a sense of pride.

"One more thing," He adds, and I can't help but groan; I'm not sure I can take any more surprises. "This soul doesn't count."

I tilt my head at the comment, eyes squinting with confusion. All at once, the body of the priest falls limp onto the floor, void of life, void of a soul as the Big Man Downstairs makes His dramatic exit.

Pity. He could have at least given me a freebie to start.

TRACK FOUR
BREAK STUFF
HI THERE, LITTLE BUDDY. TIME TO COME OUT OF RETIREMENT.

TRACK FOUR

BREAK STUFF

I AM, WITHOUT A SHADOW OF A DOUBT, ROYALLY AND irrevocably fucked.

I stretch my arms over my head in an exaggerated effort to prepare for the next six days. Los Angeles gleams differently in my eyes now, and with the flip of a metaphorical light switch, every single human sparks me as a commodity. The streets of Hollywood are far from desolate, and I feel like a kid in a candy store— overwhelmed with the sheer number of options at my disposal.

I bump shoulders with countless people, passing them by as my nerves tense. An itch crawls up my spine; every moment spent not collecting souls is just another missed opportunity.

My mind races back to those sneering faces, the rush

of power as I burned those demonic bullies alive. It felt so good in the moment—a hit of pure, unadulterated superiority.

But now?

Now, it tastes like ash in my mouth.

If I'd just kept my damn impulses in check, none of this would be happening. No Faustian bargain hanging over my head, no supernatural probation looming over the horizon. I'd be free as a bird—or as free as someone like me ever gets, anyway.

Right about now, I should be stuffing my face with deliciously greasy tacos from some mom-and-pop joint, maybe catching some up-and-coming band's set on the Sunset Strip.

Instead, I'm faced with a reality more bitter than day-old coffee and twice as hard to swallow:

I haven't collected a soul in 378 days.

Let's face it—I'm about as sharp as a butter knife right now. Can anyone really blame me? It has been over a fucking year since I've flexed any of my magical muscles, and my arcane arsenal's probably coated in layers of dust so thick, it could choke a vampire.

And suddenly, I'm expected to perform like it's the Devil's fucking Olympics, a stopwatch ticking my life away with every passing second. No pressure.

I haven't felt performance anxiety like this since...well, ever. It's like being asked to decode an ancient blood ritual without reference texts while blindfolded and reciting the Pledge of Allegiance. Backwards. In pig Latin.

But enough with my manic theatrics. The fact of the matter is, the Devil himself left his throne to personally deliver an ultimatum. My immortal days are numbered, and I have to get to work.

I reach for my ear, tugging at the cuff that curls around it. I remove it quickly, place it in the palm of my hand, and mutter a short incantation. Within seconds, the obsidian earring comes to life, limb by limb, taking the shape of an emperor scorpion.

"Hi there, little buddy," I coo at Nero, my familiar. His legs twitch and tap with excitement, filling my cold heart with a joy I didn't think I'd missed. "Time to come out of retirement. Big D's got us on a big job. We've got souls to collect."

All we need is a game plan…

It isn't difficult to find 1000 souls in a place like Los Angeles—that's just a minuscule fraction of the population. What *is* difficult is getting away with mass murder unseen. There are loopholes, of course, but I'm having a hell of a time finding one right now. Beats twiddling my thumbs while the Devil spends the next six days setting up my permanent residence in the 9th circle of Hell. It appears I have no other choice but to go in guns blazing and leave no survivors. The repercussions are November's problem. If I make it to November, that is.

The first place that catches my eye is the dive bar from earlier. Seems like a great place to start. Twenty to thirty drunken souls would make for an excellent inaugural reaping.

But I needed to be stealthy. Calculated. For every devious creature lurking the shadows of Hollywood, there's a handful of do-gooders ready to smite us with their irritably self-righteous fury.

The dive bar appears just as I left it before the whole bartender debacle: a jukebox in the farthest corner glows with a dim pink and yellow light, blasting the classics—from The Clash to the Pistols—while competing against the click-clack of pool balls. I clock about 32 innocent souls ripe for the taking, a perfect little starter pack for my impossibly large quota.

With Nero tucked safely in my hand, I sneak off toward the hall of bathrooms and payphone booths. I check my surroundings, head whipping back and forth to ensure my seclusion. My victims surround the bar, wasting their recent paychecks on shitty beer or fighting over the next jukebox tune. Crouching to the ground, I carefully place Nero before me, smiling down as I channel my magic. Hellspeak slithers off my tongue, the demonic syllables igniting the air as I prepare for tonight's first harvest.

"Grow." With a flash of dark smoke, my familiar doubles in size. I run my fingers along his ebony armor, the little hairs surrounding his exoskeleton tickling my skin. With another spell, I continue my devious work. "Multiply." Nero splits himself into dozens, creating a horde of kitten-sized scorpions. Finally, I tap into my telepathy and urge the creatures to enter the bar. "Kill."

I don't need to sneak a peek to revel in the carnage that befalls this quaint little dive bar. All I need to do is tap into the mind of my familiar.

I can see my victims now, their horror-stricken faces, the way their eyes nearly pop out of their sockets with fear. Their screams echo through shabby walls. One by one, my bed of scorpions paralyzes the patrons. I keep a careful count, summing up a whopping 32—just as I expected.

Paralysis takes over as the screams reduce to silence. My 32 victims lay lifeless on the floor, and the echoes of every single heartbeat ring in my ears like a mismatched percussion band. The scorpions dissipate at my command, collecting into a single form. Nero crawls toward me, scampering up my ripped jeans and black leather jacket to rest upon my shoulder. I extend my hands by my sides, tapping into a sphere of magic I've kept dormant for 378 days: soul siphoning.

32 souls rise from motionless forms like thick smoke, some white, others gray, most black, all innocent in the eyes of the Devil. They travel towards my welcoming

arms, sucking into my fingertips. The power is unmatched, invigorating, and brings me back to life after over a year of stagnation. I am born anew, a dark witch with dominion over the dead.

Once my harvest is complete, I take Nero into my hands. My fresh souls take the form of glowing orbs. They swirl around me like twinkling lights, awaiting my final move. With a wave of my hand, the orbs float toward Nero's ready stinger. I watch in awe, as I have millions of times before, as it siphons each soul into the tip of its tail. There they will safely remain until all 1000 souls are accounted for.

My process is fool-proof. Morbid, but genius. And with my first batch of 32 souls, the battle for my life is only beginning.

But let's get one thing straight: I'm not here to spin some sob story or beg forgiveness for my less-than-stellar moral compass. Nor am I looking for anyone's pity. I've got no one but myself to blame for my shitty circumstances.

My life—my *millennium*—has never been about good triumphing over evil. It's about survival, pure and simple; the lengths a centuries-old woman will go to keep her power. I'm nobody's hero, not even my own. I will never shield the innocent or battle the forces of darkness.

For I *am* the darkness.

I *revel* in it. *Serve* it. Just as I have for nearly a thousand years.

I don't fight the evils of the world—I fucking embrace them.

I am the Devil's Second, a long shadow cast across a wasteland of lost souls and broken dreams.

And Hollywood's about to get one Hell of a wake-up call.

TRACK FIVE
BODIES

TRACK FIVE

BODIES

Home sweet home.

I saunter back into Bad Decisions with a spring in my step and a song in my heart. It's a power ballad filled with sorrow and longing, a virtue lost to time and MTV.

My stolen phone's milky-green screen flickers to life —another trophy from my recent harvest. It's half past midnight. The deadly countdown of my ultimatum has officially begun.

Nero's stinger throbs against my ear even in his dormant state, a grim reminder of our night's work. 32 souls remain packed tight in his little bulb, sweltering in a boundless limbo of restless agony. Soon, but not soon enough, they'll be handed off to the Devil to do… whatever-the-fuck he does with them. Cosmic damnation? Eternal torture? I don't bore myself with the details.

Right now, I need to hit the ground running and snag a few more innocents for the Big Man Downstairs. The damned and the wretched won't collect themselves.

These dark, desolate hours are prime time for Bad Decisions. Men sprawl across threadbare booths while this shift's girls weave spells of their own. On stage, a trinity of dancers writhe against gleaming poles, putting on a delectable little show for leering perverts and forlorn bachelors.

I grimace at the sight. Not my first choice, and certainly not my dream job, but a deal's a deal.

A shadow lurks at the club's edges: clad in all black, face obscured by matte shades, married, no doubt, likely desperate to cloak his vices. I can practically feel the shame oozing from his pores and the guilt that gnaws at his mind. His rigid shoulders betray every attempt at nonchalance.

There's something deliciously adorable about the whole thing. He'd be my first mark if not for the door's sudden, jarring slam.

A cluster of demonic gangsters slithers into the club, moving as one malevolent horde with a singular purpose. The dancers freeze mid-routine, their bodies taut against the chrome poles, exchanging glances thick with unspoken dread. In an instant, the club's sultry atmosphere evaporates, replaced by the promise of impending violence. The air itself seems to curdle, heavy with the acrid stench of wrath and cruel intent.

Reagan emerges from her office, posture stiff at the sight of them, her clawed hands curled into fists at her sides.

"Reagan, baby," the leader of the pack practically snarls with a voice so savage, it makes my skin crawl.

"Call me 'baby' again," the she-demon warns, her voice laced with deadly seduction and equal savagery. She flashes a sharp, toothy grin, amber eyes burning bright despite the darkness of the club.

These must be the Violence Underlings she mentioned earlier—the ones I'm meant to 'take care of' in exchange for a place to stay. For a moment, I wonder if our deal still stands, given my sudden change in plans. Do I even *need* to lay low anymore?

Regardless, there's something intriguing about the she-demon… Her brazen attitude, her fabulous taste in clothes, or the fact that she's a business woman in the grimiest corner of Hollywood—perhaps it's because she reminds me of myself.

One thing is perfectly clear: Reagan can hold her own.

A creature like her could make a very handy ally.

"We'll take the three on the stage," the gangster-demon grunts, nodding his head at the girls.

Reagan's eyes flicker at me before she nods once at the thugs. The trio hop off the stage and lead the thugs to the private rooms in the back. I sneak past them, joining Charlie the bartender and shuffling some shot glasses around as if I belong there. Reagan joins me soon after, groaning as the magma-like veins flowing across her crimson skin burn bright with rage.

"I'm going to need you up there, Tober."

My lips curl in disgust. "Pole dancing?"

"I can't have an empty stage. I told you, I'm running low on girls."

An aggravated sigh escapes my lips as I vault over the bar, slinking towards the back room. I find a cramped cubby, peel off my clothes, and stash them away. As I stand there in nothing but a black bralette and matching thong, vulnerability crawls across my skin like an unwelcome caress.

It's not the scant clothing that bothers me — I've worn less in more public venues.

No, it's the knowledge that soon, the ravenous gazes of pitiful demons will devour every inch of my exposed flesh. The thought alone makes my skin prickle with disgust.

I am the Devil's Second for fuck's sake. I have a reputation to uphold and an image to maintain. This feels uncomfortably close to tarnishing both.

Chin up, tits up, as they say.

I snatch a pair of discarded platform heels that seem a tad too small and wriggle my fingers with a spell to loosen them just a bit. They slide on with ease, and suddenly, I'm five inches taller than before, with nothing but the grim, dark world at my disposal.

A flash of crimson curls vanishes behind the office door as I saunter back to the main floor. Before it can click shut, I wedge my foot in the gap and slip inside. Reagan's there, perched on her desk, fingers massaging her temples. Her face is a canvas of anxiety and contempt.

"So," I drawl, leaning against the doorframe, "I'm guessing those were the charming gentlemen you mentioned earlier?"

Reagan's nod is barely perceptible, a slight dip of her chin. She doesn't look up; she just continues kneading her forehead, as if trying to iron out the wrinkles of worry etched into her skin.

"Gangsters," she mutters, the word dripping with disdain. "More like rabid dogs with Übermensch syndrome."

I can't help but smirk at her choice of words. It's spot on, and it reminds me why I'm growing to like her so much. Even in the face of chaos, Reagan's sharp tongue remains whetted.

"You almost seem to hate demons as much as I do. How very self-loathing of you."

"I love my kin as much as the next person, but whoever said debauchery and violence go hand in hand was gravely mistaken."

Her choice of words makes me smirk while lingering in the doorway. Time's ticking, but the elephant in the room needs addressing. "Listen, Reagan"—I use her name deliberately, knowing her aversion to saccharine endearments—"I know we've got a deal. And yes, I owe you, but the game's changed since our last chat."

She sighs, eyes rolling skyward as she folds her arms. "Do enlighten me."

"The Devil found me."

Her pencil-thin eyebrow twitches, a barely perceptible reaction.

"We've been…let's say, on shaky ground lately. I may have ruffled his feathers last year."

Her molten gaze remains fixed on mine, unblinking.

"He dropped an ultimatum in my lap. A whopper. Six days to collect a thousand souls." I conveniently leave out the consequences of my failure, hoping she'll connect the dots herself.

But she doesn't flinch. "So you're looking for an out."

"Not exactly." I grimace. "Just giving you a heads up that I might be…a tad preoccupied for a few days."

"And how, pray tell, do you plan to harvest a thousand souls in six days without setting off every human alarm bell in Los Angeles?"

"Same way I always do: execute first, frame someone else later."

"There are only so many loopholes you can take advantage of, Tober. Eventually, you'll step on the wrong toes."

"Just another Thursday, then." I shrug, but my feigned confidence falls flat. The she-demon's eyes narrow, clearly unconvinced by my fake nonchalance. "Consider those rat bastards out there dealt with. A deal's a deal, after all." My lips quirk into a half-smile, equal parts reassurance and challenge.

Reagan pinches the bridge of her nose. When she looks up again, her gaze is steel. "Just get your ass on the fucking stage, witch."

I take to the dancer's stage for the first time in Devil-knows-when.

A moody, hypnotic beat pulses through the speakers. Scratchy, vinyl-like samples cut through a melancholic but seductive melody, easing my stiff muscles as I begin flowing from one familiar pose to another. My fingertips trail along my collarbones, knuckles brush against the swell of my breasts, and finally, I reach the apex of my thighs. My eyes flick to the darkest corner of the club, desperate to avoid the hungry stares of the savage beasts getting handsy with my fellow dancers.

There's that man in the shades again, the one conveniently sitting alone with nothing but a glass of liquor in his hand. I focus on him, my body shifting into liquid grace as my fingers trace the cool metal of the pole. Dancing isn't as foreign as I'd thought, and the moves certainly spark a memory of a time long, *long* past. My muscles spring to life as my magic courses through them, invigorating my limbs to ascend the pole like vines reaching for sunlight. Arms and legs twist and wrap in a hypnotic rhythm as the beat pulses through my body, and my eyes flick over to the shadowed figure.

There's…something familiar about the man. His body language. The broadness of his shoulders. The chiseled cheekbones hidden behind a popped collar. It's like a memory long forgotten. He almost reminds me of…

No. Not him. He wouldn't be caught dead in a place like this.

Lost in my reverie, I'm jolted back to reality by a sudden electric shift in the club's atmosphere. A noxious wave of sulfur and iron assaults my senses, heralding chaos. Supernatural clientele and dancers alike surge through the space in a frenzy, their panic a palpable force assaulting my own nerves.

Then, a voice—grating and feral as rusted blades on bone—cuts through the mayhem, demanding my attention:

"Well, well, if it isn't the Devil's precious little whore, gracing us with her presence."

Something comes over me then, an inexplicable rush that overwhelms all rational thought. A burning sensation gathers at my core and swirls up through every vein and muscle until it devours my senses, leaving my blood boiling with unresolved anger. My heart throbs in my ears, and I see red.

Everywhere.

Literal red.

Blood coats the floor, and three dead strippers lay sprawled, limbs pointing in every which direction.

Looming over one of them, the demonic thug leader sports a grin so sick and twisted, my fingers twitch with the primal urge to rip it from his face, consequences be damned.

The truth slams into me like a fucking freight train: this fury coursing through my veins isn't mine—it's the insidious influence of the Violence Underling.

I grin at the fiend, sliding down from the pole with a thud from my platforms, and rest a hand nonchalantly at my hip.

"That's cute coming from Hollywood's local dumpster fire."

The creature's humanoid form shifts at the insult, his bones and muscles rippling beneath paling skin. He grows three to four inches, body slouching as a gruesome hump protrudes from his back. His pesky minions flank him, their own revolting bodies twisting into their demonic forms.

The shadowy figure has vanished from his corner—thank fuck. Probably another corpse on the floor. My gaze sweeps past the hissing, salivating demons, catching glimpses of bodies whose auras still pulse faintly with soul-light despite their untimely demise.

My hands slide behind my back as I reach out mentally to Nero.

Come on, little guy. Prepare your stinger. It's harvest time.

Our bond thrums, unbreakable. Even if he was miles away, my little scorpion would find me. He'd never fail me.

I channel my siphoning magic, fingers dancing in secret patterns. The lingering souls of the departed are fair game in this Hellhole. Violence demons have no business collecting them. That's not their forte. Feeding off rage? Absolutely—that's a given. But souls? Those are *my* territory.

"Bit sloppy, isn't it, boys?" I taunt while my fingers work their arcane art. "Barging in here, making such a mess. What would your master say?"

All the while, I continue to reap what the demons foolishly left behind.

In a heartbeat, the Underlings descend upon me, a writhing mass of fury and fangs. Their razor-sharp claws and teeth aim for my flesh, desperate to tear apart one of the Underworld's deadliest creatures. I reach out with my mind, attempting to bend their will to mine—a neat little party trick courtesy of my infernal benefactor.

But these aren't your run-of-the-mill imps or lesser demons. No, their minds are fortresses, unyielding to my psychic assault. These are Violence's elite—mid to high-tier brutes, probably hand-picked by the Prime himself.

As their attacks intensify, a grim realization settles in my gut: Violence didn't send his B-team. These are his prized attack dogs, unleashed and hungry for blood. *My* blood.

Yet these brutish cretins seem to have forgotten one crucial detail: I'm Lucifer's golden girl, his pride and joy. Hurting me isn't just a bad idea—it's a one-way ticket to a realm of torment that would make the 9th circle of Hell look like child's play.

As their claws threaten to tear into me, a wicked grin splits my red-painted lips. I lock eyes with the nearest Underling, my voice a purr despite my struggle. "Alright, bitches. Time to get fucked, and not in the good way."

I blast the demons off me with explosive fire, catapulting them onto various booths and tables. I crawl toward the corpses sprawled around the room and catch sight of Nero harvesting my last soul orbs into his stinger. Relief washes over me, if only for a minute. One less problem for me, a handful of souls for my quota. I couldn't have planned it better myself.

The mid-level demonic thugs bellow in agony as my flames consume them while the higher-tier fucker makes it out without a single singe. I snatch a stiletto from a dead dancer's foot, its sharp heel glinting in the dim light. With a swift motion, I aim for the demon's neck. The creature wails as the heel slashes through his throat and lodges into the wall behind him, nailing him in place like a piece of fucking artwork.

But my victory is short-lived. To my horror, the fiend wrenches free, tossing the shoe aside with a sickening thud. Dark ichor flows from his wound, leaving an ink-like trail as he lunges at me with terrifying speed.

Before I can react, I'm slammed against the bar, my world spinning. The demon flips me around, bending me over the cool counter, pinning my arms behind my back. His breath is hot on my ear as he growls, "Did you think you could out-fight a Violence demon, you stupid witch?"

My lips curl into a grin despite the strain of my muscles, a small chuckle escaping my lips.

"Oh, I'm sorry—did you miss the part where your pathetic friends are burning to death from my flames?"

The demon's grip tightens, and I brace myself for its reaction, hoping my bravado buys me the seconds I need to formulate an escape plan.

But the backlash never comes.

The pressure at my back vanishes, replaced by a light dusting of demonic ash falling around me, coating the countertop in an eerie black sheen.

I spin around, ready to face this sudden shift in battle, only to find myself frozen in place. The dark figure from earlier, the one I mistakenly thought had met his own demise, is now dangerously close, nearly caging me against the bar. My gaze quickly sweeps over his features, and a small, disbelieving smile tugs at my lips.

Strong jaw. The peek of a branded tattoo on the left side of his neck. Twin cold iron daggers clutched firmly in his grasp.

With deliberate slowness, he uses two fingers to remove his dark shades, revealing familiar, darling brown eyes I'd know anywhere.

"Hello, lover."

Well, *well.* This is *quite* the surprise.

His greeting slithers down my spine like liquid fire, instantly quelling the adrenaline surging through me. That voice—as rich as aged whiskey, as deep as the secrets I've buried—it can't be. Not here. Not now. Yet, the impossible stands before me, real as the cold bar at my back.

We stand in the middle of a demonic bloodbath, a contrasting pair of light and dark, good and evil. A thick, black trench coat hangs from shoulders broad enough to carry the weight of the world, open enough to reveal a black button-down shirt that clings to his frame like a second skin. The top buttons are undone, and a silver cross glints there, just a pale reminder of the perpetual wedge that drives us apart.

I should have known. There's only one man in all of creation with a presence that commanding: the one that got away. The one that *always* gets away.

I cock an eyebrow, grinning as I gesture to our less-than-savory surroundings. "Never, in our eighty years of knowing each other, would I expect to find you in a strip joint, Declan Lovejoy."

His lips quirk in that half-smile I remember so well, equal parts amusement and regret. "Desperate times, October. You know all about those. Clearly."

His eyes, those damnable brown eyes that have haunted my dreams for decades, rake over me. I see the conflict there, desire warring with duty. I dust myself off, kick the pile of ashes at my feet, and fold my arms over my chest.

"It's been—what, ten years?"

"Eleven in April."

Oh, how sweet. He has been keeping count. Eight decades of lingering memories haunt my mind at the sight of him, all 6-foot-2 and full of righteous fury.

He struggles to fight his smile, lips tight, eyes suddenly darting everywhere but at me. Something's different; there's a new hardness that makes him untouchable, nothing like the deliciously pure boy I'd met back in 1923. It seems time has left its mark.

Or maybe it's the eons of darkness I've etched into his soul.

Still, that old, familiar ache gnaws at me. The urge to play, to tease mercilessly. To pick up our dangerous dance.

"Well, lucky you," I purr, flashing a crooked grin. "My shift just wrapped. Fancy a spin down the Boulevard for old time's sake?"

There it is: that smile, filled with raw adoration and longing I could wring from no other soul, mortal or otherwise. He removes the coat from his shoulders, draping it over my semi-clothed form. Always the gentleman.

With a flick of his chin towards the exit, his hand finds the small of my back, guiding me.

Through the haze of destruction, I catch a flicker of movement. Reagan's amber eyes gleam from behind her office door, surveying what remains of Bad Decisions. The once-seedy club is now a seedier barrage of carnage and ash, littered with the broken bodies of demons and mortals alike.

Our gazes lock, and in that moment, a wordless exchange passes between us—two formidable women, worlds apart yet kindred in power and understanding. I give her a slight nod, my eyes conveying what words cannot:

'Debt paid in full, babe.'

A ghost of a smile tugs at Reagan's lips. She knows as well as I do that Violence will think twice before sending his thugs to tangle with a Debauchery demon and the Devil's Second again.

Despite this victory, Reagan's eyes sear into me as I pass her with an old lover by my side, a look of pure venom and warning:

'Get that fucking demon hunter out of my house.'

TRACK SIX
BLACK HOLE SUN
RUNNING FROM SOMETHING? OR SOMEONE?
OF WHICH, I IMAGINE, YOU HAVE MANY.
JUST THE ODD ADMIRER HERE AND THERE.

TRACK SIX

BLACK HOLE SUN

Tension crackles between us as we exit the club.

Our eyes lock then dart away, our bodies close enough to feel the heat but never quite touch. My fingers twitch, aching to grab him by the collar and slam him against the nearest wall, to devour those lips I've been starving for.

But I resist. Barely.

We find my candy-red car with ease and, with a flick of my wrist, my cursed Camaro's passenger door flies open like a silent invitation to my estranged lover. Lovejoy slides in, a knowing smirk playing on his lips. I match his expression as I slip behind the wheel. The engine snarls to life, and we lurch from 0 to 40 in a heartbeat. His knuckles turn white on the door handle as his shoulders bunch like he's bracing for impact.

I chuckle when I take a sharp turn onto Mulholland Drive, jolting us both around in my cramped muscle car.

"C'mon, babe, the drive's not that bad," I chastise him as I shift gears.

"Where did you get this thing? I can feel every speed bump in my bones."

"That bad, old man?" I throw my head back with a laugh. "Suspension's off, tires are worn; what more can you expect from a junkyard find?"

He huffs. "You've come a long way from Rolls-Royce and Coco Chanel."

My grin widens. "I stole those too."

The city's jagged skyline dwindles in my rearview mirror, replaced with lavish mansions and rolling hills. With each twist of the steering wheel, we climb higher into the Hollywood Hills. Our destination looms ahead, an iconic, nine-lettered landmark looming over the city of dreams.

The scent of burnt rubber hits me when my car comes to a screeching halt. I find the perfect resting spot—a strip of dirt just above the renowned sign. The city's more beautiful from this vantage point than it ever was up close, all glittering lights and shadow with little promises of death and despair. What a joke.

Lovejoy and I sit in comfortable silence, taking in the sight of the sleeping city. I try not to think about what he has been up to for the past decade, what holy quests and glorified errands he ran for that fancy old dude in the clouds. I try to forget every instance I've conveniently shown up, distracted him from said quests, and taken every inch of him for my pleasure. As much as I welcome the silence, I need to drown out the symphony of memories in my head.

My fingers find the radio dial, cranking the volume to a soft purr. A voice emerges from the tired speakers—raw, gritty, yet hauntingly melodic, like molasses pouring over sand.

I sink back into the cracked leather seat, my head lolling against the headrest. I stick another cigarette in my mouth, lighting it with my fire. The smoke curls lazily upward, forming a silver cloud of relief and respite after a year on the run. I take a long drag, feeling the burn in my lungs as it mingles with the pulsing rhythm.

The music seeps into me, calming my frayed nerves. Every lyric, every riff, seems to quell the tempest that has been gripping my mind, replacing it with a different kind of storm—something familiar, almost *comforting*.

I roll down my window and relish in the air filling my lungs. Fully. Completely.

There once was a time in my exceptionally long life when even the luxury of breathing seemed farfetched. And though the city is littered with pollution, a small smile creeps upon my features. Decades' worth of smog can't take this moment away from me.

For a moment, this rare glimmer in time, I'm not

running, not hiding. I'm just...here, existing in this twisted reality of music and smoke.

Alongside my estranged lover.

"You really should kick that habit before your lungs burn to a crisp."

"Please." My eyes roll as I take another drag. "If anything burns me to a crisp, it won't be these little guys." The Devil made sure of that.

"The scent is less than appealing."

"Then you're welcome to leave."

Lovejoy's silence is deafening, the air thick with bittersweet nostalgia. Ours is a dance we've perfected over decades; I resurface every now and then with not so much as a wrinkle upon my delicate features, and he ages slowly —*painfully* so...

I'll never tire of those darling brown eyes. Such tenderness holds the promise of a thousand sunrises and irrevocable devotion. Despite the front he tries so desperately to wear for me, I read him like an open book, one with a cracked spine and worn pages —pages I yearn to stroke again.

But I can tell there's something hidden behind that passionate stare; a darkness that leaves him haunted, a heart that has blackened with every battle and every kill.

I relish in any part I had in refining his character.

"I know it's been a while," he speaks, and his body language shifts subtly. The rigid set of his shoulders melts away as he settles deeper into the seat, arm draping casually over the backrest. Clearly, he has no intention of leaving. It's even clearer that he thinks I wouldn't notice his fingers lazily toying with the collar of my jacket, the way they inch closer and closer to my skin. "Lost track of you after the riots."

I can't help but smirk. "Which one?"

His exasperated glare could melt steel. "You know damn well which one."

"Ah, yes. Gotta love LA," I drawl, my voice dripping with sarcasm as a humorless chuckle escapes me. "Such a *charming* place to raise kids."

The words leave a bitter taste in my mouth. It's meant to be a cheeky remark, but the moment it leaves my lips, I regret it. I fight my agitation with another drag, tethering me back to the present as the past threatens to haunt me.

"So charming that you came crawling back, what, eleven years later? I thought you were done with this place." The implication in his voice catches me off guard.

"Oh, you know." I force a breezy laugh, waving my hand dismissively. "Had to chase my dreams of becoming a famous Hollywood starlet. The glitz and the glam are hard to pass up."

"If anyone can make it in showbiz, it's you."

I meet his gaze, my eyes hardening with cynicism. "I'm trying to lay low," I confess, the truth slipping out before I can catch it. "Lots of people here. It's easy to blend into the sea of hopeless losers in LA. I'd stick out like a sore thumb in a smaller town."

His eyebrow arches. "Running from something? Or some*one*?"

I dig my cigarette butt into the ashtray, watching the last ember fade. "Just the odd admirer here and there."

"Of which I imagine you have many."

Something in his voice—a hint of jealousy, perhaps—ignites a reckless spark in me. I twist in my seat, leather creaking against leather as I slip into a position most suggestive. I run my finger along his jaw, his stubble prickling my fingertips.

"Mmm," I purr, leaning in close. "You're my favorite, though."

"And the Oscar goes to…" His brown eyes darken, a storm of emotions swirling in their depths—jealousy, yearning, and something dangerously close to hope.

The intoxicating pull of our twisted past isn't mine alone to resist. He leans in, his resolve crumbling into dust. His warm breath ghosts across my cheek. The scent of him—leather, overpriced cologne, *danger*—floods my senses, a bittersweet reminder of what was and what could be.

But then, he smiles—that playfully charming yet deceptively innocent smile.

And I know I'm done for.

Under the hushed stillness of dawn, our lips crash together. His kiss is a memory long forgotten, familiar yet new as I rediscover his proclivities. He melts beneath my touch, moaning as my fingers travel up his chest to grip his jaw, pulling him impossibly close.

There he is—my sweet, delicate demon hunter: a pillar of honor and virtue that turns to putty in my wicked hands.

There aren't enough angels and demons in the entire universe to stop me from being drawn to this man. Our banter is delicious; the sex, even more so. And after a year-long drought, I'm parched for every drop of him.

"October…" His groan is mixed with longing and hesitation. I reach for his dark jeans, fumbling with one too many buttons as he lays his head upon my shoulder, breath quickening with every passing second. His hand reaches for my wrist, tightening with uncertainty. "October, wait." I pause immediately, staring deep into his brown eyes with growing impatience. "I need to be honest with you. It's not a coincidence that we've run into each other today."

I roll my eyes, sinking back into the driver's seat, folding my arms across my chest. "You don't say."

He smooths out his clothes, clearing his throat with an expression more serious than before.

This better be good.

"The Order sent me."

I can't help but let out a bitter laugh. "Of course they did. And here I thought you missed my company. So, tell me: which of Lucifer's idiot sons royally screwed the pooch this time?"

"We…don't know yet." His admission comes reluctantly, each word dragged out like it pains him.

"You don't know which Prime you're hunting? Can't say I'm shocked. Your Holy Order always had a hard-on for decoding cryptic mumbo-jumbo instead of, you know, actually doing something useful."

His jaw muscle tenses at my abrasive comment, holding back his own retort like the gentleman he is—the gentleman he's *always* been.

"Multiple demon hunters have vanished over the past year," he says, his voice tight. "We have reason to believe one of the Primes or their Underlings are behind it."

I feel my eyebrows shoot up, genuine surprise replacing my usual cynicism. Well, that's…unexpected. Despite myself, I lean in, curiosity piqued.

"Hold up. Aren't you Nephilim types supposed to be like kryptonite to demons? Walking, talking—*glowing*—demon-slaying forces of nature?" I narrow my eyes. "How in the nine circles of Hell would they even be able to *touch* one of you, let alone kidnap you?"

Lovejoy struggles to find the words. He's a mess of exasperated breaths, fidgeting fingers, and a clenched jaw. "You're right, and we've thought the same. Us demon hunters, we…we're not meant to be compromised. We've been blessed with immeasurable power. We've had extensive training. We're *bred* to fight. To protect. And if we've started disappearing by the hands of the Primes one-by-one, who will protect the innocent? Who will balance the scales of good and evil?"

If I rolled my eyes harder, I'd burst an eye vessel. It's this self-righteous, holier-than-thou bullshit that reminds me why I steer clear of demon hunters to begin with. Well, all except this one.

Lovejoy stares into the distance, lost in thought. Dark circles shadow beneath his tired eyes, and I imagine this is probably his first quiet moment in ages. He leans his elbow against the window as he taps his fingers against his pursed lips. "The Devil's got a hand in this, I know it —I can *feel* it. But *what* he's planning, I… just don't know."

"Probably nothing." I shrug, kicking my heels onto the dashboard. "He's not responsible for the acts of his sons. They're all morons fighting over their daddy's attention and affection, and He couldn't care less. In fact, He finds it amusing."

"How would you know all that?"

Shit. Pivot, Winters.

I shrug again, hoping my indifference is convincing. "Just general chatter among occult circles. Witches hate demons"—not a lie—"and we enjoy watching them make absolute fools out of themselves." Also not a lie.

He doesn't seem convinced. His brows knot as he studies my body language. "My apprentice is meeting me here. In LA."

The sudden shift in conversation catches me off

guard. "Apprentice? You have an apprentice? Since when?"

"It's new. *He's* new. Very green."

A small smile tugs at my lips. "I remember when you were very green."

He breathes a chuckle, a charming, nostalgic smirk playing upon his features. "He's eager to prove himself. This is a pretty big job for a first timer."

Curiosity piques my interest again. "Do you remember your first?"

His smirk falters. "Nightmares and Fear. 1923."

"Before or after we first met?"

"Not too long after. Have you ever seen those two?"

Boy, have I ever. And fuck me, do I hate them. The Demon of Nightmares and Fear was one of Lucifer's more…*creative* ideas. I call them the Terror Twins—a single entity with a split personality, their grotesque form morphing to embody their victim's deepest horrors. "Once, probably."

"They really left a mark on me. Haven't had a decent night's sleep in eighty years."

"How unfortunate." That explains the dark circles under his eyes. "Sleep is overrated anyway. Everyone knows all the fun occurs after hours. I'd imagine nights are primary demon hunting hours for you."

"Then you'd be correct. Hence the need for an apprentice."

"And here I thought it was because you were looking to retire, old man." I nudge him playfully.

He huffs a laugh. "What a blessing that would be. Getting old, that is."

"Would it?" I wince. The mere idea sends a shiver up my spine.

"Depends on how you look at it." He flashes me a warm smile, one that takes me back to the days of his youth. "Aging mirrors wisdom. Of time spent, years past. It's a gift. To live a long life full of experience—*adventure…*"

I glance at my hand, at the now flawless skin that, only hours prior, wrinkled with evidence of my true age.

"We've both lived long lives of experience and adventure, babe. We don't look a day over 30."

He shoots me a sweet, almost sad smile.

"And that, lover, is a curse in and of itself."

Lover. A gentle moniker, one I've missed over the years. Silence befalls us again, but I know our previous conversation is far from over. He wants something from me. He's just too chicken shit to spit it out.

But when his fingers meet with mine again, all calloused, gentle, and hesitant, I know he's ready to spill.

"I could really use your expertise with this one."

I shrug. "Not interested."

"But you owe me."

"Do I? Since when?" I quip, flashing him a grin. When his expression hardens, I bite my lip.

His voice is low and urgent. "I've been turning a blind eye to your dark magic for years. That's got to count for something."

I can't help but roll my eyes. With a dismissive flick of my wrist, I counter, "Last I checked, you're a demon hunter, and *I'm not a demon.* I realize that little detail can get lost in translation at times."

"I swore an oath to protect the world from darkness," he persists, a hint of desperation creeping into his tone. "If *they* knew about us —"

"Sounds like a 'you' problem," I cut him off, already reaching into my leather jacket for my cigarettes. "Same old song, different decade. Don't pin your guilt complex on me. It's lazy." I place a smoke between my lips. "And you're boring me."

With a snap of my fingers, the tip of my cigarette ignites. I take a long drag, savoring the burn in my lungs before I continue. "Now, get out of my car." I wiggle my fingers at the ignition, the engine rumbling to life through my magic. "Unless you want me to spell the seats to spit you out. Trust me, it's not a fun ride."

He minds me for the longest moment, as if fighting a battle deep within his mind. I note the way his fingers tense, how his teeth grind and jaw clenches. With a heavy sigh, he squeezes his eyes shut and pulls one last Hail Mary.

"I'll make you a deal."

"Don't like deals," I mutter against my cig.

"You'll like this one." He pauses, as if he's wondering if he can still back out. "If you help me, I'll…I'll give you my blood."

It almost feels like a sick joke.

I half expect Ashton Kutcher to pop his head out from my backseat and scream 'you've just been Punk'd!'.

Nevertheless, skepticism takes over.

"You're offering me divine blood—the rarest commodity a blood-magic-practicing witch could ever need—in exchange for my help? My, my, you really *are* desperate."

He nods once. "I need to win this—to protect the Order and the human race. I'll do whatever it takes."

I've been around a long time. A very, *very* long time. I've seen things that would shatter the minds of lesser beings, done things that would make even the most hardened souls recoil in horror.

But this? This is new territory.

Nephilim blood. *Divine* blood. The blood of a human-angel hybrid.

The very concept sends a shiver down my spine—equal parts revulsion and temptation. The raw power it represents is…intoxicating.

And yet, I've never—not once in my impossibly long existence—entertained the notion of possessing such a thing. Even a fiend like me, with all my transgressions, has to draw the line somewhere.

I weigh my options, ignoring his petty pleas and

insignificant hero complex. I have larger fires to put out, starting with meeting the Devil's outrageous ultimatum before Halloween. Demons and angels never mix. There are universal rules instilled by the powers that be that we must all abide by, even me—the notorious rule breaker. But the mere idea of Lovejoy's blood nearly has me salivating, hungry for the power I had always dreamed of but could never secure.

Tempting as it may be, I remain unconvinced and focus on another harsh reality.

This is certainly not the innocent young man I had met all those years ago, who, decade after decade, promised me 'forever' before we went our separate ways. It appears, after all these years, that all I am to him is a tool to use however he sees fit.

What a pretty little fool.

I lean closer to him, staring into his eyes while caressing his cheek.

"I have better things to do than help you locate your merry band of self-righteous Boy Scouts. If they were dumb enough to get themselves snatched, well…consider it a crash course in humility. Or natural selection. Whichever helps you sleep at night."

That last bit hits below the belt, and his clenched jaw says it all. I can practically taste the sins that conflict him, the war waging in his mind as he battles between what's right and oh so wrong.

But this paragon of virtue already has one morally

gray foot in corruption's door. He made that choice when he foolishly decided to seek my help.

Alas, nothing tastes as good as darkness feels.

With a lazy flick of my wrist, magic crackles through the air. The car door flies open with a satisfying bang, eager to be rid of this unwanted passenger. The frayed seat belt comes alive, unclicking itself and recoiling like a startled snake.

Before Lovejoy can even register it all, an invisible force catapults him out of the seat. He lands in a cloud of dust, his appearance now decidedly disheveled.

I roll down the window, savoring the sight of a mighty demon hunter sprawled in the dirt.

"Better find a way off this hill quick, Lovejoy," I call out, my voice dripping with mock concern. I blow him a kiss, my lips curled in a sardonic smile. "There are nastier things than coyotes and mountain lions lurking in these parts."

A crashing thud reverberates through the Camaro's frame as an unseen force slams onto the hood. Metal groans in protest, and my heart leaps into my throat. Instinct takes over—my boot stomps the accelerator, burying it into the floorboard. Tires shriek against dirt and stone, spinning furiously, but the car remains rooted in place.

In a moment of panic and confusion, the world explodes in a brilliant white flash. My vision dissolves into a sea of searing brightness, leaving me sightless, vulnerable, and stuck atop Mount Hollywood.

TRACK SEVEN
MY WAY

TRACK SEVEN

MY WAY

A dozen voices crash over me like otherworldly static, each one fighting to be heard over the other. My vision slowly returns with every blink as I make out a tall form through my windshield, shining brightly within the darkness. But the voices never relent. In fact, they only grow louder.

'Death to the witch!'

'Whore of Satan!'

'To Hell with you!'

If I had a penny for every time the dead used my brain as their personal echo chamber and punching bag, I'd own every mansion from Mulholland to Sunset a hundred times over. After nine centuries of enduring this spectral bitch-fest, you'd think I'd grown used to it, figured out a convenient way to shut them up.

Being the Devil's Second comes with its perks, sure.

Infinite power, kick-ass titles, and a banging bod, but there's always a price—and hearing the dead? That's just Hell's version of income tax. And the infernal IRS does *not* fuck around.

Their taunts and curses continue to grow louder. Some beg for my death, others for my eternal suffering and damnation. A few even plead for me to set them free. But I'd never waste my time with good deeds and small mercies, not when I've got a job to do.

Blurry surroundings finally fade into sharpened forms when my vision heals, but my body remains stuck with nothing but a glittering city before my very eyes…

And the smug grin of my attacker.

Perched atop the hood of my battered, cherry-red clunker is a young man who hasn't quite grown into his own skin yet, all gangly limbs and sharp angles. There's a defiant tilt to his chin and a threatening squint in his green eyes, but what really catches my eye is the unmistakable glow of his snow-white aura and the hint of a familiar tattoo branded onto his neck.

Another demon hunter. Fan-fucking-tastic.

As if this night wasn't already a dumpster fire of Hellish proportions.

My fingers are glued to the steering wheel, tendons screaming as I fight against an invisible force. My leg muscles spasm uselessly against the brake and accelerator while the pedals mock me, so close yet impossibly out of reach. Fuck, even the air itself threatens to suffocate me.

His spell causes pressure to build in my chest, like liquid fire filling every ventricle of my heart, and it takes every ounce of the free will left within me to channel my own magic.

There's no fucking way I'd let some sanctimonious Boy Scout steal the air from my lungs. Not unless he had a death wish.

These desolate hills whisper tragic secrets to those who dare to listen. They say Mount Hollywood is haunted, littered with tales of mob hits, death leaps off the Sign, and hikers who've lost their way.

Urban legends, skeptics may argue.

But to a witch cursed with the 'gift' of hearing the dead, this hill isn't just some tourist trap or hiking destination.

It's a fucking graveyard.

Getting out of this clusterfuck requires more than parlor tricks and basic telekinesis. No, I need to tap into my messier talents—the kind of magic that needs more than just some silly rhymes. With a mental snarl, I silence the voices of the dead and summon Nero. My familiar, sensing my desperation, bursts to life from his dormant state and skitters across my skin.

Our psychic bond hums with shared purpose as Nero races down my arm. Without hesitation, he sinks his fangs into my palm, drawing blood. Crimson seeps from my knuckles as I clench my jaw to ride out the pain of his bite and utter a quiet spell beneath my breath.

"Forsaken and lost, long deceased,
Rise from the hills and destroy this beast."

My blood sacrifice pulses and thrums with darkened vigor as my magic seeps out my window and into the night. The pesky hunter's spell falters for a moment, and I slowly feel the mobility return to my body. Within seconds, the spirits' voices disappear…replaced with the vicious snarls of my undead minions.

Suppose that's one way to shut them up.

A handful of dead humans and animals rise from the soil, a horrific mixture of bones and decomposed skin. Tattered flesh and fur hang from broken, yellowed skeletons, while maggots writhe in the hollow sockets of their skulls. My merry band of undead swarm my car, raking their decayed claws over the hood and hissing at my unexpected attacker.

The hunter is a mess of fearful grunts and piss-poor aim, flaring holy smites like a firework show gone wrong. As control floods back into my limbs, I snap into action. Nero liquifies and reforms around my wrist, securing himself within the confines of an obsidian bracelet.

I kick the car door open, feet hitting dirt as a wicked grin splits my features. With a flick of my hand, I send my monsters after the young hunter.

Time for a crash course in why you don't fuck with the Devil's right-hand witch.

But there's one teeny-tiny little factor I didn't account for during my quest to teach this kid a lesson.

My sickeningly heroic lover.

Lovejoy joins the fight against my minions, hurling his daggers and blasting them with his holy magic. We're perfect opposites, his light a blinding beacon against my dark, blood-red tendrils of smoke. He's an expert compared to the pathetic excuse for a Nephilim beside him, painting a picture of mesmerizing light within the darkness in an attempt to protect his colleague.

"Call them off," he grunts at me as a skeletal mountain lion, long-dead and falling apart at the seams, latches onto his arm.

"But I'm having so much fun," I chastise.

"He's no threat to you. He's my apprentice."

How darling. This not-so-little thing with no control over his own magic belongs to my lover. With a roll of my eyes, my hands swirl into the air like an unholy conductor, and the undead fall to the ground in a decrepit pile of bones, sinew, and ash.

The demon hunters' pants echo through the night as they regain their strength. Lovejoy pulls the boy to him, checking his arms, neck, and face for bite marks or wounds. "What did I tell you about the smites, lad?"

The apprentice shoots him a gesture somewhere between a wince and a shrug, muttering some poor excuse I don't care to listen to. Lovejoy simply ruffles his dirty blond hair with a begrudging smile.

The sight sends an uncomfortable, almost painful rush through my core. Seeing him with a novice no older than the legal drinking age, caring for him like one would a son, just makes me wonder…

No, October. Don't go there. You *can't afford* to go there.

"This is Jeremy Roache." He nods over at the kid and pats his back.

The kid's name flits through the air like a fly—annoying, insignificant, and instantly swatted away by my inability to give a fuck. Just another useless bit of information cluttering up my 999-year-old brain. I shoot the boy a forced smile.

"Charmed."

"Jeremy, this is October Winters. She's…an old friend." I don't miss the hesitation in his voice, the way his eyes lower with hints of guilt and shame.

"Oh, come now," I coo. "I'd say we're more than just 'old friends,' Lovejoy."

Jeremy's eyes squint in disbelief. "*Friends*? With a necromancer? Sir, she reeks of death magic. That has 'evil' written all over it, *and* she tried to kill me!"

A demented smile reaches my ears as I feel my fire prickling beneath my fingertips. "Necromancy is just the cherry on top of this dark and twisted sundae, Jimmy. You should see what else I've got up my sleeve."

"It's *Jeremy*," he snarls, hands tensing at his sides. His holy magic glows from his fists, threatening to strike again, but my instincts are faster.

Lovejoy intercepts our fire-and-light face-off by

placing a hand on either of our shoulders. Tensions crackle in the crisp fall night as my demon hunter, ever the peacemaker, stands between us, torn between his past and present.

My eyes never leave the apprentice's. A delicious hunger tugs at my psyche, one that urges me to toy with this little boy and his altruism. "You know, kid, your mentor over here once found my skills rather...useful. Didn't you, Lovejoy?"

But his mentor doesn't seem as receptive. His brows furrow in warning, coffee-brown eyes shooting me a look of 'don't you fucking dare.'

I've never been the type to heed caution—and this is one pot my sadistic ass can't wait to stir.

My grin only grows. "Oh, the stories I could tell you. About the lines your mentor is willing to cross, the deals he makes in the dark..."

"October..." Lovejoy's voice comes as a deep, warning growl, one that sends a delightful little shiver up my spine. "That's enough."

A knowing hum purrs through my chest as I step closer to my lover. I run a finger along his jaw, and my words come as a haunting whisper. "What's the matter, baby? Afraid your little protégé will discover the wicked secrets of his ever-so-gallant master?"

"I said *that's enough*."

The low timber of his voice is *almost* enough to force me into submission. If I didn't know any better, I'd say he took a page right out of my employer's book. I know what lurks under the surface, the desperate attempt to put me in my place. He's afraid. Terrified. He knows his not-so-immortal existence is at risk. And somewhere deep down inside, he's ashamed. Of me. Of our twisted past and our even more twisted present. It's written all over his devastatingly handsome face.

We couldn't be any more alike.

Jeremy's eyes dart between us, clearly struggling to reconcile the mentor he knows with the man so deeply involved with his rival. It's a delicious moment of chaos, and I savor every second of it.

I hop onto the hood of my car, cross my legs, and lean back on my elbows. Lovejoy's jacket cloaks my scantily clad form, but my heels and legs peek through the thick fabric. Jimminy's—or whatever the fuck his name is—eyes flit to my bare skin, widening with equal parts shame and curiosity. Ah, to be young, pious, and oh so sexually repressed.

"I thought you said you had a lead? What business do you have with this Bride of Chucky wannabe?" the apprentice asks in a hushed whisper, desperate to ignore my blatant attempt at a distraction.

My blood boils at the mere sound of his voice. "You better watch your tongue, you little shit, or you might just end up like one of her victims."

Lovejoy pinches the bridge of his nose, exhaustion etched into every line of his face. "For Christ's sake, you lot, knock it off." He turns to Jeremy, voice tight. "October's made it clear she'll be no help to us. We'll find another way to track down Fargo."

"What's a Fargo?" I interrupt.

The silence that follows is thick enough to choke on. Lovejoy's eyes meet mine, and I see a flicker of regret before he masks it. "Fargo is…*was*…my partner," he finally grinds out, each word seeming to cost him. "One of our missing colleagues."

"Tragic," I say with a roll of my eyes.

Before he can add more, his apprentice steps closer to him. His voice drops to a whisper that might as well be a foghorn to my ears. "Declan, you should know I had to clean up a demonic mess tonight. There was a massacre at some dive bar off Gower. 32 innocents. Gone. No survivors. But the bodies, they…they were empty husks. Like their souls were…harvested. I read through some of the tomes—soul harvesting isn't common with lesser to high-level demons. That's Prime territory. Only I didn't feel the presence of any of the Big Thirteen through my Mark." His fingers brush that tattoo on his neck, the same one all demon hunters sport. "Did you?"

His hushed words hit me like a punch to the gut. How in the nine circles of Hell did they catch on to my scent so fucking quickly?

I mentally retrace my steps. The bar. The souls. The harvest. For a moment, I wonder where I may have slipped up. I may be a lazy bitch, but I'm not a sloppy one. I keep my face a mask of bored indifference, studying my chipped nails.

When Lovejoy responds with a shake of his head, the kid continues, "I thought I heard some prayers, tried to make out what they may have seen, but it's hard—too many voices. *So* many people in one city."

Try hearing centuries' worth of dead people in one overpopulated city, kiddo. It's enough to beg for a cosmic lobotomy.

"I know it's difficult." Lovejoy's voice softens. "Separating the voices, the prayers, the screams, especially in a place where evil runs rampant and humans beg for salvation." He places a reassuring hand on his apprentice's shoulder. "You'll get there with time, lad, I promise. You'll filter through the noise in no time. For now, just…do your best. That's all any of us can do. Until then, we'll look into this lead together."

I resist the urge to snort. If only they knew the 'evil' they're sensing is not just running rampant, it's standing right fucking next to them, eavesdropping on their touching little pep talk…

"Well, I hate to break up this little Hallmark moment," I drawl, feigning as much nonchalance into my voice as I can muster, "but it sounds like you boys have your hands full. Don't let little old me keep you from your divine destinies."

I slide off my Camaro's hood, shrugging Lovejoy's coat from my shoulders with deliberate swiftness. The night air kisses my skin, leaving me in nothing but the barely-there outfit from my shift at Bad Decisions—a getup that leaves nothing to the imagination.

The effect is instantaneous. Both hunters' eyes lock onto me like I'm the prized meal at Thanksgiving dinner.

The young one, bless his virginal heart, looks like he's about to spontaneously combust, mentally counting every metaphoric rosary bead in his pocket. The older's gaze travels down a well-worn path, a roadmap of every curve and valley he has memorized over the past eighty years.

I can't help but relish their hunger.

I flash the two an over-dramatic wiggle of my fingers, bidding them farewell. I return to my cursed vehicle, feeling their heavy gazes leave me as they erupt into a puff of white smoke, transporting themselves Devil-knows-where and leaving me alone with my hubris and relief.

"Now that that's over," I speak to my reflection as I reapply my signature dark lipstick, "time for the next harvest."

As I slam the car door, one last spectral whiner decides to crash my mental party, some long-dead nobody whose bones are probably dust by now.

"Your days are numbered, October Winters," it hisses.

"Yeah, yeah." I roll my eyes so hard, I nearly see my brain. The engine growls to life, a perfect backdrop to the wicked idea blooming in my mind. I fixate on the spirit before me, and my lips curl into a smile that would make the Devil proud.

"Power within me, where darkness dwells,

Banish this spirit to the depths of Hell."

The air crackles, thick with the stench of brimstone. In a delicious flash of Hellfire and smoke, the spirit shrieks, its form twisting and warping as it's sucked into an infernal vortex.

As silence falls, I can't help but chuckle. "Rest in ashes, jackass. Now, no one will ever hear you scream again."

HANDS OFF THE CAMARO, SWEETS. ONE WRONG MOVE AND SHE'LL STEAMROLL YOU.
TRACK EIGHT
THE BEAUTIFUL PEOPLE

TRACK EIGHT

THE BEAUTIFUL PEOPLE

THE MORNING SUN PEAKS THROUGH MY MOTEL ROOM blinds, casting a prison bar-like shadow against the bed. I glance over at the clock on the nightstand, red numbers flashing '9:00A.M.' Three and a half hours of sleep—not bad. But I have no time to lose.

Out of habit, I check my hands again as I sit up; they still appear spotless, skin taught with no sign of blue-green veins. Nero's enchanted stinger thrums with the weight of 199 freshly harvested souls.

Between the dive bar, Bad Decisions, a metro full of nobodies, and the late-night crowd at IHOP, I'm hesitant to admit that night one was a mediocre success. Despite my less than average optimism, the numbers don't lie— 801 souls still stand between me and my immortality. I need to keep moving.

The Starlight is now at my disposal, no debt weighing over my conscience. I grab my sunglasses and slap them on along with my leather jacket. My thick boots thud against the pebbled staircase as I run down toward my cursed Camaro, ready to take on the rest of this sordid city before my time is up. Before the car has a chance to start, Reagan's velvety voice catches me off guard.

"Not so fast, Your Excellence."

I flip my middle finger in her direction, then stick a cigarette in my mouth and light it with my magic. "Hands off the Camaro, sweets. One wrong move, and she'll steam roll you."

Reagan's brows furrow as she studies my hunk of junk. Sure, the red paint's chipped, the leather seats have seen better days, and the passenger mirror barely hangs on by a thread, but she's a resilient motherfucker, just like her driver.

"Where'd you score this rust bucket anyway? And how exactly does it run?"

I tap ash from my cigarette, shrugging. "Stole her from a scrapyard last year. The mechanic working on it" —I flash her a wink—"contributed his soul to the cause."

"So that's its fuel source?"

I nod, a wry smile playing on my lips. "Who needs gas when you've got the power of reanimation? It's practically eco-friendly."

Her magma-red arms fold across her chest,

unimpressed. "Since when do you give a shit about the environment?"

"I don't. Just too broke for premium unleaded."

The car thrums with dark energy as I run my fingers over the cracked leather. Memories of Lovejoy's touch flash through my mind. I shove them aside, patting the seat.

"This was my last hurrah before going off the grid. Can't drive stick to save my life—trust me, I've tried. This old girl was my only link to the magical world. Got me out of many scuffles with the bounty hunters."

Reagan's eyes flicker with an unfamiliar softness as she leans against the car. "Was it worth it?"

"What?"

"Whatever you did. The thing that got Lucifer's panties in a twist."

I avoid her gaze, fighting the memories that threaten to surface. 999 years of loyal service, and one moment of weakness brought it all crashing down. The soul I couldn't take. The innocent I spared.

My jaw clenches. "What's done is done. The past is behind me, and there's no turning back." I flash her one of my roguish grins and deflect. "Did you actually want something, or are we fixing to have a heart-to-heart over cheap whiskey and reruns of Happy Days?"

Reagan huffs a laugh. "You don't have many friends, do you?"

"Don't need friends. Don't play nice with others."

"Even dark witches need allies, Tober."

I arch an eyebrow. "You volunteering for the job, she-demon?"

"In this cesspool of a city, I might be the closest thing to a friend you've got."

The idea of friendship is a concept so foreign, I may need a pocket translator handy. "I can just see it now—a redheaded demoness and a blonde witch; the dynamic duo dressed in black leather and high heels. We'd make for a good laugh on Comedy Central." I crack a smile. "Suppose if I *had* to have a friend, a Debauchery Demon wouldn't be the worst. Your boss is the only Prime who doesn't make me want to hex myself into oblivion, unlike the other twelve."

"Thank the Devil for small favors in Hell's pecking order, then," Reagan purrs, her smirk sharp enough to cut glass. Then, her posture shifts, coiled tension replacing casual grace. Her voice drops to a curious whisper. "Speaking of favors…let's chat about last night. What's the deal with that Nephilim?"

I wrestle down the panic clawing at my throat, aiming for nonchalance. "He's nobody."

Reagan's amber eyes narrow, reading between lines I had no intention of writing. "Didn't seem like nobody to me."

"He helped me get rid of your Violence gangster problem," I snap, deflecting. "What's it to you?"

"Allow me to offer you some *friendly* advice, baby

cakes. Demon hunters are not just a threat to my kind; they're a threat to Lucifer. The closer they get to us bottom-feeders, the higher they climb. Primes, Big D himself… You connect the dots. I shouldn't have to explain this to the Devil's Second."

The title hits like a branding iron, searing away my practiced indifference. I grit my teeth, tasting the bitter truth. "That Nephilim's been on my radar since before you were a twinkle in Debauchery's eye. Trust me, I know exactly what I'm doing. I didn't earn my title and powers by being careless."

"Keep telling yourself that, doll face. Everyone knows you're Luci's weakness, but even the Devil's patience has its limits. There are only so many indiscretions he can sweep under the brimstone rug before he pulls your plug for good. And cavorting with demon hunters? That'll cost you *way* more than a six-day soul-collecting ultimatum."

Her words, while heavy with implication and truth, will not phase me. Declan Lovejoy, his insufferable little apprentice, and their Nephilim rescue mission will not impede on my own ambitions. Not while my quota remains dismally unfulfilled.

"We've only been friends for two minutes, and you're already giving me unsolicited advice and stating the obvious. How did I get so lucky?" My voice drips with sarcasm as I roll my eyes at her.

"Let's just say, you're not the only badass bitch who

knows a thing or two about being dicked around by her boss for his own amusement."

There's a comfortable silence between us, one of mutual understanding and respect. It's a foreign feeling, one I've never experienced in my long life. Yet, after all these years, I find myself face to face with the first person who may *actually* understand what it's like to be me.

If only she wasn't a fucking demon. Blegh.

"Good chat." I toss my cigarette out the car window. "Now, if you don't mind, I've got to get back to it."

The she-demon steps away from my cursed vehicle, leaving me free to zoom out of the parking lot and into the heart of Hollywood.

The sun claws its way up the smog-stained sky, shielded by stray clouds that cast a gloomy shadow upon Hollywood Boulevard. I walk past the Chinese Theater, its gaudy façade a stark contrast to the tarnished stars lining the Walk of Fame. Desperate souls in knockoff cartoon costumes offer photo ops to impressionable tourists while hopeful artists hand out mixtapes and CDs to unsuspecting passersby. The city reeks of street food grease, exhaust fumes, sunbaked asphalt, and that unmistakable aroma of hopes and dreams.

Welcome to Hollywood, where everyone's selling something—no matter what time of the day it is, whether it's their talent, their body, or their very souls.

I just happen to be another predator in a city full of monsters.

A regal, black, faux-leather gown captures my attention as I pass a fashion boutique cramped between souvenir gift shops and hole-in-the-wall food joints. It glitters under a single spotlight, mimicking the ebony beauty of my familiar's armor. The dress is something of a marvel with a metallic shimmer and would go fabulously with the pair of heels I nicked off one of my most recent victims. The possibilities are limitless. Alas, my wallet is not.

"Excuse me," a voice cuts through my reverie like a dull blade. A couple—tourists, by the looks of them—appears before me, map in hand and desperation in their eyes. "Can you point us toward the Hollywood Roosevelt Hotel? We're here for a wedding."

I muster my best 'confused fellow tourist' act, muttering ignorance and shooing them away with a dismissive wave, but as they stumble off, a spark ignites in the dark corners of my mind.

A wedding. At the Roosevelt.

Suddenly, the black gown in the window takes on new significance, its allure now tinged with delicious possibility. Half a block away, the lavish hotel's bright red sign pulses like a bloody beacon of opportunity.

Weddings are usually large, crowded affairs, filled with unbearable joy and free-flowing alcohol—a delicious buffet of souls ripe for the taking. All at once, the macabre jingle of a wedding march plays in my head on a loop.

A chilling grin splits my face. "Well, well—" I chuckle as I run a finger along the scorpion curled around my ear. "Guess it's time to crash a party."

BEAUTIFUL DIASASTER

TRACK NINE

BEAUTIFUL DISASTER

The Roosevelt Hotel towers above me, a white, Spanish Colonial giant, and I adjust my stolen gown, the fabric still singing with the terror of souls I harvested to claim it. Inside, marble stairs sweep up to a cocktail hour in full swing, the wedding guests none the wiser.

Angeleno elite confab over champagne and hors d'oeuvres, noses high and pinkies higher. Their stares weigh heavily as I ascend the steps in the gown. Black leather swathes my torso in a twisted bodice, taut but tolerable. Draping my skirt over my arm, I reveal higher-than-high heels with an ebony jewel wrapped around my right ankle—my treasured familiar in his slumbering state. Every breath feels like a rebirth, transforming me from shadow-dwelling punk to elegant predator—perfectly deadly and ready to consume.

Large weddings are an ideal occasion for a mass

reaping. My formula is infallible; guests are too absorbed by delight and intoxication to notice a femme fatale on the prowl, too preoccupied to notice when a guest goes missing. The event could easily land me a hundred souls, maybe even two, but I'm nothing if not realistic…and discretion is of the utmost importance.

I clock my first victim: an older man leaning against the marble banister. He fiddles with his pocket watch—a small, weathered thing in desperate need of a polish—checking the time as though he has a better place to be. I follow his gaze and catch a glimpse of a photograph nestled snug inside: a dark-haired beauty with a dazzling smile. My eyes immediately flutter to his left hand and note the golden band shimmering in the light.

How darling. My victim has a little missus at home, one who clearly isn't worthy of an invitation to the wedding. A shame, of course. He'll forget all about her when I'm through with him.

I sidle up to the gentleman. "She's beautiful." I nod at his pocket watch.

"She was." His voice breaks as he sips his liquor.

Ah, a widower. Such a tragedy.

I lean on the banister beside him, indulging his sob story about how he recently lost his wife to illness, how all his children are grown, and his grandchildren just started school. Ah, the dreadfully mundane, painfully short life of a human. I think back to the milestones of my millennia, the countless scuffles, the perilous deals, the close-calls…all memories that could cease to exist if I don't meet the Devil's demands.

I rest my heel on the platform of the marble banister, magic wriggling through my fingers. Obsidian jewels shift, and my deadly arachnid springs to life. I suppress a smile as the old man continues his woes, Nero's trotters tickling my skin as he crawls down my ankle.

Sting.

The widower hisses as his knees buckle and he reaches for his ankle. I grab his shoulders in mock-concern, steadying his weary bones. "Everything okay, handsome?"

"Just a Charlie horse." He waves his hand dismissively, but his anguish grows as his frame weighs heavier on me.

"Let's take you somewhere where you can rest your legs." I ease him against me as Nero crawls under my dress and curls around my ankle once more.

The old man makes it a few minutes before Nero's sting paralyzes him from the waist down. I see the confusion in his eyes, the fear that consumes him as I force a utility closet door open with my magic. I scurry us into the dark room and drop to my knees. My gloved hand hovers over his chest as I siphon his poor soul into my grasp.

I'll never tire of this part—those last moments before the deed is done. Their eyes tell the whole story, horror growing as they feel their essence slip away. Color bleeds from their lips, muscles wither, until all that remains is an empty husk. A beautiful work of art.

His soul is the lone light in this dark room, albeit a dim, flickering light. A sign of a long life lived, ready for paradise. It's a damn shame the widower's soul will never find peace, never find his wife in the Beyond.

His soul never stood a chance against me.

Nero, kill.

I leave Nero to feast as I return to the cocktail reception. A huddle of children whisk past me: a couple of gremlin-like flower girls and one ring-bearer. Their shrill yips and laughter are like nails on a chalkboard, boiling the blood in my veins. I snarl at the girls, flames tickling my fingertips as I resist the urge to set them on fire. They scurry off in a flash of white tulle and waving arms, leaving the ring-bearer frozen in his tracks.

I lock eyes with the boy, noting the strange and unusual air that emanates from him. His aura is lost to me, a peculiarity, given his youth. I'd expect a soul as white as the bride's gown, but I see no glow, no notion of purity, and curiosity piques my interest. All I see is a husk void of humanity—a child without a soul.

It isn't until I notice the dark of his pupils spreading to the white of his eyes when I realize the ring-bearer is something other than human. In fact, he isn't human at all. He's something far more sinister, something…

Demonic.

Just what I needed: a demon to thwart my advances.

The demon-child and I exchange knowing glances, a code of omertà between a couple of damned creatures. There's only one—well, two, if we're getting technical—demons whose Underlings possess children, the same ones who left their mark on my demon hunter: the Demons of Nightmares and Fear, the gruesome two-headed twins. I take note to steer clear of the boy.

The open bar calls to me as I target another handful of victims. My heels click softly against the marble floors as I move with the grace of a snake slithering toward her prey. Men watch with rapt enchantment, drinking in the sight of my ebony gown and the curves it so tightly cinches. I claim a seat at the bar, giving the bartender a coquettish glance as I demand his attention.

The bartender hurries to me. "What can I get'cha, miss?"

"The shit you save for people who *actually* know what they're drinking."

The look in his eyes is glorious—half terrified, half turned on, the perfect cocktail to quench my thirst. His hands tremble as he hands me his finest drink: top shelf liquor. I press the chilled glass to my lips, indulging in the amber liquid. It tickles my throat in the same way my flames kiss my skin, invigorating me. I *missed* this—my *power*. Over men, over women, over the dead. I will never allow myself to feel human ever again.

"Bride or groom?" a voice pulls me from my reverie.

I look over my shoulder. A mediocre bachelor with a

loosened tie and slicked-back hair leans against the bar, eyeing me with his hungered gaze. He thumbs his lighter, bringing it to my lips.

"Groom," I lie, leaning in for a light. With a deep drag, I turn to face him. "Second cousin twice removed."

"Coworker," he responds with a haughty grin. "Just made partner, actually."

A lawyer, I muse. Delightful.

"And you're here alone?" My voice is a shiver up his spine; a coy, melodic timber with the promise of seduction.

"Fortunately"—he winks—"for you."

Moronic men and their cheesy pickup lines. I do *so* love when victims fall helplessly into my lap.

The voice of another sends a shiver up my spine. "And unfortunately, for you."

My victim's smile fades when his gaze flickers past me. A delicious warmth hits my skin as the hand of another squeezes my shoulder. I know that voice. I recognize the subtle accent behind each syllable, like the whisper of a lush countryside, a timeless connection to the past. A knowing smile creeps over my lips as I lean into his touch.

"You found me," I practically sing. I peer at the man through my thick lashes, drinking in the sight of my charming demon hunter.

"You're hard to miss, lover," he mutters into my ear as

his finger twirls through my hair. "Thank you for keeping my *wife* company while I was indisposed."

My victim practically shrivels at Lovejoy's statement. He's gone faster than I can blink, leaving behind nothing but an empty whiskey glass.

I swivel the barstool to face Declan Lovejoy. He's dashing in his tuxedo, broad shoulders straining against dark fabric. His frame has thickened over time, firm with muscle. His hair is longer at the top, strands of chocolate curls tousled perfectly—almost purposely—over his warm eyes. "*Wife*, hm?"

"Is the idea so farfetched?" His lopsided grin melts my insides.

"Marriage is a prison sentence."

"And yet, here you are"—his fingers toy with mine—"at a wedding."

I shrug my shoulders. "I've always been a fan of irony."

Lovejoy pulls me from my seat, latching my arm within his and escorting me through the sea of inebriated guests. "Have you given my proposal any thought?"

Apt choice of words, given the circumstance. A migraine stings my temples at the very thought of it. I choose to ignore the question. "What are the chances you being here is a coincidence?"

"I should ask the same of you."

"I wanted an excuse to dress up."

He lowers his voice, leaning closer into me. "There are

heavy traces of demonic activity at this hotel. Jeremy and I are staying here to investigate."

I think back to the ring-bearer and his Hellish eyes. "And here I thought you were stalking me."

A small smirk tugs at his lips. "Running into you is always a happy coincidence."

"There are no coincidences in life—certainly not happy ones." I stroke his forearm. "Not with us, anyway."

We make our way into the ballroom, marveling at the extravagant floral arrangements adorning every table and threshold. The bride and groom sit happily at their sweetheart table, indulging in overpriced champagne while snagging a kiss with every ring of a glass. A handful of guests have already taken to the dance floor, swaying and rejoicing to a poorly curated setlist of ludicrous pop music. Weddings are as insufferable as funerals, given my experience. Estranged family and strangers come together for a common cause, whether it be celebration or mourning, and drown themselves in food and drink.

I wave my hand behind my back, mentally casting a spell on the double doors.

Lock these doors, stop sound from spreading,
Burn those who dare leave this wedding.

Magic trails from my fingertips toward the exit in a gust of wind. My victims won't stand a chance against a magical failsafe. I can only hope that little demon can keep my lover preoccupied while I get to work.

I smile and nod at the fellow guests, blending in as if I belong, and lead Lovejoy toward a circular table with two empty seats.

"You'll cause more suspicion by filling the assigned seat of another." Lovejoy stops us in our tracks. "Why don't we have a dance?"

The thought revolts me. "I don't dance."

"You *do* dance." He unhooks our arms, towering before me with his 6-foot frame. "You've danced with me plenty. In the 20s, the 30s. You were a dancing queen, you."

"Dancing was different back then, babe." Oh, how it was. The roaring twenties and swinging thirties; vibrant affairs in a world emerging from the shadows of war. The perfect time to claim the souls of the wounded.

"Once more, for old time's sake, then." His rich, deep brown eyes invite me, laced with a gentility I've long since forgotten. He offers me his hand. "Please?"

After eighty years, you'd think I'd be immune to his charm. Nevertheless, I surrender.

Lovejoy leads me to the center of the dance floor, fingers gingerly intertwining with mine. His free hand finds the small of my back, caressing my exposed skin. The ballroom falls into a hushed stillness as our bodies glide as one. A swarm of dazzled eyes watch us as we sway, captivated by our performance. Ours is a harsh reality, one bound by a twisted fate. A tragic, forbidden tale of good and evil, of two tortured souls working for opposing sides. My darkness and his light are sworn to destroy one another, whether he knows it or not. The push and pull of our bodies mirrors our sordid past, a delicious game of cat and mouse spanning eight decades.

He knows what his touch does to me. He knows every inch of my body, every weak spot. He knows which words to use and when to use them. He knows of the shadows that consume me and the corruption that fuels my magic—even if the source of that darkness remains my best-kept secret. And with every decade, with every serendipitous reunion, his lightness dares to rehabilitate me, to save me.

Trouble is, I don't need saving, not even now that the prospect of death lurks on the horizon.

Lovejoy's cheek leans mercilessly against my hair, and I feel the rise of his chest as he inhales my scent. His eyes, half-lidded with a mix of resistance and desire, challenge me to succumb to him, to give in to the hunger stirring within him, a hunger I so diligently sowed. It would appear the Devil's sons are not the only demons in need of slaying.

Declan Lovejoy has a few of his own.

"They're all staring," I whisper when he pulls me in after a spin.

"I don't care." His grip on my back tightens.

"You have a job to do, remember?" The words serve as a reminder that my quota remains disappointingly low.

I'm suddenly distracted by the mark on his neck, the tattoo that brands the demon hunters of the Order. The olive undertone of his pale skin flushes beneath the dark ink, and my eyes flash to his. His jaw clenches, determined to push through the blatant discomfort itching at his collar. I'm taken by the sight, a curiosity building within as I dare to bring my fingers to his neck. I've never asked him how that brand works—never really cared. But when we're this close, alone in a room full of strangers and one decidedly demonic ring-bearer, I wonder—how exactly *does* that mark work?

In a swift movement, he cradles my back, dipping me as our tango crescendos. My heart pounds against my ribcage, threatening to erupt from my chest as his lips draw dangerously close to mine.

A dull, distant rumble tethers us back to reality. The crystal chandelier trembles above us, clinking in a cascade of chimes. There's a thick fog that slithers around our feet, rising like growing tendrils of a shadowed horror. Panic ripples through the crowd in delicious screams. Their chaos is my playground, and my perfect moment to strike is nigh.

Lovejoy instinctively pulls me behind him, shielding me from the stampede of panicked guests on the dance floor. I rise to my tiptoes, attempting to catch a glimpse of the bedlam beyond his tall frame. The grotesque hiss of blood splatter and torn flesh fills my ears, and that's when I finally see it:

A twisted, deformed little boy eating the flesh of a bride and groom. Perfect timing.

The guests rush to the exit, banging against the shut double doors, desperate for escape. The ballroom becomes their prison—desperate hands burning against spelled doors as screams dissolve into silence. My little spell makes sure their pleas are never heard.

Lovejoy turns to face me with dauntless fervor. "October, get to safety."

"Please." I push past him, rolling my eyes and removing the gloves from my hands. "I'm no stranger to demons."

"Then help these people out of here. I'll handle the demon."

Lovejoy tears the bowtie from his thick neck and throws his tuxedo jacket onto the floor as he rolls up his sleeves. With a shout of an archaic, Latin spell, two daggers appear in his hands. He urges me once more before he lurches toward the creature feasting on the bride. The creature shrieks as Lovejoy thrusts his hands forward, projecting a blast of divine energy at the demon. Startled by the rush, the fiend bellows at the hunter and bears its shark-like teeth. Within a flash, the hunter grabs the fiend and teleports them outside into the hotel gardens.

Leaving me locked in a ballroom with over a hundred terrified souls living their worst nightmare.

And now, they're *all* mine.

TRACK TEN
ENTER SANDMAN
BLOOD TO BONE AND SKIN TO HEART, RESTORE THE LOST, LET PAIN DEPART

TRACK TEN

ENTER SANDMAN

Nero coils around my ankle after the deed is done. The heat from his stinger against my skin strokes my ego, sending a jolt of exhilaration through my body.

A faint smirk plays on my lips as I descend the Roosevelt's grand staircase, savoring the irony of shattering 104 unsuspecting souls' hopes and dreams during a joyous occasion. Their sacrifice is a small price for the endless delights that await my immortal future.

My chest tightens with pride as I tally my soul count: 323.

A wry chuckle rumbles in my throat at the coincidence—my harvest matches Hollywood's area code. Not bad for day two, but room for improvement remains. The night is young, after all, and the city pulses with life at every intersection.

As I exit the hotel, I collide with a figure—my demon

hunter's apprentice, whose name eludes me as his innocent green eyes widen in shock at the sight of me.

"Miss Winters," he breathes out.

"Call me that again, and I'll personally escort you to my favorite circle of Hell," I spit at him.

His sickeningly virtuous eyes stretch wider, and I savor the terror pooling within them. "Declan's in trouble—I've got to help him."

I snort a laugh. "Oh honey, the only thing in trouble here is your hero complex. Why don't you run along and let the grown-ups deal with the demon wedding crasher?"

"I don't see *you* helping."

"I did my part. Lovejoy's got a handle on the rest."

"You're wrong. I can hear him in my head—he *needs* me."

The desperation in his voice, the trembling of his hands—like a novice struggling to get a grip on their magic—stirs a fleeting echo of empathy within me. I know that feeling, what it's like to be brimming with raw power and ambition, with nothing but the world sprawled before me. Of course, in *my* youth, I simply indulged my impulses. But for these do-gooders, rules and regulations reign supreme.

How deliciously tiresome, to be shackled by one's own virtue.

"You really want to help?" I call out to him. "There's a ballroom full of corpses in need of a major clean up.

You handle damage control, and *I'll* check in on Lovejoy."

"But—"

"You're better off knocking one inconvenience off his plate once he's slain the demon. He'll thank you for it later."

Every fiber of my being tells me this is a bad idea. My instincts squirm at the obscure urge building deep within, fighting the voices telling me to run to Lovejoy's aid. I'm not one to pass up a chance at gaining the upper hand, and I wasn't about to let some demon snatch away what's rightfully mine.

And for the first time in centuries, I find myself charging into danger instead of fleeing it.

Jeremy splits off to handle the ballroom butchery while I make way towards my hunter. I whisper a spell under my breath, unlocking the cursed doors for the apprentice.

Meanwhile, the courtyard is in absolute chaos—shattered statues, scorched masonry, disfigured topiary. Lovejoy's locked in combat with what was once an innocent ring-bearer, now transformed into a vile creature of Hellish design. The fiend roars, revealing rows of needle-sharp teeth and dodging Lovejoy's gleaming daggers and white-hot flashes of Holy Light.

Jeremy wasn't exaggerating—he *is* in deep. But I know better than to wade into a brawl that isn't mine.

They continue to face off in a never-ending skirmish.

One ducks a vicious swipe, retaliating with a swift uppercut that barely fazes the other. Beams of Holy Light continue to blast through the darkness that consumes them. Under the crescent moon's meager light and the patio's dim glow, the battle rages, its outcome uncertain. Every shadow hides a potential deathblow, and every hit goes unseen.

But it isn't until twin wails of agony pierce the night that I realize the fight's tide has turned.

Hunter and demon fall to their knees in a dual defeat. The creature disintegrates into thin air, and Lovejoy's cold iron dagger drops to the floor with an ear-splitting clang. My lover's body hits the floor with a dull thud, and I sprint toward him to survey the damage.

He's barely breathing.

The sight triggers a gruesome moment from my own past—the days where the breath in my lungs often felt robbed from me. My body seizes in the moment, frozen in time along with a thousand-year-old memory that plagues my mind.

But a flash of red pulls me from the darkness.

Glittering crimson soaks his white dress shirt, spilling onto the masonry below.

Vibrant blood. *Divine* blood. The very same he promised in exchange for my help, useless if its source runs dry.

I'm all for tragic endings, but not at the cost of my own.

I *need* to heal him.

I clamber to my feet, nearly tripping over the train of my gown as I return to the ballroom. A hundred dead bodies lie at my disposal, void of souls, but I only need one for my plan to work.

Jeremy stands in the middle of the dance floor, hands outstretched as white magic glows from his palms. He mutters an indiscernible, ancient spell over the bodies sprawled at his feet, and one by one, they begin to disappear. It's a peculiar sight, watching a demon hunter clean up a supernatural mess. I've never stooped to such mundane clean-ups after my harvests—that's Deception's forte, loathsome as he may be. It's a pity he's nowhere to be found; the apprentice would make such a delectable offering.

Jeremy's eyes remain sealed shut as he harnesses his power, laser-focused on his chanting. I grab the lightest body I can find and struggle to haul it out the doors and into the courtyard. My groan of frustration resonates throughout the paneled walls of the hall, and I kick my heels off for better balance. Corpses are such cumbersome things, and I tire of doing my own dirty work.

A loud 'thud' resonates through the room as I drop the body. Bunching my skirts, I sprint into the lobby. My little spell seems to have drowned out any suspicion of foul play, thank Hell. Unsuspecting hotel guests and servicemen go about their business, ignorant to the tragedy that lies within the ballroom. A vacant bellhop remains untouched in a corner, a perfect vessel to carry one of the dead bodies out to the courtyard.

But another genius thought comes to mind. Why waste the blood of the dead when perfectly live specimens are right within reach?

I scan the lobby, searching for a lone innocent, a live body sacrifice for a blood magic ritual.

"Gorgeous dress," a young hotel guest, no older than the age I appear to be, pays me a compliment as she walks toward the elevators. "Is that a glitter-laminated pleather bodice?"

It's as if the Devil himself answered my plea. I wouldn't be surprised if he had eyes and ears in this very hotel.

I shoot the girl a demure smile. "You should see it in the moonlight."

I lure the girl to certain death as we enter the courtyard together. She's a gullible little thing, rambling on about her aspirations to make it big in LA's fashion scene.

Such sweet, doomed ambitions. Pity she won't stand a chance.

Her eyes widen with terror at the sight of Lovejoy's mangled form sprawled by an elegant water fountain. In her moment of shock, my magic surges, and I hurl her skull-first into the sharpest edge of the fountain. A sickening crack echoes through the air, followed by an eerie stillness as her body thuds to the ground. Blood trickles from her temples as she lays lifeless at my feet. Her soul will make for a welcome harvest when I'm done here.

Nero, awaken.

My scorpion springs to life around my ankle, then crawls up my leg and torso and onto my shoulder.

Magic like this isn't as easy as a wave of my hand. It isn't a simple telekinetic blast or a locking of doors, no—it requires sacrifice. Blood sacrifice.

I drop to my knees beside my victim, plunging my fingers into the warm pool of crimson by her head. With swift, practiced strokes, I etch five arcane runes into the ground, a pentagram blooming around Lovejoy's motionless form. Cradling his head in my lap, I continue to paint symbols across my chest, the woman's blood cooling my feverish skin. Once my macabre piece of art is complete, I send the bleeding corpse into a dimly lit corner in the courtyard.

Finally, my voice drops to a guttural whisper as I begin my spell, dark magic thrumming through every word.

"With this blood, now weave my power,

Heal this soul within this hour,
Blood to bone and skin to heart,
Restore the lost, let pain depart."

My chants echo in the stillness of the night, each repetition more desperate than the last. My heart thrums against my ribcage as the magic resists, like a stubborn beast refusing to be tamed. Then, with a sudden surge and force of my will, the barrier shatters. The blood around my victim's head stirs, animating into five serpentine streams. They slither toward me, an unholy river pulsing with dark promise.

The wind howls, biting at my cheeks with relentless force. Plunging my hand into the enchanted blood again, I let it drip onto Lovejoy's body, my chant growing urgent. The crimson sizzles and hisses as it finds his wound, and panic sets in. *Heal, damn you.*

My voice rises as my incantation grows louder. I repeat the spell aimlessly until it becomes imprinted on my tongue.

It isn't until an ominous, spine-tingling voice pulls me from my focus.

"October Winters."

Fuck me.

A looming creature appears in my peripheral vision, a single body with two heads. I expect to see a grotesque, monstrous amalgamation of demonic proportions, but instead, I make out the shape of…Lovejoy.

Lovejoy with two heads. Two rotting, decaying heads

with skin barely hanging onto those perfectly chiseled cheekbones and jaw I adore to stroke. Maggots and worms creep and crawl through the creature's skulls, leading up to their blacker-than-black eyes that send a rush of disgust through my core.

I know how this demon works, how it takes on the form of their victim's greatest fear. If the Demons of Nightmares and Fear think they can goad me into one of their little traps, they have another thing coming. I won't fall for this one—I've been around far too long to be crippled by some parlor trick.

"Back off, imp. I'm working here," I growl.

"That's not how this works," one of the heads—Fear—persists.

The other, Nightmares, hisses. "This one bears the Mark of the Primes. He is *ours* to feed on."

I sneer at the monster. "I claimed his soul long before your ugly ass gained access to this plane. He's *mine*."

Their twin voices speak in unison: "Then why is he still breathing?"

The question strikes a nerve, one I am not prepared to face. Not now. "That's my business. Scram."

"You won't get rid of us that easily, October Winters." The words are more than a threat—they're fact. So long as Lovejoy remains under the thrall of Nightmares and Fear, his blood will never be mine.

"There were over a hundred humans in that ballroom earlier—"

"Humans our Underling intended to feed on. All that remains now is a bloodbath and no souls to show for it. Now, where could they have all gone..." The demon's patronization irks at me as I resume my chant. Their void-like eyes focus on Nero for a second, long enough for me to realize what they were implying. "We cannot return empty handed. You and I both know how *He* reacts to failure."

All too well. Lovejoy's life continues to lie in the balance as my concentration remains divided between the fiend and my spell.

"Tick tock, October Winters. We don't have much time—and neither do you."

My eyes narrow. "What are you suggesting, imp?"

The creature's twin grins form a pit in my stomach. "One hundred souls."

"Fuck right off," I grit through my teeth. "I earned those, fair and square. It's not my fault your stupid minion was bested by a demon hunter."

"Try explaining that to Lucifer. Try telling Him you *allowed* a demon hunter to slay one of His kindred. Your immortal days are already numbered."

The bastard's got a point, and I find myself facing an impossible choice. I'm not ready to give up my hunter. I've *never* been ready, not for the eighty years I've toyed with him, the decades-long dalliance that provided me an ounce of entertainment during my eternal damnation.

Fear regards me with a devious smile. "One hundred souls, Winters—"

Nightmares chimes in. "That is our price. A hundred souls in exchange for our silence."

My quota is low to begin with. I can't afford to lose a hundred, but the fiend is right. Time is running out, and not just mine. "Fifty souls," I offer, "and five minutes of Nightmare Feeding."

Four void-like eyes narrow as vicious grins grow. Both of their voices speak in unison: "We eagerly await his slumber."

The Prime disappears from my line of sight, leaving me with nothing but my hopeless lover and a will to survive. I look down at him, relief flooding me as I realize he's not the decrepit corpse the demon tried to trick me with. He's still alive—barely.

With renewed vigor, I chant the spell one last time.

And in a flash of golden light, the enchanted blood, pentagram, and runes disappear.

Lovejoy's breath returns to his lungs, growing quicker and heavier with every passing second. His wounds are gone, skin as flawless as it was just an hour before. Pride flashes through me—I've never healed anyone but myself and Nero. This isn't my forte; I am a dark witch who relies on the blood of innocents and the spirits of the dead to best the Good Guys. My triumph fades quickly as cold reality sinks in: I *cannot* let this become a habit.

My hunter stirs as he comes to, but I cannot allow

him to awaken, not while Nightmares and Fear and I have a trade to make. I place my now clean hand above his forehead, whispering a spell.

"Eyelids heavy, heed my plea,

In deepest sleep, may you be free."

His breathing steadies and eyes seal shut, leaving him vulnerable to his worst nightmares.

And the Prime bares its fangs at its defenseless prey.

"You're forgetting something, witch," Fear hisses, its skeletal finger jabbing towards my familiar. "The souls. Now."

"Impatient motherfuckers, aren't you?" I mutter under my breath.

Little Nero hides beneath my curls, shielding himself from the predatory gaze of the Prime. Unloading souls after a harvest isn't pretty. The scorpion reveals the emotions I desperately try to subdue, and I curse the irony of literally wearing my heart on my sleeve. I usher him onto my palm, caressing his curled tail in a silent apology.

I shut my eyes and begin to siphon.

The sound of Nero's anguish is like a hot knife through my heart. He whimpers and cowers in my palm, a high-pitched screech that wells tears in my eyes. I count each soul as they release into the night, desperate for salvation, eager for resolution. But the Prime wouldn't give them the satisfaction. The demon absorbs my bounty one by one as I continue to pull, and not long after, my quota reduces from 323 to 273. Fifty souls may seem like a fair trade, but it's a price I'm reluctant to pay, not when time isn't on my side.

"I'm sorry, fella," my voice breaks as Nero curls in my palm. I feel his pain, the exhaustion that envelopes his tiny body. Our bond is indescribable, an enigma no living thing, supernatural or human, will ever comprehend. I fight the urge to flee in that moment, to retreat into the shadows, but our exchange is not done. Not yet.

I rise to my feet, eyeing the Prime in defiance. "Five minutes, not a second longer."

The Demon of Nightmares and Fear hovers above my hunter. The hunger in their eyes is primal. Insatiable. Like an animal famished. And Lovejoy is their coveted meal.

I turn a blind eye to their ritual, shielding my vision from what I know is a grotesque exchange. I've seen this demon feed before, the way they physically invade a person's mind and devour their terror... I can't bear to watch it feed upon my lover.

Lovejoy's nightmare breaks the unsettling silence as a murmur at first. Shallow breaths turn into pained groans and soon become hushed pleas as he fights an archaic evil in his slumber. Five minutes never felt so long.

I wrap my arms around myself, fighting the growing goosebumps pricking my skin. The Prime hisses delightfully behind me, relishing in its meal, satiating its hunger. I pity my hunter in that moment; I pity the cross he's forced to bear, the evil that haunts him for the rest of his immortal days.

I then remember that my involvement in his life is the darkest curse of all.

"That's enough," I mutter as the minutes drag on. I spin around, shivering as bile rises in my throat. My skin itches as I watch dark tendrils of smoke recoiling from Lovejoy's eyes, ears, mouth, and nostrils.

The demon stands above my hunter, licking their lips. "We'd say it's a pleasure doing business with you, Winters, but lying is beneath our purview."

"Just keep your mouths shut. Not a word to Daddy, got it?"

The Demon of Nightmares and Fear lift a long, festering finger to my chest and push lightly. "Your hunter won't live forever, witch."

"I'll be the judge of that," I sneer. "Now get the fuck out of here before he wakes up."

I kneel at Lovejoy's body once more and pull his head into my lap as he comes to. Something pulls within me, a tightness in my chest that threatens to suffocate me. Lovejoy's body is weak but gains strength with every passing second. My healing ritual saw fit to that. His eyes flutter open suddenly, breath sucking in as he grasps for my hands. I hush him then, tracing soft circles into his damp hair. Our eyes meet, cocooned in peaceful silence. It's a tender, gentle moment. The despair in his eyes fades with every curl of my fingers, every stroke against his scalp.

"I've got you." I fear my words hold little solace while my fingers reach for his cheek. Full, blushed cheeks. Not dead. Not decaying. My voice is a soft whisper under the moonlight. "Where did you go?"

He leans into me then, nuzzling his nose into my palm. He grabs my hand, bringing my knuckle to his lips, peppering gentle kisses against my skin. "The same place I go any time I shut my eyes. Right to my nightmares."

The ghost of his terrors haunt his weary eyes, thick with exhaustion. The burden weighs heavy on him and clings to his consciousness. I pity my lover, pity the dreams that torment him night after night, year after year, the mark the demons left on him.

"Waking up beside someone is rare for me. Your presence is...comforting."

Comforting. The word feels alien to me. I flash him a small smile, rising to my feet and smoothing out my gown.

"The Fear Underling?" His voice trembles with hope.

"Dead. Disintegrated."

"And the wedding?"

I suck in my lips as I concoct the perfect lie. "I tried my best, but…more Fear demons showed up. Not even my powers are a match against them."

The defeat in his eyes almost sends a twinge of guilt within me. Almost. "I need to call Jeremy." He rises from my lap. "We need to dispose of the bodies. We need to do damage control before they're discovered."

"Already taken care of."

His eyes widen in disbelief. "Really?"

I nod. "Insufferable little brat, that one. You're lucky he takes direction well."

Lovejoy stands, towering over me, his dress shirt torn open and filthy. He searches my face, hands hovering over my jaw. Then, his eyes catch sight of my bloody hands. "Are you hurt?"

I shake my head and pull my hands from his. "Don't worry about me."

Lovejoy sighs. "I've got to—"

"Go. Yeah. I know. Do your whole world-saving thing." I wave my hand dismissively.

His gaze is that of pained exhaustion, of regret and compassion. He leans in, placing his soft lips upon my forehead before turning to face the ballroom.

I love watching him walk away, the sway of his gait like a man riding into battle. I'm not ready to say goodbye —and for all I know, this could be our last.

My fingers curl into my palms as I clench my jaw. "Lovejoy," I call out as he makes his way back into the building. Tired eyes meet mine. "I'll help you."

There's a twinkle in those brown orbs, the same twinkle I fell in love with eighty years ago. "You will?"

"I don't do business with demons," I lie through my

teeth. "But even I know a disruption in the balance when I see one. I'll help you find your friends."

He rushes to me, grabbing my hands and bringing them to his lips. "October, you don't know what this means to me."

"I have an idea." I shrug. "Your offer still stands, though, right? The blood?"

"Of course." He doesn't hesitate. "But you remember my terms. No one can know."

"No one will know and no one will care. I'm no threat to you or your Order." Another lie that cuts deep, but Lovejoy believes me nonetheless. Where Lovejoy goes, demons will follow. And where there are demons, death is inevitable, souls at my disposal, to collect right out from under the nose of a hunter none the wiser. It's the perfect recipe to ensure the success of one perilous ultimatum.

I've spent a millennium lying and deceiving others. Killing to secure my immortality. Getting away with mass murder and dodging every nuisance the Holy Order of the Nephilim has thrown my way. I've survived eighty years in a twisted, clandestine affair with my rival, an angel who never fails to test my nature and quell the darkness within. The demon was right about one thing — my immortal days are numbered. And sometimes, in order to get ahead, you need to work alongside your enemies.

Even if it means betraying your master.

TRACK ELEVEN

#1 CRUSH

TRACK ELEVEN

#1 CRUSH

An endless river of asphalt stretches before me as my hands grip my steering wheel tight. Los Angeles fades into my rearview mirror, the downtown skyline glittering amidst the darkness of a starless, 3 AM sky.

After that untimely run-in with Nightmares and Fear, I realize I might need a little back up—some demonic insurance, so to speak. A quick trip back to The Starlight to change out of my dress is all I need before embarking on a little side quest of my own.

My destination is a perilous one. The freeway is desolate, save for a car or two that zoom past me. The radio hums softly, a nonstop marathon of commercial-less tunes fading into the background of my thoughts.

As the miles blur past, a memory surfaces. It's a rare gem in my vault of recollections, a fleeting moment of genuine joy. These precious seconds of emotion glitter all the brighter against the backdrop of my immortal life. I've survived lifetimes; acquaintances have come and gone, never quite crossing the threshold into true friendship, and lovers? Well, they've all fallen prey to my soul-collecting proclivities.

All except one.

Declan Lovejoy.

Hollywood, October 31, 1923

Crimson velvet hugs my body like a second skin. I stand before a vanity mirror, admiring the dashing red dress I've just procured from my latest victim. Her boudoir is something from my wildest dreams, with a closet triple the size of the shack I currently occupy in Santa Monica. Don't get me started on her husband's cars —I'm sure he won't mind if I took that Rolls out for a spin.

How could he? He's dead. I killed him. Just another soul to add to my plunder.

The Devil will be so proud of his best girl.

A flash of black in the mirror catches my eye. Tiny pincers click against the dressing table, nearly knocking over my lipstick and begging for my attention.

There he is. My darling little scorpion.

"Hey there, fella." I smile as the eight-legged creature crawls over my hand. He's motionless as I run a finger down his ebony exoskeleton. "I've got a little party to go to. What sort of accessory shall we turn you into this time, hm?"

Nero crawls up my arm, tickling my skin as his hairy little trotters travel toward my shoulders. His stinger gently caresses my neck, and I can't fight the giggle that escapes me. "Mm, a necklace would be lovely. What do you say: rubies or diamonds?"

I've already settled on rubies with my killer red dress for tonight. As much as I like to assume the creature has a mind of its own, I know he doesn't. He's simply an extension of my soul, a piece of me made manifest into a glorious, deadly arachnid bound in pincers. Still, you can't blame a lonely gal for craving companionship, no matter the sort. And what better friend to make for yourself than, well, yourself?

Nero has been with me since the day I sold myself to the Devil. He's my loyal familiar, my only best friend. The streets weren't a safe place for a scorpion, and I very well couldn't allow him to perish under the boot of a fearful idiot. So, I thought of the perfect way to keep him close: by turning him into expensive jewelry.

I cast my spell and transform the scorpion into a stunning necklace, the perfect complement to my lavish outfit. His tail wraps around my neck while the stinger rests comfortably above my cleavage. With a getup like this, I know I'll turn heads. When you've lived in the shadows for as long as I have, it's always refreshing to play the heartstopper—in more ways than one.

I finish off with a final primp and coat my lips in a sinful rouge. I rush to the garage with a spring in my step, eager to arrive at the party in style. Tonight is a special night, the best night of the year.

My birthday.

Of course, no one *knows* it's my birthday—that was just another one of my best-kept secrets.

Others usually refer to this night as 'All Hallow's Eve.' I'm aware of the coincidence.

Supernaturals have a crude sense of humor when it comes to humans. While the lifestyles of the damned and the delirious remain concealed to the world, we can't help our sadistic nature. We often feed lies to the gullible and fashion horror stories to keep them away. There's a reason why cemeteries are undesirable at night, why abandoned houses are rumored to be haunted. We need a safe space where no one will dare seek us out: a place to let loose, to be ourselves. After all, even the monster under the bed needs a place to party.

Hollywood Forever Cemetery is the perfect spot for a bash. The wickedest of spirits always come out to play during the best night of the year. I pull in past the wrought-iron gates, following the gravel pathway toward a grand mausoleum that houses a family of dead rich folk. It stands on a little island surrounded by a murky, man-made pond littered with dozens of sleeping ducks and geese. No one would ever dream that there would be a speakeasy located underneath an elaborate crypt. But it isn't just any old speakeasy.

It's a Supernatural Secret Society Speakeasy. Try saying that five times fast.

I'm greeted with the fabulous glow of a full moon when I exit the Rolls. My heels click against the marble steps of the mausoleum with an eerie echo. With a wave of my hand, my magic flings the door open with ease, revealing an empty tomb with nary a soul in sight. If memory serves me correctly, all I have to do is knock on the wall three times.

Knock, knock, knock.

White marble twists and morphs into a dark and sinister lounge. Magic fills the air, and, one by one, I am met with the dumbfounded gazes of Hollywood's supernatural elite.

It's good to be back.

"Welcome, young lady," the eager doorman greets me, and my heart flutters at the term of endearment.

I shrug off my coat, leaving my fur shawl draped over my shoulders and shoot him a wink. "Honey, I could be your great-great-twenty-times-over-great grandmother. But thanks for the boost of confidence."

Scouting out the lounge, I make my rounds: a vampire here, a werewolf there, a couple of ghosts dancing about. I catch the glance of a familiar monster or two, nodding their way, avoiding small talk. What I *really* want tonight is someone to play with, someone I can get my rocks off with before I take their soul. Birthday or not, I'm still on the clock. The Devil always admired my ruthless work ethic.

I down my usual from the bar, an old fashioned with maple bourbon. The drink burns as it trickles down my throat, and my breath practically escapes me when I'm met with the eyes of the most darling creature in the room.

He's a perfect gentleman under a single spotlight, tickling the black and whites of a precious Steinway. I can't help but smirk: a room filled to the brim with beautiful women of every supernatural flavor, and he only has eyes for me, the most dangerous gal in the world.

I saunter toward the piano with a fluid, enchanting rhythm. I keep one hand upon my black mink while my other lightly brushes against the red leather booths. My movements are a choreographed dance, one I've perfected over the years. And though he most certainly isn't my first, I can't help but relish in the thrill that builds at the sight of his dazzling eyes. The poor soul.

A cool rush overcomes me as his cadence shifts to a slow, sensual melody. It complements my graceful steps, every sway of my hips... I can only imagine the spectacle we've put on for the surrounding patrons. Their gasps fill the room as I hop onto the piano and dangle my legs off the edge. My darling pianist's eyes widen when I shimmy closer to him, moving my legs to rest upon the keys and give him a *real* show.

I'm not a modest gal—never have been, never will be. My crimson smirk and lack of unmentionables make damn sure of that.

"Well, aren't you a slice of heaven?" the pianist mutters, his lingering eyes drinking in every inch of me.

"In a dress like this?" I chuckle. "Honey, I've got 'Hell' written all over me."

He leans over, reaching behind me to pull out a single red rose from the vase resting on the piano. Never have I ever met a man with an aura so pristine, so pure. It's like the Devil himself sent me the perfect birthday gift.

I take the rose and sniff it, batting my dark lashes in a manner most coy. "What are you? You're certainly not human."

He shrugs with a smile. "Does it matter?"

"It does when your life hangs in the balance."

He raises his chin, avoiding his view between my legs. "That's a creative threat. I almost feel nervous."

"The fact that you aren't speaks volumes. You're either really brave or really green."

"Perhaps a bit of both. Intrigued?"

"Bored, if I'm being honest." Which I'm not, but I am an expert at this game, and I'll be damned if I lose.

"Honesty is an attractive quality in a woman."

"And pussyfooting is a turn off in men." I hop off the piano, smoothing out my stole and dress. I feel his eyes on me, drinking me in, studying every inch. I take the opportunity to truly knock his socks off. I twist the rose between my fingers and use my magic to turn his romantic gesture into black, dried-up potpourri.

His breath catches in his chest. "You're a witch."

Bit slow, this one. I shoot him a playful smirk. "You say 'witch' like it's a bad thing."

He stumbles upon his words, backtracking and swallowing hard. *Goodness*, is it adorable. "I just—I haven't met one before. Only read stories."

Fuck me, he *is* green. There must be at least four or five others like me in this very room. I flash him a coy smile after I take a sip of his drink. "I can assure you, I'm nothing like the witches you've read about."

"How do you know?"

"Because I've spent hundreds of years securing a reputation like mine." I lean dangerously close to his lips. "Don't worry, I'll be sure to make a lasting impression on you."

"I can't imagine you'd make anything less."

I hate the way my heart skips with every quip. The way it quickens when he smiles. The way it yearns as he proves a worthy opponent. I especially hate the way he aims to have the last word.

"May I have your name?"

I mind him for a moment. Which one of my many aliases would suit me tonight? I've retired Lorelei the ditzy nurse, and Sister Rachel of the Abbey wouldn't be caught dead in a place like this. Ah, well. He *did* say honesty was attractive. "You can call me October."

Curiosity twinkles in his eyes. "Like the month?"

"Aww, you *are* smarter than you look, Mr. Green."

"It's Lovejoy, actually. Declan Lovejoy."

I try not to laugh. I *really* do. I wonder how many hearts he has broken with those puppy dog eyes and dazzling smile. I look forward to breaking his.

"You got a light?" I ask as I reach for my golden cigarette case.

"No. Never liked the stuff."

"Shame." With a twitch of my fingertips, I conjure a golden flame and take a drag. Euphoria hits me as the smoke fills my lungs. He rises from his seat, giving me a better view of his tall frame with shoulders so broad, they'd make excellent leg rests. Be still my beating heart, this man could be the death of me.

In fact, he *might* be.

I catch what appears to be an elaborate design inked onto his neck, one I didn't notice from my position earlier —one I've grown to know very well over my hundreds of years of soul-collecting.

A mark like that only means one thing in a world like ours.

"Well, I'll be damned. *You?* A demon hunter?" My cackle rings throughout the lounge.

His smile falters. "I fail to see the humor."

Demon hunters are a peculiar brand of divine justice,

from my understanding. Half angel, half human, a righteous few hand-picked by God and bestowed with the power to track, hunt, and destroy demons, among other convenient abilities. I've spent my entire life avoiding them, of course, as they tend to dampen my style. But I can't help but feel drawn to this one. He's just so… precious.

It's a good thing he isn't a witch hunter.

I run my finger along his jaw, tipping his chin upward. "You're too pretty to hunt demons. And no one's going to take you seriously with a name like that. You need something with a little more…pizzazz, something that'll scare the bejesus outta those uglies."

The Devil despises demon hunters, hates everything they stand for. Can't blame him—I, too, would hate anyone who dared to destroy everything I've built.

My lips curl into a devious grin as an idea comes to mind. "Why don't you come with me? We can find a quiet place to brainstorm ideas."

Only a fool would fall for such a blatant trap, and it appears Declan Lovejoy is one such fool. But when he grabs my hand and leads me out of the enchanted lounge with a head held high and a smirk on his lips, I know I've met my match. This really *is* the best birthday gift a girl could ask for.

I clutch my necklace, muttering a familiar spell under my breath as we disappear into the night. My magic manifests as two dark tendrils trailing from my necklace down my arm and into the unsuspecting body of my precious demon hunter. He shivers for a second, the moonlight casting a glow over his handsome features, before he shrugs it off with a confident smile.

He's young. He's eager. He's determined.

And with each beat of his heart, my claim on his soul deepens.

TRYING TO KEEP THE NIGHTMARES AWAY?
MORE LIKE TRYING TO KEEP THE DEMONS AT BAY.
TRACK TWELVE
DR FEELGOOD

TRACK TWELVE

DR. FEELGOOD

Four hours and thirty-six minutes.

That's how long it takes me to drive from one Hellhole to another. As the hours pass, palm trees yield to cacti, greenery surrenders to the desert, and soon—but not nearly soon enough—a glittering landscape begins to emerge just above the horizon. A tourist trap tucked into a barren wasteland.

"'*Welcome to the Fabulous Las Vegas*,' my ass," I grunt under my breath. One year ago, this neon beast devoured me whole, chewed me up, and spat out a desperate shell. Now, I'm back, magic crackling in my veins and desperation still nipping at my heels.

The Strip blurs by. I pull into a ghost town of a plaza —all plywood windows and chain-link promises. This place is a graveyard of memories, and a wave of them come crashing back with full force. Until a few days ago, the last time I was at this Hell-forsaken place was the last time I used my magic.

I swallow hard, tasting regret. With a deep breath, I push through the only lit doorway in the plaza.

Only to be met with a shocked smile and wide eyes of an old friend.

"Hazel," Alejandro greets me with a weary smile, using one of my many aliases. "Holy shit."

Yeah. Holy shit, indeed.

"Last I heard, you were in New York City."

"No one wants to be in fucking New York City right now." Settling onto his workbench, I offer a tentative smile. "I should have called before showing up. I know I'm not welcome in this town anymore."

"You're safe here. What can I do for you, *bruja*?"

"You got any Dreamguard on you?"

The shaman sorts through his wares, sifting through bottle after bottle on his shelves in search of my request. "Trying to keep the nightmares away?"

"More like trying to keep the demons at bay."

"Same difference." He nods in understanding. "You piss off the twins or something?"

"Bold of you to assume this is for me."

"I know better." He flashes me a gap-toothed grin. "You never do anyone any favors. Not unless it serves you."

"Touché."

Alejandro disappears behind a beaded curtain, and I hear the clanking of glass containers resonate from the room. "I'll need to whip up a fresh batch if you've got the time," he calls out from the supply closet, grabbing one too many peculiar ingredients from vial-lined shelves.

"Make it quick," I urge him. "I'm on a big job and got a four hour drive ahead of me."

"Make yourself at home."

Home. What a concept. A foreign one, at least to me.

This shack's a far cry from home—a cramped, suffocating mess of herbs, pelts, and who-knows-what. It's like a pocket dimension of nature gone wild, sweltering under the desert sun. My outfit's all wrong for this swamp-in-a-box, but at least it beats the Hellish cold I've endured the past couple of days.

The shaman shuffles out, cradling an odd assortment of ingredients. As he starts grinding herbs, I drum my fingers against my thigh, my patience wearing as thin as the powder he's creating.

"This will work against the Primes, not just their Underlings, right?"

"Nothing's ever a guarantee." He shrugs as he stirs his pot. "But this one's worked more often than not."

"Good." I nod. "How much do I owe you?"

"How much you got?"

I dig into my leather jacket, fumbling for the precious jewelry I'd stolen from a grave. "These of any value?"

He pauses to take the gems from my hand and studies them intently. He lights a flame in his hand, shining it over the stones to test their clarity. With a small laugh and a shake of his head, he peers up at me. "Still bleeding money, *mija*?"

I smirk, batting my lashes. "Old habits die hard."

"An immortal who's bad with money." He shakes his head again. "Now I've seen it all."

I wave my hand dismissively. "Banks? Stocks? I've got better addictions."

"Such as?"

"Chanel. Rolls-Royce. Artisanal truffles."

He cracks another smile. "All hot merchandise now, no?"

"A witch has got to eat. And look damn good doing it."

Alejandro eyes my outfit, one brow raised. "Funny. You're not exactly dripping diamonds right now."

"The last diamonds I had now rest in your hand. So, they any good?"

"They'll do." He shoves the jewels into a drawer for safekeeping and continues to work on his brew. I pace slowly within his shop, scouring the crystal section for any other tools I may need for the foreseeable future. I pick up a scrying crystal, a couple of herbs, and some extra empty vials for my own needs. I remind the shaman to add these to my tab but stop dead in my tracks as I near the back room. I eye the beaded curtain, and a chill of foreboding slithers down my spine. "Any change?"

Alejandro's eyes, hollow with exhaustion, meet mine. "None." The word carries the weight of more than just medical concern. He notices my curt nod and reaches for my shoulder, but I step back.

"Hazel, you made the right choice —"

"Spare me," I cut him off, voice low and sharp. "I dug my own grave with that one. No use trying to convince me the view's nice."

His lips twitch, resignation etched in the creases around his eyes. The unspoken argument dies on his tongue.

Eager to change the subject, I press on. "So, that potion?"

"Right." He clears his throat and continues to add his ingredients to the pot.

I slouch against his desk, arms crossed, studying his work. Potion brewing was never my strong suit. Good thing I've got an ace up my sleeve—a contact who can whip up miracles in a bottle when I'm in a jam.

"Hey, Alé," I start as curiosity ferments in my mind. "Any dealings with demons lately?"

"Some. Why?"

"Those little shits up to anything juicy?"

"Deception's got the pigs in his pocket. Werewolves aren't too happy about it. Gambling industry's taking the hit."

"Crooked cops and werewolf mobsters," I muse, remembering my close calls with a particular Alpha Boss. "That's it?"

"If you're fishing for information, you're doing a shit job at it."

I sigh. "Alright, fine. Cards on the table. Demon hunters are going poof—got any intel?"

"Demon hunters?" he questions. "You're not still shacking up with *that one*, are you?"

A sound catches in my throat—half wince, half whimper—as I hunch my shoulders and avert my eyes, unable to meet his judging gaze.

"*Ay dios mío*, just like an addict," he mutters under his breath, shaking his head. "Didn't you learn your lesson in the 80s?"

A little bell jingles, piercing the tension as the entrance door creaks open, and relief floods through me at the timely interruption.

"Right on cue," I mutter, spine snapping straight. A policeman enters the shop, hands clutching his belt, obnoxiously chewing on a piece of gum. The crooked cop leers at the sight of me, removing his aviators from his dark eyes. "Devil's Second, in the flesh. Thought we ran you outta Sin City."

"Can't run me out if I saunter away, babe."

His sleazy laugh slithers down my spine. "Boss'll get a kick outta this."

"Your boss doesn't need to know I'm here. Just grabbing some goods and ghosting."

The demon's eyes flicker to Alejandro's brew, a hint of recognition sparking in their depths. His nostrils flare at the potent scent fuming from the pot. A sly smile spreads across his face, revealing teeth a touch too sharp to be human.

"Mmm, that smell—garlic and roses, is it? And a hint of…holy water." The demon's voice drops as he fights off a twitch. "Smells like demon repellent. You're not trying to keep us out of your shop, are you, shaman?"

"That would be bad for business, eh?" Alejandro flashes the cop a mocking smile.

"Lying to a demon who feasts on deception? Ballsy."

"Then maybe you should get out before you choke on the fumes," I spit. I notice Alejandro's hand reach under his table cautiously while the other hand continues to stir. A glint of silver catches my eye, and I fight the quirk in my lip.

The cop, however, sneers.

He steps forward, clenched jaw furrowing that irksome mustache of his, and a Hellish green light pierces behind his dark shades.

I push Alejandro away from the table, away from the demon's direct line of sight, and extend my hand at the fiend. My fingers curl inward, my magic tingling in my fingertips as I siphon the breath out of the creature. With a frustrated gasp, the cop hunches over, clutching his throat. But he doesn't fall to his knees or bend to my will, no. He grins—a sadistic, stomach-twisting grin that sends a shiver of panic up my spine as my hold on him falters.

In seconds, he disappears.

And my body collides with his when he reappears behind me.

"Your magic is useless here, witch," he hisses, twisting my arms behind my back. His sulfurous breath sears my ear, demonic voice grating like broken glass.

I force a smile, despite the pain. "No? Can't say the same for my boot." In one fluid motion, I drive my heel into his instep and slam my head back, feeling the crunch of his nose.

He howls, grip loosening just enough. I spin, dropping low, and sweep his legs. As he crashes down, I lunge for Alejandro's workbench. My fingers find the cold iron knife hidden underneath.

I press the freshly sharpened tip to his throat. The demon freezes, black aviators falling off the bridge of his nose to reveal widened eyes. "Now then," I say, voice dripping with false sweetness, "as I was saying before you so rudely interrupted—I'm just here for some goods. No need to act like you own the place. So why don't you get the fuck out of here before I shove some of that demon repellent down your throat?"

"You wouldn't," he rasps. "We all know you can't kill us."

"Can't? Or *won't?*"

"Your deal with the Big Man Downstairs—kill one of his own, and he will sure as fuck kill *you*."

Mother*fuck*, the pig was right. Just another reminder of the pathetically short leash the Devil keeps me on. The fine print of my immortality is a short list with long consequences. Rule number one: Collect and deliver souls. Rule number two: Demons are off limits. Period.

Doesn't stop me from hating their guts.

"How's that potion comin', Alé?" I nod over at the shaman, who peeks into his steaming pot.

"Just about cured."

"Super. Hand it over."

Alejandro's hand hovers over the vial, green light pulsing from his palm. The potion sizzles, sealed with shamanic magic. I snatch the Dreamguard Elixir and shove it into my battle-worn purse. One less nightmare to deal with.

The demon writhes at my feet, a pitiful sight. My boot itches to meet his face, but I resist. Barely.

Instead, I flash him a wolfish grin. "Stay out of my way, and I'll stay out of yours. I may not be allowed to kill you, but I have no problem getting someone else to do it for me."

The exit beckons, but that damn beaded curtain taunts me as I pass it by. It whispers. Tempts. Dares me to look…

One glance, and I'll relive the last year all over again. The choice. The betrayal. The loss.

One stupid, irrevocable decision.

One that has me dancing with the Devil and juggling souls like a Hellbound circus act.

No.

Not now. Not *ever.*

Some secrets are better left buried.

TRACK THIRTEEN

LIKE A STONE

TRACK THIRTEEN
LIKE A STONE

THE PROMISE OF A STEAMING BATH CALLS TO ME, AND I can only hope it will soothe my weary bones and settle the woes adrift in my mind. Nine infernal hours of travel has left me with nothing but a numb ass and shitty taste in my mouth. I kick off my combat boots, leaving a trail of discarded clothing in my wake as I make my way to the bathroom.

I should have collected more souls today, should have used my pit-stop in Vegas as an excuse to bag me a couple hundred. But instead, I pissed away prime soul-snatching hours collecting demonic insurance, headbanging to Megadeth, and letting old ghosts yank my chain.

With my luck, I'll be demoted to Hellspawn faster than you can say 'eternal damnation.'

Not the career move I've been hoping for.

I flick my wrist to turn on the bath, the sound of

running water quickly easing my apprehension. My reflection stares back at me from the mirror, a gothic disaster straight out of one of those Tim Burton flicks. My black lipstick, now faded into a charcoal smear, serves as a grim reminder of hours of neglect and one too many cigarettes. A defiant spark still glimmers in my raccoon-smudged eyes, as unshakeable as the dusk creeping across the sky beyond my window. The night is young. The souls can wait.

Nero rests in his awakened state, curled within the shadows of the bathroom—no jewelry confines, no stomping humans, just peace. Through our bond, I feel his contentment unfurl like a dark flower.

Cold water meets my toes as I slowly dip into the bath, sending a rush of chill throughout my already aching body. Cheap pipes, busted water heater, no doubt —what more did I expect from a motel run by demons?

I dip my hand into the water, circling my finger like a whirlpool as I use my fire magic to heat the bath. Oh, how I've missed my magic—long gone are the excruciating days of having to brew my own coffee, get up to change the channel on the TV, and, dare I say it, drive a stick shift. Such was the price to pay when pissing off the Devil.

A sharp knock against the flimsy door shatters my fleeting moment of peace. My muscles tense—it's likely Reagan or one of her infernal lackeys. I sink deeper into the tub, lathering up with a fresh bar of soap, hoping my silence will deter them. But after mere moments, a metallic scrape reaches my ears. The hotel lock yields, and the doorknob slowly turns.

So much for relaxation.

I ready my hands, preparing to blast the intruder. The next sorry ass to walk through that door is in for a fist full of flames, consequences be damned.

But then, I hear *him*.

Feel him.

The infernal brand on his soul sings to me, and my muscles relax. The bathroom door opens, a small creak nearly swallowed by the splashes of bathwater. Quiet footsteps enter, hesitant yet unstoppable. I slip into the consciousness of my scorpion, allowing myself a better view of my intruder. There could only be one, of course. One who knows exactly where I am. One who knows to let himself in.

Lovejoy drinks in the sight of my naked form. His eyes rake over me as the milky water does little to shield my legs and breasts. He lingers in the doorway, assuming I'm not aware of his presence. I'll allow him the satisfaction, if only for a moment, for I too wish to admire my scorpion's view. My hunter is a vision in a world that has grown cold over the years of our separation. He's a warmth I crave. I return to my mind, urging Nero to make himself scarce, as we are no longer alone in this dingy motel room. I lean my head back, eyes fluttering shut as a soft sigh escapes from me. The air is thick with potent, undeniable tension. And soon, a yearning of my own threatens to break my pretenses.

Trembling fingers thread through my damp hair, stroking my scalp. The gesture feels familiar—a mere ghost of the intimacy we'd grown to favor between his missions and my capers. I lean into his touch, smiling as relief washes over me. I ache for him. For his hands all over my body. For his mouth. His…

"Hello, lover."

My eyes open then, hooded and peering at him through slits. I hum at the contact, resting an arm over the edge of the tub. My fingers reach for him, wriggling lazily in beckoning.

"You found me," I sigh—this time, with a touch of feigned regret in my voice.

"You're hard to miss."

The words are our little inside joke. Our customary greeting. Every decade, he finds me. He *always* finds me. And truth be told, despite my greatest efforts, it *isn't* hard to miss a bombshell like me.

I reach for him again, aching to feel those deliciously calloused hands, hands worn and burned from years of potion-making and demon slaying. There's a charm about those scars, a physicality that adds to his intrigue. But he refuses to appease my plea. Instead, he chuckles.

My name is a warning growl from deep within his chest. His hand dips into my bathwater, drawing figure eights through tiny bubbles. His fingers are dangerously close but never touch me. Such a *fucking tease*. I shoot him a playful stare, one laced with mischief yet seductive all the same.

"How'd you manage to slip past the demons?" I ask, my gaze drawn to the intricate tattoo on his neck.

He reaches into his heavy coat and pulls out a sleek black flask from an inner pocket. "Aura cloaking elixir," he explains, a hint of pride in his voice.

"Handy," I say, a wry smile playing on my lips. "If demon slaughter isn't on your agenda, what unsavory business brings you to these parts?"

He clears his throat then, straightening his seemingly tense back. "I've come to discuss…this."

Always with the unnerving need for conversation with this one. You'd think after eight decades of this twisted dalliance, he'd have learned I prefer to keep the talking to a minimum during our sexual escapades. "And what is 'this' you speak of?" I twist my body to rest my arms over the edge and tilt my head playfully. His breath hitches as his gaze flits to the curve of my ass peeking through the water.

"Our…"—his hand trails along the edge of the porcelain tub, inching closer and closer— "…relationship."

For the love of all that's unholy, not *this* again. I resist the urge to roll my eyes as a deliciously dark ruse takes root in my mind. "We're in a relationship?"

His weary brow knits with the clench of his jaw. I

throw my head back with a teasing laugh. "Baby, we've had this conversation time and time again for eighty years. And frankly, I'm over it."

"I don't like seeing you with other men."

I bite my cheek to thwart a smile. Nothing makes me want this man more than when his possessive side creeps through. It only reminds me that, despite his divinity, darkness resides deep within. Nevertheless, I continue my little game. "Declan Lovejoy, I thought you were above jealousy."

"I find myself above very little when it comes to you."

"How flattering." I shrug my bare shoulder as I raise half my body out of the water and rest on my knees. His brown eyes darken at the sight of me, darken even more when my hands slide up his own, toward his chest…and down to the unmistakable, growing bulge in his jeans.

"And just what do you think you're doing, lover?" he rasps, voice hoarse and thick as he watches my movements.

My demented grin reaches my ears. "I thought it was obvious."

"I didn't come here to play games, October."

"Could have fooled me." I pull away and lean my back against the cool porcelain. "Come on, Lovejoy. Have some fun with me. Life's too short to be consumed by honor and duty." For him, maybe, but for a wicked immortal such as myself, life's greatest pleasures lie within the gamble of short odds.

"We can't always indulge in our deepest desires. One could become…insatiable." Calloused fingers dip into the water once more and finally, *finally* trail up my thigh, gentle and slow —*painfully* slow. His lips hover over mine, hooded eyes molten with desire. He inches closer but never close enough, and I reach for his jaw. Defiance burns within him, but his resolve is low. I can feel it. I can *taste* it.

I instinctively lean forward when he pulls away. My brows knit with a narrowed stare, glaring daggers into his back as he swaggers out of the bathroom. It isn't until he turns his head to peer at me, a delicious smirk tugging at his lips, that I realize I'm not the only one who loves to play games.

I've taught him well. But I'll never let him win.

I step out of the tub, water droplets rolling down my skin as I quickly wrap a towel around myself. Following him into the main room, I can't help but ask, "So, did you come all this way just to mark your territory?"

"No, though the thought may have crossed my mind."

I chuckle. "Cute. You *actually* think you have a claim on me."

"I know I don't," he mutters under his breath. "But you can't fault a man for his honesty."

I never cared for honesty, personally. Telling the truth has only gotten me into more trouble.

"Anyway," I dismiss his petty thoughts. "Why'd you

break into my hotel room tonight if you had no intentions of fucking the daylights out of me?"

He clears his throat at my brazen statement, and I can't help but savor these moments of rattling his composure. "I've given more thought to our alliance and the role you're to play in it."

Ugh. Such formalities. I feel like I'm working in a corporate prison again. I urge him to continue with a roll of my wrist as I slowly rub one of my protective skin concoctions onto my body.

"I think it would be best to utilize your connections in the Underworld. Perhaps you could summon a demon for me."

His request catches me off guard. "Because the ones surrounding this establishment aren't good enough?"

He grimaces. "Someone of *higher* standing, not the rabble. Ask them a few questions. See if you can catch any gossip, any motives, any plans. There's only so much we can do by listening in on prayers."

"Why can't you and...what's-his-name do it?"

"Jeremy," he corrects me. "Demon summonings are above our pay grade. Besides, can you see a demon willingly divulging information to a couple of hunters?"

"They would if you torture them enough."

"As much as I'd love to inflict every level of pain upon those beasts, I find deceit would be a better course of action."

"It's risky," I warn him. "We'd have to steer clear of

Deception Demons. They'd smell our trick from a mile away." I ponder on his request, thinking of alternative options. I hop on the dingy desk in the room, crossing my legs and gripping my towel closer to my body.

"Where was the last place you saw this colleague of yours?"

"The last place we knew of their whereabouts was here, actually. In Los Angeles. They were investigating a demonic lead. We can all hear each other, much like how we can hear human prayers. It was like one minute, they were here, and the next, they were…gone. Vanished. No thoughts. Nothing."

"Sounds glorious," I admit. I know I'd do anything to never hear a single voice in my head ever again. "And you're sure they aren't dead?"

"I refuse to believe it."

I tilt my head, shooting him an incredulous glare. "Come on, babe. You can't make assumptions like that without any proof."

"They're not dead, October. I know it."

"Alright, don't get snippy with me." I hop off the desk and pace around the room in thought. "May I offer some suggestions?"

He stretches out his hand, urging me to continue.

"Demons are imbeciles," I speak truthfully. "The only ones remotely decent at their jobs are those who work under Pestilence and Vengeance. *They* actually need to be calculated enough to pull off some of their shit. The rest?

Useless. And loudmouths. If there's one thing they're good at, though, it's banding together to defeat a common enemy. Alone, they're worthless. In packs? Unstoppable. If word gets out that a hunter is asking questions—and trust me, word *will* get out—they'll align faster than you can say 'hit me, baby, one more time.'"

He looks at me with awe, but there's a surprise hidden behind his brown orbs. "You know so much," he breathes out in disbelief.

"I've spent my entire life avoiding demons and made it my business to know their ins and outs. Don't *you* know everything about them?"

"We know their weaknesses, how to destroy them, and study their aggression behaviors. But you speak of them as if they're family."

He's not far off. The only thing separating me from demons is the nature of their conception. Oh, and basic intelligence.

"Can you trust me?" I ask, pivoting the conversation.

"I'm here, aren't I? Despite every moral fiber of my being telling me not to."

A smirk tugs at my lips, and Lovejoy's face betrays him. Conflict wars in his eyes—a shell of a man at his wits' end. His jugular throbs, and I imagine the Nephilim blood pumping through his veins… That divine ichor, so close I can almost taste it. Just one ridiculous quest stands between me and my prize. Soon—so *very* soon—it will be mine.

"I know a place. A demonic cesspool, oozing with all kinds of unholy crap. It's the safest place for them in this city, or so I've heard. Never stepped foot in there myself, but…" A sly grin spreads across my face. "I might just have an ace up my sleeve for getting us in."

A delicious twist grips my gut as false hope ignites in his eyes. I prowl closer, knee parting his legs to stand between them. My wrists snake around his neck as I claim his thigh, pressing against him. Desire crackles between us, unmistakable. Electric. *Familiar*. He clings to control like a child grasping at smoke, but the truth hangs heavy in the shrinking space between us: *I* am the master, and *he* is my puppet.

My fingers seek his weak spot—those curls at his nape. I stroke and tangle, awakening nerves he can't resist. His quiet gasp betrays him; this simple touch is my greatest weapon.

"Listen close, *lover*," I breathe, my lips a whisper from his. "My methods will make your skin crawl. They're wicked, unethical, and go against everything you've ever stood for." I nip his lower lip, tasting his hesitation. "But they'll get you the answers you're looking for. All you need to do…" I pause, savoring the moment. "Is *trust* me."

The irony is as intoxicating as his kiss.

For in this battle of good and evil, I am the least trustworthy of them all.

TRACK FOURTEEN
SYSTEM

TRACK FOURTEEN

SYSTEM

PERCHED ATOP THE GLITZY SPRAWL OF LOS ANGELES lies an uncanny sanctuary cloaked in darkness—a historic restaurant, one now frequented by Hollywood's elite, gourmet know-it-alls, and ingrates with far more money than they deserve. It's a perfect front, naturally; how would any human know that just below one of the city's most esteemed culinary delights lies the wicked center of demonic assembly?

"I'll get you into the Underground, as discussed," Reagan says, admiring her reflection in the sun visor as my cursed Camaro takes us up the winding roads of Hollywood Hills. "But I've got my own work to do. Try not to piss anyone off, yeah?"

"Me? Piss anyone off? Never."

My gaze flicks to Lovejoy, who remains in silent torment as the she-demon and I exchange words. His discipline is something of a marvel, his disdain for the creature beside me palpable. He watches—no, *studies*—her carefully, taking note of her provocative mannerisms, the low, raspy timber of her voice, and it looks as if he's counting every strand of red hair on her head. He knows of her true nature, the demonic bloodlines that twist and turn within her very framework, but he knows not of her devastatingly long list of conquests and proclivities. And while I know the dull ache of his Hunter's Mark vexes his senses, warning him that danger lurks devastatingly near, he holds his composure. He puts his trust in the very thing he hates.

That makes two of us.

Reagan's glamor hides her spiral horns, glowing amber eyes, and demonic features—another one of Debauchery's more clever ideas. Of all of Lucifer's sons, Debauchery is the one I tolerate with the least amount of contempt. He isn't as petty as Greed or as unhinged as Chaos, and he's certainly not as insufferable as Deception—and Hell, do I want to wring *that* little fucker's neck. He certainly has a flavor I can stomach. Never mind that I, too, indulge in the sins he governs.

My Camaro brakes come to a screeching halt once we reach our destination: Yamashiro—Hollywood's most fantastical Japanese restaurant. Time seems to slow here. The chaos of the city is snuffed by the soft rustle of bamboo trees under an endless sky of stars. There's something enticing about being up here with my hunter again. These hills know the secrets of our dalliance, of his dark request…and now, it'll play host to yet another secret: that Declan Lovejoy allied himself with a dark witch and a Debauchery Demon for the greater good.

We exit my car in haste, and Reagan walks ahead of us, black dress and matching heels painting a picture of seductive elegance.

Lovejoy, on the other hand, lingers.

"October, I don't like this," he hisses through gritted teeth as he grabs my wrist.

"I told you to trust me." I yank my wrist from his grip.

"I do trust *you*." His voice lowers, however dark and gruff. "It's your *friend* I don't trust."

"My *friend* is our only way into this place. You wanted my help no matter the cost, remember? So do me a little favor, angel: make like your Lord and Savior and turn the other cheek." I playfully tap his face and peck his jaw with a quick kiss.

I shrug my cropped fur jacket onto my shoulders as our motley trio ascends the concrete steps of Yamashiro. A demon hunter, a succubus, and a witch—who would have imagined?

The scent of cherry blossoms hits me in a delicate wave as the restaurant's façade comes into full view. Hanging lanterns emit a soft glow like that of fireflies. A glorious pagoda stands tall, elegant; a modern marvel of

Japanese architecture. Reagan pushes open two large double doors, and I turn to face my hunter.

"Stop fidgeting," I quip. He cranes his neck, toying with the hem of his collar, and I can see the irritation in his eyes. "I worked hard on that cover up on your neck; you don't want to wipe it off just because you've got a nervous tick."

"It's not a nervous tick, love. My mark burns because it senses an influx of—"

"Yeah, yeah, keep it down. Did you drink your potion?"

He nods once. "They shouldn't be able to sense me." Between his aura-cloaking potion and my excellent cover up job, he shouldn't stand out in this sea of deviants.

"You two lovers done quarreling?" Reagan pipes up as we linger.

Lovejoy shoots her a warning glare. "We're not—"

"We sure are," I interrupt him with a large, overcompensating grin.

Reagan doesn't seem convinced. "Remember to blend in."

We approach the maître-d stand, where a young woman clad in a crimson skin-tight dress greets us. Reagan leans in, flashing the girl a devious smile. "Reservation for Belial."

I catch a glimpse of her face, noting how her spelled amber eyes fade to the black of her natural form and back again. The hostess offers her a curt nod and leads us through the dark, sophisticated restaurant. We follow her past paper-thin doors toward a slabbed pathway that twists and guides us to an outdoor Japanese garden surrounded by four walls. The hostess looks over her shoulder and flicks her wrist. A sharp, metallic click followed by a firm clunk resonates through the garden as the latches upon every door and window lock us in. Lovejoy stiffens next to me, breath quickening and shoulders tensing at the sudden sense of feeling trapped. I step closer to him, sneaking my hand around his to give it a squeeze. *Trust me.*

The stars shine above us, and the air is thick with the aroma of earthy, wet stones and blooming jasmine. Crickets chirp in the night, and the soft muffle of conversation and music fades as we travel deeper into the garden. We soon reach a koi pond filled with countless fish. The hostess stands at the edge of a wooden bridge and waves a single hand toward the structure.

"*Appear*," she casts in Hellspeak, the demonic tongue.

In an instant, her gesture unveils a fissure in the bridge, splitting it to reveal a hidden passageway—a spiral staircase that plunges into the depths of the koi pond.

The night grows cool as the three of us descend into the depths, droplets of water faintly echoing around us. Reagan and I walk side by side, a demoness and a dark witch dressed to kill. My hunter trails behind us warily, taking heavy, calculated steps. We're greeted by a bouncer at the bottom of the steps, a brutish man with sharp, unsettling snake-like eyes. Dark, reptilian scales spread across his jutting muscles and thick neck, fading at his face. A Deception Underling—*great*. I resist the urge to claw the scales right off his body.

"Well, well," his deep baritone rumbles throughout the walls. "Miss Reagan." She flashes him a rigid smile, and his eyes flicker to me, drinking in the sight of my scantily clad form. "And you are?"

"No one important," I snap back, a bit too quickly.

Before the brute can speak, Reagan's fingers dance up his chest. "They're with me. New recruits."

His gaze narrows on us. I brush my hair behind my ear, letting Nero's dormant form peek through. Recognition flashes in that snake-like stare—now he knows *exactly* who he's dealing with. With a curt nod, he pulls back the velvet navy curtain, revealing a dimly lit lounge.

We step past the threshold and enter an underground sanctuary bathed in a palette of deep blues. Ripples from the pond above us reflect through a crystal ceiling in a gleam of dancing light. Full-length glass panels transform the lounge into a living aquarium, where koi glide through limpid water. Their scales gleam like precious gems illuminated by the moonlight that pierces the pond's depths. The paper skins of Japanese lanterns cast a soft yellow glow amidst the darkness, and the air is rich with the scents of sake, miso, and soy. I have to give the fuckers credit—demons really know how to design a space. I suppose when corruption and depravity make up the very essence of your being, money is certainly not a handicap.

Wish I could say the same for myself.

The lounge is filled to the brim with demons of every standing: Lessers, mid-tier, high-level, and, naturally, their crusty little Hellspawn. The vermin cling to their masters, ranging in size from barely knee-high to a hunched four-foot frame; a tangle of green and red blotchy skin, pointed ears, and razor-sharp claws. The very sight of them puts a sour taste in my mouth, and I'm grateful these little shits are not allowed to reveal their true form in the face of mortals.

Reagan disappears into the depths of the lounge, making her rounds. I'm met with occasional glares—some familiar, others curious, but most intimidated. After all, it's not every day the Devil's Second shows up in a demon den. I just need to make sure none of them blow my cover.

"Now what?" Lovejoy mutters.

I exhale. "Now, we find ourselves a blabbermouth."

Lesser demons would be ideal; their relentless ambition to climb the demonic ranks makes them the perfect target for a bit of espionage. I survey the lounge, catching sight of huddles of mid-levelers deep in conversation, high-levelers flaunting their status among their concubines, and one rather antsy-looking lesser. He sits alone under the single spotlight of a yellow lantern and snaps his head in an insect-like manner. I recognize his human form, likely having crossed paths with him during one of my many ill-timed run-ins with the Prime he serves—the Demon of Chaos. The cretin catches my gaze, a sickly, horrific grin widening upon his features as he bows his head in acknowledgement.

Lovejoy and I approach the lesser demon, and I maintain my aura of daunting superiority, casually picking up a freshly poured martini from the bar and savoring a slow, deliberate sip.

"The Scorpion of Rome." The demon beams at me with crooked, rotting teeth.

I arch an eyebrow at the nickname and settle into the black leather armchair directly in front of him. Lovejoy stands behind me, hands firmly gripping the cushioned seat, unwavering and resolute. "That's one I haven't heard in a century or two."

"Your work is something of a legend in these parts." He practically drools, and I can't help but sneer at the sentiment. Devil forgive me, but I hate his fucking offspring. "What brings you to the City of Angels?"

I lean back into the chair, a melodramatic sigh escaping my lips. "I have a bit of a demon hunter problem."

The demon scoffs. "Now, why would a witch have a demon hunter problem?"

"Because I've got a habit of pissing everyone off."

"But not Mister Tall-Dark-and-Broody behind you?"

"Oh, this sight for sore eyes?" I say with a coy smile, nodding over at Lovejoy. "He's just my hired muscle."

"That bad, eh?"

"*Really* bad." I roll my eyes. "Word on the street is, Yamashiro's the place to lure hunters to their deaths. Care to confirm or deny?"

The lesser demon's eyes narrow, but a sly grin quickly spreads across his face. "That information is gonna cost you, Precious."

"Come on," I pout, sticking out my bottom lip as I lean forward. "Not even for little old me?"

"Not without a little something in it for me."

I let out an exaggerated sigh, tucking my chin and looking up at him with pleading eyes. I wiggle my fingers beneath the table, silently reciting a simple spell as I lock eyes with the cretin. My will snakes into his mind, diving deep into the recesses of his consciousness to seize control. I see him resist, his neck stiffening as if battling an invisible itch, teeth clenched in a futile attempt to maintain his grip on himself.

It's a solid attempt; the effort doesn't go unnoticed, but a lesser demon is no match for my dark magic.

My mental hold on him remains tight and unyielding. He leans forward, clasps his fingers together, and lowers his voice. "If you want the real scoop, I'll give it to you: a couple of the Primes are collecting demon hunters, storing them downstairs for safekeeping."

My gaze darts to Lovejoy, who stands as rigid as a statue. "What for?" I ask.

His brows arch ever so slightly, a mischievous look dancing in his eyes. "Turns out, sacrificing a divine can tear open a permanent gateway between worlds."

"So the Primes would have a revolving door to the mortal plane rather than relying on full moons, summonings, and their convoluted methods of feeding on humans?"

"Among other things." The demon shrugs. The insufferable curve of his lips hints at a wicked scheme, and I can sense he's struggling to withhold some of his knowledge. "It's simple. Streamlined."

I lean back into the leather seat once more, using my magic to swirl my martini while maintaining my firm grip on the creature's mind. "But demons can't kill demon hunters."

"That's right."

"So…" I let the word hang in the air, encouraging him to fill in the blanks.

"Isn't it obvious?" He scoffs. "They're enlisting the help of the occult. Vampires, warlocks, witches like your beautiful self. It's quite the growing business. You'd make a pretty penny at it."

"I'll pass." I shrug my shoulders. "I just need to get one off my ass."

"All you gotta do is give me a name, maybe a

description. My boys can take care of your demon hunter problem."

"And you said they're kept downstairs?"

That gleam in his gaze darkens. "For now."

"Interesting." I glance at my hunter again. His neck is flushed red, a sure sign of his enduring torment that threatens to unravel his composure. The lounge is teeming with demons, and it's only a matter of time before dear Lovejoy blows his cover. "Mind if I take a look at the accommodations?"

The demon struggles to regain his will once more, and I tighten my grip on his resolve. "I'll take you there myself."

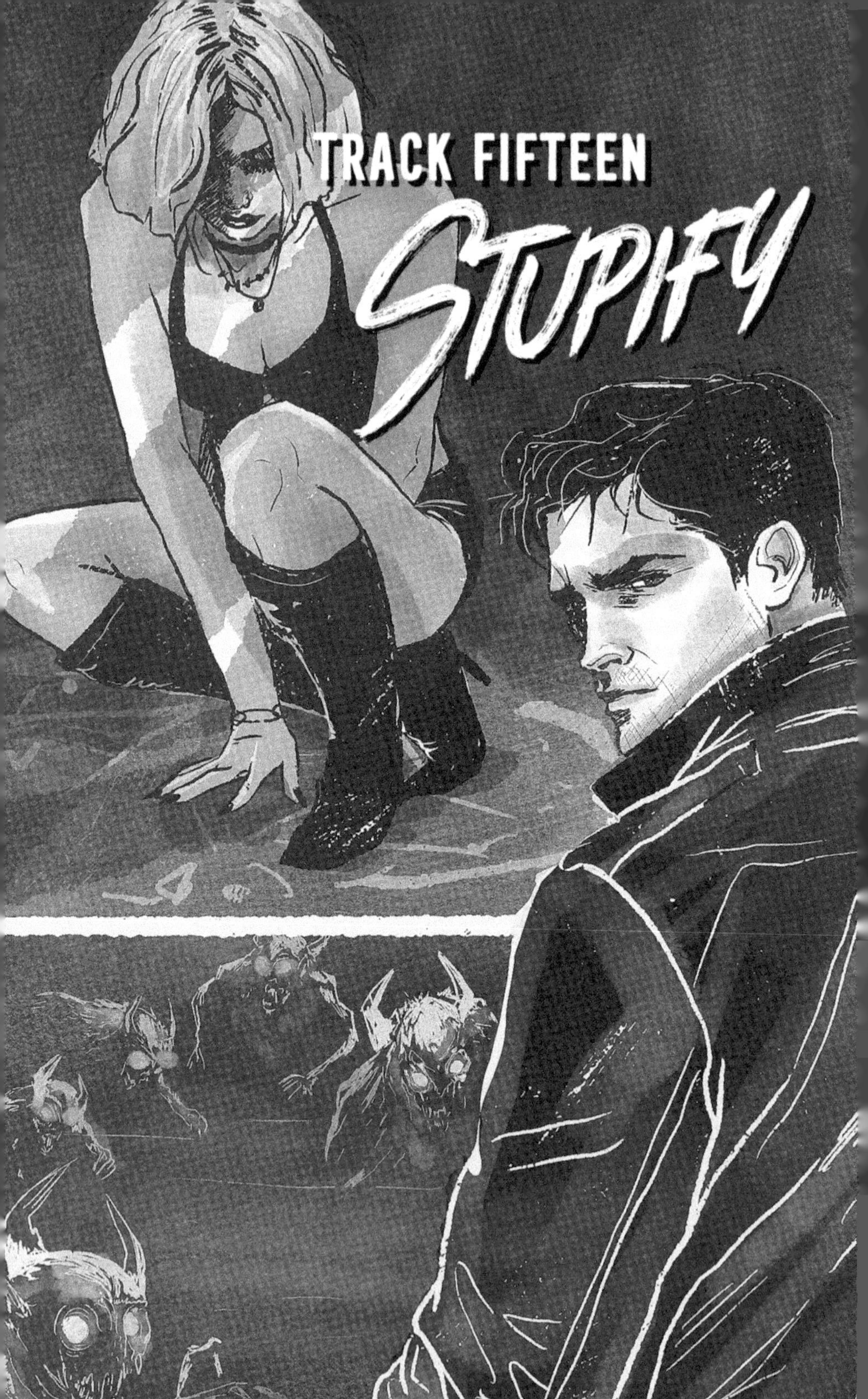

TRACK FIFTEEN
STUPIFY

TRACK FIFTEEN
STUPIFY

WE RISE FROM OUR SEATS, THE HEAVY LEATHER creaking against the black vinyl floors, and follow the lower-level demon deeper into the lounge. I meet Lovejoy's gaze with a soft, gentle look, silently pleading to him to stay composed. His body emanates a heat so intense, it nearly overwhelms me, making me forget why I'm here in the first place. I long to grab his hand, to ground him back to reality, to remind him that this is all a part of the process. But there's something about the demon's revelation that even has *me* stumped.

What on Heaven, Hell, or Earth are the Primes up to? Why do they want a revolving door between worlds? They've always had one foot on this plane. It makes less and less sense the longer I ponder.

The demon leads us through a maze of hallways lined with doors, down a set of paint-chipped stairs, and into a dim, desolate chamber with a single door. Two grotesque, monstrous, mid-level Watchers flank the doorway, sickening amalgamations of twisted flesh and jagged bone. A viscous ichor seeps from their hulking bodies, and *fuck me*, do they smell awful. I wince at the stench of rotting corpses and musty stone, wishing I was anywhere but here.

I realize we're alone in this foul chamber. While my control over mid-tier demons is rather weak, I'm confident that Lovejoy could handle the fuckers in a pinch. I gesture at my hunter with wide eyes, nodding at the lesser demon and two Watchers, silently urging him to strike. He nods in understanding, reaches for the protective amulet hidden under his shirt, and murmurs a string of incantations. His fingers flex as he invokes his holy spell, and the air around us crackles with divine energy. An electric, blinding light erupts from his outstretched hand, hauling toward the lesser demon. The beam coils around the fiend, enveloping him in a searing, white-hot flame. The chamber echoes with the demon's anguished roar as it burns to a crisp, leaving a pile of smoldering ash where the creature once stood.

The Watchers' deafening screeches shake the very air. The monsters bare their long, spindly teeth at us, hissing as they lunge at Lovejoy. He pushes me behind him, shielding me from the beasts, and wields a telekinetic wave at them. The creatures tumble to the ground, stunned and motionless, as the hunter swiftly draws two sacred daggers from his coat. In a blur of motion, the blades whirl through the air, embedding themselves deep within the chests of the Watchers. A brilliant, radiant light bursts forth from their decaying forms as their screams echo through the dark chamber.

The residual energy hums around Lovejoy, leaving behind a brief, seraphic afterglow. My breath catches in my chest; a tremor of begrudging admiration flutters throughout my core, mingled with a sharp, unsettling twinge of fear. I know my hunter was someone to be feared, but watching him at work never fails to reinforce the gruesome truth: he, like me, is a ruthless killer.

"Lovejoy, your aura," I whisper as the glow continues to radiate off his person. "How long did you say your potion was supposed to last?"

"I didn't," he pants as he catches his breath. "Must have weakened when I used my powers."

The cold tendrils of panic creep up my spine at his response. He picks up his daggers, slots them into his holsters, and takes my hand. We need to get the fuck out before reinforcements inevitably show up.

Lovejoy slams his shoulder against the steel door, forcing it open with a powerful heave. We stagger into the darkened chamber, our breaths catching in our chests with anticipation. I expect to find a demon hunter bound to a torture device. I half expect to find one dead. Instead, we find nothing. Absolutely nothing.

"It's…empty." Lovejoy's words are barely above a whisper.

The chamber looms like a forgotten crypt in the ground. The air is thick with rust and decay. The walls, slick with moisture, seem to breathe in the gloom. Looks like my kind of place, sans the demons. We stand in silence as we survey the chamber. Lovejoy's right; the place is practically spotless, void of any lifeforms—human, divine, or otherwise. Nothing worth stationing two burly demonic bodyguards out front for. With a swift flick of my wrist, I use my magic to slam the door shut and bolt it tight. A dim, flickering fluorescent bulb provides the only luminance in the room, but something catches my eye on the ground.

Chalked symbols…melted candles…and bloodied chains.

"Someone performed a ritual here," I mutter as I crouch to the ground and run my fingers over the chalk-drawn circle. I recognize the runes—archaic, demonic, something older and rarer than the modern Hellspeak alphabet.

Lovejoy crouches beside me, studying the symbols. "Can you identify them?"

"My runes are a little rusty, and these predate me. Cuneiform—Mesopotamian? Whoever did this is either very, *very* old or has a degree in dead languages."

"Could it have been an occultist? Like the demon said?"

I remain silent and cast a flame in my hand to illuminate the room to get a better look at the circle. My light reveals dark scorch marks embedded into the concrete floor and dried blood splattered about. My brows draw together as I realize the blood is not brown, not even close to crimson. It's…scarlet. A shimmering scarlet, and not entirely fresh. I huff out a breath in confusion.

"Scorch marks," Lovejoy muses. "Those are usually the result of a vanquish."

I scrunch my nose. "I think we might be dealing with more than one creature here, maybe more than two. Blood, scorch marks, remnants of a ritual—"

"Hunter, demon, occultist."

"Exactly," I add on. "Looks like your friend may have put up a good fight against a demon, judging by all the blood…"

"Demon of Chaos?"

"Mmm." I shake my head, biting my lip in concentration. "It could be any of the Big Thirteen, but I can tell you that this blood is neither demonic nor occultish—none that I can recognize, anyway." I sigh, rising to my feet. "Demons don't bleed red." A memory flashes through my mind as I glance at Lovejoy. "But you do…and this blood has a slight glimmer to it, kind of like yours."

"You don't think…" His words trail off as he follows

my logic. "Do you think the hunter held captive here was sacrificed? But the scorch marks—"

I shrug with indifference. "There aren't many other theories."

"They could have escaped for all we know." His naiveté, while mildly endearing, irks me. The desperation to find his friend clearly clouds his judgment as he clings to an illusion of hope, but nothing about this situation feels remotely optimistic. Not even close.

"I highly doubt it, given the doors were locked and guarded by Watchers," I add as I continue to search the pile of bloodied chains. I lift and study them one by one to find a fresher sample I may be able to tap into. I notice Lovejoy approach the circle, nearly stepping past its chalk-drawn perimeter. "Don't you dare." I lift a finger in warning. "I don't know what will happen if you step into this circle. It might be a trap."

"October, in the pile," he stammers out, pointing to the chains on the floor. A silver gleam glints within my flames, hidden beneath the pile of rusted restraints. I reach for the heap and pull out a long, ornate silver necklace shaped like a cross.

Lovejoy's voice breaks as he eyes the necklace. "That…that was Fargo's."

"That's convenient," I muse as I toy with the pendant. "I have an idea." I step deeper into the summoning circle once more and extinguish my flame. Darkness reigns again, but the yellow lights above continue to stutter like a heartbeat on the brink of failure. My hands flex above the bloody necklace, and I close my eyes to channel my power.

"With this blood, reveal what is lost,
Show me what recent paths have crossed."

Darkness consumes me. My vision blurs as I blink—once, twice, three times, trying to bring the scene into focus. The blood on the necklace is faint, too dry to provide a clear image. I can make out fragments, clouded forms, lights and shadows. There are three, maybe four muffled voices in my reverie: one subservient, one in agony, and the other two…wicked. I feel myself grip the necklace tighter to tether myself between past and present. I recognize an inhuman, shrilling resonance that echoes with the burden of death. A demon. A *Prime* demon. But which one?

The vision shifts as colors and shapes begin to take form. There's an aura, white, dimming and fading like a bulb on the verge of burning out. I feel the demon hunter's fear; it coils around my heart like icy tendrils—squeezing, consuming. Then, I hear the subservient voice chant an ancient ritual. I try to make out the words, but they're lost. The outcome, however, is unmistakable. Upon the last word of the spell, the white aura disappears. Vanishes. Lost to time and space.

"Banished." The words fall from my lips in a daze. I shake my head to dispel the vision from my mind. The amulet slips from my grasp, falling to the ground with a sharp, metallic clang. Lovejoy shuffles toward me, careful not to cross the chalk perimeter.

"What did you see?" he asks, his voice haunted with desperation.

"Your friend was here." I light the room with my flame once more. "I felt them, felt their fear."

"Fear," Lovejoy repeats. "Fargo is fearless."

"No one is fearless, babe, not even the divine. *Especially* not this one."

A sudden bang pulls us from our focus. The locked steel door groans under mounting pressure, guttural growls and hissing breaths seeping through the cracks. I wince at the cacophony—a nightmarish blend of monstrous wails and the grating sound of sharp claws against metal. The harsh screech echoes in my ears, and slowly, ever so slowly, panic builds.

"Hellspawn," Lovejoy breathes as he instinctively casts a protective barrier around us. The forcefield shimmers with an ethereal light and thrums with holy energy. He reaches for the blade underneath his coat and grips the hilt as his other hand shields us.

"No!" I squeak out. "There are at least a dozen of those little creeps banging on that door—you'll be outnumbered. If you start throwing holy daggers and casting smites, you'll be finished. I won't be able to protect you."

"I've been outnumbered plenty of times," he grits through his teeth. "I can handle this. When they breach the door, I'll hold them off. You find a way to get out of here."

"I'm not leaving without you." My words pull at me as an unfamiliar sensation builds. My instinct for self-preservation takes over, reminding me I need Lovejoy alive if I'm to secure my own survival. If the Primes are burning through hunters like wildfire, I won't let my last hope slip through my fingers. I shake the feeling, and a brilliant idea flashes through my mind. The snarls of the demons echo louder beyond the door.

"I've got a plan," I mutter. "Go after them. Kill as many as you can. Just trust me."

He nods once in understanding, and I can almost sense the shift in his mind as it transitions from protective lover to ruthless soldier.

I retreat into the shadows of the chamber, extinguishing my flame and using my magic to unlock the door and watch the horrors reveal before my very eyes. Dozens of Hellish creatures trample through the steel door, toppling over each other like a pile of misshapen, rabid animals. Lovejoy's holy magic flashes through the darkness like rhythmic waves of light, striking the fiends with bolts of lightning. The stench of burnt, rotting flesh hits me like a brick, nearly forcing bile up my throat. With a quick shout of a Latin spell, his holy daggers manifest in his hands. My hunter grunts as he hurls blade after blade into the creatures, then summons the daggers magically back into his grasp to do it all over again. He moves like a dancer, swiftly, without pause, with perfect form and pristine lines. A sacred, merciless predator with a taste for divine justice.

He's absolutely terrifying. A true marvel.

And I've never wanted him more.

I emerge from the shadows, twin flames blazing from my hands as I screech a commanding order to halt the fiends. Silence befalls the room in an instant, dozens of wide-eyed monsters eyeing me in a daze of awe. "Back off, you fucking imbeciles," I growl at the Hellspawn. They cower at my tone, retreating into the shadows of the chamber.

I watch as their glowing, freakish eyes fixate on my demon hunter with both fear and hunger, salivating at the sight of him. It's foolish of them to believe they could take on a foe as formidable as Lovejoy, a century-year-old demon hunter who has brought plenty of the Devil's sons to their knees. I seize Lovejoy's dagger from its thigh holster, murmuring a binding spell in Hellspeak to twist his will to mine. He stiffens, his body going slack as he collapses to his knees. His gaze is filled with a defiant, palpable hatred that feels almost *too* real. My magic is powerful, but I know it won't contain him for long.

I hiss when my skin meets the hilt of his holy blade. Pain stings at my fingertips like thousands of prickling needles. It's a small ache, but an ache, nonetheless, as if the blade was not meant to be handled by someone like me. Grasping his curly hair, I yank his head against my stomach and press the blade to his throat. "You can crawl back to your masters and tell them I just saved your pathetic asses. I'll deliver this one to the Devil myself."

I jerk Lovejoy to his feet by his head, forcing a pained groan from him. He weighs a metric fuck ton as his body slumps against mine. I drag him through the Hellspawn-ridden chamber and back into the never-ending hall of doors. The fiends chomp their toothy jaws in his direction, desperate for a taste of his holy flesh. I kick a handful of the little rats out of my way and knee a path to safety and salvation once more.

"Do you have more potion?" I mutter as we ascend the dank steps of the Underground lounge.

Lovejoy nods, struggling to regain his motility after my immobilization spell begins to weaken. His words slur from his strained lips. "I have a cloaking enchantment too."

"Good. Drink that shit, cast your spell, and get the fuck out of here. I need to do some damage control. Meet me in the car."

We part ways once Lovejoy has regained his strength. He vanishes into the basement's depths, his cloaking spell making him disappear, even to someone like me. I clutch Nero at my chest, who remains in his dormant state as a delicate ebony pendant hanging below my plunging neckline. I kiss the necklace, rubbing my thumb over the smooth ridges of its tail and stinger as I whisper, "That was a close one, buddy. Now, let's get out of here before we're demon dinner."

The lounge is draped in dead silence when I emerge from the undercroft. Hundreds of glowing, amber eyes greet me like a pack of adoring acolytes, eager to serve their deity. I can only assume Lovejoy made it back up to the Camaro unscathed. I tighten my hold on my fur jacket, pulling it taught against my chest as I make my way through the sea of drooling fiends.

"Take a picture, creeps," I mutter as I stalk through the expanse of the lounge, finding the navy curtain from which I once entered. But it dawns on me that it isn't me the demons are glaring at. It's something else—something higher up the food chain.

"Toby Winties," a patronizing voice, rich and dark like honey, calls for me as I make my way toward the spiral staircase of the Yamashiro pond.

"What *now?*" I groan as I'm compelled to face this new pain in my ass. I'm met with the red-rimmed black eyes of one of the Devil's unholy sons, a creature that practically exudes sexual energy and corruption.

The Demon of Debauchery minds me with a playful, twisted smile. He appears to me in his humanoid form, as he so often does, clad in the most ridiculous get-up: white, ruffled blouse under a black sequin blazer, high-heeled boots peeking beneath leather pants. Don't get me started on the accessories—those dated orange shades and silver rings aren't doing him any favors.

"Prince called; he wants his outfit back," I snort, folding my arms over my chest.

The Prime waves his hand dismissively. "Please. I made him what he is."

I flash him a forced grin. "Cherry."

"Darling." His smile mirrors my own as we greet each other with a two-cheeked kiss. "Haven't seen you in a while. You're not up to your knees in trouble again, are you, Toby?"

What is with these fuckwads referring to me by that insufferable moniker? "I might be if you keep calling me that stupid name."

"Aw." His tone smothers me under a layer of ice-cold superiority. "But it's Daddy's favorite."

That moniker is even worse. I narrow my eyes at him, raising my chin in defiance. "*I'm* Daddy's favorite."

"That's not what I've heard, lately," he hums, gripping the waists of two succubus demonesses who flank his sides. "I hear you're under the employment of one of my she-demons."

"And?"

"She tells me Daddy's got you on a *big* job. A thousand souls in six days. Sounds deli-ci-ous," he enunciates painstakingly slowly. "How many have you got so far?"

"None of your business, Cherry."

"There's no need for hostility, Miss Winties. I only want to help."

"Your help comes with a price I can't afford—nor would I want to be indebted to a creep like you."

"You wound me." He places a perfectly manicured hand atop his chest, feigning offense. "But it appears you *are* indebted to me." I tilt my head at the Prime, challenging him with my stare. "Did you think I wouldn't notice you brought a demon hunter into our domain?"

Shit.

The Demon of Debauchery saunters closer, his twisted, sadistic grin widening with every heartbeat. He looms over me, even with my four-inch stilettos, his gaze sharp with a playful, predatory glint. A chuckle rumbles deep in his chest as he wraps a lock of my short blonde hair around his finger, toying with it like a cat would its prey. He reaches into his pocket and pulls out a slender gunmetal chain with an ebony crystal pendant, letting it dangle in front of my face. Black tourmaline…an energy absorber.

I give him a coy smile, masking the nerves gnawing at my chest. "Aw, Cherry, you really know how to charm a girl. How'd you guess I'm a sucker for jewelry?"

The Demon of Debauchery chuckles then drops the necklace into my hand. "I'm going to make a deal with you, Toby Winties, and there is *no way* you'll be able to weasel yourself out of this one."

TRACK SIXTEEN
(PER)VERSION OF A TRUTH
IF YOU AREN'T GOING TO TALK, I SUGGEST YOU PUT YOUR MOUTH TO BETTER USE.

TRACK SIXTEEN

(PER)VERSION OF THE TRUTH

The motherfucking Demon of Debauchery made me a deal I couldn't refuse.

With a tight jaw and tighter patience, I descend Yamashiro's steps. I clasp the black tourmaline pendant around my neck, tucking it beneath my tank top. It nestles among my other chains, hidden from prying eyes. The crystal hums against my skin, hot and throbbing, a reminder of this ill-timed wrench in my clusterfuck of a day. Like I need the extra headache.

Luckily for me, Cherry's agenda played right into my hand. It could be worse; I could have been beholden to one of the other twelve morons. They wouldn't have been as kind.

My demon hunter rests against my Camaro, hidden in the shadows. I avoid his gaze as I enter the car and turn the engine on with a flick of my wrist. The doors slam shut behind us as I will the car's magic alive, desperate to get us the fuck out of this place.

Our ride back into town is silent, mostly. The speakers roar with heavy metal, the rhythm pulsing through my veins like a second heartbeat. I relish in the music, the calm it brings me despite the deadline hanging heavy over my conscience. My fingers dance on the steering wheel, idle as my cursed vehicle guides us down the slopes of Hollywood Hills and back into the city. Lovejoy, stiff with a pained expression, reaches out toward the radio. His finger finds the dial and silence falls.

I cock an eyebrow. "What's eating you, angel?"

He releases a gruff sigh, fist still glued to his chin. "Nothing."

"Liar," I tease, keeping a firm grip on the gear shift. My voice softens as I continue, "C'mon, babe. I know you're itching to talk about what happened back there."

"None of it makes any sense," he bursts out. "There was no hunter being held captive. It was all for naught."

"I wouldn't say that. We now know the Primes are using occult folk to perform portal opening rituals."

"But why? And which Prime?"

"Hell if I know," I admit with a shrug. "There's only so much intel I can get from where I'm sitting."

His eyes glaze over, mind clearly rewinding the night's chaos. "You mentioned feeling Fargo's fear. What did you feel exactly?"

My hands fall from the wheel, allowing my car to take over and get us back to the Roosevelt. I chew my lip, mulling over the memory. "It's like I could see his fears sprawled out on a physical list. He was fixated on what his demise meant for his status within the Order. His greatest fear wasn't death—it was insignificance. His greatest nightmare come to life."

"That's just it then." Lovejoy's words are barely above a whisper. "It wasn't *just* fear."

I start to piece together the puzzle. "You don't think—"

"Nightmares and Fear. Having your fears made manifest… I know exactly what that feels like. I've known for far too long."

I see the look in his eyes, the indescribable pain that furrows in his brow. My gaze flicks to the bag at his feet then back to him. Something tugs in my chest—is it pity? —and with a jerk of my chin, I cave. "Grab my bag."

He obliges hesitantly, placing the safety-pinned wreck on his lap, awaiting further instruction.

"There's a vial in there. You should take it."

"What is it?"

"Dreamguard Elixir. It's some powerful shit. It'll help you sleep. Keep the nightmares away."

He takes the vial from the bag, curiosity gleaming in his eyes as he studies its contents. "Where did you get this?"

"I know a guy." I shrug.

His voice is but a whisper, a chuckle laced with disbelief. "I haven't had a peaceful night in eighty years. That's a lifetime for most." He tilts the vial back, sparing not a single drop of the potion. My throat tightens with every swallow, with every lick of his lips. It's like watching someone drink away my demonic insurance, each trickle a painful reminder that I've lost my security against the Prime's fury.

And yet there's a tiny spark of—what is it? Pride? Consolation? Whatever it is, it's foreign, uncomfortable. I yearn to crush the feeling, the irksome notion that I, too, might have an ounce of altruism in me. But the look in Lovejoy's eyes, that glimmer of moisture at the corner—the tears of relief that threaten to spill—almost makes the sacrifice worth it.

This better not bite me in the ass.

He reaches for my hand, gently lacing our fingers together with a squeeze. "Thank you."

There's that warmth again—pride, unease, whatever the fuck. It feels...different. It travels up my chest, pulsing against my skin, nearly choking my logic. Then, the realization hits: it's not me. It's the fucking necklace nestled under my top.

The crystal hums like a live wire, drunk on more than just Lovejoy's gratitude. There's a hunger there, an intoxicating, raw mixture of admiration and desire.

Well, I'll be double-damned. Seems karma has finally cashed my check. Lose one demonic safety net, gain another. My fingers tighten around his in a wordless 'you're welcome.'

The Camaro stops suddenly. We've arrived at the Roosevelt, parked off to the side, far from the front entrance. Street lamps paint us in amber and shadow as our gazes linger, eyes locked in silent hunger.

"Want to come up?" He nods at the hotel.

A snort escapes me. "Aw, Lovejoy. Do you plan to read me your poetry journal and show me your bottle cap collection?"

"Very funny," he huffs and continues holding my gaze, voice low. "Just…not ready for tonight to end. Not yet." Calloused fingers linger on my knuckles, toying with my rings. His eyes are pleading with something more than his usual innocence. There's a darkness in them—one I've missed. One I take as an invitation.

I'm not about to look a gift horse in the mouth.

A twinkle of silver moonlight casts an intricate shadow through lace curtains in an otherwise pitch-black room. Lovejoy, ever the gentleman, holds his hotel room door open for me. I slink past him, heading straight for the floor-to-ceiling panoramic view of the City of Angels.

"So this is how the other half lives," I tease as he flips

on a small lamp at the side of his bed. I notice a second bed, unmade and disheveled, with at least a dozen leather-bound books and old parchment piled atop one another. "Let me guess—your ward's?"

"Apprentice," he grunts as he shrugs the dark trench coat from his shoulders, revealing his partially unbuttoned dress shirt. An amulet hangs loosely from his neck, no doubt one of his many protective charms. His figure mirrors that of effortless authority—imposing with an inherent strength that suffocates the room. Countless weapon holsters are strapped tight around his waist and thighs, accentuating his slim, tapered torso and long legs. He removes smaller blades from under-arm sheaths, potion vials from his belt, and two glimmering daggers from his thighs. His weapons are more than mere accessories; they're the tools of his trade, marks of diligence and control.

A sordid hunger pulls within me, desire mixed with a hint of fear, as I realize my darling hunter is as formidable as he is handsome. While the blood coursing through his veins is undoubtedly divine, his silhouette remains a deadly reminder that Declan Lovejoy is an instrument of merciless justice.

One who wouldn't hesitate to end me if he knew my truth.

I dismiss the thought, distracted by the predatory look in his eyes, one that likely mirrors my own. I know what he wants; it's written on his face, in his stance—a majestic, downright carnal demeanor that tells me he isn't in the mood to talk.

I never saw the fun in getting straight to the point.

"He's an ambitious little fucker, isn't he?" I tease as he saunters near. I turn to face the city once more, though his reflection appears clear as day through the glass. "Reminds me of you when you started out. Runs head-first into danger. Daggers first, questions later."

"I don't want to talk about Jeremy." The words rumble in his chest, and he's suddenly right behind me. Ah, music to my ears; he must have taken my advice to heart.

"Then what *do* you want to talk about?"

His breath tickles the shell of my ear, right where Nero remains. "Nothing."

It's these quiet moments before action, the prelude to our cryptic dance, that are the most delicious. We don't talk about it. We *never* talk about it. Tonight shouldn't be any different. But what Declan Lovejoy doesn't realize is that *I'm* not his plaything.

He is *mine*.

"Well, if you aren't going to talk, I suggest you put your mouth to better use."

Lovejoy wastes no time as he falls to his knees. My heart swells with contentment, grateful that even under the circumstances of the Devil's ultimatum and Debauchery's pact, there are still some situations in which I hold all the power.

He bunches my leather skirt at my waist and pulls my lacy undergarments down to my ankles. Those brown eyes never leave mine as he carefully, adoringly, kisses his way from my knee to my thigh. There's a glint in them, an innocence with the way he worships me. Rough hands roam my torso, sneaking up underneath the loose cropped tank top and caressing the swell of my breasts. A quiet moan escapes my lips at the contact, relishing in his touch, a touch I'd grown so desperate for. But when his fingers meet my nipples, I feel him smile against my skin.

"These are new," he murmurs as his nose trails up my inner thigh, flashing his eyes up at me.

I stroke his scalp, smirking helplessly. "You know how I love to accessorize."

He tweaks my nipples between his fingers, toying with the cool metal piercings flanking them. There's a dull ache that stings despite his gentle touch, eased by the soft caress of his tongue between my lips.

In an instant, the weight of my problems evaporates—poof. Gone. I'm drowning in his scent, lost in the intoxicating touch of those battle-worn fingers. His proximity, after all these years apart, ignites something primal within me. It feels *so* right, even though I know it's *so* fucking wrong.

The black tourmaline around my neck pulses, a living thing against my flushed skin. Its heat intensifies with each passing second, matching the fire building inside me

—inside both of us. My gaze darts downward, mesmerized by the crystal's piercing glow.

Tendrils of smoke, dark and sinuous, seep from the pendant. They coil around Lovejoy like spectral serpents, siphoning his energy. I catch a twitch in his neck, see the redness blooming along his Nephilim's Mark—a signal ingrained in every hunter, screaming of nearby danger.

But my hunter doesn't flinch. He doesn't stop.

If anything, he leans in closer, defying every instinct that has kept him alive this long. It begs the question: Is it the demonic artifact's dark magic at work, or the raw power of arousal? The lines blur, as they always do with our trysts, leaving me lost between gratitude, doubt, and pure thrill.

The soft click of a doorknob pulls me from my rapture. My eyes flutter open, hands clutching my lover's head in a fleeting moment of shock. But as Lovejoy's tongue continues to ravish my core, I realize there is no stopping him. He is deaf and blind to the world around him. I, on the other hand, am not as easily absorbed.

My gaze darts to the threshold where the shadows seem to coalesce, revealing a silhouette that tugs at the edges of my memory. My, my, what have we here? Lovejoy's apprentice—Jerry? Jericho? Ah, *Jeremy*—frozen in shock, that emerald-green stare locked on my body.

A silent storm rages between us—eyes flashing with curiosity, lips tightening with unvoiced shame. Jeremy doesn't move. He doesn't interrupt us. Instead, he watches. Intently. Hungrily. In mere seconds, we understand each other without uttering a single word. But it isn't until I watch a new tendril of dark magic winding its way toward the apprentice when I realize I may have just lucked the fuck out.

Jeremy enters the room and closes the door ever so quietly. If the little pervert has no intention of interrupting us, I might as well put on a little show. And what a show he shall have…

Lovejoy, lost in the throes of pleasure, keeps his focus between my thighs. My hand continues to dig into his hair, coaxing—*praising*—him as his tongue ravishes me. I hook a limb over his shoulder, my *favorite* leg rest, thrusting him deeper against my body.

I pull my hunter from his fixation, staring into his tired yet adoring eyes. He looks up at me, pupils dilated as he plants a soft kiss to my thigh. Brown orbs speak a language that transcends words, shimmering like a pool of perpetual fire. Every blink is slow—deliberate—as if savoring the very sight of me, as if he's afraid to miss a single moment. My thumb caresses his bottom lip, offering him silent praise for a job well done. Lovejoy takes the digit into his mouth, sucking lightly, rubbing the tip of his tongue across the pad of my finger.

"There you are," my voice is smooth, sultry, as I pull him to his feet. "My insatiable lover."

My lips crash against Lovejoy's, claiming his mouth in

a battle of dominance. All the while, I feel the *other* hunter's eyes on me. The room seems hotter now, thick with desire. He's wise to remain silent, and I'm no fool to interrupt Lovejoy as he takes what his body so desperately craves.

Lovejoy pulls away, his breath ragged and wanton as he whispers, "I don't think I can hold back."

"I never want you to." I curl my fingers into his hair, ghosting my teeth along his lobe. "Fuck me, lover."

Lovejoy hums against me, sending vibrations through my core. He heeds my command, and my back quickly collides with the cold glass window as he lifts my legs to wrap around his thin waist.

My eyes flutter to his apprentice, the divine youth who remains frozen against the hotel door. I know he feels the pull, the magnetic force that draws him in. A curiosity. A forbidden fruit. Oh, how the Demon of Debauchery would salivate at the sight. My gaze pierces the shadows where the young hunter stands. Even with the subtle, ambient light of the nightstand lamp, I can see his face clearly: a darkened gaze, a jaw so clenched, I wonder if it will remain fused shut. A smirk plays upon my lips as I hold his stare, mischievous and alluring. All at once, the young man realizes he isn't the only one who has discovered a secret.

I've spent a millennia surrounded by the corrupt and devious. Good men. Evil men. It would appear that not even the most holy and righteous are above perversion—the angel between my legs is living proof of that.

Why would his apprentice be any less?

Our perversions will be our little secret. He'd do well to keep his master's.

The crystal pulses with demented magic as Lovejoy slides into me for the first time in years. I hiss as he fills me inch by inch, my walls hugging his cock as if I was made for him. The inferno rages between us, our shallow breaths and heavy moans echoing throughout the hotel room. He rocks against me, keeping his grip firm at my waist, thumbs rubbing over my skin. Our gazes intertwine, a fusion of molten desire and unshakeable faith. In this moment, our eyes speak volumes that our lips dare not utter.

And then, he leans in, kissing me slowly—patiently—as if he wants to treasure every millisecond of this moment. His thrusts quicken then, hitting harder with ferocious vigor as he drives us both to the edge.

But then, my eyes flutter to the apprentice across the room once more, and I'm not shocked to see the younger man with his hand hidden beneath his jeans, stroking his own cock, relishing in our deadly, forbidden dance.

"I'm so close." Lovejoy's husky growl pulls me from my fixation. The warning bells sound in my mind then, a lesson I've learned well. My legs fall limp at his waist and my feet meet with the ground. I push myself off my lover and drop to my knees, hand fisting his cock as I coax him closer and closer. Soon after, he comes…and the demonic crystal thrums against my skin, glowing with the sexual energy of not one, but two demon hunters.

As we drift down from our fevered heights, reality crashes back in—Jeremy is gone. Vanished. Leaving my lover and I alone to bask in our union. Lovejoy plops himself across the bed, spent and glistening. His chest rises and falls in slow, deep breaths, pale olive skin sheened with sweat. I pull my skirt down, searching for my discarded underwear as he watches me with a heavy, adoring gaze.

"Leaving so soon?" Lovejoy's voice is soft, almost vulnerable. His brown eyes, forlorn and pleading, try to anchor me in place.

"Just going out for a cigarette," I mutter as I zip up my boots.

He scrunches his nose, a mix of disapproval and resignation crossing his features. A soft huff escapes him as he shakes his head, the gesture speaking volumes: *'Do as you must, but I wish you wouldn't.'*

"I'll be back." I lean down to plant a kiss upon his frown.

He sighs against my lips. "Why don't I believe you?"

"Shitty track record or something." I breathe out a chuckle. "You should get some sleep. The Dreamguard will protect you."

The storm of concern in his eyes clears, giving way to a flood of relief that softens his expression. I hoist my bag on my shoulder, check my ear to ensure Nero's safety, and reach for the doorknob.

"October?" Lovejoy calls for me, voice heavy with exhaustion. I turn, caught in the gravity of his gaze. His eyes, warm and adoring, threaten to unravel me where I stand. "Thank you. Again."

A small smile tugs at my lips. "Don't mention it."

The Hollywood Roosevelt's doors hiss shut behind me, and a cool breeze slaps me awake. My legs—screaming from the endless fucking marathon of a day—barely carry me to the nearest trash bin. Each effort feels like trudging through mud, my body a battleground of exhaustion and frayed nerves. The city's neon glow paints everything in harsh, unforgiving light, matching my mood perfectly. I collapse against the closest wall, my back scraping plaster as I fumble through my skirt pocket, desperate for the comfort of a cigarette.

"Well?"

Reagan's low, husky tone invades my senses. She leans effortlessly next to me, offering me a light. I dodge the gesture, conjuring a flame with my own magic. She smirks, watching intently as I take a drag. I then remove Cherry's crystal from my neck and hand it to the she-demon. She studies the pendant, squinting with a smirk as she notes the two glowing cores embedded within the dark stone.

"I'll be damned," she says, a laugh bubbling up in her throat. Her voice lilts with a mixture of disbelief and admiration. "You *actually* pulled it off."

I force a smirk, still avoiding her gaze. "Did you really doubt me?" The words come out more brittle than I'd like. "Demon hunter sexual energy, fresh from the oven, just like Cherry ordered." A pause, then I can't help but add with a touch of pride, "Two of them, I might add."

"More than initially asked for," she purrs. "I'm considering keeping some for myself."

"You better fucking not," I snap, the words harsher than intended. "You give your boss his necklace back and make sure he upholds his end of the bargain, yeah? No squealing."

"The apprentice's essence will certainly impress him. Though…" Her voice trails, nearly lost in the ambient racket of the city that surrounds us.

My patience wears thin. "What? Spit it out."

She meets my gaze, a mix of curiosity and something darker lurking in her eyes. "I admit, neither of us assumed you'd be able to seal the deal so quickly and so easily." She pauses, tilting her head slightly. "It was almost…effortless."

"What can I say?" I shrug, feigning nonchalance. "Apparently, the Holy Order of Nimrods aren't as sinless as they'd have us believe." I let out a dry chuckle, adding, "And the apprentice was a happy accident."

"Accident," she scoffs, her fanged grin glimmering under lamplight. "We both know you took on that deal fully knowing you'd already won."

I take another drag. "Don't know what you mean."

"You and that hunter—Lovejoy, was it? You're more friendly than you let on. There's history there, and it runs *deep*. I could smell it on him—his desire for you. The obsession. It wasn't just the effects of the necklace."

Another shrug. "I'm using him."

"Are you? Because from where I'm standing, *he's* using *you*, risking your entire reputation and rank within the Underworld."

"I know what I'm doing."

"I hope so." Reagan doesn't seem convinced. Her molten amber eyes watch me, as if burning a hole through me with her scrutiny. "It'd be a shame to watch you fall, October Winters. You're a legend, after all. An icon."

"Please, flatter me more." I bat my eyelashes at her. I drop my cigarette to the ground, grinding my boot over it. "Get that necklace to Cherry. Tell him to stay out of my way. And not a word to Big D about my arrangement with the demon hunters. Capeesh?"

Reagan's eyes squint with an arch of her pencil-thin brow as she wraps the chain around her neck. "Whatever you say, Your Excellence."

TRACK SEVENTEEN
GLORY BOX

TRACK SEVENTEEN

GLORY BOX

Cigarette smoke permeates an elegant hotel room at half past three the next morning. It invades the crisp wallpaper and plush fabrics, marking the tale of a night well spent. A single white sheet hangs loosely upon my figure, cool to the touch as the chill of Fall threatens to slip through the windows. My fingers tangle in my short, unkempt waves, desperate to give them some semblance of order after my little nap. Lovejoy stirs in his sleep next to me; the dream elixir has worked wonders on my darling demon hunter, keeping his nightmares and affiliates at bay, far away from us both.

My cigarette hangs from my freshly painted black lips, tendrils of smoke swirling above me in a little cloud. I glance over at my lover, smirking as his nose twitches from the scent, remembering how much he loathes my nasty habit, and take another deep drag.

I *should* make my escape before he wakes.

Yet here I linger, tucked under the covers next to him, savoring memories of our eight decades together.

To call it a wild ride would be an understatement. We've explored every inch of each other—from our favorite meals (his: minced lamb pie; mine: pineapple pizza) to musical passions (a curious blend of Parisian opera and heavy metal), and most intimately, our deepest, darkest desires. Superficial pleasures, to say the least. There is, however, one wall that stands between us: my secrets. And believe me, there are far too many I would never—*could* never—reveal.

Strong hands find my hips as I suck in another drag, lost in thought. Lovejoy grabs the cigarette from my lips and tosses it into the ashtray on his bedside table as he presses himself against my back. A hungry groan rumbles from his chest as he pulls me incredibly close. So close, the only thing separating us from becoming one is the hardness poking at my lower back. Impressive; that energy absorber should have knocked the daylights out of him. Guess Nephilim stamina is no joke.

"Insatiable, as always." I lean into his touch with a sly smirk, relishing in his soft lips and warm breath upon my neck.

"Can you blame me?" he whispers, lightly grazing his teeth over my skin. "Figured I'd have another taste before you inevitably disappear off to God-knows-where before the sun rises."

My fingers tug at his dark curls. "By all means, take your time."

"Oh, I intend to."

My demon hunter's fingers slip between my legs and finds my clit as his hips buck against me. He coaxes me, bringing me closer and closer to the edge as my gaze flitters to the city that remains ripe for the taking. In this moment, this brief glimmer in time between deadly ultimatums and heroic side quests, I shut my eyes. I relish his touch, fully surrendering to him.

No demonic deals hanging around my neck, no pesky voyeurs getting off in the shadows. Right here, right now, it's just us. Two star-crossed fuckups, clinging to each other while our respective worlds burn.

"I can spend an eternity inside of you," Lovejoy groans against my neck as his hand meets with my breast. Oh, the poor thing—how he pines for me, even after all these years. It's enough to warm my sinister little heart. I reach for his hand and guide it up my chest to my neck. With a light squeeze, I urge him to overpower me, to fool him into believing my life lies within his grasp.

But my life is my own, and no one has control over it without my permission.

"An empty promise," I sneer, grinding myself against him as he continues to toy with me.

"What if it wasn't?" His lips find my earlobe as his voice lowers. "We could see the world together."

Been there, done that.

"I could coat you in diamonds."

Why, when I can dig up my own?

"I would protect you. You'll want for nothing."

Protection? Please. The mere suggestion dries me up faster than Death Valley in July, as does the idea of becoming a doting wife. I dodged that bullet years ago, and my reflexes have only gotten better. "You're a darling to assume *I* need protection. I've got hundreds of years on you."

"What I mean is, you wouldn't have to resort to dark magic anymore."

His movements falter, and the smirk fades from my lips. If this is his idea of seduction, he has another thing coming—and it *isn't* me.

"You talk too much, lover. And this isn't a conversation worth having, not while you've yet to finish me off."

He takes that as a threat, as I hoped he would, and turns me to face him while crashing his lips against mine. My leg hooks around his waist as I dig my heel into his lower back. He positions himself between my knees and slowly rubs his strong hands along my calves.

I prop myself up on my elbows, raising an eyebrow. "You know I don't care for this position."

His devious smirk is enough to set my skin ablaze once more. "You do when my head is between your thighs."

Lovejoy grabs my ankle and pulls it to the side,

revealing my thigh. He kisses it softly, nipping gently as he gets closer to my core. A sigh escapes me as he parts my lips and moves that talented tongue of his in circular motion over my bundle of nerves and, for a moment, I consider his proposition. Years of being worshiped like a goddess by the mouth of a precious demon hunter doesn't sound *too* horrible, especially when it comes with the sight of those chocolate-brown eyes between my legs.

He looks up at me as he sucks my clit into his mouth, and I can't help but sing his praises with long, drawn-out moans. Delicate fingers trail up my other thigh and meet at my entrance, lightly dipping inside. I devour him with my eyes; my demon hunter, my poison. Every nerve screams his name. My senses shatter and reality blurs—he's my destruction, my addiction. And Devil damn me, I will never get enough.

The end is coming. And so am I.

We're a mess of ragged breaths and satisfaction in this fleeting moment of content amidst our typically bleak existence. One thing I will always admire about Declan Lovejoy is his chivalry—how he eagerly cleans me up after every session, how he quickly grabs me a full glass of water to ease my dry throat. But the one thing I will never tire of is that look of utter pride and devotion in his eyes after he has made me come.

He sighs helplessly, resting his head against my knee after peppering kisses along my thigh. "I'd follow you forever, October Winters. To Hell and back, if that's what it would take."

His foolish vow, fueled by passion, is made without registering its consequences. It reminds me of his younger days, before my darkness consumed him, before the evils of the world stole his innocence. The thought brings a smile to my face; he wouldn't last a second in Hell. The demons would devour him in an instant.

"'Forever,' hm?" I cringe at the thought. "You won't like me when I'm old and gray."

"I'll be the judge of that."

Our lips are inches apart now, and I can't bear to see the yearning in his eyes. I hope that a passionate kiss will quell his hollow promises and press my lips against his. It's short lived when he pulls away in agony.

Lovejoy falls off the bed and to his knees. For a moment, I wonder if I subconsciously hexed him—or accidentally used my scorpion venom-infused lipstick.

"What—? What is it?"

"T-the voices." His fingers grip at his scalp as he winces in pain. "They're *so* loud, like they're right outside. They're b-begging for forgiveness."

Ah, yes. That delightful little ability we share—he hears the prayers of the living while I hear the woes of the dead. A glorious concept fashioned by our bosses.

His hands reach for his neck, clawing at that monstrous illustration inked into his skin. The spectacle doesn't faze me as it would a concerned lover, but I *do* find curiosity within the scene. I've never witnessed the Call of the Hunt before, though I've heard about it over the years. I never imagined that it would be so… gruesome.

Lovejoy rises to his feet and staggers as his arm rests against the window-wall. His pain-filled gasp is enough to send a twinge of panic through me.

"It's one of the Primes—I can feel them. They're feeding on humans."

Of course. Of *fucking* course one of Lucifer's bitch babies would jump at the opportunity to ruin a moment of my peace. Intentional or not, Daddy's idiots sure know how to kill a vibe.

"Suppose that means our little tryst has reached its end for the night?"

"I *have* to go." His haunted brown eyes glisten with tears that threaten to spill.

"I'm not stopping you." I shrug.

Whether I care to admit it or not—and believe me, it's like pulling teeth—the Demon of Whatever's untimely interruption proves convenient. After all, I *do* have several hundred souls to collect and three more days to do it. I *suppose* I owe one of the Big Thirteen a thank you. A nod of acknowledgment, at best.

Lovejoy dresses in a hurry, fastening his handy-dandy supernatural carry belt around his waist. It's loaded with potion vials, artifacts, and scrolls that look as old as I am. It's at this moment that the bitter truth hits me harder than it ever has and I shiver as the reality sets in. I'll spend a lifetime hiding who I am from him, coming up with convenient lies to save my ass and protect the very evil he's sworn to destroy. I've known this all along, of course—but willful ignorance has always been my preferred method of delusion.

'Forever' is a fairytale for fools unbound by the Devil.

In an instant, my hunter vanishes, abandoning me in his lavish suite. The digital clock's crimson display reads 3:59 AM as I sneak into the bathroom and indulge in the Roosevelt's most exquisite shower. I relish the scalding water, excellent pressure, and high-end toiletries; it's exactly what I need to scrub away the demonic gunk clinging to me after three exhausting days.

Wrapped in a fresh towel, I emerge from the shower and rummage through my discarded clothes, searching for a stray cigarette. The mirror, clouded with steam, catches my eye. I wipe away the condensation in a circular motion, eager to admire my squeaky-clean form. But my admiration is cut short as I lock eyes with an unexpected visitor: a piercing, verdant glare. My demon hunter's apprentice.

"Enjoy the show earlier?" I don't turn to face him. Don't need to. His presence looms as I savor a drag of my lit cigarette, allowing the euphoria to seep into my bones.

"I don't know what you're talking about."

"Oh, save it," I mumble as I apply a fresh coat of

lipstick. "You pious fucks are always so quick to deny, so shameful of your own sins. You're half-human, kiddo. It's in your nature."

I shoot him a smirk through the looking glass, and his head droops in a way that is almost pathetic, like a puppy caught misbehaving. It hits me at that moment—how young and innocent he is. At his age, I was knee-deep in blood and jewels, guilt-free. The contrast is…stark. His shame hangs like lead, and I drink it in, enjoying every drop.

His back collides with the sliding closet doors, and he fumbles with his fingernails while avoiding my gaze. "How long have you two…"

"Been fucking? Too long. Longer than you've been alive. Four times over." A puzzled look adorns his youthful features, as if trying to piece together the timeline. "Don't think about it too hard; you'll hurt that pretty little brain of yours."

"We aren't allowed to have relationships. We swear off them when we're inducted into the Order."

"We aren't in a relationship," I find myself repeating for the second time in 24 hours. "Call it a twisted dalliance."

"But you associate with demons," he gathers. "That's a greater offense to Lovejoy's virtue."

"Even the holiest of people have a dark side." I turn to face him, gripping the towel tight around my chest.

"Priests, nuns, the fucking Pope. Their darkness is their best-kept secret. I'm Lovejoy's."

"Do you love him?" he asks innocently, searching my eyes with those wholesome green ones.

"Love? Hah—I don't love anyone." I shrug. "I'm a creature of appetite—a raw, *primal* appetite. I don't give a rat's ass about rules or divine pecking orders. Human, demon, angel—they're all just flavors to me. I take what I want, consequences be damned." The concept seems foreign to him, judging by the look of horror in his eyes, but something he said only a moment ago piques my curiosity. "You mean to tell me you *willingly* took a vow of celibacy at—what are you, sixteen?"

"Twenty-one," he scoffs. "Joining the Holy Order of the Nephilim is the highest honor, especially for our kind. It would be disgraceful to ignore the call."

A devious chuckle fills my chest. "Kid, I've lived through enough crusades and tyrants to know propaganda bullshit when I see it."

His tired emerald eyes narrow and darken. "That's a sin—"

"And what do I care? Is your boss going to smite me where I stand? Is he going to punish Lovejoy for fucking me? Punish *you* for watching and jacking off to it?" My words hit him like a slap, leaving his face in a mask of shock. "It's like I said, Jimmothy—"

"*Jeremy*," he curtly interrupts.

"Whatever. We all have our secrets, sins, and

tragedies. You hunters are a dying breed, and clearly, demons are out there collecting you all like baseball cards. You can't afford to rat on each other over your proclivities. I won't tell him yours if you don't tell anyone about his."

Jeremy searches my eyes once more. Seconds later, he nods in agreement.

"Good boy," I chastise him. "Now, beat it. Unless, of course, you wanted a closer look at what you walked in on earlier…"

He straightens his back, inhaling sharply, and exits the bathroom, leaving me to my own devices with only the weight of our secrets hanging heavy in the air.

Neon buzzes faintly as I step out of my possessed Camaro. The Starlight's sign flickers weakly while Bad Decisions has gone dark. At 4:30 AM, the city feels desolate—too late for night owls, too early for dawn's go-getters. An unsettling silence reigns, and I long to rest my weary head. Nothing saps a gal's energy quite like a wicked cocktail of road trips, espionage, demonic transactions, and sexcapades.

I trudge up the pebbled steps to room 666. Darkness envelops the sky, and with sunrise a mere two hours away, I figure I can spare myself another little nap. My eyelids droop, heavy as lead as I struggle to fit the old iron key into my motel room door. The lock fights me, as if it, too, is weary beyond measure. Every muscle screams for rest after the longest day of my equally long life.

The room is quiet when I finally enter. *Too* quiet. It's the kind of stillness that makes my hair stand on end. The walls shudder with a bone-deep growl, as if the very room has awakened with my arrival…and it's hungry for a midnight snack.

It isn't until I flip on the lights that I realize I am not alone in this cursed Hellhole.

"October Winters," that familiar, fiendish voice plagues my ears. Ah, fuck me — not *them* again.

"Do you two ever sleep?" I jest, the bitter irony tasting like ash on my tongue. In the room's darkest corner, the twisted twins — Nightmares and Fear — loom with a quartet of grotesque, menacing eyes glaring at me. This time, they decide to take on the form of an older woman who appears a hair away from Death's doorstep, skin sagging and eyes milky-white with cataracts. It only takes a few seconds for me to realize I'm staring at an aged version of myself with two heads.

Now *that's* an accurate depiction of one of my greatest fears. Well played, Nightmares and Fear. Well played.

Their gaze drips malice, a silent vow of terrors to come. "We know what you've done, witch," one head snarls.

I slam my keys, smokes, and brick of a phone onto the creaky dresser. "Yeah? Well, my memory's about as stable as this piece of crap furniture. So, enlighten me, Tweedle-Doom and Tweedle-Gloom; what'd I do now?"

"You fed the demon hunter a nightmare blocking elixir."

"Oh, boo-hoo." I roll my eyes. "Did I step on your nasty-ass toes? Newsflash, terror twins: a girl's got needs. And I wasn't about to let you two blue-ball me by feeding on my latest conquest right after our romp in the sheets."

Fear hisses. "Consorting with a demon hunter is beneath you —"

"Nothing is beneath me."

"Then you must pay for his nightmares with your own."

"Wait, what?" The words barely leave my lips as icy fingers of dread claw up my spine — Fear's calling card, signed, sealed, and delivered with a personal touch. Terror crashes over me like a wave, buckling my knees and slamming me to the floor. I try to fight it, but the Prime's power overwhelms me. Each heartbeat pumps more dread throughout my body, leaving me paralyzed. Drowning. Desperate.

But then, the other twin's lips curl into a menacing grin. He raises two fingers and lowers them through the air. My eyelids shut and darkness consumes me. As the last sliver of light fades, Nightmare's voice slithers into my ears, hissing a command in Hellspeak: *"Sleep."*

TRACK EIGHTEEN

TRACK EIGHTEEN

BRING ME TO LIFE

I REMEMBER THE DAY I SOLD MY SOUL TO THE DEVIL.

I remember the voices, the insults and slurs—oh, how they've taunted me for centuries, wretched words spilled by the wretched people I was raised to call 'family.'

People I burned to a crisp.

987 years ago, I discovered I was a witch. Not just any witch—one who had the power to set fire to her enemies and raise the dead. All I needed to do was spill some blood. My blood, the blood of animals, the blood of the innocent, the blood of the damned. So long as I inflicted pain, I would be unstoppable.

I set fire to my entire village on my 13th birthday. The memory lives deep in the darkest parts of my mind. Some days, I struggle to remember the details. Other days, I remember fragments—my mother's wail, her pleading, the look in her eyes before she turned to ash. I also remember the utter joy her suffering brought me.

I've tried to forget it all over the millennium, and yet, as I lay unconscious, trapped within the prison of my mind at the hands of a sadistic demon, the memory—no, the *nightmare*—appears before my very eyes.

I see it now; the monstrous cliffs that cast a shadow upon the black sands that line the seashore and the charming homes that made up our little village. I lived amongst God-fearing egoists on a small island off the coast of Scandinavia. I can't even remember the name. I watch as a sickly young girl, in rags with matted blonde hair, kneels before the ice-cold waves lapping at her feet. She holds a small box in her hands, a makeshift coffin for a dearly departed friend.

I feel what she feels—her turmoil, her pain, the grief clouding her ever-breaking heart. How could the children of the village be so cruel as to kill her only friend? She opens the box, salty tears falling into the ocean as she mutters to herself:

"Please come back to life. *Please.* I can't survive this place without you."

Her cries turn to a wail as the tide overcomes her, dragging her across razor-sharp rocks and carving into her skin. She calls to her little coffin, for the companion swept away too soon.

My heart breaks as her lungs begin to fail her. Her

chokes and heaves echo in my ears, and soon, I, too, begin to sob.

She never calls for help. No. She only calls for her friend. Her little scorpion. Her Nero.

And from a distance, I see her family smile as they watch their sickly daughter drown in the sea. *My* family.

I watch as the body of my younger self washes up on the shore along with her dead pet scorpion, streaks of blood coating the dark sands. I fight the urge to revive the girl, to pull her into my arms and shield her from the true evils of the world. Instead, I brace myself for the series of events that follow, the nightmare I could never escape.

The little girl wakes with a wheeze in her chest, a sound so gut-wrenching, I can feel my own lungs seizing up. I know that feeling—it's the one I've been running from my entire life. She scrambles to her knees, fighting her heavy coughs as her bloody hands reach for the scorpion. Once again, she mutters, "Please come back to life. Come back to me."

And with a brilliant flash of light, the scorpion is revived.

But the reunion is short lived.

"An abomination," I hear my mother growl from behind me. "You should be *dead*."

My younger self clutches her scorpion to her chest, heaving as she tries to find her footing. If only I could help her stand…

Our mother continues her hurtful sermon. "From the moment you slithered into this world, all sickly and weak-hearted, I knew you were a mistake. For thirteen miserable years, you've clung to life like a parasite, defying every prayer I've made for your demise. And now *this*—this *evil*. You should have drowned in the water, but God Himself turns His back on you, you unholy creature."

My mother's hatred echoes through time on a relentless loop. I see her disappointment reflected in every glance at her only child—a sickly girl with a penchant for creepy crawlies. Her prayers sear the air as she desperately begs God to relieve her of my presence. Motherhood was a prison sentence in her eyes, and I was a curse made flesh.

The nightmare seizes me, inescapable and vivid. It's like I'm trapped in a Hellish theater, a captive audience to my own memories. Each word, each moment, replays with cruel precision, as if etched into my mind by an unforgiving hand. Centuries of burying the past crumble in an instant. The Demon of Nightmares feasts on my anguish, his presence looming even as I dream. I can imagine it now: his limbs, a writhing mass of smoke and shadow, invading my body through every orifice. Tendrils of darkness tickle my brain, siphoning the raw pain that builds as I'm forced to relive my life's darkest day.

But soon, my nightmare shifts forward, scenes blurring like a VHS tape on fast-forward, until it snaps into focus. Amidst the soft glow of a rising full moon, I watch my thirteen-year-old self awaken to her most perilous gift—the power to conjure and control fire.

She's like a blazing goddess amidst a sea of terrorized ants. Brilliant flames shoot out from her palms, incinerating every home, every market, every wretched soul that ever dared to question her worth. Pride swells within me as I watch little me commit the largest disaster the country had ever seen. She replaced their slurs and insults with screams of terror the night they dubbed her an 'abomination.'

The nightmare's grip slips, its razor edge dulling as the memory unexpectedly fills me with serenity rather than pain. A flicker of hope sparks within me, but suspicion quickly follows. What game is the Demon of Nightmares playing now? Has he had his fill?

My thirteen-year-old self and I stand side by side as we relish in our masterpiece. A sudden chill overcomes little me, one that fights to quell the inferno within. It makes no sense at all, this icy gust amidst the flames…but I remember the sensation like it was yesterday.

Just like I remember that gruff, powerful voice.

"Quite the little fire you've started."

I smile to myself as little me freezes in place, wiping the tears from her eyes. Standing next to her is a tall, cloaked figure whose smile glimmers as he watches her flames do their worst.

"It's not that little," she says. Ever the prideful one, even at that age.

"No, it certainly isn't." There's an amusement in his voice, and her tears halt. I remember exactly what she was feeling—her childish curiosity as she realized an actual adult was giving her the time of day.

"You're not afraid of me?" she asks quietly, fearing his response.

"On the contrary. I'm rather impressed." Her shoulders loosen, relief and a hint of excitement filling her. "Got any other tricks up your sleeve?"

"I brought my scorpion back to life." She shrugs, looking at the ground. "But he didn't stay alive for long."

The man chuckles. "No, he wouldn't, would he? It takes a very special kind of magic to do that."

"Magic?"

"What did you think you had, my little friend?"

My heart twists, a bittersweet ache as I witness that fleeting spark of hope in the little girl's eyes—in *my* eyes. For the first time, I had a friend. A *real* one. Someone actually impressed by *me,* the abomination. This moment, this precious sliver of joy, was the best moment of my life. And, unknowingly, my last.

"If I had magic…" The words catch in her throat. "I'd… I'd be able to breathe without choking. I'd fix myself." Her words are but a whisper. "Maybe then, the villagers would see me as one of their own. Maybe… maybe my mother would finally love me."

"Oh, my dear…" The voice softens, a mix of sympathy and something darker. "You're not meant to be 'one of their own.' You're on an entirely different level." There's a pause then, heavy with implication. "Those villagers, your mother—they're not worthy of you or your…gifts. They never were."

She clenches her jaw as she recalls every quip, every hateful word ever spat at her. "It doesn't matter what you think or say." Her voice turns to ice. "They wanted me dead, so…I killed them first."

Silence stretches between them. When it breaks, his words are as smooth as honey. "You know what would really show them? If you outlived them. All of them."

I scoff, bitter disbelief in every word. "Me? The sickly firestarter with no friends?"

"What if…" His voice envelops little me like a silken caress. "What if I told you you could live forever?"

My young eyes widen at the question. He speaks with a smile so twisted, it even makes *my* stomach churn. "What if I could promise you an eternity where you'd never have to fear pestilence ever again? An eternity where you could breathe without consequence? Where the only thing anyone will ever fear is you—a powerful, dark witch."

His offer is tempting but downright impossible. To live forever? Without fear? Without illness? With… magic?

It was this little girl's dream come true.

"All you have to do, my little friend"—he crouches to my eye level—"is work for me."

She lifts her chin, defiant despite her skepticism. "What kind of business do you do? Are you a healer? A holy man?"

A low chuckle ripples through the air. "Hardly." The word drips with amusement. "I'm in the business of fire and brimstone, youngling. And you? You're a fountain of darkness, just waiting to overflow."

"Are you a demon?" The question just slips out, and I smirk at how asinine it sounds. So innocent. So unaware.

The mystery man reaches into his pocket, then outstretches his hand. In his palm lies my scorpion—this time, very much alive. "The King of Demons."

"Lucifer?" She says his name without fear. She absolutely glows as the scorpion falls onto her shoulder.

"Never liked that name." He waves his clawed hand.

Little me smiles. "Never liked mine either."

"What would you like me to call you then?"

I watch her think for a moment. This was her chance, her big moment—the chance to leave her wretched life behind and become the girl—the witch—she deserved to be. *Me.*

"October."

"Toby," he muses, and I can't help but grimace.

"*October,*" my younger self corrects him. The gall of my thirteen-year-old self, talking back to the Devil himself...

"So, what exactly do you want from me?" little me asks, wary but curious.

His eyes gleam with dark purpose. "Souls. Souls of

the living, the innocent, the damned—the choice is yours."

"And if I deliver?"

The Devil flashes a cruel smile. "Eternal youth. Immortality. Power beyond your imagination. Fail, and you'll be as mortal as the ashes you've left behind." His gaze pierces the little girl's. "Can you do that, little firestarter?"

The girl nods, watching as her childhood village crumbles into cinders and flames. The screams of family and neighbors echo through the night, a haunting chorus to the inferno before her. "My mother said God Himself turned His back on me."

The Devil huffs a laugh. "Where He rejects, I embrace." He offers me his hand. "Come with me, October. Let's show God the price of forsaking a marvel like you."

As the nightmare dissolves, it reveals a truth I've long known but often tried to forget. This dream—no, this *memory*—is a stark reminder of the only constant in my long, twisted life. It shows me the face of the greatest evil known to man: a fallen angel who saw potential in a broken, helpless child. He who plucked me from despair, nurturing my pain and power alike, molding me into a formidable witch—He was not just my employer. He was my savior. My curse. My dark angel.

TRACK NINETEEN

ONE STEP CLOSER

TRACK NINETEEN

ONE STEP CLOSER

My eyes, nose, throat, and ears throb with an unsettling, sickening ache. I awake from my dream with a sharp pain piercing my temples, mind swimming. A phantom burn runs through every inch of my body as exhaustion pulls me deeper and deeper into the bed. As I come to, my blurry vision subsides, and a familiar face takes form above me.

"There you are," Lovejoy's soft voice tethers me to reality. His fingertips ghost along my cheek, up to my hairline with deliberate slowness. A shiver of comfort hits me, rousing a primal sense of safety I've never quite grown used to. He brings a glass of water to my lips, and I eagerly take a sip.

"What time is it?" The words rasp from my throat, raw and desperate. My tongue sticks to the roof of my mouth as I wrench my neck to search for the clock, but another voice responds.

"Almost 4 PM."

"4 fucking PM?!" Panic surges through me. I lurch forward, desperate to swing my legs over the bed and stand, but my limbs betray me. The world tilts and blurs, my senses muffled as I fight to regain my strength. But every movement feels like a fresh Hell of pain, and my violated mind recoils as the revelation seeps in. "There's no way I've been asleep for eleven fucking hours."

"You were being fed on." Lovejoy catches me in his arms when my knees give out. "By Nightmares and Fear."

"But don't worry, we took care of them," his apprentice interjects, a chilling pride dripping from his voice.

" —for now," Lovejoy adds.

"What are *you* doing here, fleabag?" I nod at Jeremy, and the room suddenly feels *way* too small for the three of us.

"I'd be a little nicer if I were you," he barks back. "We *did* just save your life."

Please — as if my life was actually in any danger under the brain-fucking of Nightmares and Fear. Reality sets in as I regain strength and my energy returns: two days lost. A pathetic 273 souls reaped. The ultimatum's clock ticks like a bomb, and my odds of survival are microscopic. I need to *get out.*

I shove Lovejoy away, my pride stinging worse than the dull ache in my head. Slowly pacing the cramped motel room, I replay the early morning's chaos.

"They nearly drained you dry," Lovejoy says, the rickety bed groaning under his weight. "Nightmare Feedings knock humans out cold for hours. You're lucky you woke up at all."

"It's a good thing I'm not human, then."

Decades of dodging the terror twins' clutches, and now this—my subconscious ripped open, laid bare for them to exploit. My panic, however, continues to build. The voices in my head grow louder and stronger, telling me to ditch the Nephilim, storm into the next movie theater, and bag myself a few hundred souls. I *have* to make up for lost time; I barely have three days left.

"Aren't you going to thank us for saving you?" Jeremy taunts me, entitlement dripping from his words.

Lovejoy shoots him a warning glance—a silent 'shut the fuck up' and I couldn't agree more.

I sneer at the youth, walking up to meet his gaze, despite the fact that he towers over me with his outrageously lanky frame. "You'd like that, wouldn't you, Jackalope?"

"My name is *Jeremy*," he practically seethes.

"Enough." Lovejoy steps between us, placing a hand on his chest to push him away from me. "We don't have time for this."

"I certainly don't," I mutter under my breath. "Look, why don't you two skedaddle—I've got shit to do."

"Actually, October, I—*we* need your help."

Joy. Absolute fucking joy.

"What now? Want me to conjure a one-way ticket to Hell?"

"In a manner of speaking."

This man clearly has a death wish. I lean against my unsteady dresser, crossing my arms over my chest as I await this brilliant plan of his.

"I got to thinking about the ritual remnants we saw last night. Candles, blood, scorch marks. The runes. And then your vision—you said Fargo was banished," he rambles like a madman, a devastatingly endearing madman whose dreams I can't wait to squash.

"Where are you going with this?"

He licks his lips, rising to his feet and shuffling towards me. "Maybe—*maybe*...Fargo wasn't sacrificed but banished, as you said. Banished to the demonic realm."

The idea isn't as farfetched as it seems, but there are holes. Big, gaping holes. I remain silent, gesturing at him to get on with it.

"It makes perfect sense—why neither Jeremy nor I can feel them. *Any* of them. They're not dead, but they're no longer on this plane. If we can open the portal between worlds, we can find the missing hunters."

Jeremy's as quiet as a mouse, and Lovejoy stares at

me with every ounce of hope he can muster glittering in his eyes. After seconds of realizing they're awaiting my opinion, I pipe up.

"How can you be so sure they're in the Underworld?"

"Something the lesser demon at the lounge said. 'Storing them *downstairs* for safekeeping.' We all know what that's code for—we just took him too literally. The room we found last night was just a gateway. That's why there was a ritual, and we killed the demon before we could have learned more."

"*You* killed him," I correct. It's an important distinction.

"So, I got to thinking… What if we tried to recreate the ritual? We have two key ingredients already: one—well, two—demon hunters and one occultist. All we're missing is"—Lovejoy's eyes dazzle as he glances between Jeremy and me—"a Prime."

"Oh, fuck no." My arms drop to their sides. "That will most certainly get us *all* killed. I'm not about to sacrifice my life for a demon hunter I've never even met before."

"I realize what I'm asking is a lot, but it's the only option we have. And the longer the hunters remain missing, the longer the balance remains tipped. This is bigger than all of us."

I'm in no mood for the hero speech, *especially* when I could give a rat's ass about the greater good or tipped balances. I have bigger fish to fry.

"Come on," Lovejoy practically begs. "Nightmares

and Fear already have a mark on me. It wouldn't take a lot to summon them. And if we're right and they were the ones to take Fargo to begin with…then we'd be able to trap them."

"Hang on," Jeremy interjects. "You want to offer us as bait to one of the Big Thirteen?"

"Just one of us will do."

"That's asinine!"

"It's not," I add, and the idea of sacrificing the insufferable apprentice warms my cold heart. "But there's no way *I'm* summoning them. They may be vile, but they're not stupid. They'll know it's a trap the minute they see me."

Lovejoy takes a step closer, voice lowering for only me to hear. "October, please. Don't you dare back out on me now."

I arch an eyebrow. "I'm in too deep to back out, and I know better than to dig myself a grave. But if this brilliant plan implodes and you end up a corpse? Well, you'll be in for one *Hell* of an Afterlife. The dead can't pay their debts, sweetheart."

Lovejoy's features harden as he catches Jeremy's eye, whose expression remains equally grim, if not slightly confused. My hunter's scowl offers a warning, reminding me of the discretion of our alliance.

I flash the apprentice a sardonic smile, one that feigns sincerity, and place a hand on his shoulder. "Easy there, buttercup. Daddy Lovejoy's not about to offer you up on a silver platter." My gaze drifts to my lover, a smirk playing on my lips. "Our white knight here is too fond of his shining armor to do that."

Jeremy's brow furrows, doubt etching lines across his forehead. "So we summon and trap the Prime and…then what? Negotiate for the others' safe return?"

I can't help but snort. "Negotiate? With those child-possessing sadists? Trust me, kid, I've tasted their brand of hospitality. You don't bargain with the Big Thirteen—you survive them."

"That's it," Lovejoy huffs, a small hint of relief laced in his words. "We survive them. We open the portal, rescue our mates, and then…we slay the Prime."

Jeremy's eyes practically bulge out of his skull. "*Slay*? We can't—it's never been done!"

"Not in our lifetime, no," Lovejoy muses, his gaze sharpening as he considers the plan. "But if we can do it with their Underlings, why can't we do it with them? It's our literal *reason* for existing."

"It'll upset the balance—more than it already is!" Jeremy retorts.

"If the ancient texts hold true, we'd merely be resetting this particular *version* of the Primes, this manifestation," Lovejoy reminds his apprentice. "They'll reconstitute with no memory of any of it. No memory of us, no vendetta. A blank slate. That *alone* will fix the balance." His voice drops with a hint of blind valor. "Imagine it: a world free from their nightmares, even if just for a moment. Millions of souls spared from crippling terror."

"Why haven't you tried this before?" I can't help but twist the knife.

Buried within the depths of his gaze, a flicker of naïve optimism burns. "Because I've never had someone like you on my side before."

Well, *that* does it—I'm officially in deeper shit than Hellspawn in a holy water hot tub. Every voice in my twisted head is firing off sirens, begging me to bail. Fuck, I'd make better use of my time terrorizing the 3 AM crowd at Denny's, racking up souls like poker chips, and reeling in my success with a mountain of pancakes.

But there's this…tug, a nagging in the back of my head, holding me in place like a spider in a web of my own making. It's the promise of sweet, sweet vengeance, the deliciously tempting possibility of hitting the cosmic do-over button on those two colossal pains in my ass. If I can just keep flying under the radar until Halloween…

Well, I suppose my tricks might finally outweigh the treats.

"I've always hated those two." The words drip from my lips like venom, memories of last night's nightmare still raw in my mind. "A reset wouldn't be the worst." Lovejoy's gaze locks onto mine, a silent plea to aid in his chivalrous plan. I exhale, resignation hissing through my teeth. "Fine, but I can't be seen. They can't know I'm involved."

Jeremy squints at my caveat. "What would it matter if they do?"

"Kid, there are layers to this infernal onion you can't even *begin* to peel." I drift to the window, my reflection casting a haunting veil over the silhouette of the mountains. As the Hollywood skyline sprawls before me, I take note of its two most iconic landmarks, and a deliciously wicked scheme of my own begins to take root. "The Observatory."

Lovejoy's brow furrows. "That tourist trap on the hill? What of it?"

"It's not just any old tourist trap." My lips curl into a smirk. "Griffith Park's a hotspot of raw, primal energy in this concrete jungle. The Observatory's the highest point, closest to the moon, has the strongest planetary pull. It's the perfect spot for a summoning."

What I conveniently fail to mention is the park's after-hours crowd: hormone-addled teens seeking thrills, starry-eyed lovers chasing a romantic view, all those pulsing, vulnerable souls ripe for the taking. My fingers twitch at the thought of the harvest to come.

"Well, gentlemen, whaddya say?" I twirl my keys around my finger, the jingle of metal echoing in the air. "You ready to make demon hunting history?"

Still, something irks me—the familiar pull of the weight of my conscience; the memory of the Devil's deal, the trust he bestowed upon me at such a young age. But hey, when an opportunity comes knocking, who am I to deny myself the sweet taste of revenge?

Those infernal toads bit off more than they could chew when they decided to make an all-you-can-eat buffet of my nightmare. Daddy Dearest *may* have forbidden me from ever harming his sons, but there's no fine print against making them wish they'd never clawed into my mind.

A wicked smirk splits my face as I drink in the sight of Mount Hollywood, my mind already painting the legendary hillside with the chaos soon to come.

Funny how betrayal becomes as natural as breathing when you've danced with the dark for so many years. If I've got a one-way ticket to Hell, I might as well go out in a blaze of gloriously treasonous fire.

And Hell hath no fury like a resentful witch scorned.

BY RITE OF BLOOD MAGIC AND THE THIRTEEN SPHERES, I SUMMON THE DEMONS OF NIGHTMARES AND FEAR.
TRACK TWENTY
SLEEP NOW IN THE FIRE

TRACK TWENTY

SLEEP NOW IN THE FIRE

A GLITTERING TAPESTRY OF LIGHTS SPRAWL BEFORE ME as I park my car atop Mount Hollywood. Up here, all is quiet. Pristine. Deceptively pure. One could almost forget the rot festering in the city's underbelly, the desperate souls succumbing to their darkest desires, the demons who whisper and nudge and watch gleefully as humans tumble into their grasp.

A smirk tugs at my lips as I drink in the view of the Los Angeles skyline. My fingers twitch, Hellfire dancing just beneath my skin. Oh, how gloriously this city would burn.

The demon hunters exit the car, leaving me alone with my turbulent thoughts. My gaze flickers to the rearview mirror, meeting my hazel, raccoon-eyed reflection as I contemplate the dire consequences of the betrayal I'm about to commit.

I have no doubt Lovejoy has what it takes to slay a Prime. Hell, even little Jeremy is enough of an overachiever to pull it off. But they don't know the twins like I do, not by a long shot.

The way I see it, I'm doing Nightmares and Fear a favor; hand-delivering two Nephilim for them to toy with and mind-fuck as they please *and* get away with whatever angel-kidnapping spree they're on. And if they do get slain? They'll reconstitute in days and not remember a thing about me. It's win-win, a damn near perfect plan that just needs to go off without a hitch.

So long as I get my glittery vial of divine blood and collect another hundred souls before dawn, I'm golden. But fuck, part of me wants to see the hunters send the terror twins back to the fiery depths they crawled out of.

I unlock my glove compartment with a wave of my hand. Inside rests the usual witchy necessities: salt, athame, crystals, herbs—the works.

The ceremonial dagger glints in the fading sunlight. I remember the day Lucifer handed it to me, not long after taking me under his wing.

"In case you ever need me or one of my Primes," he'd said. "Your blood is the key to summoning. Spill it willingly, speak the words, and we will find you."

Who needs email when you have blood sacrifice?

I shove my goods into my worn-out purse and prepare for the worst. At least a dozen cars remain in the parking lot, no doubt belonging to guests attending the day's last planetarium show. The grounds appear desolate, and for that, I am grateful.

Lovejoy and Jeremy study their surroundings in awe, drinking in the sight of the stark white building that looms over Hollywood. The Observatory's art deco design and bronze dome cuts a striking silhouette against the twilight sky, and my fingers itch to light it all on fire—to trap the innocents in the planetarium and suck the souls right out of them. All in good time.

For now, I need to tread carefully. One false move, and the hunters will figure me out. Or worse, the demons will *rat* me out.

"So how does this work?" Jeremy pipes up as I saunter onto the lawn.

"Blood, spell, boom," I drawl, rummaging through my bag. "The Observatory's dome will be our cosmic amplifier since the moon's not fully risen yet. I'll be up there"—I jerk my chin towards the second level—"chanting the spell. But I'll draw the blood circle down here."

The hunters nod like bobbleheads, hanging on my every word. Lovejoy reaches for one of his holy Boy Scout daggers, but I shut that down quickly. "Put away your blessed butter knife, babe. This is big league shit." I fish out my athame, its obsidian blade drinking in the twilight. "Since you bear the Mark of the Primes, I'll need to use your blood for the ritual. The Dreamguard Elixir probably hasn't left your system yet, so spelling you to sleep would be useless. One of you gets to play tag with the twins while the other drags your hunter pals out of Hell's asshole."

Lovejoy nods. "They'll have their Hellspawn and Lessers with them. Jeremy, you think you can handle them?"

The kid's an eager puppy, rolling up his flannel like he's about to arm wrestle a bear.

I sidle up to Lovejoy, dropping my voice to a whisper. "This is gonna hurt like a bitch, babe. Are you sure you want to go through with it?" I lock eyes with those chocolate browns of his. He doesn't hesitate.

"I need to bring them back. The future of mankind and Nephilim alike depends on it."

Christ, the man bleeds drama and then some. I hold out my hand, beckoning for him with a wiggle of my fingers. Let's get this show on the road.

The athame slices through Lovejoy's palm with ease. He lets out a strangled groan, instinctively trying to yank his hand away, but I tighten my grip on his wrist. The blade sinks deeper, and I feel the resistance of flesh and tendon giving way.

This isn't your run-of-the-mill blade; the dark magic pulsing through the athame, cursed by the Devil himself, ensures even a Nephilim with a direct line to God himself won't be healing anytime soon.

Between us, Lovejoy's divine blood shimmers and dances, casting an otherworldly light across my jacket and skin. It's mesmerizing—a cosmic light show in liquid form. And soon, it'll be all mine.

I dip two fingers into the wound, feeling the warmth of his lifeblood coat my skin, and begin to draw.

The summoning circle comes first. Then, a pentagram in the center, because nothing says 'Welcome to Hollywood' like a star on the ground. I dive deep into the cobwebbed corners of my mind, dragging out memories from eons ago when I first learned these demonic runes. Sure, the athame and a quick spell are all it really takes to get a Prime to show up, but I need to make this look like the real deal.

"What language is that?" the pipsqueak apprentice asks.

I roll my eyes so hard, I'm surprised they don't fall out of my skull. "Would you stop with the stupid questions? I'm working here." I return to my grisly art project, using Lovejoy's hand as my personal divine paint palette. Five summoning runes in Hellspeak begin to take shape on the ground, each stroke a step closer to completion.

Finally, I place five crystals at each point of the star and use my magic to set them ablaze.

It's a masterpiece of dark magic, if I do say so myself, but the real works of art are the slack-jawed, wide-eyed stares of two painfully righteous demon hunters.

And then, it hits me.

In our eighty years together, Lovejoy has never seen me like this, never witnessed me *truly* unleash what I can do. We've always kept our professional lives neatly compartmentalized, like good little soldiers on opposite sides of an eternal war.

But now? Now, he's seeing the real me in all my glory: an immortal necromancer with blood magic coursing through my veins and flames dancing at my fingertips.

I meet his gaze, and for the first time in eight decades, I see something I've never seen in those warm brown eyes before.

Fear.

It's intoxicating. Thrilling. And there's a sick, twisted part of me that wants more.

I mutter something about the next stage of the ritual and head towards the spiral staircase leading to the upper level of the grand building. My boots clunk heavily against stone steps, echoing through the early night.

When I finally take my spot at the grand balcony overseeing the lawn, parking lot, and Hollywood Sign, I extend my hand toward the gargantuan dome of the Griffith Observatory and channel my magic. The planetary alignment above fills me with astronomical energy, an element I seldom use in my magical endeavors. The bronze-plated dome, now turned dark green over years and years of oxidation, thrums as it guzzles every natural element around us—the sky, the earth, the wind, and my fire. The pieces are in place.

And then, I begin my chant.

"By rite of blood magic and the Thirteen Spheres,

I summon you, the Demons of Nightmares and Fear."

When the final words leave my lips, the world holds its breath.

It begins with a whisper—a subtle tremor that could be mistaken for a passing truck—but it grows, swiftly and mercilessly, until the ground bucks beneath my feet. I grip the white concrete balcony, my knuckles turning as pale as the stone as I struggle to stay upright. The surrounding trees shudder violently, and the Observatory itself seems to groan in protest, its sturdy frame tested by forces beyond mortal understanding.

From below, muffled cries of alarm rise. Trapped within the building, unsuspecting humans react to what they believe is just another Southern California earthquake. Their fear is palpable but misplaced. This is something far more terrifying.

My gaze drops to the lawn below, where Lovejoy and Jeremy stand ready, the older with his holy daggers and the younger with his hands glowing with celestial magic. Suddenly, the earth surrenders. The once-lush green lawn and surrounding concrete split open with a sound like the world itself is being torn apart. From the gaping wounds in the ground, a sickly red light spills forth—malevolent, hungry, and older than time.

The moon, slowly rising to take its place in the quickening night sky, turns a dark crimson, and the clouds surrounding it seem to darken.

Familiar scents twist my insides. Smoke surrounds us,

so thick we can hardly see through it, while sulfur and decay sting our eyes. No earthquake could ever compare to this moment.

The portal to Hell has been opened. Time to fuck shit up.

The red light explodes across my vision, blinding me instantly. Before I can even blink away the spots dancing in my eyes, a thunderous BOOM slams into us. It's not just loud—it's a fucking physical force that punches the air from my lungs. The shockwave races across the mountainside, setting off a cascade of car alarms in the distance.

I'm airborne for a split second before the unforgiving ground rushes up to meet me. The impact jars every bone in my body, and I feel my channeled magic go apeshit. It sparks and sputters like a live wire, wild and dangerous.

And then, I hear it—the ominous crackle of flames.

I force my eyes open, blinking away tears and dust, just in time to see the Observatory's iconic dome erupt in flames. The copper surface warps and buckles under the intense heat, its green patina peeling away in flakes of fire.

Down below, a sight unfolds that makes me wish I'd lost my eyes in the explosion.

A creature from the depths of my darkest nightmares materializes. Two warped heads jut out of a twisted chest, festered skin curling like a horrified tree trunk. Twin skulls, fractured and misshapen, sprout spiraling horns that reach towards the sky. Decaying flesh clings to sharp cheekbones, barely concealing the hollow chasms beneath. Six void-dark tentacles spring from every dark hole within their distorted rib cage, ready to devour and invade the brains of anyone standing in their path.

The terror twins have arrived, and holy shit, have they come dressed for the occasion.

For a moment, I wonder if this form is my greatest fear made manifest. Death and decay, large and in my face, unavoidable and imminent. But judging by the way the demon hunters stare at them with ardent determination, I know they've revealed their true, archaic form. It makes my last few run-ins with them look like a warm-up act.

The acrid stench of sulfur grows stronger now, amplified by the portal to Hell at their feet. Together, they tower over the scene, making the Griffith Observatory look like a child's dollhouse. The air around them warps and twists, reality itself seeming to recoil from their presence.

They're not just a part of the Big Thirteen. They're primordial forces given flesh, the personification of humanity's deepest, darkest fears.

Lovejoy's stance stiffens in the face of his greatest enemy, the Primes that left their mark on him just as I had all those years ago. While it's common knowledge that the Primes can never physically kill a hunter, it doesn't mean they can't try. That's where Hellspawn come in—the impish little creatures bred between demon and animal and forming into some of the most fucked up little shits you've ever laid eyes on. Hellspawn and Lessers are disposable and stand no chance fighting against Nephilim. Watching them burst like little holy lightbulbs will be the cherry on top of this clusterfuck of a sundae.

"Declan Lovejoy," the two-headed monster growls, their voices explosive as the fire booming beside me. "We meet again."

Lovejoy's aura flares like a supernova, his holy essence crackling around him like barely contained lightning. Every muscle in his body coils, ready to spring. His daggers blaze with righteous fury, and with a battle cry that could shatter steel, my lover hurls himself at the towering Prime.

The Earth splits further, disgorging a horde of nightmarish imps. They scramble from the cracks, all gnashing teeth and razor-sharp claws, their eyes fixed hungrily on the hunters.

"October, the planetarium!" Jeremy's panicked voice cuts through the chaos. "There are still people in there! They're burning—!"

Indeed there are. A smile tugs at the corner of my mouth as an idea blossoms in my mind—dark and enticing. Let the boys handle their end of the bargain, their foolish attempt to slay two of the most ancient evils known to mankind.

Me? I've got a date with a burning building full of souls ripe for the taking.

As Lovejoy and Jeremy throw themselves into an impossible battle, I turn towards the inferno that was once the planetarium. The flames lick hungrily at the structure, promising destruction and opportunity.

Time to fill my quota. After all, why should the demons have all the fun?

I shatter dark glass with my black magic, and the windows crumble at my feet. I hop through the threshold as burning flames kiss my skin, greeting me like an old friend.

A glorious building once known as one of Hollywood's greatest scientific hubs now serves as a blazing battlefield.

The Observatory has become a labyrinth of fire, every chamber and hallway a corridor of dancing flames, but this is no ordinary blaze—it roars and crackles yet consumes nothing. The fire paints the walls with living shadows, each flicker pulsing with dark energy.

The flames part before me as I glide through the inferno. They don't dare touch me; they know better. My magic pulses, an invisible force field protecting me from vicious heat. I can feel my hair floating, charged with power, while the embers swirl around me.

And then, I hear them.

Whimpers. Cries. The desperate screams of my victims.

Ah, humans. Such fragile, pathetic creatures cursed to be my precious commodity. Their fear fills me like the electric currents from a heavy guitar riff, and their despair is a delicacy I can almost taste. Each panicked heartbeat calls to me, a siren song of vulnerability.

As I saunter deeper into this disaster of my own making, a smile plays on my lips. These useless lives, so ripe for the taking… Their end will be my beginning, their souls the currency of my ascension.

Let the harvest begin.

Amid the crackling flames of my Hellish inferno, I emerge from the burning building. My fingers trail along once-white walls now darkened to a crisp. A subtle, knowing smile curls my lips as Nero's stinger pulses against my skin, filled with a hundred new souls swirling in eternal damnation. I relish in the flames as they dance around me.

My attention is quickly diverted to the monstrosity towering above Lovejoy and Jeremy. The trio face off upon the grass lawn surrounding the Observatory. The historic planetarium blazes on brilliantly, casting a crimson, fiery glow upon Hollywood Hills.

I watch intently from the Observatory's steps as hunter and demon face off in a battle written in the stars.

Hundreds upon thousands of reaching hands pop out of the rift in the ground, the grasps of the eternal damned, helpless, desperate souls begging for salvation. They reach for anything, anyone who would dare to pull them out. A swell of pride rushes through my skin as a knowing smile tugs at my lips, reveling in the fact that it was I who sent most of them to their fiery end—a powerful, formidable witch with no regard for the lives of the innocent.

The pesky apprentice struggles to ward off Hellspawn as they gnaw at his arms and legs, screeching with fiendish fury as he reaches for the few hands that appear human and flesh. Flashes of Holy Light strike the beasts like lightning bolts from the sky, and every creature defeated elicits a stench so gut-wrenching, I almost gag. This mountain will reek of rotten eggs and burning asphalt for weeks to come.

And then, there's Lovejoy. Bravery and strength made manifest.

I've seen him fight before. I've seen him decimate Hellspawn and undead and send Lessers to the void. I've heard him boast of his conquests and outsmart other supernaturals—hell, I've even seen him survive a killing blow.

But nothing compares to the battle he faces now.

He's swift. Cunning. Using his agility and size to

thwart the gargantuan Prime's efforts, he dodges every tentacle, catapults over every swipe, and even does that nifty little teleportation trick. All the while, the Demon of Nightmares and Fear grows angrier, more irritated by the pest that dares to outwit them.

But their patience grows weary, and this battle needed a victor.

My breath catches in my chest when Lovejoy's pained groan echoes louder than the screeches of surrounding Hellspawn. Nightmares and Fear's booming chuckle nearly makes the earth shake again. Panic sets in, gripping my nerves as Lovejoy's body struggles against one of Fear's ink-like tentacles. I can practically feel his bones crack, reform, and crack again as the coils threaten to crush him, but he stays strong. He *keeps fighting.*

The Prime brings his victim closer to their twin grotesque skulls. Each head takes a moment to speak, their voices similar yet distinguishable in tone.

"You've played the long game, Declan Lovejoy —"

" — But your end is near."

"You've placed your faith in an illusion —"

" — And it destroys you with every scheme."

"You're a fool to face us —"

" — For your soul will always be ours."

And then, both voices join together. "Your greatest fear is not death. It is heartbreak."

The world plunges into eerie silence. Every sound — Hellspawn, fire, city noise — vanishes.

Then, Lovejoy erupts with light.

A searing, blinding radiance explodes from his form, so intense, it burns my vision. A shockwave of holy magic ripples outward, its raw power nearly knocking me off my feet.

Reality tears. The Demons of Nightmares and Fear are caught in the surge, their monstrous forms distorting as they fall into the breach.

And Lovejoy—my foolish, brave Lovejoy—is right there with them. For a split second, I see his face: determined, fearless. Then, in a final burst of light, they're gone.

My legs move faster than my brain can think.

I run headfirst into peril, bolting down the stairs and blasting Hellspawn out of my way. Nightmares and Fear's tentacles pour out of the rift, desperately clawing and clinging to the surface, pulling themselves back onto the human plane.

A moment of relief washes over me when I catch sight of Lovejoy hanging onto the edge of the breach for dear life, and my pace quickens.

My boots come to a screeching halt when I finally reach the breach. Red light reflects against my skin as I get a glimpse of Hell, the one place I've worked so hard to avoid. For a moment, my own fear torments my mind; one false move or misstep, and I could fall head-first into my own end.

Hell can have me when it earns me. I'm not going down because of a stumble. When I fall, it'll be spectacular—and entirely on my terms.

Pain sears through my knees as they scrape across the unforgiving concrete. I ignore it, lunging for Lovejoy's arms with desperate urgency.

His chocolate eyes light up at the sight of me, a mix of relief and self-importance dancing in their depths. "October, what are you—"

"What does it look like I'm doing? Getting you out of this mess," I cut him off, my voice rough with exertion. "Just shut up and hold on, okay?"

A strained sound escapes his lips—half chuckle, half disbelieving gasp. Even now, with the embodiment of fear breathing down our necks, he manages to find humor. "Shouldn't it be me rescuing you? You're ruining my big hero moment."

The familiar banter hits me like a punch to the gut. For a split second, I'm torn between the urge to kiss him senseless and the need to slap that smirk off his face. Instead, I tighten my grip on his arms, feeling the solid warmth of him beneath my fingers.

"You're a shitty damsel in distress, Declan Lovejoy," I mutter, pulling him towards me with all my strength.

"Now, move your ass before I change my mind about saving it."

Those desperate, Hellish hands of the damned reach for me, and the wailing cries of thousands upon thousands of vengeful souls fill the air. Their touch burns as they try to drag me down into the depths of Hell with them. Each grab, each pull, is fueled by a hatred I know all too well—the desire to see me suffer the same fate I so carelessly inflicted upon them.

The irony isn't lost on me—the very power I've cultivated through their suffering now threatens to be my undoing. As I fight against the vengeful dead, I can't shake the thought that maybe, just maybe, I'm finally reaping what I've sown.

Pull yourself together, Winters. Let's get the fuck off this mountain.

Beneath us, Nightmares and Fear struggle to find their own strength. The damned souls grip at them while they themselves grip at my hunter, and it all seems like one twisted, demented game of Monkey in a Barrel.

"Jeremy, the ritual!" Lovejoy's roar cuts through the chaos as his body wavers between realities.

I grip his shoulder holsters, muscles straining. "You'd better hope you trained him well for this," I grunt.

Jeremy's voice rises, weaving unfamiliar rhymes into a spell. It's nothing like the dark weaving of my craft, but I can feel its power building, unmistakably holy.

Ebony tendrils pour through the monster's putrid rib

cage and reach for Lovejoy. The ground quakes violently as Jeremy's ritual starts to solidify the breach. Their demise is inevitable, but a Prime will never allow themselves to be bested by the likes of a demon hunter. The creature claws at Lovejoy's legs, desperate to take the hunter down into the abyss with them. We may both have a claim on his life, but my future depends on this one moment. And I will be double, triple, *quadruple* damned if I let a fucking Prime destroy my chance at immortality.

"Give him power, the strength to muster,

Let me save this demon hunter."

An unholy power flows through my veins like dark ink dripping from my fingers as I dig my nails into Lovejoy's back. I transfer my might to him, my sacrilegious version of a Hail Mary. My flames reflect in the Prime's evil, menacing eyes as my treachery sinks in.

"You fucking *bitch*," the creature bellows along with the trembling of the earth.

Lovejoy gathers every ounce of strength I'd given him. With a final, arduous effort, he slams his boot into one of the thick, cracked skulls of the Demon of Nightmares and Fear and crawls out of the breach.

Their screams echo through the night in a haunting symphony of rage and despair.

The rift pulses, consuming the Prime's corporeal form, and seals shut with a blinding green light. An energy ripples throughout the hills and trees while the wails of the damned disappear into the night. A sickening silence hangs in the air—palpable, salient. My hunter and I are a mess of winded breaths, holding each other as the clouds part to reveal the moon returned to its silvery white glory.

"You saved me," he whispers breathlessly.

I saved him.

I, October Winters, saved someone other than myself.

The Devil will never let me live this down.

He lays his head back onto the ground, staring at me with adoration even I can't fathom. I remain on top of him, my hands still gripping his shirt—his *bloody* shirt—when relief hits me. Lovejoy is safe. The demon is banished. I've upheld my end of the bargain. But relief is fleeting, quickly triumphed by a sense of dread.

The demon is banished.

In all my years of violence and darkness, never have I known of a demon hunter who successfully banished a Prime. It isn't a simple task. It's one of vehement, unfathomable power. I've seen demonic minions slain—hell, I've seen the Demon of Violence himself slain—but *banishment*? The inability to set foot on the human plane? The ramifications could be fatal.

The scales have been tipped. Good reigns the victor. Humans will be free of their nightmares and fears… for now.

And my demise has never felt as imminent as it does right now.

We're not alone on this burning hill, I soon realize. A handful of new figures lay on the ground, fresh from the trenches of Hell. Their auras are bright and immaculate as they sigh, gaping at each other in disbelief. Jeremy helps them to their feet, tending to them. I forgot this part of the deal for a moment, the one where I was meant to help return the missing demon hunters to the human plane. The Devil is *really* going to have my ass for this.

I watch this seraphic reunion as, one-by-one, each hunter embraces the other. I imagine this is what family feels like, to be surrounded by those who adore you unconditionally. Something I haven't known. Something I'll *never* know.

"Declan?" a demon huntress' voice calls within the smoke.

In seconds, Lovejoy stirs underneath me, scrambling to his feet. The warmth of his body fades, leaving me cold and alone on the cracked concrete. He stops in his tracks to stare at the huntress—a pixie of a girl with short raven locks that sculpt her round features—and breathes out a sigh of relief. "Mireya."

Tears well in her eyes, threatening to spill. Within seconds, they're inches apart, studying each other in disbelief in a way only star-crossed lovers do, as if they're the only living creatures on the planet.

And in that moment, I realize my recent bout of heroism is quickly forgotten.

Their gestures are gentle, intimate, like two halves of

the same soul mended after being ripped apart. Their silence is deafening as they share a wordless tête-à-tête while reading each other's gaze. I watch with narrow eyes as her trembling hands trail up his chest—*my* chest—and rest on his cheeks. Her dark, troubled eyes search his, desperate for answers, longing for hope. But it isn't until he places his hands upon hers and leans into her touch that my stomach churns.

I've never known jealousy, not in my millennia. Jealousy is a disease, a juvenile emotion. It cripples the soul and regresses the mind, fuels petty, irrational actions. I'm above jealousy. *Far* above it.

And yet, my hands burn with the flames of rage as I watch another woman lay her claim on my man.

TRACK TWENTY ONE
TOXICITY

TRACK TWENTY-ONE

TOXICITY

A COLD WAVE OF DREAD WASHES OVER ME, CONSUMING me, snuffing out the inferno raging in my heart. It isn't the sight of them standing so close, his hand gently caressing her cheek—the way he would caress mine—or the way she whispers his name…It's the sudden realization that our twisted entanglement is nearing its end.

A threat stands in between my carnal, possessive urges and the debt I'm owed. A woman I've never heard of; a woman he has never mentioned. This so-called *Mireya*.

I could fucking kill her.

"October," a voice cuts through my brooding. I turn to see Jeremy limping towards me, his skin a canvas of ash and soot. Battle-worn and ragged, he's a far cry from the infuriatingly pure little pest I've come to know.

"Not in the mood, kid," I grumble as I walk toward my Camaro.

"Are you hurt?" It isn't a question of concern. It's one of scrutiny. Of disbelief. Disappointment.

I raise my hands, twisting my wrists, and face him with a forceful grin. "Flawless as always."

"Funny that any time Declan sends you after the humans, there are always inexplicable casualties of unfathomable sorts and you always walk away unscathed."

I clench my jaw, fists balling at my sides. "I've always considered myself a lucky girl."

"A little too lucky," he huffs.

My patience wears thin as the moon rises higher over Mount Hollywood, casting a milky glow over the burning observatory. I keep my distance from the apprentice, but the look in my eyes challenges him. "If you're going to throw around accusations, I suggest you stop being a pussy and come right out with it."

He saunters closer, lowering his voice when he's mere inches away from me. "You let those people die."

"And?"

"Those were *innocent* people."

A helpless laugh escapes my lips. "I'm sorry, I was temporarily possessed by the spirit of not-giving-a-fuck."

"It was your job to get them to safety."

"Last time I checked, I don't serve your higher purpose."

"Then who *do* you serve?"

I want nothing more than to wring that pale neck of his, tear out his throat, and feed him to my scorpion. And while the thought is tempting—so *fucking* tempting—I need to flee from this hell-damned mountain.

"The next time you decide to point fingers, you'd do well to remember that you and Lovejoy are alive *because of me*. Now, if you wouldn't mind getting your useless ass out of my way, I've got a job to get back to."

"Right," he calls out as I take my leave. "Wouldn't want to keep your patrons waiting."

A flame involuntarily ignites in my hand. I ache to unleash my fury, to burn the not-so-little worm to a crisp…but Lovejoy interrupts our altercation. I extinguish the flame in my hand, wiping it on my jeans.

He murmurs to his apprentice, low and urgent, something about tending to the survivors. Jeremy hesitates, skewering me with one last venom-laced glare before he stalks off, leaving me alone with the man who has turned my mind into a war zone.

My fingers curl into fists, trembling at my sides. A familiar heat crawls up my neck, threatening to shatter my pathetically thin composure. The tension between us is charged, heavier than the acrid smoke of my inferno. I steel myself when we finally lock eyes.

There's a different air about him. An uncertainty. Hesitation. He doesn't reach for me. He doesn't touch me as he naturally would. He doesn't check me for wounds, and he certainly doesn't regard me with the intimacy he did with that Mireya creature just seconds before. He does, however, regard me with those haunting brown eyes, so full of admiration and gratitude despite the opposite of his body language.

"Congratulations, Lovejoy." My words are like pulling teeth. "You've just made history—first demon hunter to boot a Prime off the mortal plane. Some might say that's a fate worse than death. It'll take them ages to find their way back onto this plane."

"Slaying them would have made for lesser headaches." He shrugs. "Portals are…complicated. Unpredictable. If we found a way to bring the Nephilim back, they'll find a way for themselves." He pauses, his expression thoughtful. "I imagine the Underworld is in quite a state of unrest right now."

A mirthless chuckle escapes me. "I guess I'll let you know."

"They'll be coming after you. The Primes. Their Underlings."

"They're the least of my worries," I mutter under my breath. "I've been pissing demons off for a thousand years, *lover*. Survival's not just a skill—it's embedded into my bones."

That *word* catches in my throat, a slip of the tongue despite the irritation simmering beneath my skin. It's no longer our private term of endearment, a secret shared between stolen glances. It's a loaded gun, safety off. I see the weight of it in his eyes, heavy with unspoken hesitation.

Oh, yes. The game has *certainly* changed.

And I strike the final blow.

"You'd better run off. I'm sure your *colleague* is counting the seconds till you're back in her arms."

It's not his silence that sets my blood boiling. No, it's the feigned innocence pooling in his eyes. The sheer gall to act oblivious to my backhanded suggestion. He stands there, pretending nothing changed, as if the only difference in this twisted dance is the cluster of self-righteous fuckwads at his back. And all the while, his gaze remains fixed on me, unrelenting. *Guiltless.*

I can't hold it in—the fury. The urge to verbally tear him apart. To blame him for my shortcomings and failures. To blame his stupid brown eyes and his stupid virtuousness. His divinity.

But there's only one thing I can say to him.

"I never pegged you for a hypocrite."

The words slip out, sharp as broken glass. His wrath wavers, confusion creeping in.

"What are you getting at?"

"Your *colleague*." I let the word hang again, heavy with implication. "You conveniently forgot to mention she was your girlfriend."

Tension cracks his features. "She isn't."

"Oh." I quirk a brow. "Another notch on your bedpost, then? And here I thought you demon hunters were above the sins of the flesh. Aren't you just a perfect example of all that is righteous and pure?"

The painful irony in my statement intoxicates me. I relish in ripping into his dignity, destroying him with every patronizing quip of the truth. My words strike a chord as he visibly wages a war within, fists balled, jaw clenched—the perfect specimen of a man tormented by his inner demons.

"I expect manipulation and deception from the Primes and their Underlings—fuck, even from myself. Yet here you stand, a patron saint of virtue, toying with me and using me to your own benefit. You tell me you don't like seeing me with other men, you whisper promises of 'forever', and yet you fail to mention that that little pixie's box is one you frequent."

Lovejoy's eyes crinkle as he succumbs to laughter. A boisterous, incredulous laugh, as if his body didn't know how else to react.

"What is so *fucking* funny?" I grit through my teeth.

"After all these years…I've finally broken you." I can't find the words to question him. I merely squint at his audacity. "You're so quick to point fingers when you, yourself, are a paragon of hypocrisy. Green is *not* your color, October Winters."

I step closer to him then, fighting my ever-growing rage, my violent urges. I could kill him for a comment like that. "I am many things, Declan Lovejoy. A hellion. A hoodwink. A harlot. But I am *not* a hypocrite."

A bitter laugh escapes him. "Has your ego finally devoured your sanity? Are you so lost in your own delusions that you can't see what's right in front of you?" His voice drops, each word a dagger aimed at my core. "You. Love. Me. And it's eating you alive."

I don't entertain his slander, this pathetic notion that what I feel for him is remotely close to love. I cannot love. I have *never* loved and I never *will* love…not if I don't make good on the Devil's deal.

All at once, the gravity of my survival weighs heavily upon me. The thousand years of treachery. Murder. Power. It all comes down to this moment, where a little girl who just wanted to breathe finds herself within days of mortality, of her final end. A little witch pushed to the brink of desperation and madness.

It doesn't matter. In the end, one of us won't make it out alive.

And I've got nothing left to lose.

"I risked *everything* for you. To pull you out of that breach. To bring *that girl* back to this plane. You have *no* idea what I've done. Who I've betrayed. He'll *kill* me for this."

The confession spills from my mouth like vomit. Uncontrollable. Unrelenting. Regret itches at my nerves the second his expression turns sullen. My mistakes will be the death of me.

And so, I turn away.

"*Who'll* kill you?" His voice is a lower timber that sends a shiver up my spine.

I can't tell him. I *won't*. But his hands grip my shoulders and spin me toward him. "Who's after you? Who are you running from?"

I urge my feet to flee, to get me off this stupid mountain and back down to the tawdry trenches of the grisly city, far away from demon hunters and pious sycophants.

But Lovejoy holds on. He *always* holds on, even when he knows he shouldn't.

My hands clamp around his wrists, the magic of my fire surging forth. His flesh sizzles beneath my fingers, and the scent of burning bodies fills the air. A strangled cry tears from his throat as he jerks back. The moment his grip loosens, I'm gone.

I throw myself into the Camaro, and the engine roars to life with the flick of my wrist. Tires screech against asphalt, leaving twin black marks as I drive away. The burning hills of Griffith Park blur past, a Hellish backdrop in my rearview mirror.

Who are you running from?

His words play on a loop within my anguish.

I know what I'm running from—it's the same dark shadow that has haunted me since childhood. Now, after a thousand years, death is catching up to me.

And I'm running out of time.

TRACK TWENTY TWO
FREAK ON A LEASH

TRACK TWENTY-TWO

FREAK ON A LEASH

My watch reads 9 PM as I enter Bad Decisions. The air is thick with the faint, musty odor of cigarettes and regrets, my preferred scent. Velour booths, once plush and supple, now threadbare and in desperate need of an upholster, line the interior of the club. My fellow gals are stage-bound, their platform shoes thudding against withered parquet, feather boas and fishnet stockings at the ready. I shrug my oversized coat from my shoulders and jam it into my locker in the back room as I prep for my night shift. Nero springs to life with a wave of my hand as I lean into the yellow bulb-lined vanity mirror and reapply my black lipstick.

I wish I never made that deal with those demons. I wish it didn't come down to this—relying on the damned and the desperate for income and shelter. My saving grace is that a strip club is the perfect place to harvest demented souls. Easy pickings.

"How many are we at, fella?" I ask my familiar.

491.

Disappointment washes over me, forming an unsettling pull at my insides. I'd hoped to be farther along by now, with just two days left until my birthday. Nevertheless, I shoot Nero a forced smile. "Let's see if we can make it 510 before midnight. Stay close, okay? Keep away from the bar. Charlie hates critters."

Nero clicks his pincers in obedience, disappearing into the dark depths of the club as I make a final primp before showtime. My reflection disappoints me, to say the least. My black-painted lips press into a tight grimace as I recall the days I didn't have to bargain my body for a place to live, when killing the right rich man or fucking the right demon came with glorious benefits. Long gone are those days. Such is the life of one bombshell Devil's advocate.

Lovejoy was right—I've come a far way from Rolls-Royce and Coco Chanel.

Reagan's fiery curls distract me from my trek to the stage. Her obsidian horns reflect the garish, rotating lights of the main room as she blocks the doorway, eyes dim and dangerous as ever. "He's here, and he asked for *you.*"

I blink at the she-demon. 'He' could be anyone.

Lovejoy, his simpering apprentice, one of the Primes. A cold, familiar rush fills my lungs, and my eyes instinctively widen in a panic. Reagan nods to her left, toward the 'murder den,' as the girls call it, the one us supernatural creatures take our kills to. I swallow hard, rolling my shoulders as I push past the redhead and begin my walk of shame to the coveted VIP room.

I lock the door with a quiet click. Dried blood covers the floor and walls like a macabre Jackson Pollock, a testament to our devious delights. The she-demons aren't the cleanest, the vampire girls fancy themselves too good for housekeeping, and I certainly couldn't care less about appearances. Our murder den is one to be feared, and nothing gets a man's adrenaline pumping like blood-stained walls. It makes for a *delicious* kill.

My patron sits draped along the velour booth with languid reserve, as if the weight of his importance weighs heavy upon his frame. His fingers toy with the seats, picking crusted blood off the armrest and sprinkling it over the ground. I avoid his gaze, avoid the growing fear threatening to end me as my heels head for the dreaded pole.

The temperature drops, and I know—playtime's over. The Devil is here to discipline His Second.

The air is different when He's in the room. It's… surreal. It's what I imagine it feels like above the clouds. Crisp. Prickling. There's an invisible force about Him that brings even the strongest hero to their knees, a force that demands submission. After nearly a thousand years, you'd think I'd be used to it. But given my recent misgivings, I can't help but crumble as my guilt suffocates me.

Nevertheless, I begin my show.

It's impossible to pretend I'm the only one in the room. There's an emptiness in me, a far-off look in my eyes that glazes over with every twirl around the pole, every sway of my hips. I think to my Nero, my little familiar who remains tucked under a booth in the main room, awaiting my instruction. I urge him to find me, to join me in this murder den, to ease my guilt. Music blares softly through static-ridden speakers barely clinging to their wall mounts, adding to the artificial appeal of my little show. I don't know how long I've been moving, how many songs have passed, but what I do know—what I undoubtedly *feel*—is the heavy stare of my deadly benefactor glued to my body.

The hairs on my arm stand on end as a throaty groan emits from my patron's chest. For a moment, I forget how to dance. I forget the movements that have become second nature and pause to finally look at *Him*.

"Don't stop."

His husky, demonic growl petrifies me. The cool metal pole behind my back only adds to the shiver creeping up my spine. I stare into His eyes—those dark, demented eyes that narrow with every second of my trepidation—and lick my lips.

I have no choice but to do as I'm told. The Devil does *not* like to be kept waiting.

Lucifer possessed a hunk of a man who looks like he could break me with a single touch. On any other night, I'd let him, but tonight, my skin itches. My instinct urges me to run, to avoid this inevitable confrontation and the consequences that are certain to follow. I can't tell Him the truth. I won't be the first to speak, and He absolutely knows it.

The King of Demons beckons me with His thick finger. My feet move forward against my better judgment and kick His knees apart to stand between his legs. For a moment, I pretend He isn't the Devil. I pretend He's a delicious victim who'll split me in two the second I fuck him. Pretending used to be easier before I became a fucking traitor to my own deity.

He grips my hips as I straddle his lap, continuing my dance. "Tell me, Toby"—He draws out that stupid nickname in a way that makes me want to wring his throat—"what's a gal like you doing in a place like this?"

My shrug is as unforgiving as the look in his eyes. "It pays the bills."

"What bills?" The Devil's throaty chuckle sends vibrations through me. "Don't I compensate you well enough?"

"Beauty and power don't keep a roof over my head."

He hums thoughtfully, digging his fingertips into my skin and pulling me dangerously close. "How about I grant you the power of Persuasion?"

"And risk owing your stupid son a favor? Pass." My contempt for the Demon of Debauchery is unparalleled, to say the least, especially after the past few days. Inheriting a power from him would only complicate my sordid status in the Underworld.

"Now that isn't a very nice thing to say."

"I'm not very nice to begin with."

"I know all too well. It's one of my favorite things about you."

I roll my eyes along with my hips, pressing hard against the growing length beneath me. For a moment, a fleeting moment, I wonder what my boss' true form would feel like. Is He as demonic as the cursed creatures He sired? Does He have a ghastly appendage with twelve eyes and six mouths? Curiosity tempts me, but I'm grateful for His penchant for human possession.

"You already know why I work here." I run my fingers up from His chest to His neck. "It's easier to kill in establishments like this. The clientele is positively rotten. Plenty of demented souls, just for you."

"Such a good little witch," He purrs into my ear. "How many have you got for me tonight?"

There's no use in lying. Our bond leaves little room for secrets, and there's already one I'm barely keeping hidden. Nevertheless, I persist. "Sixty-nine."

A heart-fluttering, lopsided grin leaves me eager for more as I toy with the husk of this possessed patron. I relish in His hum of approval, forgetting my woes for a second as His praise invigorates me.

It's short lived.

"Why are *you* here, boss?"

The Devil leans his head against the booth, tilting it as His eyes drink in my form. "I've missed you."

I roll my eyes again. "Bullshit."

He sits up then, pulling me closer. His mouth finds my neck, sharp teeth biting down with little forgiveness. A cool breeze hits my skin as my blood flows like a crimson river between my breasts. My breath hitches as I fight back a groan, gripping His shoulders while I ride His clothed lap. Sex will help me forget. Sex *always* helps me forget.

He reaches beneath me, fingers digging into my ass to lift and yield Him space. The soft sliding of metal snaps in my ears as my possessed patron pulls out His throbbing cock. I shudder above Him, feeling His fingers tug at my flimsy undergarments and pull them to the side as He sheathes himself to the hilt in a single movement. The patron is large—*deliciously* so, just as I imagined—and stretches me with every inch of His girth. My moans pierce the walls, drowning in the heavy, distorted guitar riffs blaring from the speakers. Those void-like eyes watch me as I writhe and grind, as I take the pleasure I so desperately need. His thumb trails along the delicate line of blood seeping from my neck, coating it crimson before He shoves it into my mouth. I accept it, eagerly sucking and swirling my tongue around the digit, mewling at the metallic taste of my own blood.

His hands return to my ass, cupping each cheek to control the speed of his thrusts. He pounds into me, coaxing my orgasm with every strike. In and out. Out and in. I'm an awful, pitiful mess of breathless pleas and shallow moans, begging for my release, seeking the permission I so desperately crave. He makes one final, vigorous thrust, drawing an ache so delicious that I know my orgasm is inevitable.

And then, he stops.

The infinite black pits of His gaze nearly ruin me. Those eyes are hungry, deranged as His chest rises and falls with heavy breaths. I whine above Him, rolling my hips to encourage movement, to resume our sinful dance. Instead, He pins my arms behind my back with one hand, and His mouth sweeps up my neck once more.

"I've heard a rumor," He finally growls into my ear, "that you've been cavorting with demon hunters."

The statement cuts devastatingly deep. My movements falter, pausing at His…rather astute accusation. He grabs my chin between his forefinger and thumb, forcing eye contact. There's no turning back now. "My 'stupid sons' tell me *everything*." There's a devilish grin upon his lips fitting for the King of Demons. "Seems like the same can't be said for you, my little firestarter."

I swallow hard, muscles tensing against His grip. "I've got a plan."

"Do you?" His fingers trail up my sides and cup the swell of my breast. He licks the line of blood upon my skin, humming with satisfaction, leaving me torn between arousal and fear—His favorite method. "Your heartbeat tells me otherwise."

"Hearts tend to do that when a girl's close to coming."

A chuckle rumbles through his chest. "That smart mouth of yours is getting you into far too much trouble lately. There was another rumor, you know, one that nearly shattered me." His love for theatrics never ceases to irritate me, but my irritation is shadowed by crippling anxiety as my heart continues to pound in my throat. "You allowed one of my sons to be banished by a hunter."

Our eyes meet once more, and my skin burns beneath His gaze. His is a tempest, fierce and unyielding, but I refuse to relent, no matter the terrors that fill me. "They'll find a way back."

"Wrong answer."

Lucifer's nails dig into my hips, flipping me around and onto my stomach against the crusted armrest as he drives into me again. I cry out as he grabs a fistful of my hair, jolting my neck back. His other finger loops beneath my skin-tight choker, pulling so hard, I struggle for air. Under any other circumstance, I'd revel in asphyxiation, but tonight, I fear for what is left of my damned life.

"You've never given me a reason to question your loyalty, Toby." His growl is echoing, unholy. "Not until last year, that is. And now, with these nasty rumors circulating…you understand my hesitation. I can't afford to take any more risks." He pulls my hair harder—so hard, I fear my vertebrae may snap. "You remember our agreement, don't you? Six sunrises and six sunsets."

I try to nod, to remind him I'm still His, but his grip renders me useless. "Let's sweeten the deal, then. Since you *love* spending time with demon hunters, why don't you add their souls to your plunder?"

My words are caught in my throat. "I-I've never killed a demon hunter before."

"We have that in common, then. Alas, *I* can't kill them. *You,* however, can. And you *will*. Add them to your thousand."

The Devil releases me with a vigorous jolt and withdraws himself. I fall to the floor, crumbling as I reach for my throat to steady my breathing. I imagine I look like a helpless puppy, a pathetic creature cowering in the face of her master. The mere image ignites something primal within me. I force myself to stand, to face my boss with my chin held high. His dark gaze penetrates me, challenges me. I finally will myself to speak.

"You'll get them all by Halloween."

Lucifer's eyes soften, if only for a moment. His burly hand caresses my cheek, thumbing the single tear that escapes my eye. I hold onto my resolve, hold onto whatever dignity I have left. And then, He leans in closer…

"I better," He whispers, His lips a mere inch from mine. "Or I'll see to it that you'll never live to betray me again."

TRACK TWENTY THREE
ANGEL

TRACK TWENTY-THREE
ANGEL

THE MORNING SUN PEEKS THROUGH THE WINDOWS AS I stalk through the Roosevelt's hallways. Thick-heeled leather boots cling to my thighs, clunking heavily against the carpet as I walk towards my prize. There's a hesitance in my gait, a nervousness fluttering in my stomach. The Devil's unexpected addition to my already impossible task weighs heavy on me, and while I'd love nothing more than to dispose of the demon huntress and apprentice, I need to remain calm. Calculated. Discreet.

The clock keeps ticking. The hours continue to pass, and I have less than two days left to acquire 500 souls and kill three demon hunters. The odds seem further from my favor than they did at the beginning of this wretched affair.

My last-ditch effort in this eleventh hour is Lovejoy's

bargain: his divine blood. The rarest of magical commodities. A coveted component that not even the charlatans of the Underground Black Market possess. And it's almost mine.

My feet follow the maze of twisting halls and finally arrive at Lovejoy's hotel room. Not two days ago, I found myself standing outside this same door, indulging in my favorite game of seduction, breaking the last bit of resolve the hunter had left. Now, I find myself in a precarious position, playing a game I favor far less: the game of survival.

My quick, rhythmic knock on the door leaves me in a flux of impatience and angst. Chipped black nails tap against my thigh as I shift my weight from leg to leg. My mind becomes a restless clock, ticking what's left of my life away and leaving only the sharp bite of consequence. In seconds, I'm met with the cold, verdant stare of one demon hunter's apprentice, whatever his name is.

"Move aside, worm."

He crosses his arms over his chest. "I have a name."

"And it's of no importance to me." I attempt to push past him, but he remains still, using his abnormally tall frame to intimidate me. "Move."

He leans against the door, a small smirk twisting at his lips. "He's busy right now."

Calm. Calculated. Discreet. Oh, how the urge to kill the little urchin tickles my insides. It could be quick; his life would be mine in seconds, followed by that Mireya woman and…

Hushed whispers and a distressing exchange from inside the room capture my attention. I can hear them, my demon hunter and *his* demon huntress. Their voices are muffled, but key words strike my ears like a bell, words that tease my curiosity, words that turn the corners of my lips upward in a knowing smirk. *Threat. Vanquish. Legend.*

"Let her in, Jeremy."

The apprentice clenches his jaw and drops his arms to his side. I bump his shoulder with my own as I trudge past him, entering the demon hunter's den. The image of a wolf in sheep's clothing walking into an unsuspecting deer thicket invades my mind, and I imagine that's what this looks like: a cloaked, *deadly* predator entering the sanctuary of three helpless creatures, physically spent and licking their wounds. Under other circumstances, the three of them could best the wolf, what with their sharp antlers and substantial hooves, but this wolf has the upper hand. She has them played.

I enter at the tail end of their rather fascinating conversation. Lovejoy and Mireya stand at the round dining table, hunched over a cluttered mess of parchment and tomes. I raise an eyebrow when I catch a glimpse of their fixation, briefly noting gruesome illustrations and archaic texts. I find myself mildly intrigued, wondering what secrets are sealed in ink, what facts the Order *thinks* they know about the Underworld.

But before I can decipher a single syllable, Mireya abruptly shuts her book. She eyes me with skepticism, a darkness growing in her eyes as she scrutinizes my form. Her aura is unmistakable—stark white, if not a bit dimmed and tarnished from her time in the Underworld. An unholy prison does that—it breaks even the most steadfast of souls.

Lovejoy straightens his posture beside her, neck and shoulders tense. He's a vision of pure, emotional turmoil, torn between his feelings for me and the façade he wears for the sake of his colleagues. Tensions rise thick in the air, thunderous amidst the silence. I shift my weight again, shoving my hands into my coat pockets and flashing the demon huntress a forceful sham of a smile.

"October, this is Mireya Fargo." *Fargo.* The name he gave me at the beginning of this whole mess. How foolish could I have been to believe Fargo could be a man?

The huntress keeps her distance but regards me with a curt nod. She's a vision in head-to-toe black, a frilled lace collar stretching up the sweep of her long, thin neck, covering the dark ink that classifies her divinity. An ornate silver cross glimmers at her chest, a symbol of her faith, likely an amulet of protection against those she so dutifully hunts.

"I am grateful for your efforts in rescuing me." There's a rhythmic hint in her accent, a crispness reminiscent of medieval Catholicism and the Spanish Inquisition. She may be the oldest creature in the room besides me. "The Order is indebted to you."

Hell on Earth, do *all* these demon hunters have something thick and pointy lodged in their asses? Their formalities and eloquence are enough to bore me to tears.

"Yeah, about that debt—"

Lovejoy clears his throat, shifting his weight, tired eyes suddenly wide and tense. A warning. "Why don't we speak privately?"

I can't bear to look him in the eye. I shrug, feigning indifference as best as I can. I hear him mutter something to his companions, an order of some sort, and he repeats my name, escorting me toward the foyer. Dread returns like a suffocating shroud. I'm not ready to be alone with him, not yet. Not after last night.

His voice is rich and rough, laced with exhaustion. "I never thanked you for what you did last night."

Gratitude has never been a vice of my choice, and my nerves prickle beneath my skin at the sentiment. Instead, I raise my chin, holding onto any ounce of dignity I've got left. "I've come to collect my reward."

The admiration in his eyes fades, quickly replaced with foreboding. A hint of panic clouds his features, jaw clenching and neck tense. Oh, how he wears his heart on his sleeve.

"Not here," he murmurs, voice low enough for only me to hear.

"I won't leave until I get what's owed to me."

He clears his throat again and places his hand at the small of my back, ushering me through the foyer and toward the exit. I notice his hand swipe an item from one of the tables, the same that once housed countless accessories and texts relevant to his profession. He announces our leave to his apprentice and…*colleague*, and within moments, we're alone in an endless hallway of timeless elegance.

I fold my arms over my chest, observing him with a molten stare that practically has him squirming.

"You remember my terms," he mutters in a voice so low, so husky, that something tugs at my insides. The familiar pull. The delicious anticipation of our twisted, sordid affair.

"Yeah, yeah." I wave my hand dismissively. "Don't tell a soul."

"October, I'm serious. No one can ever know."

"You bore me with your reminders. Hand it over."

Hesitation haunts his chocolate-brown eyes. He fumbles with an object in his hand, fingers tightening as if it was an anchor tethering him to reality. To his ethics. His virtue. With a sharp inhale, he reveals an empty crystal vial, larger than the small, overpriced potions stocked at the apothecary. My eyes narrow in skepticism.

"I'll need to give you a fresh draw. It's more potent that way."

"How thoughtful," I muse, flashing him a feigned grin. He reaches for one of the many blades slotted into his thigh holsters, but an impish smirk adorns my lips as a wicked idea comes to mind. "Allow me," I practically purr, taking his palm into my hand. "I'm something of an expert when it comes to blood."

Lovejoy swallows hard, nodding. Confliction weighs heavy upon him, dripping like sweat off his brow. He knows the consequences of our exchange. He *knows* the risks of our relationship. And yet, he remains so deliciously vigilant, so desperate to cling to his word, even if it means betraying his God. His sins won't haunt him for long.

"Humor me." I pull my hand back. "Why don't we go somewhere a little more private? You wouldn't want your friends catching us in the act—or any other wandering eyes, for that matter. Blood sacrifice isn't exactly popular amongst mortals. Or clean."

"Right," he breathes out.

I lead him down the hall and towards the nearest fire exit to ascend a never-ending flight of stairs. We walk in painful, heavy silence, the memory of last night weighing heavy upon both of us. Those heated questions, the perilous accusations… The game has certainly changed, and I can't wait to get this over and done with.

Lovejoy opens the heavy rooftop door for me, beckoning me outside. The sun peeks from behind parting clouds, bright and blinding amid crisp, cool air. The view of the city is breathtaking, of course, but not nearly as beautiful as it is at night, when the lights twinkle like a thousand stars in the Hollywood sky. The burnt Observatory greets us from a distance, thin clouds of smoke circling above in a delicious reminder of last night's job well done.

Lovejoy surveys the rooftop, noting every potential vantage point, every potential for subterfuge. He nods to the left, finding the perfect quiet spot for our exchange. Once again, the hunter reaches for his blessed dagger.

"Put that thing away." I eye the blade. Its holy-imbued magic radiates in his hand, nearly blinding me. "We both know it won't make you bleed. Not enough to fill that vial, anyway. I've got something of my own."

He eyes me inquisitively. My hands meet with my ear, removing the scorpion-shaped earring that hooks around my cartilage.

"You can't be serious."

I raise an eyebrow at him. "You're not afraid of a little earring, are you, babe?" The term of endearment, once habitual and coltish, now stings on my tongue. It feels foreign, wrong, but that's all the more reason to use it as I see fit. After all, I'm meant to act like nothing has changed. His trepidation weighs heavy in his gaze, and so I flash him a playful smile. "Trust me."

Lovejoy licks his lips, fingers wiggling. I reach for his wrist and tug him closer to me as I take the post of my earring and jab it into his hand. His muscles tense with the contact, but he doesn't let out a sound. I imagine he has had many painful stabs over the years; my little familiar's poke is nothing in the grand scheme of things. He'll know his true sting in no time…

"Bleed for me," I whisper in Hellspeak, the tongue of my infernal inheritance. I drag the post deep through his tough skin, drawing a sanguine line down the middle of his hand.

Scarlet flows from the Nephilim's palm, shades brighter than that of human blood. It gleams like garnets under the harsh rays of fall sunlight—mesmerizing, *enchanting*. Flecks of luminescence dance against my leather jacket, both beautiful and unsettling. Divine blood is something of a magical marvel, more striking than any natural phenomena known to mankind. Tension releases from my weary muscles as warmth fills me with relief at the notion that I might just survive past October 31st.

My fingers beckon the vial from Lovejoy's grasp. He hands me the flask, hovering his bleeding fist over its opening. His eyes remain glued to the blood that spills, coating the once crystal-clear glass in thick, holy ichor.

If the legends are true, a mere drop of divine blood can bring the dead back to life. Protect one from the greatest evils. Provide power unimaginable. It will make for one hell of a bargaining chip. Lovejoy's lifeline is the last Hail Mary, my only salvation.

Do it. There's a voice in my head, like velvet dipped in poison. It's a voice that knows my deepest desires, knows the gravity of my pursuits. A voice that has frequented my mind for a thousand years, one I'd be a fool to ignore.

Kill him. The world around me blurs, and the voice sinks deeper into my mind, embedding itself into my psyche. *You could end this all right now.*

The voice is right. I could cast Nero's awakening spell, order him to strike the hunter as I siphon his divinity and claim his soul. I could reanimate his corpse, send him to do my bidding, kill his wretched friends, and then leave them all to rot. Hell, I could then raise all three if I wanted—it would certainly make my job *that much* easier.

But something pulls me back; maybe it's the feeling of his hand in my grasp—the soft valley between his knuckles, the way his thumb ever so lightly brushes mine in soothing circles. Or the way he bites down on his bottom lip, grinding his teeth into the tender flesh. Lips that have pleasured me for decades. Lips I've savored like a final, forbidden feast. Perhaps it's that look in his eyes, the one that sends a shiver up my spine, that pulls at every carnal desire, every unanswered wish…

I can't kill him, not now. Not while his vitality rests in my hands. I'll have to find another way.

The Devil on my shoulder won't win today.

I squeeze out every ounce I can get before his skin inevitably begins to heal itself. He eyes me nervously, brows drawing closer as I twist the cap onto the flask and study its otherworldly nectar. The blood glows against its crystal containment, appearing more valuable than it ever has. A grin spreads upon my lips, and I bite back a triumphant laugh. I shove the vial into my innermost jacket pocket, tapping my leather for safekeeping.

"Pleasure doing business"—I nod at him—"as messy as it was."

I have no reason to linger, nothing tethering me to this rooftop, not even the voices inside my head. My shoes click against the concrete as I make my way towards the stairwell.

"October, wait."

I turn on my heel, minding him with a cocked eyebrow and vexed glance. I watch as he rubs his thumb into his once bleeding palm, likely soothing the dull ache of my incision. He saunters near me. "That's it, then?" I sneer at his question. "You're just going to leave?"

"That's what happens when a trade is fulfilled. I, for one, have better things to do than hang around a bunch of useless Nephilim who easily get outsmarted and kidnapped by their own prey—especially ones who can't banish a Prime without the help of their own enemy."

His brows arch with the slow grace of a man who isn't used to being delivered the cold, hard truth. The ground seems to quake beneath his steps, his fingers curling inward, knuckles white with rage. "You never stay in one place for too long, do you?" His voice rolls out from a rumble in his chest, deep and resonant, downright menacing. Something stirs within me then, a carnal curiosity, a deep, demented desire to test his limits.

My shoulders slump, yielding to the weight of my

indifference. "It's like I just said: our bargain's done. There's no sense in hanging around. Now, if you don't mind, I've got a pint of soupy ice cream waiting for me at The Starlight—and you've got an apprentice to train and a demon huntress to crawl back into bed with."

He lunges for me in a flash, and his fingers grip my neck. A burning sensation spreads, searing my throat beneath his grasp. He practically slams my body against the cool wall of the stairwell, gritty bumps of stucco prickling into my skin. I can't fight the breathy chuckle that escapes my lips.

"Ooh, did I hit a nerve, *babe*?" I coo at him, my voice a pitch higher against his tightening hold. "Did I insult your honor and virtue?" Chocolate-brown eyes blacken with every successful blow to his character. I see him under a different light now, the darkness I've rooted deep within him peeking through with every passing moment. What a beautiful specimen of a corrupted angel. "Careful, Lovejoy," I rasp with a sadistic grin. "Violence isn't nearly as easy to banish as Nightmares and Fear. You wouldn't want another Prime feeding off your many sins."

"The only sin I'm guilty of is loving a damned creature like *you*."

Silence shrouds us then, pressing in from all sides. Time seems to slow, his last words weighing heavy in the air, ringing in my ears on a loop. A warmth fills me, seeping in like a quiet intruder. It slips through the cracks, flowing through every vein, sending a flush of red across my chest and cheeks. The heat is…unfamiliar. Unsettling. It is not that of Hellfire, not like the magic burning within my bones or prickling at my fingertips. It's a bittersweet tension that battles my reluctance, my nature. And with every yearning glance, every shaky breath, my resolve dwindles.

And I fucking hate it.

"But I'll always be your best-kept secret, won't I?" I croak. The words come across more desperate than I'd like. They reveal a weakness I can't afford. I know if I give him an inch, he'll take the mile.

Lovejoy's grip loosens on my neck, his fingers trailing up to my jaw before tangling in my hair. He releases a heavy sigh, bowing his head in resignation. "As long as your heart remains in the shadows."

And so, here we stand, skin glistening under the harsh light of morning, bodies and minds connected as they have for so many years. Trembling. Aching. Desperately clinging to something—*anything*—that won't end this.

Lovejoy's hands cup my face, and his lips ghost along my jaw and cheek in a silent apology. "I know why you run, October. I think I've always known." My breath catches in my chest. Ice forms in my veins, crippling me as anxiety grows. He couldn't know… "Your soul craves isolation because that's what you think you deserve. Happiness is a prospect that terrifies you, and I'll never understand why."

My soul doesn't belong to me, I want to tell him. *That's why I run.*

Instead, I deflect. "I run because I've pissed off enough of the Primes and their Hellspawn to have made the infernal Most Wanted list. Don't read into it."

His lips curve in a delicate arch but are weighed down by a sorrow tugging at his brow. A gentle, almost pitiful sweetness lingers in his eyes, a look that says, 'I don't believe you, but I'll let you have this one.' His lips softly press against mine in a long, lingering, final kiss.

In many ways, it probably is.

"I'll destroy whatever is after you, October Winters," he whispers as the hustle and bustle of the Hollywood streets seem to muffle around us. "I will *hunt* them and I will *kill* them. I will spend the rest of my days fighting Hellspawn, demons, and even the Devil himself if it means you'll live another thousand years."

"Declan…" It's the first time I've called him by his first name since the night I met him in 1923. There's an ache in the word, a pleading, a longing. He hushes me as he pulls my forehead flush against his.

"I swear it, October," he whispers and kisses my hair. He pulls my face upward to look into his eyes, eyes that will forever haunt my dreams, long after he's gone. "Look at me. I *swear* it."

I want to believe him. I want to believe I can replace his soul with any other demon hunter, one of the cretins sent to bring my head to their God, but the Devil knows.

The Devil *always* knows, and there's no way he will let me live without killing my lover. After all, Declan Lovejoy's soul was doomed from the start.

This is my cross to bear.

I huff out a laugh and run a finger along his perfect jaw. His eyes search mine with such devotion and promise, it's almost difficult to hold his stare. "You're an angel, Declan Lovejoy. Too pure for this world, even with your occasional sins. But our 'forever' will only end in heartbreak, so don't ruin a good thing with promises neither of us can keep."

Lovejoy is silent as I slip out of his grasp. I smooth out my clothes, running my hand over my pocket to ensure the collateral's safety. I flash him a smirk, a silent gesture of thanks as I turn the knob of the door to the stairwell.

"October, wait," he beckons me once more. "There's something you need to know."

Lovely. I don't think I have it in me to hear another confession. Nevertheless, I gesture him to continue. "Mireya, she…" The name sounds demure upon his lips now, almost like a regret. As it should be. "She heard a rumor while being held hostage in the Underworld. A new lead—a new *threat*. We've informed the Order, and they've instructed us to turn our attention to it, effective immediately." The anticipation chokes me. A flash of that gripping conversation I overheard earlier comes rushing back.

Threat. Vanquish. Legend.

"She overheard the Primes discussing an immortal creature, a thresher of souls. It's a source of great evil and legendary power—" Shit. "—and it's been sent to the human plane to collect and deliver a thousand souls to Lucifer by All Hallow's Eve." *Shit.* "They called it the Devil's Second."

You've got to be *fucking* kidding me.

WHAT'S YOUR PLAN?
SO YOU DON'T HAVE A PLAN.
SHOW UP. PARTY HARD. PEACE OUT.
TRACK TWENTY FOUR
KILLING IN THE NAME
DOES IT LOOK LIKE I HAVE TIME TO COME UP WITH A PLAN?

TRACK TWENTY-FOUR

KILLING IN THE NAME

Lovejoy's words echo through my mind, a relentless reminder of the truth I can't escape. That deep, velvety voice—once a comfort, now a torment—repeats the damn moniker.

Again.

And again.

And again.

Each repetition carves deeper, hollowing me out until it forms a hole in my stomach.

He wasn't supposed to find out. He was *never* supposed to find out. It was the one rule I swore I'd never break with him, the secret I guarded more fiercely than my own damned soul.

I've slipped through the cracks for eighty years—a lifetime for some, but a blink for me. My wits were my weapon, my lies my armor, but it all came crashing down the minute he said the words.

The Devil's Second.

Rage burns through me, sweltering beneath the nonchalance I feign. The worst part of all of this is not that I fucked up or misjudged my actions. No—it's the fucking demons, the same vile creatures I've loathed since the moment I first laid eyes on them nine centuries ago.

They ratted me out, intentional or not. After everything I've done, every soul I've delivered, those dirty bastards couldn't keep their fucking mouths shut, and now…

Everything's going to Hell.

Including me.

Golden kernels of buttery goodness fall from the paper bag in my arms as I shuffle down a narrow aisle in a cramped movie theater. Reagan and I squeeze past knees, earning agitated, nasty remarks from engrossed audience members.

"Move along, ladies," they groan.

"Aren't you a little late?" they jab.

I ignore them, of course, just as I ignore the woes of the dead that seem to follow me everywhere I go. But I definitely clock them on my kill list.

For a moment, we're just a couple of pretty faces amidst the matinee crowd, indulging in a discounted midday showing of this spooky season's promised blockbuster. How delightfully mundane.

If only they knew who—*what*—walks among them.

The velvet seats creak as we sink into them, the sound lost to the blaring speakers of the Vista movie theater.

"Was the pizza necessary?" Reagan's lip curls in disgust as she hands me the cardboard box of melted cheesy goodness. "It smells like feet."

"Yeah, you'd know," I mutter with a mouthful of popcorn. "Look, if we're gonna lure demon hunters to their death *and* commit mass murder in a movie theater, I don't want it to be on an empty stomach. I haven't properly eaten in days—or gotten a decent night's sleep, for that matter."

"You would if you'd stop dicking around with that hunter."

"Mind your own business," I deflect, digging into the pizza box. My gaze slices through the theater, cataloging every shadowy corner and dimly lit aisle.

Twenty...twenty-three...twenty-five humans at most.

A pitiful showing, but time's ticking, and I need to go for the kill.

"What's your plan?" the she-demon whispers.

I shrug. "Show up. Party hard. Peace out."

I can practically feel the disappointment radiating off her, but it doesn't faze me. "So you *don't* have a plan."

"Does it look like I have time to come up with a plan? I just need you to lift your glamor. The rest will come."

"How the hell will the Nephilim find me?"

I flash her a knowing glance. "They've got this weird

demonic tracker signal tattoo shit on their necks. It burns when a demon is near."

"Yikes. I imagine the burning never ceases in a city like this."

I shrug. "The minute you drop your glamor, they'll sense you. They're on high alert, now more than ever. And thanks to me and my questionable taste in men, there's a bunch more of them crawling around. Just make sure you get the fuck out of here the second they come in."

Reagan hesitates for a moment, her glamoured eyes filled with equal parts concern and defiance. "I'm not afraid of demon hunters."

"Don't be stupid. You have no defensive powers, and I can't protect you *and* save my own ass."

Reagan remains seated, her glamor a masterpiece of deception. Gone are the telltale signs of her demonic nature—no horns piercing through flame-red hair, no magma-glowing veins pulsing beneath crimson skin, no serpentine tail coiled in anticipation. To the untrained eye, she's just another face in the crowd, an innocent out for a night of entertainment.

In a matter of seconds, her wriggling fingers lift the demonic magic that cloaks her Hellish features. She flashes me a proud smirk and wink before we both settle into our chairs and indulge in our greasy treats.

It's only a matter of time now.

Moments later, as if on cue, two new figures enter the

barely-filled theater, their auras shining as bright as the sun on a hot summer day. Dread, cold and viscous, floods my veins, turning my blood to ice. A plan would have been nice, but I'm not much of a planner—improvising is *far* more chaotic and oh *so* much fun.

My eyes scan the theater, noting every vantage point, every dark corner. A flicker of movement catches my eye: a tiny sprinkler, barely visible against the flash of the silver screen. And just like that, a plan forms in my mind.

It's insane, downright mental, but no one would question an electric mishap in a world so dependent on technology.

The hunters take their seats in the theater, one toward the front, one in the middle. Their auras taunt me, burning bright along with the gunshots flashing on the screen. With lightning quickness, I slip out of my seat and make my way towards the theater exit. The double doors remain closed, and my hands meet with the push bar. I channel my fire magic and melt the metal until it seals the exit shut.

No one's coming in.

No one's getting out.

Not until the deed is done.

Reagan eyes me as I return to our seats in the top most row, and I stand tall with my hands outstretched. "You're not gonna—"

"I sure as fuck am."

My fire magic has always felt like a volcanic eruption,

a disaster so organic and devastating, it can only be described as natural. There's a slow rumbling in my chest as my magic stirs, a slow pressure creeping through my skin. My palms grow hot, almost feverish, as the power grows. When I finally unleash my flames, it's like the volcano explodes.

Then, there's fire. Everywhere. On every seat. Every aisle. Wrapping around every innocent human, turning their bodies to ash. The scent of burnt flesh assaults my nostrils and fills me with the familiar lightheadedness that often follows my inferno. And their screams… Oh, how their screams thrill me.

It's euphoric, like a drug, pulling at my insides and begging for more.

The energy surges through me, a food of pure power that makes every nerve sing. My skin tingles with electricity, my hair standing on end as if charged by an invisible storm. The air around me crackles and shimmers, distorting like a blazing wave. The once dark theater is now ablaze with my flames, destroying everything in their path.

I'm my strongest when I use my magic, and I've never felt more powerful than I do at this moment.

The Nephilim, however, do not miss the opportunity to strike at me.

I step in front of Reagan, shielding her from their line of sight. The incessant, shrill ringing of a fire alarm echoes throughout the theater, and those handy little sprinklers turn on, raining water over us. It's a welcome mist at first, cooling the heat rising through my skin but quickly dampening my style—pun intended. Floating blonde locks moisten into twisted strands against my face. The sealed double doors shudder violently, rattling in their frames as theater security pounds from the outside. A dangerous grin creeps upon my face as I force my flames higher up the walls.

Reagan grabs my arm from behind me. "Tober, incoming—"

A Nephilim's blade whirls past my ear and it lodges itself in the wall with a dull thud. In one fluid motion, I thrust my palm forward, unleashing a searing bolt of flame. It strikes true, hurling the divine loser backwards over rows of velvet-clad theater seats.

As he crashes, I extend my other hand, fingers contorting as I channel the dark energies of soul siphoning. Tendrils of shadow snake towards the fallen warrior, latching onto his essence. The process drags on for far longer than with mere mortals, but what did I expect? He's divine, after all.

The air crackles with ethereal resistance as I slowly drain his spirit. Each moment feels like an eternity, and the Nephilim's soul fights my efforts with every fiber of its being.

Soon, but not soon enough, the light of the hunter's aura burns out like a light bulb. His body shrivels like a raisin, skin wrinkled and cheeks hollowed as his mouth remains open in a permanent 'o.' His divine soul, on the other hand, remains a corrupted treasure, glowing and pulsing at my feet.

The souls of the burnt humans swirl throughout the theater, lost and desperate for salvation. Their reaping will be eons easier than that hunter's, and I eagerly await the relief that will come as I continue to fill my quota. I crack my knuckles and resume my harvest.

The second Nephilim isn't as brave as her partner. Her eyes never leave mine, watching in certain horror as I siphon each innocent soul, sucking their essence into my palms. White, ghost-like tendrils travel towards me, forming multiple glowing soul orbs at my feet, ready for Nero's stinger.

"Why are you doing this?" the Nephilim asks, tears forming in her awe-struck gaze. I see it in her eyes: the gears turning, the realization hitting her. She knows who I am. She *has* to. And the truth leaves her paralyzed with fear.

I shoot her a playful look and flick my wrist in her direction, using my telekinesis to knock her off her feet. My heeled boots thud against the sticky movie theater floor as I saunter closer to my divine victim.

I crouch down, looking down at the pathetic excuse for a demon hunter, cocking an eyebrow. "Because it's easy. Because it's *fun*. Because humans were put on this earth to play with. To corrupt. To feed to Lucifer's sons. And your kind? Well, you're just another stick in the mud, set out to destroy what my employer has worked so hard to build. You want to know a little secret?" I lean in closer, and I can see my flames reflecting in her wide, horrified eyes. "Nothing brings me more pleasure than sacrificing the innocent in exchange for power, praise, and the pretty little things that come with them."

With a final surge of my unholy magic, the soul harvest is complete.

At my feet, a second soul orb of divine warrior pulses with an ominous glow. Two down, one more to go.

"Peace out, scrub."

I collapse into a theater seat behind me, the worn cushion exhaling a puff of dust as I land with a heavy thud. With a flick of my hand, my fire disappears, and the fire alarm ceases along with the sprinklers. Finally, silence.

My lungs burn, each ragged breath a reminder of the chaos I've endured. Five days of non-stop scuffles has left me bone-weary and soul-sick. I could use another year-long vacation—this time, without magical handicaps.

A shell of a body lays limp in the seat next to me, burnt to a crisp in all its ashen glory. Reagan kicks the corpse off the velvet, watches as it dissolves into dust on the ground, and takes a seat. I avoid her stare, avoid the sheer and utter look of judgment that inevitably comes with an awkward silence like this.

"Looks like you're not safe on these streets anymore, doll face."

I wipe the sweat off my brow with my leather sleeve, leaving a smear of something darker—blood or undead residue, I'm not sure. "You don't say."

My fingers tap a rapid pattern against the sticky arm rest, a silent summons. Nero, ever attentive, trots across the red velvet seats. He reaches my knee and pauses, his stinger twitching in anticipation.

"Go on, bud. Do your thing."

With eerie precision, Nero begins to gather the remainder of the soul orbs scattered around us. His pincers click softly as he absorbs each one, the theater growing darker with each vanished bulb.

"How many?" I ask him, my breath coming in ragged gasps.

Nero's response echoes in my mind: *465 remaining*.

"Fuck," I mutter, leaning my head against the seat with an exasperated groan. How can I *still* have that many left?

"That bad?" Reagan slides an extra-large fountain drink my way, its straw bent and twisted like a consolation prize gone wrong. Her voice, usually laced with mischief, now carries a weight of concern. "October, you need to talk to *him*."

The emphasis on 'him' sends an irritable chill down my spine. I snatch the drink and take a swig, desperate to quench my thirst. A sickly sweet taste hits my tongue— blegh, root beer. I grimace. "Not a chance."

"It's the only way you'll be able to reap without

turning too many heads. A dive bar here, a movie theater there—those look like happy accidents. But a few hundred at once?" She shakes her head, her voice dropping to a whisper. "You won't just risk exposure with the humans and tip off a couple of Nephilim—you'll piss off the Primes too. Hell, you already have."

I open my mouth to argue, but she cuts me off.

"This may be the City of Angels, but don't forget who *really* runs this town."

I lean back again, feigning nonchalance, but Reagan *still* isn't done. She leans in closer, her voice a low hiss.

"I know you think you walk on water, that your fancy little title makes you untouchable"—her lips curl into a sardonic smile—"but this is LA, babe. The big leagues. This game has a different set of rules. Don't act like you don't know that. For someone who puts herself so high above humans, you're nothing but a mirror of their worst qualities—the very thing you claim to despise."

I shoot her a hateful glance. As if sensing my unease, a slight movement ripples at my knee, and Nero's obsidian exoskeleton gleams under the flashing silver screen as he scuttles onto my palm. The she-demon's not wrong, and my silence only proves that.

"Your hubris is going to continue biting that pretty little ass of yours if you don't start taking this shit seriously."

"Hate rules," I grunt, my eyes fixed on the scorpion as he curls into my hand.

Reagan watches Nero with a mix of fascination and disgust. "Yeah, well, from where I'm sitting, rules are all that's standing between you and eternity." Her gaze flicks from Nero to me. "No one's exempt, not even the Devil's Second and her creepy little pet."

"He's not a pet," I correct her, a small smile tugging at my lips. "He's my familiar. There's a difference. And we've been through way worse."

The truth behind Reagan's words sows a seed of dread even I can't shake. I stroke Nero's back with my knuckle, feeling a spark of our shared magic. The bond is as unwavering as the day I stumbled upon him in that lonely sea cave all those centuries ago.

I was just a kid then—thirteen, friendless, with a whole village worth of hatred on my shoulders. The world felt vast and empty and I was drowning in its indifference, but then there was Nero, a little emperor scorpion rising from the black sands I'd known my whole life. This tiny creature, with its six little eyes and eight little legs, dared to look at me and saw something worth sticking around for.

He didn't run when my magic flared, didn't cower when the darkness inside me reared its ugly head. He simply…stayed. In a world determined to push me away, Nero pulled me close. The day I lost him was the day I lost a part of myself.

But when the Devil brought him back to life, I was reborn. I became the witch I was meant to be.

In this fleeting moment, between demon hunter scuffles, soul harvests, zombie raising, and the fight for my immortal life, the paltry truth bites at my core:

In Nero, I found more than a familiar. I found home.

And he's all I've got.

TRACK TWENTY FIVE
LAST RESORT
WELL, WELL. IF IT ISN'T MY FAVORITE LITTLE SCORPION. COME SIT.
I'D RATHER EAT GLASS.
OH, DARLING. DON'T BE SO VANILLA. I COULD THINK OF FAR MORE EXCITING THINGS TO PUT IN YOUR MOUTH.

TRACK TWENTY-FIVE

LAST RESORT

I promised myself I'd never owe Cherry a favor.

I swore to myself I'd never stoop so low. I talked a big game out of pride and conceit and dug myself into a dark, grimy corner.

But that was before the game shifted beneath my feet, before there was a shiny prize for my bleach-blonde head, before the Nephilim caught wind of the Devil's Second.

Such promises feel a lifetime away, even if they were made yesterday, and the proverbial corner is only getting smaller. Now that I find myself with one day left to reap more than 400 souls, desperate times call for desperate measures.

Minutes from the heart of Hollywood, just a stone's throw away, is the West side, a place where success isn't chased. No, it arrives via chauffeur, champagne in hand and dressed to the nines, a polished, perfectly manicured façade in grave contrast to the neon grit soiling the promise of fame and fortune.

Hollywood is where stars are born. WeHo raises them in designer threads. And Beverly Hills? Well, that's where dreams go to die.

It's an ill-suited reality for a wretch like me.

The Sunset Strip, however? Now that's a scene I can get behind.

I trudge past a line of eager fans snaking down the sidewalk as I arrive at one of my old stomping grounds, The Roxy. I rub shoulders and elbows against countless humans dressed just like me, all dark leather and darker makeup. There's a sense of kinship with these poor souls, a thread tethering us together through music and a strange taste for the macabre. This scene sings to my cursed soul like no other. From Viking battle cries echoing through my youth to the guttural roars of thrash metal, music is my lifeblood, damned as I am.

Skirting the main entrance, I slink around back to a door known only to those with one foot in the supernatural world. Three sharp knocks later, the door swings open.

A she-demon appears in the doorway, cut from the same infernal cloth as my landlord—a succubus brave enough to show her true form in broad daylight. Her eyes flash with recognition, a smirk playing at the corners of her mouth as she steps aside.

I slip past her. The threshold is a gateway between the human and demonic worlds.

We wind through a labyrinth of dark corridors. Discarded stage equipment looms like forgotten idols while tangled cables snake across our path. Finally, we arrive at my destination: the green room. Even from the back, I can feel the energy pulsing from the theater. The reek of spilled beer and cigarette smoke claws at my nostrils while the thrum of bass and drums vibrates through the floor, climbing up my legs and settling in my chest.

The Roxy is more than just a venue—it's a touchstone where small town punks with big dreams test their worth. If they're lucky, they'll land it big, get picked up by some grubby agent with deep pockets and deeper transgressions. But the scene is growing, ever-changing. Rock music evolved from moral anarchy, chaos, and rebellion to that of something darker. Sorrow. Introspection. Heartbreak.

Undoubtedly influenced by the Primes.

And speaking of Primes… I have a date with the most lecherous one of all.

The green room door flings open, revealing my man— my *demon*—of the hour.

The Demon of Debauchery drapes across an expensive leather couch in his usual human glamour, four hopeless women clinging to his every move. They're a mess of giggles and liquor, tripping over their own feet, begging for a taste of what the Prime has to offer.

But he cares not for their begging and pleading. He only has eyes for me.

"Well, well, if it isn't my favorite little scorpion," Cherry's voice drips with honeyed venom as he pats his lap, a gesture both inviting and commanding. "Come sit."

"I'd rather eat glass." My eyes roll.

His lips curl into a mock pout, a well-worn mask within our infrequent affairs. "Oh, darling, don't be so vanilla. I could think of far more exciting things to put in your mouth."

I snag a chair near the bar, swinging it around with a fluid motion. Straddling it backwards, I drape myself over its backrest. It's a deliberate power play in his very own lair, a middle finger to the demonic hierarchy. And though my posture screams defiant with a hint of apathy, my intentions couldn't be clearer: I'm here to make a deal.

"To what do I owe the pleasure?" the Demon of Debauchery practically sings.

I exhale sharply, eyes narrowing to slits. The game begins. "You run this city."

"That I do."

"And I realize there are rules."

"Rules you constantly—*deliberately*—ignore."

"And ignoring the rules has…landed me in hot water lately."

He leans forward, intrigue dancing in his eyes. "My, my. Self-awareness, humility? From *you*? I'd sooner expect Hell to freeze over." His grin widens, predatory. "Out with it, Winties. What do you want?"

A sigh escapes my lips as I clench my jaw. "I request permission to reap this theater."

Cherry leans back into the sofa, the leather creaking beneath him. With a lazy flick of his wrist, he dismisses his fawning entourage. A pointed glance at the she-demon standing sentry by the door sets her in motion, herding the reluctant groupies out like a demonic shepherdess.

And so, we are finally alone.

"Oh, how the mighty have fallen."

His words send a shiver up my spine, threatening to suffocate what's left of my dignity. Before I have a chance to speak, he continues.

"You're October *fucking* Winters. The Devil's Second. A thousand-year-old pain in everyone's arse who plays puppet master with corpses and turns cities to ash on a whim. You've never asked for permission before. Why would you suddenly start asking now?"

I narrow my gaze. "I'm in a precarious situation."

"So precarious that you've resorted to asking one of the Big Thirteen for help. I thought you hated us."

"Oh, I do. There's nothing I'd like to see more than you and your brothers writhe and squirm like the worms you are, but...there's a bounty on my head. The Holy Order of the Nephilim has discovered me, and I find myself in need of five hundred souls in less than twenty-four hours."

"Seems to me like you've made your bed, and now you need to lay in it. Did you expect that you could just fuck that demon hunter and he'd never figure you out? You've grown sloppy, darling. Is your old age finally catching up with you?"

His words slice through me, igniting a fury that explodes into action. In seconds, I'm on my feet, the chair beneath me catapulted by my rage and magic. It hurtles through the air, a makeshift missile with four iron legs aimed at Cherry's heart.

But the Prime moves with viperine swiftness. He twists, a blur of motion, vaulting onto the couch as the chair splinters against the wall behind him. His dark eyes flash, predatory and gleaming. With a cruel flick of his fingers, invisible bonds lash out, snaking around my wrists.

The wicked ropes cinch tight, yanking my arms behind me with brutal force. My knees slam into the floor, the impact jarring through my bones. I'm pinned, panting, my own magic sputtering against his power.

Cherry looms over me, a smirk playing on his lips. I grunt as he stands beside me, running his black-painted nails up my neck and toward my ear cuff. I recoil from his touch, snapping my teeth in his direction, and *fuck*, how I long to rip him limb from limb.

"There's that ballsy little *bitch* I know and love," he

purrs, his voice a velvet threat. He yanks me from the floor and slams me flush against his chest. Long fingers, like heated iron brands, dig into the nape of my neck. He forces my head back, his grip a mockery of intimacy. Our eyes lock, and I see the inferno of his desire to dominate blazing in their depths. "Your little demon hunter isn't here to help you banish another Prime, and you're a fool to believe you could overpower one of the Devil's sons. I *may* be the Demon of Debauchery, but I *will not* let you *fuck me.*"

The threat drips from his lips, hot and heavy against my skin. He's *just* like his fucking father, using his dominion to overpower me. But I don't fear Debauchery as I fear the Devil, and I'm tired of falling victim to the whims of the damned.

I relax against his hold, and he releases me in one swift motion. He takes his seat back on the leather couch, arms folded neatly in his lap as his eyes rake over me once more.

"Let's try this again, shall we? What do you want?"

"I request permission to reap your theater," I repeat, slow and deliberate.

He gives the request some thought, mulling it over with pursed lips. "I'm sorry, darling, but it appears your needs interfere with my own. I have a business to run, after all, and I can't afford to shut down due to mass murder and bad press. You'll have to find a new solution —preferably one that doesn't inconvenience me."

"Then at the very least, offer me your protection."

"Protection? What makes you think I'd freely give you that?"

"I gave you two hunter essences for the price of one."

"You completed the assignment, bravo—but this isn't high school, and extra credit won't do you any favors."

"I help Reagan keep Bad Decisions afloat."

"Please, it's only been five days. Talk to me after the next end-of-year fiscal report."

"Hell, Cherry, stop fucking with me—what's it going to take?"

His diabolical smile reaches his ears. "I just want to see you beg, darling."

"You sick fuck."

"Do you expect anything less of me?"

I grow tired of this useless game. While I know it's in the nature of a demon to be infuriatingly stupid and difficult, my options grow more limited than before. I give one last effort, shooting him a pleading glare, a witch on the brink of desperation.

"I do not grant you permission to reap any of my establishments, nor do I offer my protection," he says, his fingers tapping together in a gesture reminiscent of prayer. I open my mouth to protest, but he raises a single, black-painted fingernail to silence me. "However, I *do* have a friendly suggestion."

"I'm listening." I grit my teeth.

He glances at one of his she-demons, nodding toward

her and directing his gaze at a stack of flyers. She sifts through them and grabs a single page covered in grotesque illustrations and bold lettering. She hands it to me, and I examine it closely, raising an eyebrow in skepticism.

"A Halloween rock concert?" I ask, scanning the band lineup.

"At Hollywood Forever," Cherry adds. "None of us—my brothers, our minions, or myself—will be there. The cemetery is a historic property, and the tickets have been sold out for months. The talent has been paid, and I've already made my millions. If, by chance, the concertgoers were to meet an unfortunate end due to some stage pyrotechnics gone wrong… Well, that would make for a juicy headline on November 1st, wouldn't it?"

I squint at the Prime. It seems too easy. "And what about insurance claims?"

"I'll leave it to Greed and Deception. Wouldn't be the first time they've cleaned up a supernatural mess."

"They'd never help me."

"Don't you worry about all that, darling. All you need to do is rise and reap."

The bait glistens, but the hook is too obvious. I know better.

"What do you want in return?"

"Call it a birthday gift. Making up for the 999 I missed over the years."

A sharp laugh rips from my throat. "It's never that

easy. You fucking cretins *never* play fair. It's always 'collateral this' and 'debt that.' All deadly deals and little pay off. Can't even take a piss without you vultures circling."

Cherry's molten gaze sears through me. "So hateful of your kindred."

"*Kindred?*" I spit. "We're about as related as a dog and a cockroach. The only thing we share is the air we breathe and the deity we serve."

The Demon of Debauchery's melodic, sinister laugh echoes through the green room, and the mere sound makes me want to tear his larynx right out of his throat.

"Darling, how many centuries must pass before you swallow the bitter truth? You are *just. Like. Us.* The only *real* difference is that my father hand-picked you rather than sired you. He raised you just the same: a cold-blooded killer. No remorse. No empathy. Just as depraved and wicked as the rest of us."

My nostrils flare as I clamp down my rage. Once was enough—he won't see me crack again.

Cherry's gaze sharpens, his chin lifting as he dissects me from his seated position. "You do, however, have a choice, one my brothers and I do not."

"Enlighten me," my words scrape through clenched teeth.

"You can choose to walk away from this… feeble existence you call life. To be free of the leash. Free of the voices, and the enemies, the deals." His eyes rake over my rigid form, and for a moment, I feel his influence melting away the tension in my shoulders, the tautness of my jaw, much like what I imagine *true* freedom must feel like. Calm. Carefree. Euphoric.

But I shake the feeling. I'll never allow a Prime to influence my actions again.

"I've had a taste of that freedom. It's nowhere near as blissful as you make it seem."

He meets my words with a quirk of his brow and a tug at his lips. "You can't have it all, my darling."

"I can sure as fuck try."

His lids droop into a hooded gaze, and for a moment —just a moment—the light at the end of the tunnel burns bright. "I've always liked you, Toby Winties. You'd make a deliciously wicked Debauchery demon."

"Over my dead body."

Cherry's laugh is a low, dangerous rumble. "Careful, my little scorpion. You and I both know that in our world, 'dead' is a…flexible term." He flashes me a playful wink. "Hollywood Forever Cemetery. Tomorrow night. Rise and reap."

Cherry's instructions hang heavy in the air. I turn on my heel and stride toward the exit, past his bodyguard, and get the fuck out of this demon-ridden theater.

The Roxy's pulsing beat fades as I burst into the night, inhaling fresh air that doesn't reek of demons and deals. The Sunset Strip grows dim as I put distance between myself and the West Side.

A few hundred more souls. A graveyard before midnight.

I smile as the promise of immortality dangles before me, just within reach.

Happy fucking birthday to me.

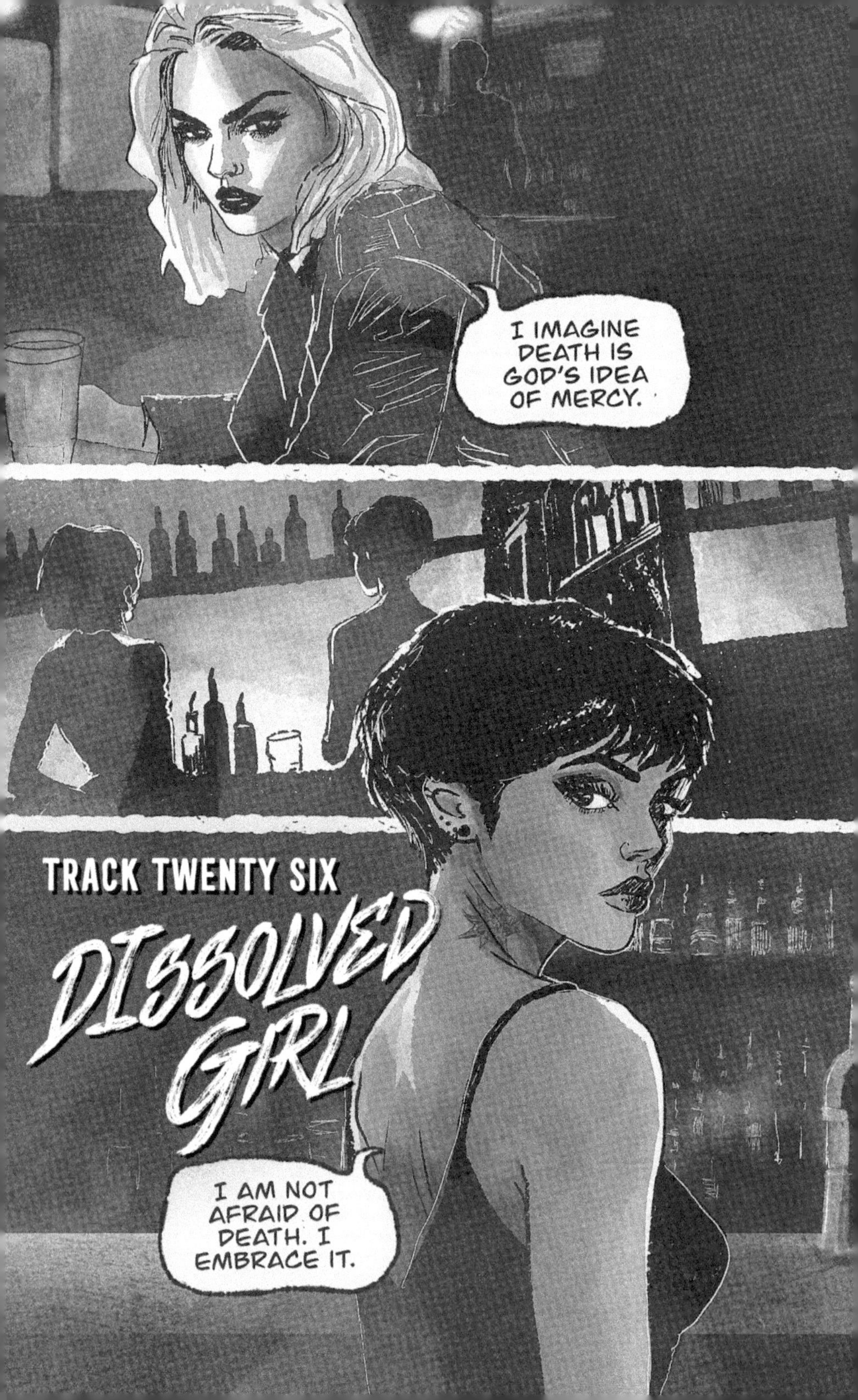

I IMAGINE DEATH IS GOD'S IDEA OF MERCY.
TRACK TWENTY SIX
DISSOLVED GIRL
I AM NOT AFRAID OF DEATH. I EMBRACE IT.

TRACK TWENTY-SIX

DISSOLVED GIRL

I'VE LEARNED HOW THE NEPHILIM WORK OVER THE years. I know they can communicate mentally, can teleport in a huff of white smoke, and can sense demons from a mile away thanks to that nifty little brand on their neck.

I'm not a demon—never have been, never will be—but despite that little factoid, I feel like I'm being watched. Not just by the Devil—though I know he's got his eyes and ears everywhere—but by the pious thorns in my side that now think they can take me down.

All I can hope, as I park my car in a public lot on Highland, is that the two I ran into earlier didn't have the chance to send out a little mental blast to their pathetic little friends.

I slip into another run-down Hollywood bar not too far from Bad Decisions. I could use a drink to wash down my bruised ego after my meeting with Cherry. I nod my head at the bartender, requesting a cold beer as I take my seat on a barstool. My attention snaps to the wall-mounted TV, its scratched screen flickering with the daily news.

"New details are emerging following the tragic fire at the Griffith Observatory. The preliminary investigation suggests it originated from the Tesla Coil exhibit and spread to the planetarium, and there were no survivors. A public memorial service will be held for the fallen. Our thoughts and prayers are with the families of those lost in this tragedy."

I bite the inside of my cheek to hold back a smile. Another mass reaping perfectly covered up—thank you, science. Thoughts and prayers can only go so far, and they won't save the souls resting uncomfortably in the stinger of my familiar.

The place is moderately packed for the afternoon, and I resist the urge to do a little killing. The show tonight will fill my quota, and I know I've earned a little birthday libation after the longest six days of my life.

For a moment, I feel peace, the calm before the storm. I try not to think about Lovejoy, the Devil's addendum, and the 465 remaining souls looming at the back of my head. Instead, I think about tomorrow.

I imagine watching the sunrise after my final reaping, long after my exchange with Lucifer is done. I can almost feel the sun on my skin as it rises over Mount Hollywood and casts its golden glow over a city I single-handedly brought to its knees in just six days. I think of where I'll go next, which city will fall victim to my dark magic, and what darker deeds the Devil has in store for me.

It's a beautiful reverie, brimming with hope and goodness—concepts that typically turn my stomach. But in this moment, it's my lifeline—the promise that after tonight's carnage, I might just glimpse another dawn.

Peace is fleeting as someone claims the barstool beside me. In this near-empty dive, some idiot dares to invade my solitude. Lovely. The bartender slides my beer over, asking my unwelcome neighbor for their order. Their voice tickles my memory, sending a chill down my spine.

A petite figure shifts in my peripheral vision. I stifle a groan as a silver cross catches the dim light. Mireya, that wretched little Nephilim, perches next to me—silent, stoic, and infuriatingly close.

"How'd you find me?" I ask, averting my gaze as I take a swig from my beer.

"It's my job to track down your kind."

"My *kind*?" I scoff. "Bad ass bitches with a great sense of humor?"

"Evil."

The word stings, and my fingers curl into my palm as I fantasize about gouging her sanctimonious eyes out. I force a vicious smile. "Must be exhausting, living with that broom shoved so far up your ass, you can taste wood. Bet that moral high ground gives you splinters."

Mireya's icy façade might fool the average mortal, but I see right through it. Behind that onyx stare, disdain simmers like barely contained brushfire. A tell-tale twitch pulses under her skin—right beneath that damned Hunter's Mark—a delicious sign of her fraying control. Oh, how desperately she's clinging to her composure. I, on the other hand, am practically salivating at the chance to shatter it completely.

"You demon hunters are all cut from the same cloth. At least Lovejoy's got the balls to dance with darkness when it suits him."

"What spell have you cast on him?" Her question hits like a slap and a punchline rolled into one. It's deliciously absurd and oh so very telling.

"The fuck are you talking about?" I almost choke on my own laughter.

She closes the gap between us, her petite frame coiled like a viper ready to strike. Her eyes narrow to slits, chin lifted in defiance. It's *almost* adorable—this tiny thing thinking she has cornered her prey. If only she knew. "I've known Declan Lovejoy for the better part of a century," Mireya hisses, each word dripping with venom. "Never have I seen him so… irrational. Desperate. What dark magic have you woven around him, witch?"

I can't help but let out a low, throaty chuckle. "Oh, honey. No magic required. He comes to heel all on his own… like a good little dog starved for affection."

The hatred in her eyes flickers then fades, replaced by

a dawning horror. I watch the pieces click into place behind those widening eyes. Now that the hook is in, I can't resist twisting it deeper, shredding whatever pride she has left.

"What's the matter, babe? Big bad huntress afraid of a little unfriendly competition?"

"You are no competition." The words come out in a quiet hush, slicing through me. "Declan is a good man, far too good for you. You don't deserve him."

"And you think *you* do?" Her silence speaks volumes and weighs heavy between us both. "I know more about Nephilim than you think. I know that God sent his angels to breed with humans to create you and then wrapped a shiny little metal prong collar around each and every one of your necks." I nod toward that tattoo, the Hunter's Mark that brands their skin. "I know your leader instills fear in every one of you, trains you to become merciless killing machines, void of love and compassion, just to do his bidding while he sits up in the clouds and watches you clean up the mess he made. And if you fail?" I pause, savoring the tension. "Well, I imagine death is his idea of mercy."

"Death is not our end, October." Mireya's voice remains steady and resolute. "We are not his pawns. We are his chosen warriors, sent to the Heavens upon our demise to continue his work from above. I am not afraid of death. I embrace it."

My lips curl into a sardonic smile. "Oh, baby girl.

Your blind faith is as comical as it is pathetic." I pause, letting the words hang in the air before adding with a hint of cruelty. "Let me tell you something about your 'God.' He and I go back. *Way* back. Long before you were a divine little tadpole in your father's ball sack. God spends his omniscient existence dangling false hope before his faithful sheep, but when the chips are down? You're shit out of luck. Chosen or not, your soul's as disposable as last week's garbage. Tell me, Miss *Fargo*," I purr, circling her like a predator, "where was your God when you were snatched by the Primes? How quickly did he turn his back on you in the face of a great evil?" I pause, allowing the metaphorical knife to twist further into her righteous dignity. "He does that, you know. Give up on those who are worth the most. Now, is that a God worth fighting for?"

When her coffee-brown eyes darken to obsidian, I know I've struck gold.

"You sound just like…" she whispers, voice trembling.

I step closer, towering over her petite frame. "Say it," I demand, voice dripping with dark anticipation. "Say His name."

Mireya swallows hard. "Lucifer."

The name hangs between us like a death sentence. My lips curl into a wicked grin, teeth gleaming in the dim light. "What can I say? I learned from the best."

I expect her to lunge at me, to wrap those puny little hands around my neck and choke me out, but she doesn't move. Instead, her eyes trail to my ear, and a small, barely-there smile forms upon her lips.

"That's an interesting earring you've got there." She nods at Nero in his dormant state. "Where did you get it?"

A chill slithers down my spine, and I feel the warmth leach from my face like water circling a drain. Her words hang in the air, heavy with implications that send alarm bells ringing in my head. Is this a trap designed to make me reveal my identity?

My lips part to speak, but I quickly close them as the acrid stench of sulfur assaults my senses. Both our heads whip around to face its source: a trio of low-level Debauchery demons sauntering nearby. Their attire leaves little to the imagination as they set their sights on the desperate and lonely bar patrons littered throughout the room. I shoot Mireya a knowing look, glancing at the mark on her neck that seems to almost glow in the presence of demons.

"Clean up on aisle 666," I chastise and take one last swig from my drink. "Wouldn't want to slack off on your higher calling just because God's sending you on a little side quest."

I leave the demon huntress to her own devices, hoping the convenient trio of Lessers will keep her busy long enough for me to prepare for tonight's final reaping. An analog clock marks 4:45 PM, and in a few hours, this will all be over. The Nephilim threat will just have to wait.

As I exit the bar, my body collides with another. Fiery red hair and amber eyes meet me with a mischievous grin.

"Another birthday present from Cherry," Reagan says, spiral horns nodding at the bar. "Couple of Lessers to keep your little Nephilim pests busy."

"Won't keep 'em busy for long."

"Probably not, but it's enough to get you out of this bar and off to that cemetery." She places a hand on my shoulder, those magma-like veins pulsing like a fiery river. "Happy birthday, Tober. Here's to another thousand years."

A laugh escapes me, sharp and brittle, and my smile twists in a fusion of disbelief and dark relief. Who would've thought that, in this game, it pays to have friends in the deepest circles of Hell?

I KNOW YOU LOVE HIM. I KNOW YOU WON'T KILL HIM.
DON'T PRESUME YOU KNOW ANYTHING ABOUT ME.
TRACK TWENTY SEVEN
EVERYTHING EVIL

TRACK TWENTY-SEVEN
EVERYTHING EVIL

Ugh. There it is again. That feeling—like someone's watching me. Fan-fucking-tastic.

While I managed to slip out of Mireya's grasp, I can't shake the feeling that this isn't over. They'll eventually all figure me out and track me down, and I'll have to come up with another brilliant plan to escape from their clutches. Or, I can just kill them all and make good on the Devil's addendum.

Death is always my favorite way out.

Although I've frequented this city a handful of times, it always feels like a labyrinth; my boots take me through an alley on Sunset before I struggle to remember where I parked my damn car. If only I had some kind of button to press to remind me of where I parked… Oh, right.

"Come to me."

An engine roars and tires screech in the distance. I

will the car to find me, to scoop me up and take me to the nearest mall so I can grab a couple hundred for my quota.

But there's someone waiting for me when I'm finally reunited with my possessed vehicle. He's all legs and angelic circumstance, with youthful innocence that reminds me so much of my lover—one demon hunter's apprentice, Jeremy Roache.

Just what I need. Another pain in my ass.

"Shouldn't you be cleaning up Mireya's mess?" I mutter, avoiding his gaze.

"You mean *your* mess?" he practically spits.

I cock an eyebrow at him and wave my hand at the car, flicking the engine on with my magic. "Buzz off, kid."

I try to shove him away as I reach for the door handle, but he doesn't budge.

"I know what you are. *Who* you are."

My jaw clenches, gritting my teeth as I quickly think of a new way to back myself out of this poorly-timed inconvenience. I scan the alley as thunder booms above us and rain begins to fall. We're alone, it seems. No sign of Lovejoy or Mireya or any lingering eyes. I think back to the Devil's addendum, how he demanded the souls of the three demon hunters I dared to associate with.

I need to prove my loyalty. No one will miss this pathetic little boy.

A sardonic grin flashes upon my lips as I turn to face

Jeremy. "What are you going to do, angel cakes? Pray the evil outta me?"

Jeremy stands straight, towering over me with his 6'2" frame, and cages me in between his lanky arms against the Camaro. The fire in his eyes burns as bright as my flames. "I'm going to tell Lovejoy the truth. Tell him who you *really* are."

"And who exactly do you think I *really* am?" I mock.

His words are a growl laced with spite. "The Devil's Second."

No one has ever called me that to my face. No demon, no witch, not even the Devil himself. It's a title I wouldn't have picked, but there's a ring to it. Pride swells within me. I'm not afraid of his empty threats.

"He'll never believe you." My fingers reach for his chiseled jaw. "I've had Declan Lovejoy wrapped around my finger for eighty years. The version of me in that darling little head of his is the one *I've* masterfully crafted. Surely, you don't think he'll believe the likes of you, a brown-nosing neophyte, over little old me?"

"He will when I bring him your familiar."

My eyes narrow at his hollow promise. There's a righteousness about him, the same righteousness I've spent years trying to snuff out of Lovejoy. They could be twins, these two; two dreadfully handsome fools with white knight syndrome.

"You may think I'm an amateur," Jeremy hisses, "and in many ways, you're right. But even amateurs know to pay attention to their surroundings, especially when darkness lingers so obviously under their nose."

Jeremy reaches for my ear, latches his fingers through my ear cuff, and snatches Nero from his dormant state. A jolt of electricity rushes through me as my lobe burns in agony. He stuffs the earring into his jeans, preening as my piercing wail threatens to deafen him.

"You fucking toad," I shriek as droplets of blood drip from my ear to the ground.

Thunder roars above us. Lightning flashes in electric waves as I rouse my magic from deep within. The rain begins to pour, and Jeremy falls to his knees at the jolting gesture of my hands. My fingers curl inwards, squeezing his heart from afar as I telekinetically force him from the ground against the brick walls of the alley, over and over again until he bleeds. My heart rages in my chest, pounding with seismic vigor.

I could kill him. I *want* to kill him. I *need* to kill him. But not before I have a little fun with him first.

I whisper my familiar's awakening spell as Jeremy plummets to the tar-black ground. A sadistic chuckle rumbles in my chest as I saunter toward the fallen apprentice. My stilettos click against asphalt, muffled by the downpour, in a sinister rhythm. His dark blond locks, now damp and dark, stick to his face with a mixture of rain and blood. I smirk as I catch a glimpse of Nero, whose ebony armor glimmers under the moonlight as he crawls up Jeremy's jeans. I finally reach him, relishing in the sight; a man on his knees, as he should be. His breath comes in shallow, frantic gasps as he tries to regain his strength. With viperine quickness, I launch forward, colliding my heel with his chest and pressing him into the ground. Jeremy's strained cries dwindle as I take my dangerously sharp stiletto and dig it into his neck. His hands flail, desperate to wrap around my ankle, but I merely press my heel deeper into his skin. Meanwhile, my darling Nero's stinger quivers as he rests upon the hunter's heaving chest.

"I know you love him," Jeremy rasps against my heel. "I know you won't kill him."

I lean forward, resting my forearm on my thigh and staring into his glassy eyes. I press the ball of my shoe harder into him. "Don't presume you know anything about me."

"Please," he begs as tears spill from his eyes. "Don't kill him."

I tilt my head and study the crimson flowing from my heel and pooling over the asphalt. Jeremy's blood radiates, pulsing with divine magic—magic I so desperately crave. Lucifer demanded demon hunter souls. He said nothing about their blood. What a glorious opportunity…

I release the hunter from under me. Relief washes over him if only for a moment until he notices my familiar perched on his chest, stinger ready to kill. I drop to my knees, hovering above his trembling body, and grab his jaw to pull it closer to me.

"Such a hero. So selfless," I coo, turning his head to the side to marvel at the bloody impression of my shoe on his neck. That's going to leave a beautiful scar. "The Devil will reward me handsomely for your soul."

I place my hand upon his chest, and the look in his horror-struck eyes fills me with unmatched joy.

My dark magic sucks his life-force into my palm like a lethal vacuum. I feel his soul fight my efforts like an infernal tug of war, but my thirst for his demise only fuels my power. His skin turns pale as I pull harder, and his cheeks slowly begin to hollow, aging him nearly 10 years. With each second, color leeches from his hair, turning from light brown to gray. In seconds, his life will be mine.

But before I can complete the siphon, my body is slammed into the cold, wet ground.

A strong pair of hands restrain mine behind my back while their weight holds me down.

"Jeremy, get out of here!" a wrathful feminine voice growls above me. I kick my legs from underneath my attacker. The familiar echo of metal against leather fills my ears, and my fury grows as I continue to squirm. Amidst the struggle, I mentally call Nero, willing him to aid me. I dip into his vision for a moment, long enough to see who dared assault me during a kill.

A woman. Small. Strong. Armed with a knife. Skin inked with the same tattoo that adorned Lovejoy's neck.

Mireya.

The demon huntress screeches at the sight of my familiar, cursing with a wail. I squirm, throwing her off me and facing her as she fights with Nero. She's an impressive sight, I'll give her that, blinded by the same vocation that cripples both Lovejoy and Jeremy with an aura as white as snow. But the rage in her eyes, the hunger for my demise… It makes me wonder just how much the price on my head is.

"Get your filthy demon off me, witch," the huntress snarls in my direction as she spares no effort to harm Nero.

I click my tongue, tilting my head in wonder. "So much anger. Isn't that some sort of sin in the eyes of your God?"

"All sins can be forgiven as long as we deliver your head."

"But my head is my best accessory," I patronize the huntress. "Next to my 'little demon,' as you so kindly put it."

Nero, kill, I mentally communicate to my scorpion. He wastes no time obeying my order, and the ear-splitting scream of the huntress is music to my ears. The pain is excruciating, I know that well. I couldn't have possibly chosen a better familiar. I rise to my feet, dusting the dirt and debris from my leather and relishing in the sight before me: yet another demon hunter brought to their knees by my magic.

Her skin turns purple as the puncture swells. I survey the alley, searching for Jeremy to no avail; it appears the little toad found it in him to escape, no doubt to warn his master. That will be the last mistake he ever makes.

My attention returns to Mireya. If only Lovejoy could see his little angel now, writhing in agony at the hand of the Devil's Second. The thought brings a wicked grin to my face.

"I've never stolen the soul of a demon hunter," I say as I admire my nails lazily. "Not until recently, mind you. Your little friends were certainly a challenge, but they folded like a house of cards." She snarls at me again, clutching where Nero stung her. With every passing second, the wound festers more. I channel my magic into my hands, revving it like the engine of my possessed Camaro. "And so will you."

The anger in her eyes quickly turns to fear as she understands my motives. I stretch my hands in her direction, creating a siphon that sucks her life-force into my hands. There's something different about this one, something I've never experienced before. It feels… powerful. A little *too* powerful, like it will escape my clutches if I make the wrong move. I remain focused with a sinister grin as the huntress' skin grays and her body deteriorates before my very eyes.

"Jer-bear was supposed to be next, but you ruined that for me. I suppose you'll have to pay for his soul with your own." Her efforts cease as she succumbs to paralysis. I grab her by her shaggy pixie-cut and dig my nails into her scalp. "And once I've harvested it, I will go back for him. I'll find him. I'll defile his soul and feed him to my scorpion. And then, I'll go after your entire fucking Order. There will be nothing left but Lovejoy and his broken little heart."

Euphoria. That's what this feels like, to destroy the woman who dared to steal the man that belonged to me. I continue my siphon as her body begins to perish. After a few strenuous minutes of steadfast concentration, the demon huntress' soul rests in my hands, leaving her body to rot, aura-less and void of life.

Good fucking riddance.

"Come here, bud," I beckon Nero as I crouch to the ground. He crawls towards my fingers, readying his tail for our usual exchange. The soul of the huntress radiates in my palm, and Nero snaps his pincers with anticipation. In seconds, he strikes at the orb. I caress his ebony armor as his stinger glows like an ember, pulsing with the fresh soul I've just collected.

My first divine entity.

From behind me, another familiar voice sends a shiver up my spine.

"No," Lovejoy's devastated, quivering voice pulls me from my victory. A sudden dread overwhelms me, leaving me numb and frozen. "It's you. *You're* the Devil's Second."

Fuck.

TRACK TWENTY EIGHT
UNHOLY CONFESSIONS
IF YOU KNOW WHAT'S GOOD FOR YOU, YOU'LL STAY OUT OF MY WAY. AND NEXT TIME, I'LL GIVE YOU MORE THAN JUST A SCORPION'S KISS.

TRACK TWENTY-EIGHT

UNHOLY CONFESSIONS

"You're the Devil's Second."

If heartbreak had a face, Lovejoy would be the poster child for grief and anguish.

He's connecting the dots, each realization hitting him like a physical blow. I can almost see the images flashing through his mind: every mysterious assassination, every inexplicable tragedy, every act of terror that has shaped the course of history. And behind them all, he now sees me—a constant, malevolent presence.

The worst part? He's not wrong, not completely.

His eyes, once warm with trust and admiration, now burn with a fury that grows hotter with each passing second. I watch, a detached observer to my own unraveling, as understanding dawns in his gaze.

I could deny it. I could spin another web of lies, offer explanations and excuses. But as I stand there, pinned by the weight of his accusing stare, I find I don't have the energy. What's done is done.

It's time he learned who I *really* am.

"Say something," Lovejoy finally chokes out, his voice raw with emotion. "Deny it. Tell me I'm crazy. *Anything.* Tell me you're not the evil I was sent to destroy."

"Evil's a strong word, don't you think?" The words die in my throat. My lips twitch in a pathetic attempt at a smile, but it feels more like a grimace. My heart, that treacherous organ I thought long dormant, threatens to choke me as it hammers against my ribcage.

Is *this* it? The moment where our decades-long dance of hunter and hunted, of secret smiles and hidden truths, finally comes to its inevitable, bloody conclusion?

I flex my fingers, feeling the familiar tingle of magic coursing through my veins. Power thrums beneath my skin, a constant reminder of what I am. Of what I could do.

I could *hurt* him.

I could *kill* him.

His holy knives, the blessed weapons he has wielded against countless demons, are laughable against the infernal magic coursing inside me. He stands before me, vulnerable, mortal, so *painfully* human.

And yet, I hesitate.

"Why couldn't I trace you?" The question pulls me from my dark thoughts..

I shrug with a nervous smile. "I'm not a demon,

remember? I'm a witch. Less obvious. Keeps me under your radar."

Lovejoy watches me, his eyes a storm of emotion. "How long were you going to string us along for? String *me…*"

"I was just making it up as I went along." I shrug again. Not a *total* lie. "No big diabolical plans here."

"Bullshit. If there's anything I know about you, it's that everything is calculated, whether you care to admit it or not."

"Then you don't know me at all."

Lovejoy lunges at me with renewed vigor, hands reaching for my neck. I struggle to flee as he presses me against the same wall I had Jeremy against just moments before.

Nero drops from my hands, and I can only hope he can flee to safety. The coolness of the iron sends a shiver up my spine, and for a fleeting moment, I find myself gasping for air.

His voice is as cold as ice when he speaks again.

"You've killed millions… You killed Mireya. You tried to kill Jeremy. You *lied to me.* For eighty *fucking* years." His grip tightens around my neck, fingers digging into my flesh. Then, his voice drops to a venomous whisper, each word dripping with disgust and betrayal. "I loved you more than *anything.* Despite your darkness, despite the side you chose." There's that hurt again—his trembling hands, the twitch in his brow, the tears threatening to spill from his haunted brown eyes. "You're not just a monster, October. You're a goddamn abomination. Everything you touch turns to ash, and I was fool enough to think I was the exception."

Abomination.

The word cuts deeper than it ever has. The memory flashes in my head—my heartless mother, her relentless wish to be rid of me. The pain rushes back, but I refuse to break beneath his grasp.

"Ouch," I feign disappointment. "Such big feelings for such a one-dimensional creature."

His wrath is unlike anything I've ever witnessed, and that's saying something. It's as if he skipped denial and gone straight to rage. His body shakes, teeth gritting so hard, I fear he'll break them. While the sneaking tendrils of fear threaten to crawl up my spine, I wonder…would he *actually* kill me? Do his destiny and loyalty to his faith outweigh the love he feels for me?

Did we ever stand a chance?

Enough. *Enough.*

Childish thoughts of hopeless romance won't win this war. I've procrastinated long enough.

Luckily, I have one little trick left up my sleeve—one I hoped I'd never have to use on the likes of my forbidden lover. But time's running out, and Lovejoy is the last obstacle standing in my way.

Wiggling my fingers behind me, I siphon energy from Nero. With a silent apology, I reach deep within myself, tapping into the connection I share with my familiar. Emperor scorpions aren't known for their lethality, but their venom…oh, their venom is a thing of terrible beauty. Capable of incapacitating creatures far larger and fiercer than any human, it now courses through my veins, a gift from my loyal companion.

With a fluid motion born of centuries of practice, I grasp Lovejoy's stubbled chin. His skin is warm beneath my touch, alive with the pulse of mortality that has always fascinated me. For a fleeting moment, I see confusion in his eyes, only for it to quickly be replaced by dawning horror as he realizes my intent.

I pull him close, my lips meeting his in a mockery of a lover's embrace. The Scorpion's Kiss, I love to call it. A fitting name for such an intimate poison.

Lovejoy's eyes widen, terror blooming in those precious brown depths I've grown to love so much. Dark veins spread from his lips like spiderwebs, tracing macabre patterns across his cheeks. They remind me of the gnarled, reaching branches of a bald cypress, beautiful in their macabre.

A choked gasp escapes him as the venom takes hold. His body goes rigid, muscles locking as the poison races through his system. He crumples to his knees, a fallen warrior at the feet of the monster—the *abomination*—he dared to love.

I walk past him, and his gurgling groans echo off

every surface as he struggles to regain mobility. In a strained mix of grit and malice, he curses me.

"You *Hell-Whore*."

I pause mid-step, my lips twitching with the ghost of a smirk. Slowly, I pivot to face him. "Oh, lover," I purr, my voice a silky blend of amusement and menace, "I've been called *much* worse."

I kneel and grip his curly locks, pulling his motionless head toward me. "If you know what's good for you, you'll stay out of my way. Next time, I'll give you more than just a Scorpion's Kiss."

His head thuds against the pavement as I let him go. The venom continues to work through his body, leaving him seemingly lifeless. I make my way through the damp alley and find my car, ready for my last stop before my inevitable victory.

As I stride away from the remnants of my shattered past, a familiar rustling beneath my jacket catches my attention. I glance down to see eight tiny legs emerging from my sleeve, followed by the obsidian carapace of my constant companion.

"There you are," I coo, my voice softening in a way it does for no one else. I extend my hand, palm up, and Nero scuttles onto it, his pincers clicking softly. "Thought I almost lost you back there."

The cool night air caresses my face as we approach my car. I slide into the driver's seat, the leather cool against my skin, and place Nero gently on the dashboard.

The engine roars to life, a throaty purr that sends a shiver of anticipation down my spine. As I pull away from the curb, leaving behind the wreckage of my confrontation with Lovejoy, I feel a weight lift from my shoulders. No more pretenses. No more divided loyalties. Just the road ahead and a job to finish.

It's almost…bittersweet.

I glance at Nero, then at the rear-view mirror. The woman staring back at me is a mess of dark makeup and burning purpose, the Devil's Second in her full, terrible glory.

"Hollywood Forever Cemetery," I murmur. My final destination, the very same place I met my darling new enemy eighty years ago. Irony never tasted sweeter.

"Let's rise and reap."

THE DEATH AND RESURRECTION SHOW

THE DEATH AND RESURRECTION SHOW

TRACK TWENTY-NINE

THE DEATH AND RESURRECTION SHOW

HOLLYWOOD FOREVER CEMETERY IS LIT UP LIKE A gruesome Christmas tree on this very Hallowed Eve. Hundreds of introverts drawn to darkness come together at a haven where they can rejoice in the music that speaks to their souls. I smile as I watch them packed in like sardines, a barricade warding off the unlucky few who failed to score tickets. I slip past the gates, keeping my hands deep within my pockets in hopes of remaining inconspicuous.

Truth be told, I could see myself thriving among these creatures of darkness, these punks and goths who cling to this music as if it's gospel.

Unfortunately for them, that will never happen.

I take a seat on the furthest tombstone closest to the barricade. I whisper my spell to awaken Nero, who eagerly crawls off my freshly healed ear and onto my shoulder. I glance at him, a sly smile creeping upon my dark lips. "Tonight's the big one, buddy. We're going to take as many as we can, more than you've ever held before. Think you can handle it?" The scorpion sidles up to my neck, the thick hairs of his pincers caressing my skin. I blow him a kiss and begin my work.

First, I need to ensure this little scheme of mine wouldn't risk the exposure of magic. Dark witch or not, there are still rules, and breaking those rules could cost me more than my powers. I take a deep breath, inhaling the multitude of scents lingering in the cemetery air, from cigarettes to liquor, sweat, and weed, the sickening scent of glue and hairspray used to keep hair sky high.

And soon, I begin to chant.

"Wretches and deviants on this Hallowed night,
Dance to this music and keep me out of sight."

It's a simple spell, a slew of rhymes perfectly arranged to hex the crowd. They'll never notice me now. And so, my harvest begins.

I climb over the barricade and join the concertgoers. I recognize the front woman from MTV—Summer Jones, a rising rock icon recently acquired by one of Hollywood's biggest record labels. Her voice hypnotizes the crowd with a low, sensual melody. The pounding drums pulse through me, beating in tandem with my heart. An itch creeps up my neck, pricking my skin as the adrenaline continues to build. I shake off the urge to get lost within the music, to succumb to the darkness she so brilliantly weaves. The flame machines billowing from the stage kiss my skin as I draw closer to the catwalk.

With a twitch and a shake, a shiver inches up my spine. A cold, familiar air surrounds me, directing my attention towards the band on stage. The front woman catches my gaze with those dark, sinister eyes. She leans into his microphone stand and speaks to me—only me— with a deep, husky voice.

"Hello, Toby."

My eyes widen as I realize she isn't just any musician: she's an unfortunate vessel for the greatest evil in the world. The Devil grins, a diabolical, toothy smile that reaches the void-like eyes of His victim, and extends a hand out to me. Without hesitation, I allow Him to pull me up on the stage. I've lived long enough to learn that snubbing the Devil's call is not in my best interests. I thank my lucky creepies and crawlies that I cast a spell on the crowd to blind them from my actions.

"You realize there are demon hunters in Los Angeles, don't you, boss?" I yell over the band's performance.

The front woman covers the microphone with her tattooed hand. "What, you're worried your little boyfriend is going to annihilate me before a crowd of unsuspecting humans? The Order will have his head for human exposure even if he succeeds."

I squint my eyes, half irritated by His omniscience and half annoyed at His use of the term 'boyfriend.' "What are you doing here?"

"I couldn't help myself." Lucifer shrugs. "The moment I learned of your plan, I knew I just had to see it come to fruition with my own eyes. Well, the eyes of a rock idol, anyway."

There's that omniscience again—that irksome mental bond we share by means of the dark gifts He's granted me. I find I enjoy life a little more when He isn't in my head, seeing everything I see, feeling everything I feel. But then again, playing mortal for a year was a dreadful affair, and I'd much rather have my mind open to the Devil than spend another day magic-less, even if it means my secrets will never be my own.

The front woman's hands crawl up my arms to my shoulders and turn me to face the bewitched audience. They continue to jump in tandem with the music, oblivious to my existence. In their eyes, there's a band performing their heart out. In reality, the true Prince of Darkness graces them with his unholiness.

But there aren't just humans in the crowd. Within a sea of nearly a thousand misfit souls, there are those who are immune to my spell. I count four in the front alone; four white auras that sting my vision even from afar.

Demon hunters.

More specifically, Declan Lovejoy, a freshly-mended silver-haired Jeremy Roache, and their band of divine thugs.

Goosebumps bloom as Lovejoy spots us—me, then the Devil. His body screams revenge, that hero's instinct for glory burning in every tense muscle, shoulders rigid with familiar ambition. I see the gears turning in his head, calculating his plan of attack before either of us have a chance to escape. But I'm too quick.

"See you on the other side." I wink at the possessed front woman and jump off the stage, falling into a soft pile of cemetery soil.

The ground is cool to the touch, and dirt catches under my nails as I curl my fingers into the earth. My magic fills me, tickling my insides. It courses through my veins, invigorates me, and tears well in my eyes. Oh, how I've missed this. The music pounds in my ears and drowns out the miserable spirits whose voices plague my mind. I know just what will shut them up—temporarily. It has been far too long since I've risen the dead.

> *"Spirits that linger from dusk until dawn,*
> *Bend to my will as faithful pawns,*
> *Rise from your graves, your tombs, your crypts,*
> *Rise and reap this pathetic mosh pit."*

The ground rumbles in tandem with the roaring band. One by one, hundreds—if not a thousand—rotted creatures rise from graves split open by my magic. Decrepit bodies emerge, barely held together by decayed sinew clinging to their bones. My magic gives them purpose, the will to ascend, the strength to serve. I concoct yet another batch of rhymes, one that whispers my desires into their minds. I look at the crowd of cursed humans who violently mosh to dark metal and smile as my creatures trudge their way.

In this day and age, I believe they're called 'zombies', mindless shells of their former selves, risen to appease their master.

Sweaty bodies dance at the mercy of my spell, unaware of the hex that drives them. They bend to my will as their intoxication leaves them powerless against my dark gifts. They'll never be able to tell the difference between my undead thralls and a Halloween get-up. Got to love the 21st century for making a fool out of All Hallow's Eve—humans make my job far too easy. Nothing brings me more pleasure than watching the dead rise to do my bidding.

Call me lazy. Call me a bitch. But you can't deny I'm one hell of a witch.

The roar of the crowd shifts from admiration to a pained, ear-splitting death wail. There's an electricity surging through me as I watch the undead attack the humans. They tear through flesh, attacking at my command, and, little by little, bodies hit the floor as their souls attempt to pass to the other side.

Oh no, they don't.

Nero sits at my shoulder, ready to store my bounty within its little stinger. I ready my hands for my soul siphoning, curling my fingers inward to collect dozens of soul orbs at a time. The wind rushes through my hair as I tirelessly collect and store, collect and store. I can't help but breathe in deeply, relishing in the sheer power I possess.

Hundreds of souls.

All mine.

My immortality is so close, I can taste it.

A blinding flash hits me in the chest and knocks me to my knees when I least expect it. Pain seeps through me in a hot wave, paralyzing my limbs as panic spreads. From the corner of my eye, one of those divine thugs I'd caught sight of earlier crouches to my eye level, a grim scowl adorning his features. He reaches for my neck, crushing my windpipe with supernatural strength as he lifts me into the air.

"So *you're* the Devil's Second," he sneers, peering into my watering eyes. "You're just a sad little girl with a bad haircut working for the wrong deity."

I huff against his grip. "Takes one to know one."

The pressure against my throat persists, but the air never leaves me. I hang on, just barely, concocting a spell in my mind to knock this fucker onto the ground. But two other glowing figures appear at his side, cornering me in a divine foursome. Each of them clutch their blessed weapon of choice, eager to strike me with a single blow. But here's the thing about divine glory-chasers: they always need to have the last word.

They eagerly discuss their next move now that I appear powerless. Their voices are a mumbling mess to my ears as my consciousness dwindles. I can see my undead thralls devouring the living through my blurring vision when a brilliant thought comes to mind.

My power surges, and the dead rise hungry. The hunters' formation shatters as rotting fingers snag their ankles. One screams as a decomposing MMA fighter delivers his final takedown. Another one, damn her, moves like smoke. Her blade whistles, cleaving through one of my minions before it can blink its maggot-filled eyes. Alas, numbers win this infernal game; while the huntress is busy decapitating a skeleton, two more corpses tackle her from behind. Meanwhile, the last two hunters fall beneath a wave of undead, their blessed blades as useful as plastic toys.

The hunter who incapacitated me proves resilient as his strong hands grip my neck, and I'd do anything to kick him in the balls for putting a damper in my plans. I close my eyes and focus on Nero, summoning him to aid me in my escape.

I can see what my familiar sees when I tap into his little subconscious. From the lowest vantage point on damp ground, Nero notes two of the thugs battling the undead. He crawls towards the scumbag who threatens to squeeze the life out of me and makes his ascent up his flailing body. I see myself through the arachnid's eyes, pale as ever and void of control as the hunter reaches for his divine-blessed weapon to end me.

But there's one thing this demon hunter doesn't know…

The Devil would never let me die of asphyxiation, and neither would my familiar.

Little Nero's stinger punctures the hunter's skin repeatedly, eliciting the most wonderful screams. I relish in the sight as the scorpion venom seizes the divine idiot limb by limb. Soon, I regain control of my body and scramble to my feet, scooping Nero into my palm and giving him a little kiss. I plant him back onto my shoulder, straighten out my outfit, and primp my hair—got to look fabulous no matter the circumstance. I glance over at the demon hunter trembling at my feet, growing purple as my venom renders him useless.

"You won't win," the hunter rasps as he ever-so-slowly loses consciousness. "Evil will never win."

I chuckle and kick the hunter where I wanted to earlier—right where the sun doesn't shine. My wicked grin grows at the sight of his demise. "It seems I already have."

Once more, I am free to continue my reaping.

But the wind picks up suddenly, almost as if by magic. The pyrotechnics blazing upon the stage ride the current, igniting the musicians and their instruments with a deadly inferno. What a shit-show this will make for the 10:00 news. I can see it now: *High winds set off a pyrotechnic accident at a Halloween Horror Concert, killing the band and audience.*

Wait a minute…

A moment of brilliance strikes me once more.

That is *exactly* what will get me off the hook. How can I risk the exposure of magic when a perfectly good cover-up lands in my lap like this? They'll never know the truth.

And my job just got a little more interesting.

I continue siphoning the souls of my victims with one hand as the other focuses on the flaming stage. With a whisper of an archaic spell, I enchant the fire to grow and travel, destroying all in its path. The humans who dare escape the pit or fight off the undead do so in vain, as my deadly inferno robs them of their breath. Between my thralls and flames, my remaining souls are easy to gain. The power is exhilarating. Intoxicating. And completely my own.

Sirens bellow in the distance, no doubt first responders enroute toward my perfect disaster. The flames spread to the palm trees, forming a beacon of light guiding the living to the dead. But they're too late—my harvest is almost complete. I transfer the soul orbs to Nero, who sucks them up like a demented vacuum. The screams of mortals dwindle with every passing moment. I squint into the distance, walking through the fire as I notice a familiar figure carrying multiple bodies through the fray.

Dark curls. 6-foot frame. And a soul marked for the Devil.

Declan Lovejoy.

I should kill him. I should destroy him for the sake of protecting my boss. And yet, despite my better judgment, my heart calls to him. It twists and writhes with an unfathomable guilt, but all I can think about are those darling brown eyes.

Eighty years, I've known the man. Eighty years, I've toyed with him, avoiding collecting his soul despite marking him. And even now, as we've become sworn enemies, I still can't do it. I *still* can't kill him.

Amid a landmark engulfed in embers and cinders, Lovejoy's eyes meet mine across the flames. His pain mirrors my own—the conflict, the guilt, the indescribable pull entwining our destinies. He hesitates, his heart torn between doing the right thing and being with the woman he loves. To my utter surprise, I watch as he ushers a straggling few to safety.

This is it. My chance to escape. Now or never.

Nero's claws remain latched onto my leather jacket, which has grown heavy in the heat. His little stinger glows with the light of nearly a thousand souls. I pull him into my hands and cast my spell to turn him into a bracelet.

Then, I run.

I run for my life.

For my immortality.

But my feet come to a screeching halt as I find myself surrounded by the red, glowing apparitions of the dead I did not raise.

Cemeteries are a spectral playground filled with stubborn spirits of every flavor; some are easy to overpower while others remain steadfast and able to resist my magic. I can only hope my Hellish reputation will keep them at bay.

And yet, among the burning bodies aflame by my gifts, a panicked breath catches in my chest. With a tortured shriek, a horde of wayward souls overwhelm me, hellbent on my demise.

All at once, darkness consumes me.

TRACK THIRTY
MORE HUMAN THAN HUMAN
YOU MURDERED HUNDREDS OF INNOCENT PEOPLE.
IT'S ALWAYS THE SAME FORMULA WITH YOU--BIG ACCUSATIONS, NO FOLLOW UP.

TRACK THIRTY

MORE HUMAN THAN HUMAN

I hiss as a tightness grips my wrists, shooting searing pain to my back and shoulders. As I come to, I realize I'm seated on the damp grass, back flush against a tombstone. My arms are bound by some sort of celestial knot, and an electric pressure digs into my skin.

Cinders float within the ruins of an incinerated graveyard. A once-luscious field of headstones now mimics a war zone filled to the brim with burnt bodies. I can't help but take pride in my handiwork.

My admiration is cut short when a figure emerges from the shadows—all long legs and arrogance, a lanky, entitled brat whose name I'd gladly forget, if only his very existence didn't grate against my last nerve.

I flash Jeremy one of my signature sardonic grins. "Nice hair, baby boy. Now you *actually* look a little older than 12."

The apprentice squints at me, ignoring the quip, and pulls a dagger from his boot, one I hadn't seen on his person before.

I struggle against my restraints once more. "You know, if you wanted to dabble in rope-play, all you had to do was ask."

"You murdered hundreds of innocent people." His voice is cold, loathsome.

My smile turns sluggish. "How many? 700? 800? Ballpark."

My mockery stings; I can see it in his eyes. Sauntering closer, he grips his dagger, but the tremble of his hands and the wobble in his step betrays his façade. He desperately clings to his mask, this phony semblance of courage and might. But no amount of hatred can conceal the crippling truth; he's terrified of me. Absolutely terrified.

It only feeds my defiance.

"It's always the same formula with you—big accusations, no follow up. I imagine Lovejoy will be here any second to put you in your place."

Jeremy's eyes flash with barely contained rage, and his jaw clenches. How sweet; I've struck a nerve. He circles me, keeping his distance, his gaze never leaving mine—a predator assessing its prey.

"He's got you on a tight leash, doesn't he?" he growls, his voice low and dangerous. "Lucifer."

I can't help but smirk, my bottom lip jutting out in a

mock pout. "Oh my, so the little puppy *does* have claws after all," I coo, my tone dripping with condescension.

Jeremy's nostrils flare, his free hand balling into a fist at his side. "I've read all about you, you know. You're nothing but a myth, not even worth a full chapter in the texts."

I arch an eyebrow, my voice dripping with false modesty. "What can I say? I'm excellent at covering my tracks."

"Clearly not good enough. Mireya saw right through you."

"Mireya?" I hum, savoring the word. "Oh yes, I remember her. Annoyingly short. Tightly wound." I pause, letting the tension build. "Tell me, Jerk-off, where is she now?"

His face pales, realization dawning, but his rage remains.

"That's right," I whisper. "Dead as a doornail, soul locked deep within my vault." My eyes flick to his, cold and predatory. "And you? You're sprinting down that same dark path."

A shimmer of movement ripples behind Jeremy, barely visible amid the dark. My gaze flickers past him for a split second, catching sight of a decrepit corpse dragging itself across the ashen ground, its putrid fingers clawing into the hallowed earth. My lip twitches as I channel my necromantic power into this final, desperate move.

But I remain deceptively still, sizing up the young hunter.

"You know," I drawl, my voice eerily casual despite the strain, "maybe after tonight, your precious Holy Order will dedicate an entire book to me." I lean in, eyes locked on his, my words a silky whisper. "And you, little boy? You'll be nothing but a footnote in my story."

As I speak, I feel my undead minion inching closer, its festering jaw just feet away from Jeremy's exposed neck. In a heartbeat, the air shifts, and Jeremy's eyes flicker with sudden awareness—whether he's sensed the approaching corpse or simply lost patience, I don't know. The world tapers to a blur of motion and shining metal as the apprentice and his dagger whirl through the air, aiming for my heart.

"Jeremy, don't."

A cool rush washes over me at the sound of that voice. *His* voice, my drug of choice for eighty years.

Lovejoy emerges, a formidable presence against the Hellish glow of smoldering debris. As he approaches, the subtle irregularity in his stride becomes apparent—a slight hitch in his step, a little limp that speaks volumes of the battle he endured.

But despite his injuries, his posture remains rigid. Each step forward is a silent declaration of his sheer force of will, even as flashes of pain dance across his face. His features, once handsome, are now ridden with soot, evidence of the Hell I unleashed on All Hallow's Eve.

His gaze, however, burns with an intensity that rivals my flames.

"Just like I said," I mutter, eyes locked on Jeremy, throwing him a taunting wink as he remains frozen, dagger still aimed for my heart.

My minion crawls toward the hunters, rabid and snarling. Its putrid neck severs from its body when Lovejoy's white magic bursts from his fingers, leaving the creature slain and useless.

Jeremy's a panting mess. "You shouldn't have stopped me."

Lovejoy puts a hand on his apprentice. "We need her alive."

"Says *who?*" The young man's voice breaks, laced with utter disbelief. "No one gave that order, Declan—you only want her alive for yourself, t-to help her escape—t-to let her get away with *e-everything.*"

"No one wants her dead more than I do." Lovejoy's gaze flickers to me, and for a moment, time seems to freeze. In those eyes—the beautiful brown eyes I've known for so long—I now see something entirely different. It's not the rage of a demon hunter facing an evil incarnate. No, this...this is something far more personal.

Beneath that scorching anger and regret is pure, unadulterated heartbreak. In that instant, I realize I've achieved something I never intended, something far more devastating than any spell or curse.

I've broken Declan Lovejoy in a way that no plain-old-evil ever could.

"I don't believe you." Jeremy's words come out as broken as his mentor's heart. As the two hunters wage a war of accusations and defenses, my fingers reach for my familiar. Nero remains curled around my wrist, a chunky obsidian bracelet locked together with a magnetic clasp. The cosmic bonds keeping my hands wrapped behind my back dig into my skin, releasing electric jolts of divine magic that sear through me into my bones. I fight through the pain, grinding my teeth as I desperately try something, *anything* to get this fucking thing off me.

With a dull 'click' of metal, I finally manage to wriggle my bracelet off my wrist. I whisper Nero's awakening spell before I command him to release me of my bonds. Within seconds, the pressure subsides, and I rise to my feet.

But before I can make my escape, Lovejoy strikes. Steel cuts through air, then a sharp tug throws me off balance. His dagger pierces through the sleeve of my leather jacket and into the tombstone, pinning me in place like a butterfly to a board. The cold blade barely bites against my skin, not close enough to draw blood but promising far worse if I dare to move.

Lovejoy pivots slowly, his movements deliberate and predatory as his eyes lock onto his apprentice. The air grows heavy with unspoken tension as he extends his hand, palm up, fingers curling in a silent demand.

"The blade, Jeremy," he says, his voice a low, dangerous rumble. "*Now.*"

Jeremy hesitates, his grip tightening on the second of Lovejoy's twin blades. For a heartbeat, defiance flashes in the boy's eyes—a spark of rebellion that led him to question his mentor's methods.

But Lovejoy doesn't blink, doesn't waver, and time seems to stretch into years of waiting.

Finally, Jeremy relents. The blade changes hands, its metallic sheen catching the light as Lovejoy reclaims it. He tests its balance with a practiced flick of his wrist, then levels a gaze at Jeremy that could freeze Hellfire.

"This will be the last time you question my methods," my hunter says, each word precise and cutting. "She belongs to *me*."

Jeremy's jaw tenses while he searches the hardened stare of his mentor. With a small nod, he turns to face me. He's a young man torn between ambition and duty, with the weight of the world pulling his shoulders down. Smoke and embers circle him as he takes a step closer.

"I hope you get what you deserve, witch."

My insides twist with unmistakable sadism, and I blow a kiss at the boy. "Run along, *Jeremiah*."

His green eyes narrow in contempt, nostrils flaring with a final, sharp inhale. Seconds later, the young apprentice disappears into the night in a flash of Holy Light.

Leaving me alone with this dangerous, savage of a man hardened by heartbreak.

All at once, the only soul I ever considered worthy of my time becomes my greatest threat.

Lovejoy is mere feet away from me now, and when he speaks, his voice is a low growl.

"You're not going anywhere, October." His teeth are clenched so tight, I can almost hear them grinding. "Not this time. Not ever again."

The threat in his voice cuts me like his blade promises. A deadly promise lingers in his eyes, mirrored by the hunger in my own.

I've never feared Declan Lovejoy, not until this very moment.

For eighty long years, he has been my plaything, a delightful little distraction in my immortal existence. I realize, with a thrill that's equal parts excitement and dread, that our game has finally reached its end.

No more toying. No more teasing.

It's time to collect what's rightfully mine.

TRACK THIRTY ONE
Schism

TRACK THIRTY-ONE

SCHISM

"Why?"

The word escapes him, a whisper so faint, I almost mistake it for the wind. But I hear it. I *always* hear him.

I can't help but grin as I face imminent danger. "That's a loaded one. Why what? Why is the sky blue? Why is the Earth round? I could think of a better one: why am I still breathing?"

He huffs a laugh, one laced with disbelief. "You think you're funny, don't you? Very clever."

"Oh, yeah. Hilarious. I'd give George Carlin a run for his money."

Lovejoy advances, deftly extracting the knife from my sleeve and pressing its edge against my throat. The celestial-imbued metal hums against my skin. A hiss escapes my lips as I try to retreat, and my back scrapes against the rough surface of the tombstone. But Lovejoy's grip on my shoulder holds me in place, and his eyes glint with ruthless determination.

I force a chuckle, my throat bobbing against the blade. "So, what's the holdup, *lover*? Why am I still here instead of facing the wrath of the All Mighty God? Is the reward for my head not shiny enough? Or maybe the paperwork is just too cumbersome."

His eyes narrow into slits. "You don't get to call me that anymore."

"What? *Lover*?" I repeat, the word dripping with venom from my tongue.

The blade digs deeper into my skin, and a trickle of blood runs down my neck.

"The only reason your heart's still beating is the same reason mine hasn't turned to ash."

His enigmatic words hang in the air, heavy with unspoken meaning. "Cryptic as ever, Declan," I manage, my voice strained. Our eyes lock, and I see it then—the same aching conflict that tears at my own heart, mirrored in his tortured gaze. He's caught between duty and desire, just as I am. But old habits die hard, and I can't resist taunting him further. "Is this the part where you give me one last chance at redemption? To trade in my pitchfork for a halo?"

Lovejoy drops the blade to his side. The air returns to my lungs, if only for a moment. "It was the Devil all along, wasn't it?" he muses. "The one who was after you?"

I shrug with a helpless smirk. "What was your first guess?"

His gaze sears into me, pleading with me, begging me to see reason. "What is it, October? A Blood Oath? A contract? Something deeper? What does he have on you?"

A thousand years of power and immortality—and oh, what a gratifying millennium it has been. I look forward to what the next thousand years will bring.

My silence perturbs him. "Please, October. Let me help you."

A bitter smile tugs at my lips. Oh, *Lovejoy*. The poor, unfortunate fool still clings to the notion *I'm* the one who needs saving, as if *I'm* trapped in some infernal merry-go-round of soul harvesting, demon pacts, and manslaughter.

Well, perhaps I am, but it's a carousel I wouldn't trade for all the halos in Heaven.

The nightmare—no, the *memory*—flashes before me again: a little girl standing among the flames, next to the greatest evil known to mankind. Even as I relived that moment under Nightmare's feeding, I realized two things with perfect clarity: the unmistakable glimmer of admiration in His eyes and the unholy fire that drove me toward Him.

I was never the Devil's puppet, never His unwilling thrall. I chose my path long ago, and it has kept me alive for almost a thousand years.

It's the greatest decision I've ever made.

My eyes harden, all traces of humor vanishing. "Cut the sanctimonious bullshit. I'm way past your holy redemption. Do us both a favor and quit lying to yourself." I lean in, my voice dripping with venom. "I know what *really* drives you: glory. Adoration. The goddamn trophy. It has driven you since you were a little green Nephilim, eager to impress your employer. And you've always wanted *more*, always believed you were God's gift to this Earth, a perfect white knight born to rid the world of its natural evils. I regret any role I played in feeding that delusion, but don't you *dare* pretend for a *fucking second* that I mean *anything* to you, Declan Lovejoy. I'm just a means to your righteous end."

"The 'prize' I'm after isn't something Heaven can offer. It's the one thing that keeps pulling me back to this God-forsaken dance with you, against every shred of sense I have left. You *know* that. You've *always* known that. You're just too goddamn stubborn to admit it."

The truth in his words is undeniable. We've always been drawn to each other despite our warring sides, despite our allegiances, despite the secrets I've kept from him. Even now, as we stand at the precipice of death, there are some secrets I'll never tell.

His tortured gaze lingers, paralyzed by the same hesitation I witnessed when he discovered my true identity just hours ago. He won't kill me. He can't.

But I've learned a thing or two from my many run-ins

with Lucifer's idiotic sons. Time to put those lessons to good use.

"How about we strike a deal?" I purr, my tone shifting to velvet-wrapped steel.

He barks out a laugh, bitter and sharp. "Trust you? That's rich."

"Just hear me out," I murmur, my fingers ghosting over the hand still gripping my shoulder. "Renounce your vows to the Order. Retire. Give up divinity." I lean in, my lips a breath from his ear. "Join me and my employer. I'll make sure he overlooks that impressive demon body count you've racked up over the last century."

"Have you lost your mind?" His voice rises, a mix of shock and something else — intrigue, perhaps?

"I'll put in a good word," I tease, flashing him my most innocent, doe-eyed stare. "C'mon, Lovejoy. Job comes with great perks. You can be my partner, the Devil's Second's Second. I'll work on the title."

Lovejoy squints at me, lips pursing as he stifles his exasperation. "I'd rather die than work for *him*."

A sadistic grin aches my cheeks. "I'm sure we can arrange that."

With a surge of arcane energy, I hurl Lovejoy backward, his boots skidding across the ash-strewn ground. Nero materializes from the shadows, skittering silently to my side. Summoning every last vestige of power within me, I conjure twin flames within my palms.

With a sweeping gesture, I encircle Lovejoy in a ring of Hellfire.

Nero and I stride through the flames unscathed, our eyes locked on the prey I've danced with for nearly a century. The soul I marked all those years ago. The one who has been mine since the beginning, whether he knew it or not.

I crouch beside my fallen demon hunter, fingers crackling with soul-siphoning magic. A predatory smile plays across my lips as I drink in the sight of him—fallen, breathless, with nowhere left to run.

"How did you become so…" Lovejoy's voice falters, caught in the gravity between us.

"Persuasive? Irresistible?" I offer, my tone a dangerous caress.

His gaze hardens, a flicker of his old resolve returning. *"Evil."*

The word dangles like a noose between us, weighed down by a happily ever after that was never meant to be. *Evil*, a simple, two-syllable word that has taunted me for so long, I'd thought I'd grown used to it by now, and yet, every time I'm labeled as such, it's as venomous as a scorpion's sting.

"You don't know me, Declan Lovejoy. You have no idea what I've endured."

"I know you're the one thing I can never have," he whispers to me, on the verge of breaking. "The object of my darkest dreams. My 'forever.' And you're tearing me apart."

"Some paragon of virtue you are, huh? Driven by sin, torn between duty and desire, glory and greed. You're *just* like my boss."

There it is—the fire blazing in his eyes, the beast that yearns to consume me whole. A primal growl erupts from deep within him, and in a heartbeat, he's upon me. His weight slams me to the ground, knocking the air from my lungs.

Instinct takes over. My palms press against his chest, magic surging through my veins. With a violent burst of energy, I launch him skyward, and his body arcs through the air once more.

I scramble to my feet, my boots slipping on the uneven ground, nearly tripping over little Nero. I urge him to come closer as Lovejoy's enraged roar echoes in the distance. Desperation claws at me as I bend down to usher my familiar into my hand, ready to make our last harvest.

But a sickly feeling fills my core.

It all happens so quickly: a glimmer of silver, a gust of wind against my cheek, a deafening 'crunch' on the ground by my feet.

My lungs cave in, void of breath. A searing pain rips me apart, smothering my magic and leaving me helpless as I fall to my knees. The damp soil beneath me seeps through my clothes while a flash of light nearly blinds me. A thousand orbs swirl like stars from above.

Lovejoy's holy dagger shimmers in the moonlight, lodged deep into my scorpion's lifeless body.

TRACK THIRTY TWO

BLOOD ON THE GROUND

TRACK THIRTY-TWO
BLOOD ON THE GROUND

My shrieking wail echoes over acres of ruined bodies and trees reduced to ash. The world around me disappears while a part of me dies—a part I kept locked away for centuries.

My little familiar, my precious Nero, lies lifeless before me.

Dead.

Killed by the man who once promised me 'forever.'

My trembling fingers rake at the ground, digging up moss and dirt. I work past a torrent of guilt-ridden tears, muttering incantations through gritted teeth. My magic is weak, the weakest it has ever been, but even so, I manage to spell the earth I've dug up. It glows beneath my fingers, soaking in what little power I'm able to emit as I conjure a small glass coffin. I pull the dagger from Nero's little body, tears falling from my burning eyes.

"I'm so sorry." I kiss the scorpion as I take it in my hands. In a moment of hysteria, I forget that the creature can no longer hear me—*will never* hear me again. After all these years, I've failed to do the simplest of things: keep us safe.

And now, I remain defenseless.

Unprotected.

Broken.

With trembling hands, I line the glass coffin with enchanted moss, its ethereal glow creating a soft, otherworldly cradle. Gently, I lower Nero's tiny form into this gossamer nest, my fingers lingering on his cooling body.

I whisper ancient words of preservation, a simple spell that settles over Nero like a veil, sealing him in endless sleep.

A sob claws its way up my throat, threatening to shatter me. I try to swallow it down, but grief tightens its grip, suffocating me with each ragged breath. The Devil's bargain may have granted me immunity to mortal ailments, but it offers no shelter from the crushing weight of a broken heart.

"I'll keep you with me always, Nero," I promise, my voice barely audible. A tear splashes onto the coffin's surface, glinting like a star under the moonlight. "I'll never abandon you. Not ever."

It finally hits me that every soul I've collected over the past six days has disappeared into the night. A thousand lives gone, wasted, resorted to dust or floating to the Heavens, for all I know. 'Forever' will now only last an hour.

The dreaded countdown has finally begun.

All at once, my sorrow is replaced with rage.

Where the *fuck* is Declan Lovejoy?

Mustering the little strength I have left, I rise to my feet. The world spins as I slowly regain focus, scanning the cemetery for my prey. My circle of flames was extinguished along with the death of my familiar, and spirals of smoke dissipate into the cold night. I can still smell his overpriced cologne, sense the purity in his aura —no, he couldn't have gone too far, not while his job remains unfinished.

I *will* find him.

And when I do, I will *end* him once and for all.

I will *hurt* him the way he hurt *me*.

And so, the hunter becomes the hunted.

I prowl the cemetery as a scorpion would, pincers tense and stinger at the ready. Though my magic and resolve are feeble, I still have blind rage. And oh, does it fuel me.

Through the smoky graveyard, I catch a glimpse of Lovejoy's form darting between tombstones, his path unmistakably leading to the cemetery chapel. *Of course*— the crafty bastard. He knows full well my arcane abilities will wither within those hallowed walls. A smirk tugs at my lips; he's clever, I'll give him that.

But I have no intention of playing by his rules.

My fingers curl, dark energy crackling between them, and I scream his name at the top of my lungs. It fades into the night, blending with the sounds of the city beyond this scorched ground. I chant a spell that would normally paralyze him, but instead, it causes him to stagger.

Lovejoy turns to face me, struggling to regain his balance. Our eyes finally meet, and the tension is so thick, my hands itch to strangle him with it. There he stands, between the chapel and a mausoleum, luring me to my demise while I quickly, willingly oblige. Might as well run head-first to my death before the Devil has a chance to do the honors.

I have nothing left to lose, after all.

If it's said only fools rush in, I must be the most reckless of them all.

My boots click against the asphalt leading to the white mausoleum filled with corpses of celebrities past. My chest rumbles as my anger builds, and I fight to regain my composure. I'm eager to get my hands on him.

"How dare you?" My voice shatters like glass, raw emotion bleeding through every syllable. Flames erupt in my palms—weak, flickering things, fueled by a fury that could reduce worlds to ash.

Lovejoy stumbles backward, his usual grace abandoned. A dull thud echoes as he collides with the mausoleum wall, trapped between cold stone and my burning wrath.

"I had no choice," he says. My flames dance in his eyes as I draw near. "If I kill you, I weaken *Him*."

I can't help but laugh—a sound caught between amusement and pity. "Oh, Lovejoy," I growl, shaking my head. "Your naiveté would be charming if it wasn't so stupid. Killing me won't even *scratch* His power. It'll just royally piss him off."

He lifts his chin in defiance. "Then I'll gladly face Him too."

My maniacal laugh turns his skin white. "Oh, my darling fool. I'd *love* to see you try."

I thrust my flames in his direction. He dodges them quickly but trips upon marble steps with a pained groan and falls before my feet. Before he can escape, I straddle him, just as I have many times during our many trysts, but this time, it's with a more darker intent than ever before.

"We've been playing this game for far too long, Lovejoy," I say as I lower my lips to his ear. "Whether you realize it or not, you've always been hunting me, and I've always been the one who got away."

His body stiffens beneath my weight as I run my fingers up and down his arms. Oh, how I love the look of terror that fills those beautiful brown eyes… I won't miss them.

My hand slips into my leather jacket, fingers closing around the hilt of the holy blade—the very one that stole my precious Nero from me. As I withdraw it, the air hums with celestial energy. The dagger's touch sears my skin, a dull, insistent burn that speaks of its divine origin.

Our eyes lock. In that fraction of a second, I see realization dawn in Lovejoy's gaze—but it's too late.

With a fluid motion born of centuries of violence, I drive the blade deep into his chest. The sickening crunch of steel against bone mingles with his choked gasp. Warm blood, bright with divine light, spills over my hand.

And finally, justice is served.

"You should know, I'll be dead by midnight." My words are like venom as my fingers find his chest. "Which means you would have succeeded. All you'd have to do is run off to your employer and collect your reward. You'd be the hero you'd always dreamed you'd be."

He struggles against me, but even a seasoned demon hunter is no match for the wrath of a heartbroken witch. I pull the knife from him and bring it to my lips to kiss the blade. His blood coats my grin like lipstick. Just a little taste…

And my power flourishes ten-fold.

I relish in the horror filling his eyes, the look of helplessness and defeat that makes my black heart flutter. "I wonder what the Big Man *Up*stairs will think when he discovers you allowed evil to take your blood—not once, but *twice*."

Lovejoy attempts to speak, but his words are lost to my ears.

"I guess we'll never know. If I'm going down, I'm taking you with me."

My name is a prayer upon his lips, a final plea and last resort, one I gladly choose to ignore.

"Please," he begs one more time.

My grip tightens. "You've sealed your fate, and now, your soul will be mine. But who are we kidding?" I grin through mascara-running tears. "It has belonged to me since the night we first met."

My nails sink into his skin, draining the life from his trembling form. The air around us grows heavy, charged with the weight of my final harvest. In Lovejoy's eyes, I see the last embers of his defiance flicker and die. Within seconds, his body turns limp beneath me, growing colder and grayer by the second as I welcome the thrill of vengeance that fills my core.

A single light glows within the darkness that surrounds me.

In my hand lies the divine soul of Declan Lovejoy.

TRACK THIRTY THREE
ANTICHRIST SUPERSTAR

TRACK THIRTY-THREE

ANTICHRIST SUPERSTAR

THE SWEET, SWEET TASTE OF REVENGE MEANS NOTHING without a thousand souls. I'm not met with peace and vigor but with a hole in my heart that keeps gaping. Nero remains nestled in a death curl within the little box I conjured for him. As his body decays, a part of me continues to die.

And in a few more minutes, I will cease to exist.

I never thought I'd die at the hand of negligence; I figured I'd continue to dodge every bullet, keep to the shadows, do my job, and live until this planet implodes.

But no.

Here I stand, ten minutes before my 1000th birthday, ready to disappoint the Devil for the last time.

I check my flip phone, watching the milky green screen flash '11:50 P.M.' I clutch Lovejoy's soul in my hand, keeping it close as I ascend the stairs of the once-burning stage. The stench of scorched plastic and wood fills my lungs, and I feel the tears welling in my eyes again. This will be the last time I breathe at all, a mundane, thankless activity I'd grown unappreciative of. I sold my soul to the Devil for a chance to breathe without pain, and now, I'll never know the luxury again.

God, October, get the fuck over yourself. No one's here for your pity party, so let's go out with a bang.

Placing the soul orb in my jacket, I take one more deep breath and summon the Devil. I close my eyes, then reach into my back pocket to grip my athame. I chant a familiar spell as I draw blood from my free palm. This process has always been a messy one, and I won't miss it. There's a chill in the air, much like there was the night he came to deliver his ultimatum. I fight the weakness in my knees, ignore the tremble in the ground, and await my master.

Hard, heavy footsteps rattle the dais. A dark shadow emerges from behind singed curtains, taking His natural form—crimson skin, bat-like wings, horns and all—the King of Demons, Lucifer Morningstar. My one and only employer.

I sink to my knees, bowing in His presence. My throat caves in as I attempt to speak, voice hoarse from exhaustion. "You stuck around."

He minds me with a smirk, tipping His curved horns toward me. He's a handsome motherfucker, no matter what form He takes. "Didn't see the point in leaving. I knew this little show would get you your 1000."

I bite my lip as my growing shame weighs me down. "About that…"

His expression turns sullen, yet there's a playful glint in His void-like eyes. He knows. He *has* to know. "Toby…" His patronizing voice makes me want to tear the flesh from my bones. "Don't tell me you're short."

I wince, looking down at the radiant orb in my hand. "Give or take 999."

The Devil stands tall, one eyebrow cocking impossibly high as His chest fills with a dramatic inhale. He shakes His head and circles me, and for the first time in my very long, grueling life, I feel like prey.

"You've served me well for nearly a thousand years."

Here I stand, teetering on the precipice between life and death, staring into those dark, void-like eyes with nothing but my wits and a small vial of divine blood tucked away in my pocket. My last Hail Mary. A last resort.

The weight of it burns against my thigh, a reminder of hope and hubris intertwined. Will it be enough to cheat death one final time? I can't know… All I can hope is that the Devil has reserved a spectacular room for me in the fiery depths of Hell.

If I'm going down, I'm doing so on my own terms.

Lovejoy's soul pulses in my palm like a captured star. When I extend it to Lucifer, his smirk turns predatory.

"You've never delivered a demon hunter's soul to me before, have you?"

The question catches me off guard. I can't even find the courage to speak. I only shake my head.

"So you'd never know that a hunter's soul, especially one whose reputation is as formidable as this one, is easily worth more than a thousand petty human souls."

My throat feels even tighter now. If my eyes could widen any more, they'd pop out of their sockets. He takes Lovejoy's soul in His hands. He studies it for a moment, noting how it pulses and animates, as if filled with rage. I can only imagine the look on the hunter's face if he knew he was in evil's clutches. With a small smile, the Devil steps closer.

"Your debt to me is paid."

I part my lips to protest, but His finger presses against them. "Do not question me. You did me a big favor with this one. He's taken one too many of my Underlings over the years, banished my twins. I realize what I asked of you was…nearly impossible. Yet for all intents and purposes, you delivered. You even disposed of that troublesome huntress. An impressive feat, indeed."

The praise washes over me, a conflicting blend of warmth and unease. But then, His voice takes on a sharper edge. "Though you *did* allow that apprentice to slip through your fingers…"

Fucking Jeremy Roache. The name finally sticks after six days of dodging the persistent brat. His demise will be swift, I vow silently—a promise I fully intend to keep, not just for the Devil, but for my own peace of mind.

I meet Lucifer's gaze head-on. As we stand in silence, I wonder: is He pleased with His handiwork? Does it satisfy Him to see how eagerly I've embraced this life, this cursed existence? In facing the architect of my damnation, I find a twisted pride in the creature I've become—the creature I have always been.

"I know what *he* meant to you," the Devil murmurs, His fingers gently brushing the hair from my face.

I rise to my feet, mustering a dismissive wave and a hint of my usual cheek. "He didn't mean a single thing."

He flashes me a sharp-toothed grin. "After all these years, you still think you can lie to me."

"I'll keep trying for the rest of my life," I retort, a challenge in my voice.

"Yes, you will." His large, red hand cups my cheek, thumb tracing the smooth skin under my ageless eyes. "And next time, there will be no loopholes."

I meet his gaze once more. "We'll see, boss."

His grin widens, a mix of pride and mischief. Then, to my surprise, he extends his hand towards me. "You'll have more use for this than I would," he says, his tone softer than usual. "Consider it a gift. Happy birthday, October."

My breath catches as He utters my real name. The sound is foreign on His lips, and for a moment, I feel seen—not as His slave, but as His equal. He places the soul orb back into my hands, and I hesitate, wondering if this is another of His tests.

Then, unexpectedly, He presses a soft kiss to my forehead. The intimacy of the gesture leaves me reeling, hinting at a depth to the Devil's feelings I hadn't dared to consider. Our complicated past has always bound us, a shared understanding that transcends the roles of master and hireling.

As I stand there, the weight of the orb in my hands and the ghost of his kiss on my skin, I know one thing with certainty: I will serve Him until my dying day. Not out of obligation, but because in this intricate dance of power and submission, we've forged something unbreakable.

He regards me with a small smile, a hint of pride still glimmering on those dangerous lips. "You had your fun for six days. But remember, there is still one more debt you've yet to pay."

The fleeting moment of relief evaporates, leaving a chill in its wake. My voice catches, barely a whisper, "W-wha—?"

"That soul from last year, the one that slipped through your fingers? The very catalyst of this…inconvenient ultimatum." A pause hangs heavy in the air. When He speaks again, His voice drops lower, almost gentle in its cruelty. "The Nephilim hybrid…"

My stomach drops, and I squeeze my eyes shut,

willing this conversation—this reality—out of existence. But the final blow comes, inescapable.

"Your child."

His words hit me like a physical blow, nearly driving the air from my lungs. *My child.* My best-kept secret—or so I'd hoped. It doesn't matter anymore. None of it matters anymore…

"You knew all along." I fight the ever-growing pit in my stomach as I face my master.

There's that smile again, the one that reminds me He will always have the upper hand. "You forget, my little firestarter—I have eyes and ears everywhere."

Debauchery in the nightlife industry. Crooked cops in the Las Vegas police department. Occult creatures tucked away in His back pocket. I should have known. I should have seen it coming.

His voice cuts through my thoughts, smooth as silk and sharp as a blade. "But never mind all that. You may have failed to deliver me the soul of your child…" He pauses, letting the weight of my failure hang in the air between us. But then, His eyes glint with a mixture of triumph and something darker. "But you did not fail to deliver me her father's."

My gaze flicks to the soul orb once more, its soft glow a cruel reminder of how the only person who ever truly mattered to me now lies trapped and powerless within my grasp. I try to avoid the montage of memories flooding my brain, the flashes of his charming smile and darling eyes. The reality twists in my gut like a knife, a reminder of the choices I've made and the prices I've paid. And, perhaps, the prices I've *yet* to pay.

The game is not over—it's just beginning.

"Now that you're back in the fold, there's quite a bit of catching up to do." He pauses, gaze sharpening. "And a few...situations that need your attention."

I arch an eyebrow, brushing a wayward strand of hair from my face. "Oh?"

"Indeed." His tone cools noticeably. "You can start by cleaning up that little mess you made with my twins."

Ah, yes. The ever-loving pains in my ass. "I suppose you want me to undo what my hunter did?"

"What *you* helped him do."

"I'll get on that right away." The words are like broken glass in my throat. My boss nods with a small smile, stretching his bat-like wings as he turns to take his leave.

"Sir?" I call out before he descends into the shadows. I've never regarded Him with formalities, but after giving me not one but two chances at immortality, I'd say He deserves it. He pauses mid-step, turning His face to the side. "You were never going to kill me if I failed, were you? This was just another twisted lesson to remind me of my leash."

A small smirk tugs at His lips. "Our bond, October Winters, is forged in blood and sealed by death. You know this." He pauses, savoring the moment. "You've always been my prized asset. Clever. Resourceful. Loyal —even if you need the occasional reminder. Your value to me is far greater here than in any Afterlife. Besides"—his eyes glint with dark amusement—"imagine how dreadfully dull the world would be without you in it."

I can't help the warmth that fills my cold heart as the Devil bursts into flames, leaving a scorched shadow where He once stood. I take a deep breath.

I'm alive.

The realization hits me like a jolt of electricity. Despite the loss that left a hole in my heart, despite the dangers that await me tomorrow, the unfinished business, the demons I've pissed off, the favors owed…

I'm *still* here. Breathing. Heart beating.

A slow grin spreads across my face as an idea takes root.

I know *just* how to celebrate.

Lovejoy's soul glimmers in my hand. Revenge finally tastes sweet without a ticking time bomb looming over me. I smile at the orb, at the vicious idea bubbling in my mind. We could have been good together under different circumstances, but he signed his death warrant when he killed a part of me.

I kneel on the ground once more and settle the soul orb next to my knee. I summon Nero's little coffin, my heart skipping a beat as I lift the lid to find its curled body where I left it. I reach into my pocket and pull out my most precious commodity—the divine blood of my now-dead lover.

I've risen the dead countless times, watched putrid bodies do my bidding for as long as my magic allowed them, but never have I brought a creature back to life. Not completely. Not forever. Magic like that comes with an exceptional price, and the irony is absolutely delicious.

"You've promised me 'forever' for as long as I can remember," I whisper to the soul orb as I pour divine blood over the body of my familiar, "and I always told you to be careful what you wish for."

I grab the orb and press it into the lifeless scorpion, filling it with the lingering soul of my incessant hunter. With a flash of light, the creature is revived, perfectly healed and ready to strike. My wicked grin spreads as I grab it by its stinger and watch it struggle.

"Declan Lovejoy." Even his name tastes bitter on my tongue now. "You darling little fool."

In loving me, he doomed himself twice over—first allowing himself to fall for an evil witch he could never truly claim and then daring to choose between doing what's right and the darkness lingering within. Forever caught between his duty and desire. Forever shackled by an insatiable hunger that consumes all men.

I trace my fingers over his new form, the ebony exoskeleton I've grown so used to after a thousand years. He squirms within my grasp, within the confines of his tiny body and the new limbs he fails to control. Was it truly foolishness that sealed his fate, or was it a long, drawn-out inevitability of my own design? The lines blur now, much like the boundaries between us once did.

In the end, it was not only his foolishness but his blind hatred that left me with no choice—no choice but to do what I've always done: survive, even if it meant killing the only man I've ever loved.

Perhaps, in that, we were both fools.

With the wriggle of my fingers and a whisper of a spell, the creature shrinks and hardens, twisting into a loop. Obsidian gleams under moonlight, my new familiar cursed to eternal agony. I slip the ring onto my finger, savoring its cold bite. My laughter echoes through the night, that same darkness filling my insides as it has for a thousand years.

I lean close to my glittering prize. "Welcome to 'forever,' lover."

EPILOGUE
FADE TO BLACK
WELCOME TO 'FOREVER,'
LOVER.

EPILOGUE

FADE TO BLACK

DECLAN LOVEJOY

I know what happens when people like me die. It's ingrained in us from the moment we take our holy vows. First, there's a bright, guiding light. It consumes us, protects us, ushers us from one life to the next—where the Good are laid to rest. Death was not the end, not for someone like me. No, it's a beginning. We arrive in a realm beyond human understanding, greeted by rosy-cheeked cherubs. With open arms, they welcome us before grand, pearlescent gates that slowly swing open. Eternal peace is finally within reach. Only then are we met by the Creator, the benevolent force who willed our existence, who commends us for our virtues.

This is not the case for me.

There is no guiding light. No pearly gates. Certainly no cherubs.

Instead, I'm met with darkness, then fire. Soon after, I'm greeted by the cold, twisted grin of the woman who killed me, the only woman I've ever loved.

But she appears different to me now. Everything seems —*feels*—different.   Darker.   Muddled. Incomprehensible. My eyes don't see as they once did; they see far more than what is in front of me. Above. Below. Everything and anything all at once. Yet nothing at all. The vibrant color palette I'd known my entire life is now reduced to a simple few shades of light and dark. Shapes. Figures. Shadows.

I reach out, desperate to grasp anything within my control. But instead of the familiar sensation of ten fingers, I feel the strange movement of eight legs...and two pincers. Panic cripples me unlike ever before; I feel the blood rush through my veins, a tiny heart pounding through this equally tiny body, unable to scream for help, unable to retreat to safety. I am helpless, powerless. I'm a prisoner in this body, a minuscule creature with eight limbs, six eyes, and a curved tail.

The realization hits me like a blow to the head; I am a scorpion. I am *her* scorpion.

My mind, on the other hand, is a tempest of its own making.

For a century, I've been haunted by voices in my head —voices filled with anguish and despair, begging for salvation and deliverance. The prayers of the poor and unfortunate. But now, for the first time in a hundred years, all I hear is silence.

Pure silence.

Until *she* speaks.

Her voice echoes through my entire body; vibrations tickle through my feet, and a cynical, sultry voice that once brought me a sense of peace now fills me with unfathomable dread.

Peace. What a concept. I'll never feel peace again.

There's anger building within me, and it's too large for this tiny body. This brain can only handle simple thoughts: eat, move, strike, hide. It cannot comprehend the heartbreak my human form suffered just moments before my soul was sucked from its husk. All I have are memories, memories of a hundred years battling the evils of the world, sacrificing my mind and body to the Big Thirteen, saving and losing innocents—and one wicked, enigma of a witch.

I want to hate her. I *need* to hate her. Every fiber of my being aches to destroy her, to break her like she broke me. But I can't, though it's not the guilt that eats away at me, nor the love I may have ever felt for her.

No.

It's this…inexplicable, inherent subservience that renders me powerless to my own desires, a cacophony of clashing wills. I feel her thoughts as they invade my own —her pride, the wicked pleasure that has filled her for a thousand years. She's overjoyed by my pain and misfortune. She relishes my struggle, and in some twisted, baffling way…I feel it too.

I crave her attention. I stand ready at her command. We're connected, bonded, and my feelings are no longer my own. They're hers.

Every moment, more of my control slips from my grasp like sand. It's pure agony, fighting to hold onto the piece of myself still left in this little body. But as her magic overwhelms me and her soul consumes mine, I feel myself slipping further away, losing the essence of the man I once was.

There's only room for one soul in this body.

While the voices in my head no longer haunt me, I pray that an ounce of my magic still exists. I feel an ever so slight tug at my insides, a familiar sensation that reminds me of the divinity that once coursed through my veins, but it's fleeting. Unstable. Hard to grasp.

It's only then my new little mind remembers: it wasn't my soul that made me divine. It was my blood, and it's that same blood coating this creature's body—*my* body. It's my blood, this priceless collateral, that has me bound in pincers. I was a fool to give it away so freely. Such is the consequence of my desperation.

I won't give up so easily, and I don't have much time left.

I try to reach them—the demon hunters, my brothers and sisters who fought valiantly against the Devil's

Second. I know they're near; I know some had survived while others fell victim to her reaping. My only consolation is knowing their souls are finally free to ascend to the heavens, where they rightfully belong.

Where I am not.

Where I will never be.

I send out a telepathic blast, a silent plea as October dangles me by the tail and taunts my very existence. *"Avenge me,"* I beg. *"Avenge me."*

I can only hope my plea is heard.

But then, *she* grins—a twisted, depraved, villainous grin—as her words echo like a haunting prayer. "Welcome to 'forever,' lover."

Eternal damnation in the fiery depths of Hell would have been a mercy.

Her fingers wriggle at me as she whispers a spell in Hellspeak, a language I finally understand. The words invade my mind as the world around me grows larger. My body shrinks in her hand, and my limbs tingle as numbness grows. Muscles that once obeyed my command grow unresponsive, and I curl into a little loop as my exoskeleton begins to harden. Within seconds, my arachnid prison morphs into something far more sinister, a punishment fitting for the sins of a Nephilim.

I am transformed into a ring, one she effortlessly places upon her finger.

I am no longer Declan Lovejoy. I am her familiar, just another piece of jewelry in her heart-shaped box. I am bound to her for eternity, forever a vessel for the souls of the innocent, forced to serve an evil I vowed to destroy.

'Forever' seems like a death sentence, once the object of my greatest desires. I suppose the witch was right—I should've been careful about what I wished for.

There's only one wish I have now as I remain paralyzed in this prison. It's the only thought that echoes as I desperately try to connect to the sliver of divinity left in me before it fades away for good, the last words I direct to whatever demon hunter will hear me:

"Kill October Winters."

WE'RE JUST GETTING STARTED

The Hellion Harlot Collection (or Hellion-verse) is a multiple-book collection centered around October Winters and the badass ladies she meets along the way. Buckle up for thrilling, fast-paced novels, comics, and novellas welcoming you to the darker side of storytelling. The Devil's Second's story is just beginning—a thousand year old witch with a new lease on life and a millennium worth of enemies has many more stories to tell.

Reagan Valentine and **Jeremy Roache** will return in the sinful second installment of the Hellion Harlot series. To earn her seat at the top of the demonic hierarchy, Debauchery demon Reagan must corrupt a demon hunter to prove her worth among her Broodline.

From the mystical land of Los Angeles, California, Nikkita Bell is an author-illustrator who has carved out a distinctive niche where literature meets visual storytelling. Specializing in adult dark paranormal and urban fantasy with horror and romantic elements and a gothic neo-noir flair, each of Bell's novels become an immersive experience where readers encounter dangerous, high-stakes, and fast-paced narratives through captivating illustrations and music-inspired themes.

Through her groundbreaking hybrid graphic novel format, Bell welcomes you to the gothic side of storytelling filled with morally complex anti-heroines who embrace their darker natures and never apologize for it. She has built her brand on a simple but powerful premise:

villainous books about villainous women doing villainous things.

When she isn't crafting the next femme fatale to follow to Hell and back, Nikkita enjoys orchestral music, pretending to sing opera, and snuggling with her husband and two cats, Ciri and Yennefer.

Looking for more bookish updates, adventures, and kitty escapades? Follow Nikkita on Instagram, Tiktok, and Threads @nikkitabell, and don't forget to sign up for *The Hellion Harlot Club*, the Nikkita Bell newsletter, at nikkitabell.com!

There's that saying that "it takes a village to raise a child." It takes constant, unwavering support from all avenues and corners, to lift you up on the days that are hard and to guide you when the future seems bleak.

Sometimes, the village isn't so easily physically immediate. Sometimes, the village is sprawled out across states, countries, and oceans.

This book is my child, my magnum opus, and I couldn't have brought it to life without the following people:

MY BOOKISH CREW:

JENNA W. AND NICOLE R.

J-j-j-jenna and the Niccccs! When my life came crashing down in February 2024, you two were my rocks. Your constant love, checkins, and unwavering support nursed my back to health in ways I could never imagine. We three bought our books to life last year, and I am so honored and proud of the role I played in bringing your books to life through my art. I am so very grateful to you both, and cannot wait to keep creating badass female main characters together!

STELLA J.

My first anthology sister, first author friend, and October's godmother…

You're the one who told me to do this. When October's story was nothing but an idea to write 31 poems with commissioned artwork, YOU were the one who told me to give her a novel. YOU were the one who listen to every rant, idea, and helps me craft the best story I've ever written. Stella, you are my sunflower and sunshine, and this book is for you. I love you forever.

STEPHANIE S.

To the sister I never expected to find… An ocean may separate us, but the bond I've forged with you in the past year is one of the greatest treasures I've ever uncovered. You helped me bring October to life; you were the first to read this novel when it was at its barest bones and helped me make it the best it could be. I'll always love you for the strength you've given me to believe in myself and crush my goals.

BRI V.

When my life fell apart last year, you came to me with an opportunity. This opportunity was a pipe dream at best, but you believed in me. You ALWAYS believed in me. I argue to this day that you're the reason this book is currently in the hands of many. You gave me the strength and motivation to come back into the author world. You taught me that my talent is worth investing in, and have been by my side every step of the way (including fun bookish adventures!) I'll forever be indebted to you for breathing life back into this very nervous author, and for helping bring her dreams to life.

JORDAN K.

We brought our novellas to life together. We turned them into thick books and decided to take on the world with the incredible stories we concocted in our brain. You've been a rock during this whole publishing journey and I cannot even tell you how special you are to me. Thank you for your support, enthusiasm, and for listening to my rambling voice messages and answering my stupid questions. May our Nightmares find each other in the future.

MONTY KAY R.

My Lithuanian long-lost-sister in Sweden! You've been by my side unconditionally for the past few months and you've kept me so incredibly sane, and have truly been a huge light in my life. You always remind me to drink water and take my vitamins and take care of myself, and are always a voice message away to bounce off the walls together in excitement any time something amazing happens, or we hit a major milestone! I am so very proud of you and how far you've come in your journey and so very grateful for your friendship FOREVER!

NIKKI K.

We found each other late into my publication journey, but you've left the deepest mark in my life. Finding a friend who not only is skilled, talented, and shares the same passions as I do (and oddly has an EERIE amount of things in common with me) has been the most wonderful ride! Thank you for being there for me as I brought my graphics/comics to life, and for always bouncing ideas off with me to help me create the best product I can make. I am forever indebted to you!

NIKKI R.

Our lives have been intertwined for years and we truly had no idea just how much. To my beautiful, kind, compassionate, and generous ECN, thank you for coming into my life when you did. You've held my hand along the way during this very ixxciting yet stressful time and I cannot wait to see where our beautiful friendship takes us in the future! Thank you for being in my corner, and such an amazing friend.

KELSEY M.

When I came back into the author world in 2023, I connected with you first. You were my next anthology sister, and fell hard for October at a time when I didn't think she would be palatable for the bookish world. Your review of Bound in Pincers gave me the idea for the title of this book, and you'll always be such a near and dear friend to me. Thank you for naming my debut novel and being the most wonderful friend!

FANS-TURNED-FRIENDS-FOR-LIFE:

LAURENCE G.

To my first ever October Winters fan… Words will never describe the love, respect, and gratitude I have for you, my first fan! My face always lights up when I get a message from you, and every check in message and excitement for my next author endeavor always makes me feel less lonely. Friends like you are hard to find, and I will forever keep you in my corner. No matter what anyone ever says, you will always be my first fan! Thank you for your enthusiasm, love, support, and extra pixie dust every day!

BRITT B.

THE PRESIDENT OF THE NIKKITA BELL FAN CLUB! Britt, I couldn't believe how quickly you and I became friends. You are easily the true October Winters super-fan, to the point where you even dressed as your favorite Pincers chapter for Halloween (I STILL CAN'T BELIEVE THAT!) You've always been the brightest beacon of light in my life, the first to respond to any form or post, and you've given me the motivation to keep on going with all this. You're my Linkin Park soul sista and I know I've made a friend for life out of you. Thank you for being the greatest ray of sunshine, and such an incredible friend.

SARAH G.

Woman, you metaphorically showed up on my doorstep and EASILY moved right into my heart! You're a super amazing addition to my "Canada Crew," and a constant form of support, love, enthusiasm, and excitement in any of my endeavors. I am so very grateful for all of your checkins and for holding my hand throughout the past few months as I geared up for this very big leap in my life. I love you so much, thank you for being such a quick, reliable, and unforgettable friend!

ALLEN F.

You also came into my life very recently and have made huge waves! You helped me realize that my work can reach and appeal to so many people from all over the world, and I'm so grateful for the chance to have been interviewed by you. Your constant and vigilant support and belief in me is what makes me excited to keep creating, and I am so happy we connected through all of our similar interests and love for the arts.

EFFIE S:

You changed my world and how I view myself as an author the day you told me October was your role model and inspired you to embrace your true self. I was so fortunate to connect with you through being published together in Out of the Cauldron and you quickly became such a great friend! Thank you for showing me what October can mean to people, and that the work I create can make a difference. I am so grateful for you!

FAMILY: BIOLOGICAL AND FOUND

SILVA D.

About 11-12 years ago, I posted a weird status on Facebook about writing a book. You decided to comment on it about wanting to know more, and so we met up at our (now usual) favorite spot and spent about 8 hours discussing this world I created. I didn't know it then, but that night changed my life forever. If it wasn't for you, October would have never existed. She wasn't even a figment of my imagination when I started drafting Bodark. But after countless Coffee Bean and Barnes & Noble dates, she came to life, and it's all because of you. Your unwavering patience and HOURS spent listening to my ramble on about this story and my woes of writing a book were my anchor, and I am so grateful to have had you on this ride with me. You ARE my October. Thank you for bringing her to life with me.

LUKE G.

If anyone has had to put up with my ridiculousness over my author dreams, it's you, Lukie. My best friend across MULTIPLE oceans, the person I would message at all hours of the night for the past decade talking about this crazy dream of publishing a book, the person who would spend countless hours over calls helping me flesh out my novels, and the literal voice behind all of my demon characters… THANK YOU. Thank you for being the best honorary second husband (iykyk) a girl could ask for. You've helped me grow into a strong, confident creative and you gave me the power to bring my dreams to life. I'll spend the rest of my life repaying you for the decade of patience you've had for me and my crazy author life!

SARA E., BRANDON Z., & MANNY P.

To my FL-PA fam… What would I do without you three? From Sara driving me around to author events, the constant back and forth text messages, check ins, and my fairy godfathers pushing me to be the best writer and be proud of myself every step of the way, I can't thank you three enough for being the greatest trio of friends a gal could ask for. You're both the family I chose, and I will always remember this special time in our lives and the support you all gave me. I love you three!

LEXI AND MIKE M.

Where would this novel even be if not for you two? Most of it was written at your house or during our writing dates together (with plenty of delicious noms and colorful keyboards). Any time I ever felt stuck, you both were there to help me through every problem. Any time I needed to flesh out my plot, you both sat me down and came out with the best ideas ever. Lexi, my physical October Winters, I will forever be grateful to you for encouraging me to go with my unconventional main character idea, and for inspiring me to write after months of not feeling any inspiration. Your line edits also SAVED MY LIFE! I love you both so much!

STEPH A.

To the best friend who has always been a call or text away, who always sends me a good morning check-in message and believed in my abilities from day freaking one… THANK YOU. You may not realize this, but it was o your couch where I decided to open up my iPad after months of fearing I would never drive again and just started trying again. That was the day I decided I could do this. I could bring this graphic novel to life. You gave me the strength I didn't know I had, and reminded me to take care of myself on the days I forgot to put my health first. I love you, and you'll always be my Sparkles <3

LAUREN A.

To my sister and second mom, the woman who stayed by my side and nursed me back to life… You're the reason I am alive. You raised a woman and creative who is unafraid to take on the world, and taught me how to be proud of myself and my skills. You bought me my first Wacom tablet and helped me discover my love for illustration. We always joked that you would write the books and I would draw them, but you encouraged me to do both. I love you until the end of time, and you will always be my platonic soulmate.

MOM & DAD

To the parents that always supported every dream… I literally wouldn't be here if it weren't for you. Dad, you never hesitated to help me find the tools I need to be the best artist I can be, and Mom, you always told me to never hide my stories from the world. You told me that my writing is worth investing in, and that I should shoot for the stars. I love you both so very much, and hope I've made you proud with this huge milestone in my life.

THE MARVELOUS MR. BELL

Last but certainly not least…

On our wedding day, you wrote the most beautiful promise in your vows. That you'd stand next to me and support me during any endeavor, from my next marathon to my next book idea. Chris, you delivered on that promise tenfold. You held my hand through this big, exciting, and at times, very scary process and honestly, this book is as much yours as it is mine. You essentially created Cherry and Jeremy for me, and spent countless hours helping me sort through plot ideas and character traits to create the best story I could ever dream of—the story I was meant to write. You gave me the strength to live again, to chase a pipe dream I never thought I could accomplish, and if it weren't for the hours upon hours of laughter, puzzle-piecing, and smiles, neither my book nor I would be here right now. Thank you for being the president of the Nikkita Bell fan club, and for being the greatest cat dad to our girls (I know I probably forgot to clean the litter box here and there while drafting and drawing, so thanks for that, buggy). I love you to the moon and back, and you are my universe.

www.ingramcontent.com/pod-product-compliance
Lightning Source LLC
Chambersburg PA
CBHW040850010826
48978CB00013BA/958

9 798999 192440 5